Joy to Noel

TRACY BAACK

Joy to Noel

Copyright © 2025 by Tracy Baack

All rights reserved.

ISBN ebook: 979-8-9905554-9-5

ISBN paperback: 979-8-9905554-8-8

Cover Design by Parker Spencer at Author's Best Friend

Joy to Noel is a work of fiction. Names, characters, and incidents are products of the author's imagination and intended to be used fictitiously. Any resemblance to actual events or persons, living or dead, is entirely coincidental—except for Hamlet, the cat.

No part of this publication may be reproduced, distributed, or transmitted in any form or by any means, including photocopying, recording, or other electronic or mechanical methods, without the prior written permission of the publisher, except as permitted by U.S. copyright law or the use of brief quotations in a book review.

For permission requests, contact Tracy Baack at info@tracybaack.com.

For Meili Joy

Go take the world by storm

Author's Note

Merry Christmas, dear Reader!

This book is the second in the Christmas in Noel series. If you haven't read *Saved by Noel* yet, I'm here to give you a chance to stop, drop, and read book one! You'll have such a greater appreciation for this cast of characters if you meet them in Clara and Clark's story first. Madison will be here (impatiently) waiting for you when you get done.

If you'd prefer to just forge ahead, Liam wouldn't blame you for being too intrigued by Madison to backtrack now. I tried to drop enough breadcrumbs of information from the first book to keep you from getting totally lost.

Thanks for celebrating my favorite time of year with me. Now, on to Christmas!

Content Considerations: This is a closed-door, kisses only romance. There are brief mentions of childhood bullying and postpartum depression.

Prologue

MADISON

I like Christmas a normal amount.

I have nostalgic childhood memories of celebrating with my family. I enjoy watching Christmas movies each year. I own an average quantity of decorations that I put up while listening to Christmas music every November.

You know, a *normal* amount of fond feelings for the holiday.

My best friend is an entirely different story.

Clara has enough Christmas spirit to single-handedly power Santa's sleigh. The creators of Buddy the Elf probably shadowed her for character inspiration.

Case in point—last year, Clara's Christmas spirit saved a whole town. Like something out of a Christmas movie, she rallied a dying town to create a Christmas festival worthy of its Yuletide name. Well, the town's Yuletide alter ego, considering that Noel isn't actually pronounced *No-el*. It's technically pronounced *Nole*, rhymes with hole. But Clara convinced the grumpy mayor (who descended from the town's founding father) to embrace the Christmas connection. Together, they saved the town of Noel, Arkansas from its path toward extinction. Of course, Clara and Clark fell in love in the process. One year later, they're now getting married during the very same festival.

See? Like something out of a Christmas movie.

Or, should I say, like something *into* a Christmas movie—considering Clara adapted her real-life experience into a movie script being produced by the Heartmark Channel this year. Her holiday spirit launched the inspiration for her lifelong career dream and led her to the love of her life.

I've spent all of Thanksgiving week here in Noel helping Clara put finishing touches on the festival decorations that will double as wedding decor. Practically everyone in the small town has pitched in, and many will be at the wedding tonight.

"Mads, do I look okay?" Clara asks. "Not just okay—do I look perfect? I need Madison Wheeler honesty. Don't spare my feelings."

"When am I ever not honest?" I reply, making Clara smile. "You are the epitome of perfection. Hottie McScrooge is going to swallow his tongue when he sees you."

Clara laughs at my old nickname for Clark, her soon-to-be husband. When Clara first purchased her cozy cabin in Noel to use as a writing retreat, she met Clark through a serendipitous mishap. Their spark of attraction was nearly snuffed out when Clara discovered that Clark was her opposite in a lot of ways—including his general dislike for the holiday season. He earned that "McScrooge" nickname fair and square, although he's really come around since then. Clara has a way of bringing out the best in people.

And she really does look perfect today. Her strawberry-blonde curls are swept into an effortless updo, subtle makeup brings out the blue of her eyes without covering up the freckles spread across her cheeks, and her wedding dress is exquisite. The cream bodice is simple and strapless, and the full skirt with endless layers of tulle ends just above her ankles, perfect for an outdoor wedding.

Clara nearly dripped runny mascara on the sample dress when she tried this one on at the bridal boutique. The tulle is the perfect homage to Clara's late Aunt Gloria, a professional ballerina who never had any children and had doted on Clara just as much as her parents. It was the inheritance money gifted by Aunt Gloria that enabled Clara to buy her writing cabin in the woods.

We've been getting wedding-ready all day, along with her other bridesmaid, Sydney. Clara had a playlist of Christmas love songs on loop, and I've had to stop her from getting teary-eyed more than once. Thankfully, her makeup has stayed intact, and she truly is a vision.

"I'll go make sure that Clark is ready for the first look," Sydney says to Clara. Syd is a Noel local, married to Clark's best friend, Davis. She's Clara's closest friend here, though I will forever maintain best-friend status. Unfortunately, I still live in Kansas City, while Clara moved to her cabin in Noel full time earlier this year. It was a tough pill to swallow, considering that she was my boss as well as my best friend, but she's living her dream come true.

As Syd leaves the room, Clara turns to me and smooths an errant strand of hair I didn't know was sticking up. I'd opted to pull my long, brown hair into a sleek ponytail instead of a more elegant updo. Clara stands a solid five inches taller than my 5'3" stature, allowing her to see the top of my head better than I can in the mirror.

"Thanks," I tell her. "You ready for this?"

Clara's eyes mist over. "So ready. Thanks for being by my side today."

"*Every* day," I emphasize. "But you are not supposed to be crying before you even see Clark. Stop being sentimental!" I wave air at Clara's eyes as she laughs, and we're interrupted by Syd and Davis coming in to give us the go-ahead.

The ceremony will take place at the pavilion in the center of the festival grounds, but Clara wanted their first look to be in Mistletoe Lane, an alley off Main Street that's decorated with sprigs of mistletoe hung from crisscrossing strands of lights overhead. It's the place where Clara first confessed her feelings for Clark a year ago, even though it took him a couple extra weeks to admit his own.

Sydney, Davis, and I accompany Clara on the short walk from the town hall to the first look location. Clark's other childhood friend and groomsman, Beau, waits for us at the entrance to Mistletoe Lane. Clark stands at the other end, back turned away from us. I give Clara's dress a final floofing, then nod to the photographer that she's ready. The four of us in the wedding party hang back a respectful distance, wanting to give Clark and Clara a modicum of privacy (but also, we're the intrusive type of friends).

Initially, it took some convincing for me to get on board with Clara's feelings for Clark. When she first discovered that he was the mayor of Noel and was obstinately opposed to hosting a Christmas festival, his borderline rude behavior toward her put his name on my naughty list.

But he slowly won me over as he revealed his inner softie behind that stoic exterior—a soft side that's now openly on display. He wipes tears from his eyes as he watches Clara walking toward him. Her back is to me, but I'd bet all my money that Clara is crying her way to him.

I smile as I watch Clark take her hands and twirl Clara around before pulling her in for a kiss. Clark's gain may come at my loss, but I could never wish anything but happiness for them.

Kicking off my shoes at the door, I walk across the room and flop down on the bed inside the tiny cabin, exhausted. The lights of the small Christmas tree in the corner provide adequate illumination without turning on the overhead light. The exposed wooden beams of the ceiling give a log cabin vibe, but the whitewashed shiplap walls keep the space fresh and airy.

These cabins on the outskirts of Noel are primarily used by tourists during the summer for the river floating season, but they become mini Christmas oases for people to rent during Christmas Fest. There are two rows of A-line cabins of varying sizes with a gravel drive through the middle, dotted with fire pits.

Noel is a *very* small town nestled in the woods along the Elk River in Northwest Arkansas. The residents here are some of the kindest, most down-to-earth people I've ever met. I might be the slightest bit biased, considering how the town welcomed Clara into the fold as one of their own. Next year, Christmas Fest will begin the day after Thanksgiving, but the entire town voted to delay the kickoff this year so that Clark and Clara could have the magical wedding of her dreams.

It was a perfect celebration of love and Christmas—just what Clara wanted. A casual dinner followed the ceremony, giving the newlyweds the chance to mingle with guests before they ducked out at eight o'clock. I'm not sure if the early curfew was the result of their eagerness to be alone on their wedding night or Clark's general aversion to large crowds. Likely a combination.

Sighing, I stand up long enough to change out of my cranberry bridesmaid dress into my flannel Grinch pajamas. The cozy bed tempts me to dive right in, but my conscientious nature wins out. I take time to brush my teeth, remove my makeup, and wash my face.

Once I'm tucked under the covers, my thoughts immediately start picking apart my maid-of-honor speech. Davis struck the perfect balance between sentimentally reminiscing and positively roasting Clark during his toast, and I question whether mine was equally as captivating. When my mind begins rewriting portions of the speech, I cover my face with a pillow and beg my thoughts to quiet down.

The speech is over. You can't change it. Be quiet and go to sleep!

CHAPTER ONE

Madison

DECEMBER

"What reindeer threw up in this place?"

Clark's tone borders on horrified as he scans the interior of the bar. It's been transformed into a holiday wonderland, lit up by thousands of lights with hundreds of ornaments and candy canes hanging from the ceilings. Tucked around the tables, Christmas trees and statues cram into every available inch of space. The menu has even been Christmasified, with dishes renamed for classic Christmas movies and festive cocktails crafted solely for the season.

Clara smacks him on the arm. "Are you kidding? This is incredible!" They're visiting Kansas City for her annual birthday celebration with her parents—attending *The Nutcracker* ballet three days before Christmas. I arranged for an early birthday gift in the form of a reservation at one of the many Christmas pop-up bars that are wildly popular in the Kansas City metro area.

"I knew you would love this," I tell Clara as the hostess leads us to our table. "Please appreciate the effort it took to get a reservation months in advance."

"Best birthday gift ever," Clara assures me. She turns to Clark. "I wonder if we could convince Ben to do this at the Deer River Bar for next year's Christmas Fest. How cool would that be?!"

Clark groans. "Please, no more additions to Christmas Fest. The bar is the one haven for locals to escape the tourist chaos. We can't turn it into a tourist destination too."

Clara ignores his protest. "I'm sure Ben wouldn't mind the extra flush of cash. I'm going to ask him," she says as she starts taking photos and videos of the space with her phone.

"By the way, your movie turned out ah-MAY-zing! Not that anyone is surprised," I say.

Clara beams. "Thank you! It was so crazy to see my story come to life on the screen."

"The first of many," Clark chimes in. "Heartmark hit the content jackpot when they discovered you, hon. So, Mads, how's work? You holding things together without Clara there?"

I'm the proofreader for WritInc, a company that creates written content like newsletters and postcards for clients around the country. No file heads to the printer without passing through me first. Clara used to oversee the entire writing department, but her move to Noel meant a new manager for me.

"I'm doing what I can. Work life would be infinitely better if they had hired literally anyone other than Chad to replace Clara," I say with an exaggerated sigh. "You might be a little Grinch-y at times, Clark, but Chad is the Abominable Snowman. Not the nice version after his teeth are pulled."

To his credit, Chad did fire the lazy writer who consistently took advantage of Clara's overly accommodating nature. But that's about where Chad's credit ends, considering he's overbearing and micromanages everyone's every move. He's also downright rude—and that's coming from someone who tends to blurt the honest truth before I think through whether it should be an inside or outside thought.

As much as I dislike Chad, it's a solid job that I'm amazing at, if I do say so myself. Catching mistakes is my greatest superpower, an innate skill honed through years of professional training and constant practice. Pointing out other people's flaws comes naturally after decades of ruminating on my own.

Clark and I both recognize the unnecessary guilt welling up in Clara over leaving WritInc, and Clark rapidly changes the subject. "Are you going to Nebraska for Christmas?" he asks me.

I nod. "Yes, I'll leave tomorrow. Nothing like a four-and-a-half-hour drive through corn fields to get you in the Christmas mood."

"The solitude of a long solo drive doesn't sound so bad," Clark says. "I'd choose quiet corn fields over busy pop-up bars any day."

Clara leans over to kiss his bearded cheek. "I know you would, babe, which makes me extra grateful you came tonight. You're the most selfless husband ever."

A smile breaks through Clark's gruffness, and he turns his head to return Clara's kiss. I kick his chair under the table. "Ugh, stop it with the PDA, you two," I tease.

"Can't help it when I'm married to this gorgeous woman," Clark says, still making googly eyes at Clara. He turns back to me. "Will you get to see your whole family for Christmas?"

"Yes, my sister's family will come to the farm, too, which means I'll get to spoil my cutie niece for a few days," I answer. JoJo is the most adorable two-year-old there ever was, and I'm not just saying that because I'm biased. I don't get to see her nearly often enough, even though my sister, Caitlin, isn't too far away in Omaha, Nebraska. At least, not as far as my parents and younger brother, Chris, who's taking over the family farm. They're deep in rural Nebraska, surrounded by acres of the family's farmland. Chris is married to his high school sweetheart but doesn't have kids yet, which means JoJo gets the full only-grandchild spoiling for now.

"How long will you be in Nebraska?" Clara asks. "I don't suppose we'll see you again until after we get back from our honeymoon in January."

"Probably not," I say. "I'll be in Nebraska until the twenty-seventh, but then I'll be back to work. And figuring out if I want to find a new roommate to replace Amy or a new place to live."

"Oh no," Clara replies, eyebrows knitting together. "Amy's moving out? You know you can't handle rooming solo with Ivy. You'll lose your mind."

"I already lose my mind with her on the daily," I groan. Ivy is one of those clueless people who doesn't adhere to social norms. She tends to push the boundaries of acceptable behavior. It's impossible to number the random men, animals, and questionable substances that have circulated through our rental house due to Ivy's whims. "Amy and her fiancé are moving to Texas after the wedding, so she won't be renewing the lease with us at the end of February."

Clara gives me a sympathetic look. "At least she gave you plenty of notice. You could always move to Noel!" Clara says with a wink.

"Ha ha," I say, rolling my eyes. "I already moved to the city from one small town. As much as I love you, I'm not about to reverse course."

CHAPTER TWO

Liam

FEBRUARY

"**E**xcuse me? I'm going where?" I ask.

My boss glances at his computer. I appreciate the extra step of confirmation because I'd really like his first statement to be incorrect.

"Yes, Arkansas. Noel, Arkansas, to be exact," Cal confirms. "One of our subsidiaries, Pure Fur All, opened a new pet food production plant there a few months ago. Apparently, the plant manager was a total disaster and made a mess of the entire thing. You're going to fix it."

I pinch the bridge of my nose, squeezing my eyes shut.

I'm a fixer. This is what I do. This is what I excel at—swooping in to clean up other people's messes. Ruthlessly rearranging personnel and systems until things are running smooth as butter. Then, I hightail it out to the next fiasco. Sometimes I'm able to resolve the issues remotely from Holden Incorporated's headquarters with a few drop-in visits on site, but bigger messes require my in-person presence for weeks or months at a time.

I just got back to Houston after a two-month job in Arizona optimizing an organic laundry detergent production line. I'd hoped to have a small reprieve at the home office before being unleashed on the next screwed-up factory. *Honestly, why are there so many idiots in charge of running things? I suppose it's job security for me. Even if it means I never get to stay in one place for very long.*

"You're the best we have, Liam," Cal says. "And this one's a major issue. Probably not a quick fix. We need our best on the job."

"I know I'm the best," I blurt before sighing, hands on my hips. "I just don't want to spend months in some podunk Arkansas town."

"Well, unless you're interested in a demotion to a different position with less pay, you'll get in your car and drive to Arkansas. You have two weeks to enjoy Houston while you wrap up paperwork from your last gig and prep for this one, but then I expect you to get out there, podunk town or not," Cal says with a no-nonsense tone. When I don't answer immediately, he adds, "Liam? Should I contact HR about open positions?"

Gritting my teeth, I glower at Cal. "No. You know I'll do it. Email over the files so I can research what I'm walking into."

"Already done," Cal replies. "And Angie has arranged lodging, although it may be a temporary solution depending on how long the job takes."

My brow furrows. "Will I not be staying in the same rental as the previous plant manager?"

"Nope. The town is too small to have very many rental options. The manager was driving in from Bentonville every day, which was likely part of the issue. Talk to Angie if you want more details," Cal says as he takes a seat behind his desk. His form of dismissal.

"Fine," I practically growl as I exit his corner office. Angie's desk is right outside, but she accurately reads my expression and doesn't attempt to talk to me on my way out. I beeline to my own small office, which sits empty the majority of the year. Once my computer is powered on, I open the files for the Pure Fur All plant and click the "print" button. I prefer to mark up physical papers for my initial deep dive into failing facilities.

I spend the rest of the day working on reports from the Arizona job and leave the office at five o'clock sharp. I don't bother getting housing details from Angie because I'd rather live in denial about going to Arkansas for as long as possible. *Hamlet is not going to be happy about leaving again so soon.*

Striding through the parking garage, I click to unlock my black Yukon Denali, stowing my leather satchel in the back seat. On the short drive to my apartment, my phone rings with a call from my sister, Hana. I send an auto-reply letting her know I'll call her back. Stopping to grab takeout from one of my favorite Tex-Mex places, I reach my building and take the elevator up to the eighth floor. The second I step through the door, Hamlet comes running over, meowing loudly in greeting.

Crouching down, I run my hand across his striped gray fur, and he arches his back into the touch. "Hi, my friend," I say, and he meows in response. He sniffs the bag of food in my hand—not because he thinks I'll give him any, but because he thoroughly inspects every new item brought into his space. When he's done, he leans back into my hand, meowing again. "My day was okay. You're not going to be very happy with me when I tell you what happened, so let's not talk about it yet."

After filling Hamlet's dish with the expensive food for his sensitive stomach, I sit down at the table with my own dinner. I video call Hana and prop my phone up against the napkin holder in front of me.

"*Annyeong*," she answers in Korean. "Or should I say 'cheerio' now that I'm in London?"

I roll my eyes at her. "Well, 'cheerio' is used as a farewell, not a hello in the UK. But a simple 'hi' will suffice since we both speak American English as our primary language."

Hana harrumphs. "I'm trying to pretend I fit in here as effortlessly as you can. I didn't have the luxury of spending my first eight years of life living in London like you did. *Halmeoni* always wants to talk in Korean, and it's hurting my brain to think so much. How did you do it?"

"Well, growing up bilingual isn't exactly the same as you attempting to learn more Korean now as an adult. Dad never really made us speak it casually at home outside of lessons, so you're at a disadvantage," I reason before taking a bite.

"Yes, let's blame that instead of my brain's slow processing speed," Hana jokes. "How is it being back in Houston? Was Ham happy to get home?"

"Stop calling him Ham," I chide.

"What? I shortened all of our cats' names—Ophie, Rosie, Gilly. Just be glad I call him Ham instead of Hammie," Hana retorts.

"Hamlet is less of a mouthful than Ophelia, Rosencrantz, or Guildenstern, so I think you could do him the courtesy of using his formal name," I say. "And yes, he is happy to be home. He immediately walked around the entire apartment rubbing against every piece of furniture. Unfortunately, he'll be disappointed when we load up to leave again in two weeks."

A banging sound comes from the background of Hana's video. "What was that?" I ask as she rolls her eyes. "Just *Harabeoji* pounding the wall between our rooms. He thinks I'm still a little girl and should be going to bed at eight o'clock. Living with our grandparents while I'm studying here is great for my bank account but not so much for my freedom."

Doing the math in my head, I say, "It is getting late there. You probably *should* go to bed."

"Just because I'm a post-grad student doesn't mean I've graduated from my undergrad schedule habits. The night is young!" Hana says, a little too loudly. Another bang sounds. "I'd better hang up and pretend to be asleep. Or sneak out," she adds with a wink.

I narrow my eyes. "Don't you dare. You've been there less than two months, so you don't know enough yet to stay out of trouble." I met Hana and my parents at a ski resort in Flagstaff for Christmas, and then she left for London shortly after the new year. "Tell Halmeoni and Harabeoji I said hello. Well, tell them tomorrow."

"Will do. Love you, Liam," Hana says, blowing a kiss at the camera.

"Love you too."

I quickly finish my dinner, and the second I take my last bite, Hamlet jumps into my lap. He rubs his face against mine, purring softly. I scratch the white fur on his chest, and his purrs increase in volume.

"I missed you too. You need to enjoy the short reprieve at home. Because we're heading to Arkansas."

Hamlet narrows his seafoam green eyes at me and gives a disdainful *meow*.

CHAPTER THREE

Madison

"What do you mean 'let go'?" I ask, incredulous.

"I mean that today is your last day with the company. You'll have three months of severance, but we expect you to have things wrapped up and cleaned out by the end of the day," Chad says. If I'm not mistaken, there's a hint of glee in his voice.

"But why are you firing me? I've never been written up. Has my quality of work dipped?" I ask, demanding more answers. I turn my gaze to Mr. Douglas, the COO and Chad's boss. "What grounds do you have to terminate my employment?"

Chad heaves an annoyed sigh, but Mr. Douglas at least has the decency to look uncomfortable. Mr. Douglas is the one to respond, "Don't think of it so much that you're being fired as your position is being eliminated. We'll happily give you a glowing reference as you seek new employment."

I narrow my eyes as I pull my hair into a ponytail. "What do you mean the position is being eliminated? You can't send out hundreds of pieces of mail each month without them being proofread first. That would be absurd. Clients will riot."

"I have it handled," Chad replies with a huff. "I know how to do my job."

After shooting daggers at Chad, I turn my gaze back to Mr. Douglas, staring until he offers more of an explanation. I've worked for WritInc for seven years with no complaints against me. I'm far too meticulous and dedicated to my work to receive any criticism.

I deserve an explanation.

Mr. Douglas finally cracks, shifting uncomfortably in his chair. He clears his throat before saying, "Chad has assured me that we can utilize AI tools in the final proofreading step of our content creation process."

My blood begins the rapid-boil process. "You're replacing me with AI?" I clarify, stuffing down my anger to keep from yelling.

Chad rolls his eyes as though I'm a toddler throwing a tantrum. "It's a simple way to cut costs and make our process more efficient. This is a business, not a charity, after all. The bottom line is the bottom line."

"Well, now, it's not quite so cut-and-dried as that," Mr. Douglas cuts in, a feeble attempt to soften the blow of Chad's statement. "But the owner of WritInc has asked me to eliminate unnecessary spending, and Chad convinced me that—"

"That I'm unnecessary?" I blurt.

"Stop acting like you're a victim here, Madison," Chad says. "It's not personal—it's business. We were told to make some moves to cut expenses during the first quarter, and it's nearly the end of February. It's not like we let you go right before Christmas. The severance package is generous, and as Mr. Douglas said, we'll provide a positive reference to help you on your way. If you need any assistance packing up today, let me know."

"You think this is just business, but this is a *bad* business move. I catch all sorts of errors that AI won't recognize as mistakes. You're going to send out subquality content and upset our customers. This is a stupid decision," I insist. Chad only glares. I cut one final glance to Mr. Douglas, willing him to step up and reverse this course. He averts his gaze.

"I won't be needing your help, Chad," I seethe as I rise to my feet. "I've always been perfectly capable of completing my work on my own."

Spinning on one heel, I storm out of Mr. Douglas' office. With each step I take toward my cubicle, I tamp down the anger welling up behind my eyes. *I will not cry. I will not cry. I will not give Chad the satisfaction.*

When I open the door of our small rental house, I'm met with the smell of burnt . . . sewage? My brain doesn't even have a classification for whatever this scent is. I'm afraid to know what Ivy is doing, but I'm more afraid to *not* know what Ivy is doing.

Poking my head into the galley kitchen, I find her muttering to herself in front of the stove. The exhaust fan is on, and something black sits on a plate next to the stove.

"Um, what happened here?" I dare to ask.

Ivy looks over at me. "I saw a recipe to make crispy durian, but I think I heated the coconut oil too high, and the whole thing burnt. My date tonight is vegan but an adventurous eater, so I wanted to show him I'm a versatile cook."

Versatile, maybe. Cook, no. Of the three of us roommates, I'm typically the one who cooks meals.

Except now it's just the two of us. Amy moved out last week, leaving me alone with Ivy. I've hemmed and hawed over whether to move out or find a new roommate to balance out Ivy's . . . Ivy-ness. But this is the final straw. I'm ready for a permanent respite from Ivy. Not to mention I won't be able to afford rent in a couple of months.

"Ivy, I'm not going to renew our lease. I've decided to find somewhere else in the metro to live," I declare.

She glances over at me and gives an indifferent shrug. "No problem. If all goes well on the date tonight, maybe I'll move in with him." Ivy looks back to the blackened pan in front of her. "Maybe I'll suggest we try that new vegan restaurant that just opened." She pulls out her phone and walks away toward her room, texting as she goes.

Making zero moves to clean up the mess (and smell) she's left behind.

My eye twitches as I fight the instinct to dispose of her experiment and hose down the kitchen. *It's not your problem. Make her do it.*

I close myself in my room and drip some lemon and peppermint oils into my diffuser to try to cover up the smell, at least in my little space. Flopping spread-eagle across my navy bedspread, I groan. When that's not enough, I cover my face with one of the coral throw pillows so I can full-on scream.

What could I have done differently to prove my worth? How could Mr. Douglas listen to Chad's stupid advice? Using AI is a terrible idea. I'm light-years better than AI. Aren't I? How could I have worked harder to prevent this from happening? What did I do wrong?

Rolling onto my stomach, I attempt to smother my thoughts but really only succeed in smothering my mouth and nose. Grumbling, I sit up and grab my phone.

ME

Free to chat??

CLARA

We're on our way home from checking in on Pops. I'll call you as soon as we get to the cabin.

Pops, the elderly man who serves as a surrogate grandfather to Clark, is cantankerous in the most superlative way. I love him.

His house is only a few minutes away from Clara's cabin—everything in Noel is only a few minutes away—so I know it won't be long until she calls. As I wait, I start to regret reaching out to her in the first place. I don't want her to feel guilty for leaving WritInc. Even if this never, ever would have happened on her watch.

Replace a professional proofreader with AI?

Clara would never.

But she's my best friend, and everything about my life is falling apart. I'm not usually one for overly-dramatic theatrics, but losing your job *and* the roof over your head on the same day seems to land fairly high on the "life-falling-apart" scale.

Even though I technically chose to lose the roof over my head. Ivy and her shenanigans forced my hand.

When my phone rings, I answer it by saying, "I was fired today, Ivy nearly burned down the kitchen with horrid-smelling fruit, and I'm going to be homeless in two weeks. My entire life is a giant failure."

"Wait, hold on," Clara responds. "Back up a second. What do you mean you were fired?"

"I mean that Chad, the heartless robot who replaced you, convinced Mr. Douglas that I could also be replaced by a robot," I say, launching into an explanation of my crappy day. Clara responds with frequent gasps of shock and hums of sympathy, making me feel like maybe I'm being just the right amount of dramatic.

"Mads, this is terrible! Oh, I never should have left WritInc! If I was still there, this absolutely would not have happened," Clara says, genuine remorse in her tone.

"Stop it," I chide. "We've been over this so many times. You deserved to chase your dreams. And they're coming true! As much as I hated you leaving, it was the right thing to do. I only wish that Mr. Douglas had found someone other than Evil Chad to fill your position." I sigh. "What am I going to do, Clara? I have some savings built up and a severance package, but this feels like I'm starting back at ground zero. Nowhere to live. Nowhere to work. I'm twenty-nine years old—I shouldn't be homeless and jobless!"

"Take a deep breath. We're going to figure out a solution. What do you *want* to do?" Clara asks.

I swallow down the fear that knots my throat at her question. Because I'm not sure I have any clue what I *want* to do.

"I guess I'll start searching for open positions tonight. I'm nervous that more and more places will be going this direction, though. How hard will it be to find a proofreading position?" I wonder aloud. I've never really been interested in *writing* original content—I like *perfecting* content. Apparently, the demand for my particular talent is dying out.

Clara makes a disapproving noise. "You didn't answer my question. I asked what you *want* to do?"

I'm silent for a beat, searching my mind for a response other than the big, fat "I don't know" that's front and center in my thoughts.

"That's not the most important question right now," I redirect. "What I *need* to do is find any reliable position that offers insurance and a steady paycheck and job security."

Clara is quiet, and I'm not sure if that's a good or a bad sign for me. I put the call on speaker and sit up to pull my hair back into a ponytail. I stare at my fingernails, painted a shade of plum, except for the middle fingers, which are painted blush pink. I used to follow the trend of painting each ring finger in a complementary color, but after Chad started working at WritInc, I switched to my middle fingers. My tiny form of silent protest while I had to play nice to my superior.

Too bad "playing nice" got me nowhere.

"Mads, you were always so insistent about me chasing my dreams. You constantly pushed me to stop helping everyone else and go after what *I* wanted," Clara begins. I hold my breath. "But have you ever even stopped doing what you *should* do long enough to figure out what your dream is?"

I huff. "As happy as I am that you're living your movie-script-writing dream, not everyone has to have a big dream to live. Sometimes it's okay to put your head down and just clock-in and clock-out of a mundane job. Sometimes the right thing to do is the responsible thing," I reason.

"But always doing the 'responsible' thing doesn't make you immune from the rug being pulled out from under you," Clara says, and I can *hear* the air quotes in her voice. "Just look at today," she adds.

I grunt. *Since when do I grunt? Why did I just grunt?*

"Hit a little close to home?" Clara asks, voice dancing.

"I don't know the right answer here," I say. A feeling I strongly dislike.

"Well, it seems like the stars have all aligned to give you a window of freedom to explore the possibility of chasing a dream. Why not try going out on your own with editing and see where it takes you?"

I dismiss the suggestion. "You mean offering independent editing services? That's so risky. Who's to say I could ever find enough independent proofreading jobs to make a livable income?"

"Who's to say you can't?" Clara counters.

"You know, cost of living in Kansas City isn't exactly cheap," I grumble.

Clara gasps. "Come stay in Noel for a little bit while you give it a go!" When I audibly scoff, she doubles down. "I'm serious! The cabins that James rents out for Christmas Fest and the summer float season are sitting empty right now. Maybe he'd let you stay in one for a couple of months while you mine the depths of your soul, searching for your dream."

I roll my eyes but stifle a smile. "You've been writing too many Christmas-miracle movie scripts."

"I'm serious, Mads," Clara says. "I'll talk with James. What would it hurt to come here for a couple of months and see if you can get some traction? Dip your toe in and see if an independent career could be the dream you didn't know you had?"

When I don't immediately say no, I'm shocked to realize my subconscious is actually considering this option. *This makes no sense, though. Revamping your résumé and applying for every open position you can find would be the much more responsible way to approach this setback. Networking to find someone looking for a roommate. Consider moving back home if you can't find an affordable housing option—that would be responsible.*

My mind recoils from the thought.

"No." I don't realize I've said the word aloud until Clara tries to argue. "Wait, I wasn't saying 'no' to you. I was saying 'no' to my thoughts."

Because I *don't* want to move back home. If that's the "responsible" thing to do, then call me irresponsible.

"Okay. Talk to James, and let me know what he says," I tell Clara, and she squeals. "I'm not saying this is my long-term solution, but I'm willing to give it a brief trial run."

CHAPTER FOUR

Madison

MARCH

I sigh heavily.

No, that's not a strong enough description.

I heave a guttural expulsion of carbon dioxide.

I'm about thirty minutes outside of Noel, and my parents are going to drive my sanity off a cliff.

"I really don't think this is a smart idea. At the very least, you could have come here while you tried to look for a job and fiddle with this side hustle idea," my dad says, his voice loud through the speakers of my car.

Mom hums her agreement. "We still have your room set up just like you left it when you graduated. You know you could come back here while you figure out your life. It's the smart decision."

I'm tempted to pull over to the side of the road so I can massage my temples. Or pull out chunks of my hair. My parents are kind, loving people who mean well. They just don't *hear* themselves a lot of times.

"I already told you—they're letting me stay in the cabin basically for free. I'm paying a minimal utilities fee. So I'll still be able to save most of my severance paychecks for the next couple of months, and then I'll evaluate if this is something I really want to pursue," I explain (again, for the tenth time). "I thought through this decision like a responsible adult. I'm not going to be filing bankruptcy this year."

They continue their litany of objections, but I tune them out. I really don't need them poking holes in my decisions—my own brain does plenty of that on its own. My mental list of all the ways I'm potentially torpedoing my life is twice as long as anything they could possibly come up with.

Mercifully, a call from Clara beeps on my phone. I jump on the opportunity. "Oh, Mom, Dad, I've got another important call coming through. I'll text you later once I'm settled in. Love you!"

I barely give them time to say quick goodbyes before I end their call and transfer to Clara. "My darling friend, you have impeccable timing."

Clara snorts. "Um, okay. I was just calling to find out your ETA."

"I'm about fifteen minutes out. Am I in the same cabin I had during your wedding week?" I ask.

"Yes. James was going to rush to get the Christmas decorations taken down, but I told him to leave them up," Clara says.

I pull a face, even though she can't see me. "They haven't taken down the Christmas decorations yet? It's the first week of March. Even *you* have your Christmas decorations put away by now."

"First of all, you know I have a few little decorations that stay up all year. But I think James and Becky were enjoying a slower pace catching up on life after managing the cabin rentals and her coffee shop for so many months. Busy tourist season pretty much runs from May through December around here now," Clara says, and I can hear the pride in her voice. Her vision for Christmas Fest is what enabled so many of Noel's businesses to stay open longer. "I'm sure they'll be boxing up the decorations from the rest of the cabins over the next couple of weeks, but I told him to leave them up in yours. A little inspiration might help with your dream-finding quest."

Now I'm the one to snort. "Clara, *you* are the one who is constantly inspired by Christmas. Not me."

"Just you wait. I think an extra dose of Christmas cheer might be just what you need," Clara says confidently. "Clark and I will meet you at the cabin to help you settle in."

"I really won't need much help, considering most of my belongings are in a storage unit. But I'll be delighted to see you," I reply.

I hear a bark in the background, followed by Clark's voice shushing Chase, his dog that acts more human than canine half the time. "Are you bringing Chase with you?" I ask. "I could use a dose of Chase's emotional support today."

"This is going to be okay, Mads," Clara says. "It's going to be better than okay—I think this is the first day of the next era of your life. Just wait and see." When I don't say anything in response, Clara adds, "But yes, we'll bring Chase."

Ten minutes later, I pull up in front of the tiny cabin that was my hotel a few months ago. Staying in semi-familiar surroundings will at least give me a semblance of normalcy. I see Clark's truck parked outside already, along with a car I assume must belong to James or Becky.

The second I step out of my car, Chase bounds over to greet me. I crouch down to scratch his chest and wind up full-on hugging him. He sits still, resting his chin on my shoulder like he knows this is exactly what I need.

Chase always knows.

When I stand, Clara is there for her hug, and I start to feel a little less anxious about this leap of faith. Clark is *not* a hugger, but he gives me a quiet nod of welcome. Becky comes out of the cabin carrying a bucket of cleaning supplies.

"Welcome back, Madison!" she says. "We're excited to have your spunk around town again. The cabin is all freshened up and ready for you. Since Clara said you wanted the Christmas decorations"—I spear a look at Clara, who smiles serenely—"I left those up, but we can store them away at any point if you change your mind."

"Thanks, Becky," I say. "I really appreciate you letting me stay here."

"Oh, it's better than sitting empty! There's plenty of wood stacked on the main log rack at the end of the row of cabins if you want to use the fire pit. Call or text me if you have any issues," Becky says. "And just FYI, there's going to be a guy moving into the cabin across from yours tomorrow. I didn't want you to be startled!"

Clara's brow furrows. "Who else would be renting one of the cabins at this time of year?"

Clark jumps in to answer instead of Becky. "The pet food factory is sending in someone new to oversee things until they hire a new plant manager. According to Beau, the last guy royally screwed things up."

Although he's no longer the mayor of Noel, Clark is somehow still in the know about everything going on in the town. Then again, small towns lend themselves to *everyone* being in the know about *everything*.

Becky nods. "Yeah, he's not sure how long he'll be here, so he opted to rent one of the cabins for now. You know there's not much available by way of rental properties in Noel."

"They should hire Beau to be the plant manager," Clara announces. She shrugs when we all turn to look at her. "Just saying. I know he's only the head engineer of machinery, but I bet he would do a great job."

Clark grunts. "Beau did move back to Noel specifically to work at the factory. I wouldn't want to see it shut down due to mismanagement. He'd be back in the same position he was in when they moved away from Noel after the meat-packing plant closed. But I'm not sure if the bigwigs at corporate companies ever hire internally at small-town plants or if they always insert their own lackeys."

"Cynical much?" I ask Clark, quirking an eyebrow.

"Well, I think it could happen," Clara declares. "But for now, let's focus on getting you unpacked, Mads."

It takes all of five minutes to unload my car, and then Clark starts carrying loads of firewood from the main rack to the small one at the side of my cabin. Clara helps me unpack clothes into the dresser and onto the hanging rod next to the bed. "*Ooo*, where did you find this dress?" she asks, holding up a coral mini dress with an A-line flared skirt. "Let me guess, thrifting?"

"Ding, ding, ding!" I say as I zip up my suitcase and store it under the full-sized bed. "I don't suppose there are many thrift stores in Noel, huh?"

"Certainly not of the caliber you're used to finding in KC," Clara admits. "There's one place on Main Street that accepts and sells second-hand clothing, but you'd have better luck driving over to Bentonville."

The possibility of exploring wholly new-to-me thrift stores sparks excitement in the core of my being. The "Queen of Thrifting" title bestowed upon me by my friends was a hard-earned recognition. People who don't know me well sometimes make the mistake of asking about my thrifting "hobby," only to hear a passionate spiel about the effects of consumerism on the environment. Purchasing second-hand items whenever possible seems to be the only *reasonable* decision. A choice so obvious, I never understand why people need so much convincing.

Now that everything is unpacked, I look around the small interior of the cabin. The kitchenette has a small fridge, a sink, a microwave, and a single burner hot plate. A tiny table with two chairs is tucked next to the kitchen cabinets, and there's a cozy bench seat with throw pillows by the door. It will be the perfect place to sit and read when the weather is nice enough to leave the door open.

As much as I hate to admit it, the lingering Christmas decorations do add a touch of magic to the space. I remember helping Sydney find some of these decorations at thrift stores in KC to prepare for the first-ever Christmas Fest. The theme of this particular cabin is one of the more whimsical twists on traditional Christmas decor, which is why I picked it as my hotel room during the wedding week. Tiny white twinkle lights are tacked along the wooden beams of the ceiling, accentuating the simple architecture of the cabin. Syd really does have an eye for design.

I love the natural twigs and the sprigs of faux silver berries mixed in with more traditional Christmas greenery, which is hung with restraint around the space. The tiny flocked tree has a mix of silver, navy, and bright pink ornaments along with white lights. I remember how cozy the cabin felt lit by only the Christmas tree, and I'm grateful to have a best friend who knew what I might need even better than I did.

Clara claps her hands, jolting me out of my reverie. "What do you think? Come to dinner at the Deer River Bar with us? Maybe you can help me convince Ben to do the Christmas pop-up idea this year," Clara says with a devilish grin.

Giving her a mini-salute, I say, "Lemme at 'im."

CHAPTER FIVE

Liam

There's not a trace of the sun left by the time I pull into Noel. Although I got up to leave Houston at 6:00 a.m. and made all of my stops efficient, the nine-hour drive was lengthened by frequent road construction. The only bright spot of the long trip was the fact that I made it through an entire audiobook about business optimization.

Hamlet glared at me from the passenger seat for the whole drive. He'd occasionally sniff around the vehicle after using the portable litter box on the floor of the backseat, but the familiar surroundings bored him quickly. Then, it was back to his disapproving stare. We've done enough of these road trips, though, that I'm immune to his expressions of displeasure.

As I pull up to the address Angie supplied, I'm shocked to find not one but *many* cabins in two rows. "What in the . . . ?" I wonder aloud, drawing Hamlet's attention. He perks up and props two paws on the window to investigate.

I open Angie's email about housing to read the entire thing. When she initially sent it, I simply copied the address into the Yukon's GPS. Angie did spell out the fact that this is a tiny cabin on a campground with multiple units rented by tourists during the summer float season. There's a note that she requested the largest unit, along with the cabin number and instructions to find the key under the doormat upon arrival.

Small towns. Of course, the key is under the mat, available to anyone.

Closing my eyes, I blow out a calculated breath. *You can do this, Liam. You're going to fix this as quickly as possible, and then you're going to get out.*

My cabin number is easy to find, considering it's the only one with the porch light turned on. Parking in the designated spot to the side of the cabin, I step out of my car and stretch. As I do so, I notice a soft glow of light inside the cabin directly across from mine. When my gaze catches on the small front window, a shadow ducks out of sight.

The rest of the cabins appear empty, which makes sense for the beginning of March. Even in the milder climate of the South, it's not exactly river tourism season. At least, I wouldn't want to live next to any tourists crazy enough to float the river at this time of year.

I hear an irritated *meow* from Hamlet and turn to see him glaring at me from the driver's seat. Scooping him into my arms, I say, "Let's check out the new digs. Don't expect to be impressed."

Unlocking the cabin, I push the door open and peruse the space. It's all open concept with a small kitchenette and a bathroom door along one wall and a full-sized bed at the back of the room. The whitewashed walls are accentuated by a black metal spiral staircase that leads to a loft overhead. I assume there's another bed or two up there that could house kids if a family was staying here. The interior is clean and modern—not what I was expecting from a river cabin in small-town Arkansas.

Hamlet breaks out of my arms and begins a thorough sniffing of our new temporary home. He meows and looks over at me pointedly. Shrugging my shoulders, I admit, "You're right. It's not so bad." He continues his inspection of every square inch while I read the welcome card with notes about amenities left on the counter. On the plus side, there's Wi-Fi at the cabin. On the negative side, I'll have to use the laundromat in town since there's no washer and dryer. *What are the odds of them having a decent dry cleaner here?* I wonder.

I make quick work of hauling my suitcases and garment bags in from the SUV before locking it behind me. Maybe the cabin owners feel secure leaving their property unlocked, but that doesn't mean I'm going to.

Unpacking doesn't take long, although I have to carry some of my suits to the loft since the hanging rod by the main bed isn't very large. I pour some food and water into Hamlet's dishes before setting up a small litter box in the bathroom.

Although I'm exhausted from a full day of travel, I'm also wide awake. Taking a seat at the small dining table, I pull out my notes on the factory, reviewing the list of key employees I'll prioritize speaking with after an all-hands meeting Monday morning. The faster I can assess the current state of the plant, the faster I can figure out how to fix it. And the sooner it's fixed, the sooner I get the heck out of Arkansas.

I wake early after a solid first night's sleep at the cabin. I have to admit—the bed was far more comfortable than I'd expected. The modern furnishings appear to have been upgraded fairly recently, so I can't really complain about this living situation. Hamlet is going to get incredibly bored being cooped up in such a small space, but he'll have to deal with it since he's a strictly indoor cat.

Never, ever would I recover if he got lost outdoors and something happened to him.

Looking at my surroundings on the phone map, I scout a running route. After downing a glass of water and refreshing Hamlet's water dish, I put in earbuds and head out the door, tucking the key into the pocket of my joggers.

Thirty minutes later, I slow to a jog as I reenter the cabin grounds. There's certainly something to be said for beginning the morning with a quiet run through the trees along a riverbank. Far more relaxing than dodging countless other runners on city sidewalks. I'm walking slow circles in front of my cabin to cool down when I catch movement out of the corner of my eye.

Removing my earbuds, I turn to see a petite woman marching toward me. Her long, brown ponytail swishes back and forth behind her as she approaches, a determined expression on her face. She stops in front of me, the top of her head just reaching my chin. Tilting her head back to meet my eyes, she holds out a hand.

"Hi, I'm Madison Wheeler," she states. "I figured if we're going to be living a few yards away from each other for the foreseeable future, I may as well introduce myself right away."

I meet her outstretched hand with mine and say, "Liam Park. Nice to meet you, Madison." As our hands drop from the handshake, I can't help but run my eyes over Madison in a quick but thorough appraisal. She can't be more than 5'3" since I'm only 6'0", but she carries herself with the presence of a 5'10" woman wearing four-inch heels. The flecks of honey-gold in her light brown eyes seem charged with energy as she tilts her chin up.

"So, you're the corporate know-it-all the bigwigs sent to fix up the pet food factory, huh?" Madison says as her eyes run a similar assessment over my physical stature. My lips twitch in a half-smile at her straightforward comment.

I play along. "Corporate know-it-all, at your service. And what exactly is the story of why you're staying in a tiny cabin for the foreseeable future? Glamping addict? Social recluse? Leader of the tiny house movement out to show the rest of us the error of our materialistic ways?"

She rolls her eyes in a way that indicates she's not offended—she's stepping up to the verbal challenge. My smirk grows, and I crack my neck as she inhales oxygen to fuel her response.

"While I *am* a huge proponent of minimalistic living, I'm also a realist when it comes to modern necessities." After scanning me head to toe once more, she adds, "Although, I have a feeling I'll have some thoughts to share about the number of suits you own."

I lick my lips and tilt my head to one side. "I'm wearing athletic clothes. How could you possibly make that kind of assumption?" I make a mental note to move more of my suits up to the loft in case she ever comes inside my cabin.

Madison motions toward my face. "It's the haircut. And your whole vibe." The corners of her lips turn up slightly as she teases, "Along with the fact that you're a corporate business guy currently wearing luxury workout gear."

I hide the fact that I'm impressed by her perceptive assessment. "Maybe I simply appreciate quality over quantity."

She arches one of her striking eyebrows, holding my stare. My smirk turns into a reluctant smile. "And maybe I like suits."

Madison snaps her fingers and points at me with a sly smile of her own. I turn the conversation back around. "You never answered the question though. Why *are* you living in a tiny cabin?"

The light in her gold-flecked eyes dims the slightest bit. "I'm afraid I'm a total cliché," she answers on a sigh. "I'm here to rediscover myself, or whatever dramatic phrase they're calling it these days when your world falls apart and you're forced to reassess the meaning of life."

My expression softens in proportion to the dimmer switch in her eyes. "I'm sorry things fell apart." She shrugs and looks away. I stoke the fire back into her spirit. "Not sure exactly why you chose backwoods Arkansas to do your self-rediscovery, but to each her own, I suppose."

Her eyes flash back to mine, gold flecks rejuvenated. "I'll have you know that Noel is a very special town." Now I quirk an eyebrow at her, and she takes a small step closer. "My best friend saved this town from extinction and fell in love with the people here in the process. By proxy, I love them too. So watch yourself, Mr. Exec."

I close the space between us with my own small step forward, forcing her to tilt her head back further in order to maintain that fiery eye contact. "I'd argue that Pure Fur All saved this town from extinction. But you're entitled to your opinion."

Madison narrows her eyes and *tsks*. "You have so much to learn about Noel. I'm kinda excited that I get a front row seat to your education." The smile lines at the corners of her eyes crinkle as she gives a warm smile tinged with a drop of evil grin. "It was nice to meet you, Liam. I'm sure I'll see you around."

As she whirls around to walk back to her cabin, I call out after her. "Good luck with the journey of self-discovery."

She waves a hand in the air without looking back. I may be salty about being back in Arkansas, but at least I have someone to make my time here interesting.

CHAPTER SIX

Madison

How is it that one inch of movement can make your muscles feel like they're ripping apart? Let me tell you—barre class instructors have somehow figured out that answer.

My legs tremble uncontrollably as I will myself to finish the final ten seconds of plié pulses. Clara maintains her perfect posture on the other side of the portable barre set up in her living room. Either her time training at ballet school created lifelong muscle memory, or I am more out of shape than I thought.

I'm sure muscle memory is the more scientific explanation.

When the instructor on the video *finally* gives the cue to extend our legs and stretch, I lean my full weight against the barre. "Remind me again why we like this torture," I command Clara, focusing my full energy on stretching the pain out of my quads.

"Because both of us hate running, and you got tired of men hitting on you at the gym," Clara answers as she gracefully balances on one leg and pulls her other foot up to stretch her quad muscles. "Did you not keep up your membership at the barre place we went to?"

The video instructor has moved on to arabesque leg lifts, and while Clara continues with her, I remain doubled over the barre. "Did I keep paying for a membership? Yes."

Clara gives my elbow a quick swat with her hand. "But you didn't keep *going* to classes?" she clarifies.

"I mean, how loose of a definition of the word 'going' are we using?" I evade. Clara gives me her best version of a glower, which isn't saying much, considering she's one of the sweetest human beings to ever roam planet earth.

"It wasn't as much fun without you," I say. "Well, if 'fun' could ever be the correct adjective to describe this muscle torture."

She shakes her head at me but smiles. "Why don't we cut it short today and skip to the cool down stretch?" she suggests, turning to her laptop to skip the video ahead.

"No, no, I can do it," I falsely protest, my voice an odd falsetto. When we're done with the cool down, lying on our backs in a full-body stretch, I roll to my side to face Clara. Propping my head on a fist, I say, "I met my new and only neighbor this morning."

Clara abruptly sits up and swivels to face me, legs crisscrossed. "And?"

"Liam Park, self-admitted know-it-all executive who's obsessed with suits but has zero cares for the environment," I declare. She knows to wait for the reality version of the story.

"He did ooze executive confidence but seemed like a decent enough guy. Tall but less tall than Clark. Clean-shaven, black hair in one of those preppy haircuts you'd imagine all the guys at Oxford have. Although, he was returning from a run—and had the athletic body to show for it—so I'll have to withhold my final judgment on his hair vibe until I see it styled." Clara nods along, and I'm grateful that she knows me well enough to not assume I'm interested in this guy just because I noted so much information about his physical appearance. This is simply what I do with everyone I meet.

I add, "I can see why he was sent here to clean things up. He didn't buckle a single inch throughout the conversation."

A laugh escapes from Clara's throat before she can cover her mouth. "Good gracious, Mads. What did you subject him to?"

I exaggeratedly sigh. "Nothing too outrageous. Just poked and prodded his confident exterior a little to see how well it held up."

"And?" Clara asks.

"Confidence stayed fully intact without coming across like an arrogant piece of work. Although, he definitely has stereotypical negative assumptions about small towns, as any lifelong city dweller might. So he's in for a rude awakening when he realizes how legit the people of

Noel are," I observe. "I have to say, my life just got a lot more interesting having him as a neighbor as I tackle life."

"Speaking of, what's on tomorrow's to-do list for tackling life?" Clara asks.

I sit up and mirror her pose. "Aww, I love that you assume there are daily to-do lists. It's like you know me or something." Clara kicks my knee, and I hold up fingers as I list off tomorrow's agenda. "A of all, decide on an official name for my business. B of all, investigate the official business-y registration what-nots that have to happen to make me for real. And C of all, secure a web domain. If there's time, I'll start the actual website-building process."

"You are nothing if not ambitious," Clara muses. "We could get a head start on your list. Let's brainstorm name ideas! Do you have any thoughts on what direction to take it?"

I sputter a breath through my lips. "Eh, I'm not sure what the best course of action is. I could do something punny about words. Or I could choose something professional and posh like 'Something-something Editorial Services.' I haven't decided what's more likely to catch people's attention."

Clara stares up at the ceiling. "Why not make it more personalized? Something with your name?"

I scoff. "'Madison Wheeler Editing' doesn't roll off the tongue."

"Then use your middle name. Something with 'Joy' in the title could sound pretty. 'Joyful Editing Services,'" Clara offers, and I make a face.

"Nooo, way too cheesy, Clara," I say, but I chew on my lip as I give it more thought. "I suppose I could keep it ultra simple and brand the business as 'Madison Joy Editorial.' That does sound a little more appealing."

"I love it!" Clara affirms. "Let's act like your business is officially called Madison Joy Editorial all day, and you see how it sits in your mind when you're lying in bed tonight."

We spend the rest of the afternoon talking about Madison Joy Editorial like it's already a real, thriving business. Clara accompanies me to the local grocery store, Noland's, where I purchase enough staple foods to stock my small fridge and pantry. We catch up with Emily, whose husband owns the store. Emily used to work the register every day but has cut back her hours now that she's the town mayor. She gives me the same welcome back to Noel that everyone has so far. Being associated with Clara means I'm a recipient of warm enthusiasm, even if I haven't earned it myself. After dropping Clara off at her cabin, I return to my tiny one.

Although Clara invited me to stay for dinner, I declined. I know Clark well enough to assume that his energy is drained after socializing all weekend as a part of my official "welcoming committee." Also, he's ridiculously obsessed with being married to Clara. He's going to be ready for a quiet night alone with his bride.

As I unload groceries from the trunk of my car, I can't help but sneak a glance at the cabin across from mine. A light is on inside and the black SUV is parked out front, so I assume Liam is there. Even though I could easily loop all the grocery bags on one arm, I purposely make two trips on the off chance that Liam might come outside. I'm curious to see his styled hair so I can confirm my assumptions and pat myself on the back for astute observation.

To my mild disappointment, his front door remains closed, so I shut mine behind me. I put groceries away but decide I'm not really hungry enough to make dinner yet, so I pull out my laptop instead. Opening up my spreadsheet to-do list, I click tomorrow's tab. It feels satisfying to check off the box next to "Choose Business Name" a day early.

However, checking that box opens Pandora's box in my mind.

Who am I kidding, thinking that Madison Joy Editorial is somehow going to instantly take off and cover all my life expenses? This experiment is doomed to fail. If I couldn't prove my value to the company I'd faithfully served for seven years, then how am I going to convince total strangers to contract with me?

You're kidding yourself, Madison.

I'm seconds away from slamming my laptop shut and packing up my stuff when I glance to the side and see the tiny Christmas tree set up in the corner. Walking over to it, I turn on the lights, followed by the strands of twinkling lights strung overhead. I turn off the overhead fixture and soak in the dreamy glow.

Clara made her dreams happen here. Maybe a touch of her Christmas magic will linger long enough to help me achieve mine. Well, once I figure out exactly what my dreams *are*.

I decide to fully embrace Clara's Christmas spirit and turn on a jazzy Christmas playlist. I've always admired jazz musicians and their ability to improvise their own notes, to truly go with the flow instead of following sheet music. Pretty much, the polar opposite of how my brain works.

Tackling the technical business tasks is sure to rouse my inner critic's voice talking me out of this whole thing, so I decide to go a creative route instead. One of the graphic designers from WritInc offered to create a logo design for me when she heard about my plan to try freelancing. I compile a document of inspiration photos and color palettes I like.

I title it "Madison Joy Editorial."

CHAPTER SEVEN

Liam

*M*eow.

"It's not too much," I say to Hamlet. He's sitting on top of the closed toilet lid next to me as I assess my appearance in the mirror, straightening my tie. "I won't wear a tie every day, but this is my first day meeting all the employees. They need to know what level of professionalism I expect."

Hamlet slow-blinks before shaking his head. *Meow.*

"I've taken your opinion under advisement, but I'm going with my gut, like always," I say. He pounces to the floor as I turn off the bathroom light. He's already eaten breakfast, but I double-check his water dish. I give him a serious look as I add, "No causing any trouble today. Just because this is a small space doesn't mean the rules have changed—stay off the counters and the table. You can sleep and play with your toys on the floor. Got it?"

After sniffing the air with disdain, Hamlet rubs against my ankle, and I reward him with a scratch under his chin. "See you tonight, friend." I remove the protective sheet from the lint roller next to the door and quickly roll it over my dark navy suit. All of my suits are expertly tailored, but this is one of my favorites with the subtle plaid pattern. The fit is perfection, and I can alter the precise look I'm going for based on the color of shirt I pair with it.

Today is plain white accented by a pale blue tie. No-nonsense without coming across as over-the-top serious.

Looping my leather satchel bag over my shoulder, I lock the door and turn around to find Madison sitting in an Adirondack chair in front of her cabin. At least, the mass of brown hair piled into a bun and poking out of a blanket mound looks like Madison's. Hands holding a steaming mug are the only other body parts visible from the layers of fabric bundled in the chair. She shifts when she hears me, and the blankets droop enough to glimpse her smirking face.

"Called it," she states.

Once again, I can't resist taking the bait. Taking a few steps closer, I ask, "Called what?"

Madison simply raises her eyebrows. "It's okay, the whole Henry Golding vibe is a good look for you. You could be his doppelganger."

"Untrue," I say. "Henry Golding is of Malaysian descent. I'm half-Korean. We look totally different. And there's nothing wrong with nice suits."

"Just accept the compliment, Liam," Madison counters. "Being told you look like Henry Golding is one hundred percent a compliment. And I never said the suit was bad. Or the haircut. I simply said, 'I called it.'" She sits forward in her chair, the blankets falling from her shoulders. "Actually, can I tag along for the day? I'd love to watch you walk into a factory full of Noel residents dressed like that. I'm pretty sure it's 'Bring Your New Neighbor to Work Day' anyway."

Fighting a smile, I shoot back. "Don't you have an existential crisis to work through today?"

"*Oof*, low blow, Liam, low blow," Madison scoffs as she falls back against the chair. "How about I work on my issues and you work on yours, and we'll compare who's made more progress at the end of the day?"

"I'd hardly call my job an existential crisis. I think you have an unfair handicap if we're going to be comparing progress," I say.

Madison stands, rolling her shoulders forward to better anchor the blanket around her. As she steps closer, I notice that her mug doesn't contain coffee, but liquid the color of an orange sunset. Before I can comment, she says, "Based on the power presence you're heading into the factory with today, I'd wager you have more than a few issues to solve. This kind of aura"—she motions up and down my body—"could only mean one thing: you mean business. And you need the rest of the employees to mean business. Which means things must currently be a mess."

I ignore her shrewd observation and make one of my own. "Oolong or white?" I ask, tipping my head toward her mug of tea.

A smile plays at the corners of her mouth. "White."

I quirk an eyebrow. "Sure you don't need something stronger before tackling a day of existential crisis management? I have fresh coffee beans inside."

Madison waves me off. "Not only is tea far superior to coffee, but you also don't have time to make me coffee. You'd better go make a dent in your to-do list. Good luck."

I begin taking backward steps away from her as I say, "I don't need luck. I have everything I need right here." Tapping my temple, I give Madison a wry grin. "But thanks for the well wishes anyway. I'll see you later when you admit that I accomplished more than you."

I replay my conversation with Madison as I drive the few minutes to the production facility. I'm always intrinsically motivated to lead out and work hard to get a job done—not to mention the added motivation of getting *this* job done in order to get out of Arkansas. But this new productivity competition with Madison is the extra *zing* of dopamine pumping me up for the first day on the job.

Angie got my full-access ID badge for the facility programmed before I left Houston so that I wouldn't be slowed down today. I despise being slowed down. After buzzing myself into the building, I briefly introduce myself to the receptionist, ready to walk right past. When she abruptly stands in greeting, I'm forced to pause.

"Hello, Mr. Park, we've been expecting you," she replies. "I'm Amanda. Let me just notify Mr. Olson that you're here so he can show you around. You're a few minutes earlier than expected."

Although mildly irritated that she thinks I need a babysitter, I force a close-lipped smile and wait. As she picks up the phone and dials, I mentally scan my list of important names. Mr. Olson—first name, Beau. Head engineer over machinery. Noel native who temporarily moved away when the old meat-packing plant shut down, only to return when the current facility opened. Several positive recommendations on his LinkedIn profile. Family man with a wife and three children.

I could rattle off similar summaries of all the key employees, thanks to two weeks of diligent prep work. After all, if I'm going to swiftly and decisively win the chess match, I need to understand what pieces I'm working with. I've memorized the key players—what I don't know is how this plant managed to fall grossly behind production goals while bleeding out a disproportionate amount of money.

Yet. But I intend to figure it out quickly.

A man with red hair and a matching beard makes his way toward me. He's dressed in a basic pair of navy pants and a white button-up shirt embroidered with the Pure Fur All logo. As he reaches the front desk, he holds out his hand in introduction.

"Mr. Park, I'm Beau Olson. We're glad to have you here to help get things in better shape," he says. I meet his firm handshake, appreciating his honest welcome. He gestures behind him, "Would you like me to give you a tour of the facility?"

"I will be looking around the entire plant but not immediately," I answer. "Where is Mr. Singer, the floor manager?"

Beau's brow furrows as he glances at Amanda. "Uh, Mr. Singer hasn't worked here since the beginning of December."

Of course, they sent me outdated personnel information from this train wreck of a facility. How much more of my prep work was worthless due to incorrect reports?

"If Mr. Singer is gone, call the new floor manager, please. I'd like to talk with him or her first thing," I state.

More nervous looks between Beau and Amanda. "We don't have a floor manager right now. A replacement for Mr. Singer was never hired."

Closing my eyes, I sigh heavily. "You mean you've been operating without a floor manager for three months?" They reluctantly nod. Under my breath, I mutter, "No wonder this is a dumpster fire." I rake a hand down my face and then look at Beau. "First, I'd like to address all the employees here who are able to temporarily leave their stations. Is there a space conducive to a quick all-hands meeting?"

Beau nods and turns to Amanda. "Why don't you make an announcement for everyone who's able to gather in the empty wing in fifteen minutes?" She immediately picks up the phone to dial the all-call intercom number, and I follow Beau out of the reception area.

"There's an unused wing in the facility?" I ask Beau. "Why would there be usable space sitting empty?"

Beau explains as we walk. "The meat-packing plant that was here before took up more space than the machinery needed for the initial cat food production line. I guess the Pure Fur All execs figured they could expand later if they wanted to."

"Good thing they didn't start off maximizing the space, considering how poorly things have been run so far," I observe. Beau's shoulders slump slightly, but he doesn't argue. He leads us through a door and flips on lights that illuminate an expansive room. The floors look like they were coated for eventual production with proper drains installed, but otherwise, the space is untouched.

"What did you think of the former plant manager?" I ask Beau while we wait for the rest of the employees to join us. Testing his level of candor.

Beau shrugs. "Mr. Wilson? He wasn't the type of guy to make a strong impression. I honestly didn't interact with him a lot."

My eyes narrow. "You're the head engineer overseeing all the machinery. But you hardly interacted with the plant manager?"

To his credit, Beau maintains his composure, aside from tapping one foot. "Your presence here is an indicator of how good of a job Mr. Wilson was doing at managing the factory."

"But you didn't deem it appropriate to push for more interaction? To force more attention when there were issues?" I press. In reality, I already know that Beau was one of the proverbial whistle-blowers alerting Pure Fur All of John Wilson's negligence. But he doesn't know that I know this. And I need to know what kind of backbone the guy has.

Beau squares his shoulders. "I pressed for more oversight through every channel available to me. When Mr. Wilson was unresponsive, I ultimately went above his head with my concerns. I take my job and my responsibilities very seriously, and I don't appreciate any implication otherwise," he says, a hint of defiance in his tone.

Good.

Nodding my approval, I reward his mettle. "I'd like you to give me a full tour after the all-hands meeting. I have a list of further questions I'd like on-the-ground insight on."

Beau clears his throat and stands a little taller. "Can do. You'll need to remove—"

"The coat and tie, and put on a hard hat," I cut in. This isn't my first production line rodeo, after all. I don't want Beau or anyone else thinking I need my hand held while I'm here.

"Yes, sir," Beau responds just as a wave of people flood into the space. Eventually, I see Amanda enter and give Beau a nod, seeming to indicate that everyone with the flexibility to leave their stations has arrived. There are probably seventy-five or so people standing around, so I make my way up a staircase at the side of the room to stand on a platform in order to be clearly seen and heard. Everyone from janitors to packaging line workers to machinists are gathered, staring at me with varying levels of scrutiny and distrust.

"Thank you for stepping away from your posts for a few minutes, even if it means going back through the hygiene sanitation process before reentering the production floor," I begin. I notice a few facial expressions shift from open cynicism to veiled curiosity.

Yes, I do my homework. I do whatever needs to be done in order to take control of the situations I walk into. Even if it means watching boring videos about sanitation processes in pet food production facilities—after all, we can't have microbes or bacteria being transferred into our beloved pets' food.

I certainly wouldn't want any contaminants in Hamlet's food.

"My name is Liam Park, and I work for the parent company that owns Pure Fur All. I have years of experience assessing and improving the operations of failing companies and facilities, which is what I'm here to do," I say. "I'm going to cut to the chase—this is a failing facility. You're somehow underperforming and overspending in egregious fashion, and I'm here to find out precisely how that's been happening. Then, I'll make whatever changes are necessary to fix it."

People shift nervously on their feet, darting glances at fellow employees. This is the part where people inevitably start to fear for their jobs, their livelihoods. Considering the recent history of the town, I'd wager that fear is amplified to an even higher degree than usual.

"I'm not here looking to axe anyone's jobs—not without good reason. If there's fat, I'll trim it. But I'm not convinced that's the issue at hand. More likely, I think there were several ways that the former plant manager was mismanaging production, and those are probably processes that we can fix. What I need from each of you is your transparent honesty about how things were run—what you were asked to do or not do, what your daily responsibilities looked like, anything unusual that you noticed. In return for your honesty, I'll do my best to optimize this plant's efficiency without cutting any jobs. Understand?" I ask.

Heads nod, and I make direct eye contact with as many individuals as possible as I sweep my gaze across the room. I've been standing up straight, feet shoulder-width apart, for the beginning of my speech. Now, I take a second to unbutton my suit coat and lean my hands on the railing in front of me, adopting a slightly more approachable stance. I need these people to both respect *and* trust me enough to speak truthfully when I ask questions.

"I'll be meeting with employees from every department over the next few weeks, shadowing positions and asking questions. If you have thoughts to share that you think would be beneficial in solving the puzzle here, please feel free to initiate a conversation any time. Amanda will be able to schedule a meeting on my calendar," I say.

Did I clear that with Amanda ahead of time? No. But I have no doubt she'll figure it out, if she's worth her salt. Her eyes widen with surprise, but she straightens her shoulders and nods as though she was completely prepared for this responsibility.

"Please fill in anyone from your department who couldn't leave their stations and those who work the other shifts. An all-company email will be sent out by the end of the day. Thanks again for taking these few minutes away—now, let's get back to it," I end, and the low mumblings of conversation fill the room as people file out. My list of mental notes lengthens as I observe demeanors and facial expressions, cataloging the people with the most influence who I should prioritize meeting with first.

I pull the reMarkable tablet out of my satchel, ready to take a boatload of notes. Loosening my tie as I turn to Beau, I say, "How 'bout that tour? I don't want to waste any time."

After all, I have a productivity competition to win.

And a small town to escape.

CHAPTER EIGHT

Madison

Pressing my palms to my eyelids, I slowly count to three.

When I blink open, the steadily-building pressure of a headache still resides behind my eyes. Apparently, three seconds of respite doesn't magically fix twelve straight hours of staring at a computer screen.

Working by the glow of Christmas lights in lieu of a brighter overhead light could also be a contributing factor to the eye fatigue. I'm not sure how to explain it, but the combination of the Christmas decor around me and the snowy coffee shop ambience video I looped on my tablet has kept my mind in the zone for this marathon workday. I've been too heavily influenced by my best friend.

Clara did bring me lunch, and we sat outside at a picnic table in the crisp air for thirty minutes. But aside from that brief break, I've been working nonstop on today's to-do list. The first (and most critical) item on the list—officially registering my business—slowed me way down when I realized I needed a physical address for the application. Which I currently lack. I had a long debate with myself over whether to use a friend's address in KC, Clara's here in Noel, or my parents' in Nebraska.

Which led me to a mental argument over whether I should even bother officially incorporating a business right away. I could MacGyver my way through for now with PayPal invoices to my personal bank account, especially since I may abandon this idea altogether in the not-so-distant future. At the very least, I might have a permanent address attached to my existence by the time I decide to do this long term. I could wait and make things official then.

But even as the rebel devil on one shoulder argued with the rule-following angel on the other, I always knew which side would win out. If I'm going to do this, I'm going to do it right.

Hence, hours of productivity lost to the black hole of pesky physical address requirements. I ultimately decided to use Clara's address (with her permission, of course) since I'm physically located in Noel for the short term. I'll need access to the documents mailed to the supplied address. I can update it later when I move back to KC.

Although filing the application to register Madison Joy Editorial as a legitimate LLC took up way too much time, it's a satisfying checkbox to mark off on the to-do list.

Glancing at my watch, I see that it's nearly 9:00 p.m. A reasonable person would turn off her computer and wind down for the night. But reasonable people don't have friendly "I can accomplish more than you" competitions to win. Clicking open a new tab in my browser, I navigate to the host I've chosen for my website so I can claim a domain name. I can tackle the actual web design tomorrow.

I've been debating between two possible web addresses: a straight-forward madisonjoyeditorial.com or a succinct mjeditorial.com. I think I'm leaning toward the latter, and I have the domain name pulled up on the browser when I'm startled by a knock at the door. That's not a light, hope-I'm-not-imposing Clara knock. It's a strong, self-confident knock.

I bite back a smile and walk the few steps to the door. I couldn't know with certainty that Liam would actually check in tonight to compare first days . . . but I'm not surprised in the least. And I may be just a tiny bit delighted.

Swinging the door open, I *am* surprised by the catch in my chest when I see Liam's end-of-day appearance in contrast to his but-toned-up suit this morning. As in, the suit jacket is literally unbuttoned. The blue tie that was so professionally knotted this morning is now draped around his neck as he leans one hand beside the door.

That hair is still perfectly styled, though. Posh, magazine-worthy hair.

Thankfully, Liam doesn't seem to notice my double take of his appearance because he's doing his own double take of my surroundings.

"Whoa, why is it Christmas in your cabin?" he asks, bypassing any perfunctory greeting. "You are aware what month it is, right? March is way past acceptable for leaving up Christmas decor. And *way* ahead of early decorating."

"It's a long story," I say with a sigh. "Side effect of being best friends with the queen of Christmas spirit. But I'm assuming you didn't pop by for a long story about Christmas spirit and dreams coming true."

Liam pushes his weight off the door frame and casually drops his hands to his hips. "I did not. But I admit I'm intrigued now."

Raising an eyebrow, I sniff. "I'm afraid you'll have to earn that story," I say as I shift my weight to one foot and rest a hand on my popped hip. "Now, Mr. Exec, did you come to gloat or admit defeat?"

One corner of Liam's lips twists into a smirk as he reaches into his leather satchel. "I never admit defeat because I never lose," he says, holding up a thin tablet.

My eyes light up as I reach for the tablet, effectively pulling him inside the cabin since he doesn't let go. "Is that one of those paper tablets that converts your handwriting to text?"

Liam surrenders the tablet to my greedy hands and closes the door to the draft outside. "Yes. I got a reMarkable tablet two years ago and have never looked back."

I try not to drool. There's something especially satisfying about marking edits with a real pen on real paper. But, as someone who cares about the environment, I don't like unnecessarily printing out documents.

"I'll admit I'm getting a little green-eyed here. As an editor, I would love marking changes by hand and having them convert to text. I wouldn't kill my eyes staring at a computer screen and could sit in a comfortable chair instead of being tied to a table. Could have saved a lot of headaches over the past several years," I say, turning the tablet over in my hands.

"That's what you do? Editing?" Liam asks, holding out his hand for the device.

I nod, meeting his gaze. "Proofreading and copyediting, mostly. Different than line editing," I say. When he quirks an eyebrow, I add, "What? Now you're intrigued by the difference between editing stages?"

Liam's eyes bore into mine as he remarks, "I'm intrigued by a lot of things."

I ignore the thrilling shiver that surges through me.

His eyes drop to the tablet as he powers it on. "I can see how it would be appealing to an editor," he says, then gives me a brief rundown of the features.

"What made you want something like this instead of a regular laptop? Computers seem much more executive," I quip.

"I write by hand a lot faster than I type," Liam replies.

I brace myself. "Liam Park, do not tell me that you don't have proper typing technique."

His eyes dance mischievously as he leans in, pointing to himself. "I'm a hunt-and-peck typer, through and through."

I groan, covering my ears and squinting my eyes shut. "I think you just ruptured my ear drums with that admission. I'm appalled."

Liam shrugs. "Hasn't held my career back in the slightest, despite your dismay. Besides, this is much more conducive to taking notes while walking around a factory than a laptop," he says. He waves the tablet in front of me like a taunt and adds, "As evidenced by the twenty-two pages of notes I have from today alone."

Scoffing dramatically, I motion toward my laptop on the small table next to us. "Well, I created a brand-new business from nothing today, so who's the real productivity victor here?"

Liam glances at the table then back at me, an evil gleam in his eye. "All I see is a jazzy Christmas ambience scene on your tablet. I hardly call that a productive work day, despite whatever long-story explanation you have to tell me."

Smacking him on the arm, I huff. "You have definitely *not* earned that long story yet. Your insight into Noel's Christmas magic will have to wait. I'll have you know, I wrestled with US government regulations and won," I say, pointing at the laptop.

He looks more intently at the screen, which still displays the web domain site. "MJ, huh?" His eyes meet mine again. "Is that what your friends call you?"

"No, absolutely not. I'm calling the business 'Madison Joy Editorial' because Madison Joy rolls off the tongue more smoothly than Madison Wheeler. My friends call me 'Mads,' but my middle name does not come into play with nicknames," I say. When his eyes narrow slightly, I narrow my own. "Maybe 'Joy' isn't the appropriate nickname for my saucy attitude."

"Maybe," he says, holding my pointed gaze. "Or maybe it's perfect, MJ."

I roll my eyes to break the spell of Liam's eye contact. "Regardless, I maintain that starting a new business is a more impressive achievement than twenty-one pages of notes," I say.

"Twenty-two," Liam corrects. "Twenty-*two* pages of notes."

I wave off the correction. "Just admit defeat," I assert, returning my hand to a popped hip.

"Never," Liam murmurs. "Is a business *really* valid if there's no website to prove its legitimacy?"

Ugh, that's such a good point. I absolutely don't trust a business with no online presence.

I pin him with my best glare. "We'll call day one a draw, Mr. Exec, but we may need to clearly define the rules of this competition for the future," I state.

Liam shrugs one shoulder. "If you insist, MJ. Now, if you don't mind, I have twenty-two pages of notes to review and consolidate, so I'll leave you to your relaxing Christmas vibes."

As he steps backward, I realize for the first time how closely we were standing to each other. An odd wave of disappointment cascades through me at the empty space between us now. Shaking it off, I raise my chin. "I'll call your notes review and raise you one web design. See you tomorrow, Liam."

Did I stay awake until 1:30 a.m. fighting with a web design platform?

I'm exercising my fifth amendment rights.

Did I still set an alarm so I would have time to make a cup of tea and be casually sitting in my trusty Adirondack chair when Liam leaves for work?

Like I said, fifth amendment.

While proofreading the copy of a website to make sure it's error-free is absolutely in my wheelhouse, *designing* a website is not a natural strength. But I am a resourceful, determined individual—and you can learn how to do virtually anything on YouTube these days.

That means I ended day one with one bona fide business website, and I think that certainly tops any amount of note compilation that Liam may have accomplished last night. My late-night hours still count toward day one since we're counting days by the hours awake and working, not the official date shown on your phone. At least, I say so.

I take a long sip of my English breakfast tea, brewed extra strong, with a splash of cream and a drizzle of honey. A higher caffeine content was necessary after a short night's sleep.

I'm intentionally sitting at an angle instead of directly facing Liam's cabin. While I do enjoy taking in the peaceful woodsy scenery, my gaze frequently drifts to his cabin. Ever since he came over last night, I've been itching to get a peek inside his living space. I want to confirm all of my gut instincts and assumptions about him (and count his suits, for good measure).

That's the *only* reason I'm dying to go inside his cabin—because I love proving myself right. However, I am socially aware enough to not be a psycho knocking on his door demanding entry in the early morning. I'll bide my time until the appropriate snooping opportunity presents itself.

When I hear the click of Liam's door opening, I quickly school my features into a natural, aloof expression. Staring off into the scenic distance.

"Morning, MJ," his smooth voice calls.

My aloof expression is instantly spoiled by an eye roll. "Stop calling me MJ," I say as he strides my way.

"Why? Did a childhood bully call you MJ? Or does it have some other traumatic association from your past?" he asks.

"Well, no."

"Do you have a general aversion to the initials?"

"No."

"Then why can't I call you MJ?" he presses.

I harrumph. "I don't know. I've just . . . never been called that before. It's always Madison or Mads. MJ makes me think of Michael Jordan or Michael Jackson—it doesn't fit me," I assert.

Liam's eyes sparkle. "The two Michaels, huh? Two icons of their fields, powerhouses of presence. I think the shoe fits."

A genuine smile spreads across my lips before I can sassify it. Liam holds up his phone and says, "Besides, mjeditorial.com is official and everything. Now the shoe definitely fits."

My eyebrows shoot up. "You looked up my website?"

"Obviously," Liam says. "We both knew you weren't going to go to sleep before you had a website. Not after our conversation last night." He adds the final remark with a self-satisfied smirk.

I match his expression as I stand and step toward him. "Let me guess—all nineteen pages of notes meticulously sorted and converted to your computer?"

"Twenty-two pages—you're purposely getting it wrong now," he quips back. "And yes, I sorted through all my notes and came up with two pages of questions and next steps in the investigation for today. Although, I would have done that last night regardless of your added motivation. But living across the gravel lane from you certainly isn't harming my productivity. If I accomplish everything on my to-do list today, it's going to take more than a completed web design for you to claim victory."

"We'll have to compare the number of checked-off items on our lists at the end of the day. Make the competition a little more objective," I say.

Liam narrows his eyes and angles his head like he's considering what I've said. "I don't know—it seems like comparing a business startup to fixing a broken system is innately subjective. Surely we can both agree to take into account the amount of time tasks require and be honest in our assessments," he counters, a confident gleam in his eye.

As he's spoken, he's slowly walked closer to me, and the morning breeze picks up the musky scent of his cologne, wafting it through my senses. His plain, dark navy suit is paired with a baby blue shirt, sans tie today. I suppose the full suit was just a day one look.

"Black tea?" His question breaks me out of my focus on his appearance, startling me with how close he is. I glance down at the mug in my hands as he continues, "If you needed more caffeine, my coffee offer is a standing proposal."

"Thanks, but no thanks," I say. "I prefer tea."

"I gathered as much. But an artisan cup of black coffee could be a special treat, even for a tea person," Liam says. He starts to back away toward his SUV as he adds, "Just let me know if you ever need a cup."

My attention sparks as I recognize the appropriate snooping opportunity that just presented itself. "Tomorrow," I quickly state. "I'll try a cup tomorrow. If only to prove to myself once and for all that tea is the superior morning drink."

"I accept the challenge," Liam says with a wry grin. "Good luck winning the productivity day on your inferior caffeinated beverage, MJ."

He shuts himself in his car before I can come up with a sarcastic reply. He gives me a two-finger salute from the steering wheel as he drives past me, as if acknowledging his victory in the verbal sparring ring this morning.

Marching the distance to my cabin (all six feet), I psyche myself up to have the most productive day on record. I might need to forgo the Christmas ambiance video today in lieu of some angry-girl music to get my sass back in full swing.

Chapter Nine

Liam

"You're not in trouble. Just walk me through your routine," I urge the timid man in front of me. He operates a forklift, unloading the deliveries of frozen meat into the freezers and then loading the pallets of packaged food onto the outgoing trucks.

As he talks me through his responsibilities and literally walks me along the paths he drives, I take notes on my tablet. Looking at the tablet temporarily distracts my mind, reminding me of my conversation with Madison last night. I quickly brush the thought away and focus on my current surroundings.

To some executives, it might seem like a waste of time to walk through the responsibilities of a forklift driver. But in order to create and optimize standard operating procedures, I first have to assess how things are currently operating. From the very beginning: unloading the raw ingredients—to the very end: loading the finished product.

Somewhere along the line, procedures have been breaking down here. And I won't know where until I walk through every detail. When I received the initial reports from Cal, my boss in Houston, I was scratching my head as to how a production facility could be so off the mark on daily targets and so far in the red financially in such a short time.

When I'm finished taking notes on the unloading and loading processes, I stop through sanitation before entering the room where raw ingredients are mixed. An employee explains the different parts of the machinery—grinding the meat, mixing in the added nutrients and other powdered ingredients, and adding liquid until the slurry is the right consistency to be tubed onto the conveyor belt to go through the baking and cutting process.

I'm not sure I'll be able to look at Hamlet's food the same way again after seeing it in slurry form. I may skip lunch today.

Beau gave me a detailed tour of the entire facility yesterday, taking care to explain each piece of the machinery for me. The floor plan design and machine installation were handled by an outside company that specializes in optimizing efficiency in pet food production facilities. So, while I'm not expecting to find any breakdowns in the machine efficiency, I still want to be thorough in my assessment.

For today, I talk with employees at each hands-on phase of the process, from mixing ingredients to packaging to quality control. Tomorrow, I'll speak with the sanitation specialists who clean the machinery and the engineers who fix it when it breaks.

The employees I've interacted with so far have been courteous and helpful, if a little spooked. It's obvious that the previous closure of the meat-packing plant has everyone on edge about me being here. Like I represent an existential threat to the town's future.

I don't know how to reassure them that their jobs are safe other than to figure out what went wrong here. On the surface, the mismatch in production and spending doesn't make sense. My gut tells me something's off, and I don't like it.

After working through lunch, I take a break in the office designated for the plant manager. After yesterday's digging, I decided I should probably make myself at home here. I wish I could sit down with the previous plant manager and ask some pointed questions, but he's been unreachable since being fired. Instead, I call up the chain at Pure Fur All to request a more detailed report from a comparable facility.

"I'm sorry, sir, I can't just turn over sensitive financial information like that. I hope you understand," the representative tells me.

Exhaling a calculated breath, I press. "No, *you* don't understand. I've been sent to this location by Holden Incorporated—the company that owns Pure Fur All—to ensure this facility starts hitting target numbers and turning a profit. I can't do my job without comp numbers from another facility to compare and see where it's going wrong. I need these reports sent to me yesterday."

"Um, I'm sorry, I'm just going to need to check on your authorization," the man stutters, mumbling something about a supervisor. I inhale slowly, pinching the bridge of my nose. Incompetency and inefficiency sit at the top of my pet peeves list.

"Listen to me carefully," I cut in. "You're going to write this down—Liam Park, Executive Operations Specialist with Holden Incorporated. Currently stationed at the production facility in Noel, Arkansas, with full authorization and access to *any and all* information I request. You're going to run this information by whoever you need to run it by the second I hang up, and you're going to have those reports emailed to me by the end of the day. Got it?"

"Uh, yes, sir, I'll do the best I can," he says.

"Please do," I reply and end the call. I pick up a tennis ball from my desk and toss it at the wall a few times, bouncing questions around my mind in the process. Dialing Amanda on the office phone, I ask her to track down Beau and send him my way.

As I wait for Beau, I continue tossing the tennis ball until I miss catching it. Rather than stand to retrieve the dropped ball, I pull up Madison's website on my phone again. The site was bare-bones basic this morning when I first searched for it. I'm curious to see if she's made any progress on the design. After all, I need to know what kind of productivity race I'm in for today, even if the judgment is subjective.

The site looks mostly the same as before, but that doesn't mean she hasn't been hard at work today. She probably tackled other tasks. I suppose I'll find out tonight.

Stop thinking about how Madison is spending her time. Focus on your own tasks, Liam.

My admonishing self-talk is interrupted by Beau's knock on the open door. He pokes his head in and says, "You wanted to see me?"

I motion toward the empty chair across from my desk before I think better of it and stand up instead. "Never mind, don't sit. Walk with me. I think better when I'm moving," I say, and Beau dutifully follows me out of the office. I make my way to the empty wing where there's plenty of open space to walk and talk without interruption.

Flipping on the lights, I start walking a circle around the room at a brisk pace. Beau falls into step beside me and asks, "So? What do you think is the problem?"

I shake my head, frustrated that I don't have the answer. Even if I've only been here for two days.

"I won't draw final conclusions until I finish my full investigation, but I don't think there's just one problem. There are probably several little problems—maybe some big ones in the mix. It's not adding up, and that makes me uneasy," I say, and Beau nods. "I requested more information from Pure Fur All that should have been sent to me from the beginning. But until they get their act together and send me comprehensive reports, I can't make any fully-informed assessments."

I spend the next thirty minutes walking laps around the empty room and peppering Beau with questions. I need to know if and how any processes or routines changed from the time the plant opened in October to the manager's firing at the beginning of last month. If I'm going to take control of this mess of a factory, I *need* all of the facts—gaps in information are one of my personal circles of hell.

Beau is eventually called away to fix an oven that isn't heating to the correct temperature. I divert him back by my office to grab my tablet and tag along to watch their problem-solving process. After about twenty minutes, Beau has the oven working again.

"How many pounds of food did we just lose during the time this oven was offline?" I ask. Beau and the other two men look back and forth at each other, making varying noises of ignorance. I square my stance and pin them with a look. "None of you know how far behind you just fell in these sixty-three minutes?" More embarrassed looks. "Every single employee should know exactly how many pounds per hour this factory should be producing. So you know exactly how much money you're wasting every time there's a delay."

After a few more darted glances between them, Beau clears his throat and speaks up. "Breakdowns in machinery are unavoidable. These types of temporary delays are expected."

I resist the urge to roll my eyes by pinching the bridge of my nose instead. "I'm not saying that machine breakdowns are unexpected. I'm saying that you all are *expected* to know your facility's targeted production capacity, so you have a sense of urgency to get back on track when breakdowns happen."

Beau squares his shoulders. "Just because we don't know the exact number of pounds lost doesn't mean we don't work to fix issues as quickly as possible. We have integrity to do our best work regardless of the precise amount of loss."

While mentally giving Beau good marks for standing up for himself and his coworkers, verbally I reiterate, "I expect everyone in this facility to know the answer tomorrow—how many pounds of food are lost each hour when there are processing delays?"

Pivoting on my heel, I head back to my office without further comment.

After another late night in my office taking a preliminary look at the comp information Pure Fur All sent, I pull onto the gravel "road" between the rows of cabins. As I park beside mine, I notice that Madison's car is gone, and her unit is dark. I'm surprised by the disappointment that sinks like a rock in my stomach.

I dismiss the sensation—it was just a pleasant surprise having someone around to process my day with yesterday. A stimulating conversation with someone who constantly rose to the challenge. It was an abnormal outlier, not a routine I should expect.

As I unlock the door, I can hear Hamlet's yowling through the walls. He must have had quite the exciting day if he can't even wait for me to come inside before he starts telling me all about it. Opening the door carefully, I find him waiting right inside. "Hi, my friend," I say as I reach down to scratch his chin. He rubs against my ankles, continuing his constant meowing.

When I bend down to remove my shoes, Hamlet leaps onto my back and settles on my shoulders as I stand up. "Missed me, huh?" I ask as I walk to the kitchenette. This blazer will definitely need a trip to the dry cleaner now.

"Why don't you tell me about your day while I make dinner?" I tell Hamlet as I reach a hand up to scratch his chest, which is positioned right next to my ear. He meows the entire time I heat up a bowl of spicy ramen noodles. *I really need to figure out some better meals if I'm going to be here for a while. Take-out options are sorely lacking. Especially healthy ones.*

As much as I'd hoped to be in and out of this town as quickly as possible, it's looking less and less like a quick fix. *At least I have Madison's feisty presence keeping me company so I don't completely lose my mind here.* Hamlet meows extra loudly in my ear as if he could read my thoughts. "Sorry, buddy. You're right—I always have you to keep me company. I'm sorry I haven't been around much. I'd hoped that putting in a few long days would magically fix the problem here and we could get back to Houston. But that's not looking very promising. I swear I'll try to be around more."

Hamlet meows loudly once more before jumping off of my shoulders and padding over to his food dish. *Meow.* I smile at his demanding demeanor and scoop dinner into his dish. "Trust me, Hamlet—you don't want to know what that food looks like before it makes its way to you."

Meow.

As we eat our respective meals, I send a text to Hana to see if she's awake to chat, even though I hope she's asleep. Ten minutes later, my phone rings with her video call.

"Hey, Night Owl," I say.

She forgoes a greeting altogether. "Where are you?" she asks, narrowing her eyes and leaning closer to the screen.

"In my temporary residence for my latest assignment," I reply, withholding as much information as possible.

"Is this like some sort of studio condo or something?" she asks, and I realize the bed is visible behind me based on the angle of my phone screen.

"Something like that. How are classes going?" I inquire, hoping to change the subject from my current location.

"But *where* are you? Where's the latest assignment located?" she presses.

I roll my eyes and deflect by accusing *her* of deflecting. "Are you saying classes aren't going well? Are you getting too distracted by all the men with British accents to focus on school?"

"You're making things up!" she huffs indignantly. "I'll have you know that I received high marks on my first big research paper about *The Canterbury Tales*. And you know they're grading more harshly than a university in America, so I essentially got the equivalent of an A."

"Oh, I know this, huh?" I tease. "I think you're just making excuses, and the accents are distracting you from A-quality work."

"Ha ha," she says. "What would you know about distractions? You never get distracted by the women around you, even though I try to convince you to pay attention."

I shrug. "There's no point in paying attention when I'm constantly moving around. And I'm never home in Houston long enough to go on more than a few dates with someone. It wouldn't exactly be chivalrous to start a relationship and then ask her to wait around until the next time I'm home for a few weeks."

"You don't *have* to keep gallivanting around all the time, constantly saving the business world from self-destruction. Surely you could find some catastrophes to avert from the same home base," Hana says, shaking her head in disapproval.

I don't know what possesses me—possibly that disapproving head shake—but the words "I have met an interesting girl here" are out of my mouth before I think to stop myself.

Hana immediately sits up straight and leans forward. "What?! You're interested in a girl?"

I give her a taste of her disapproving-head-shake medicine. "You're twisting what I said. I said I 'met an interesting girl,' not, 'I'm interested in a girl.'"

"I think you're splitting hairs," Hana says, grinning. "Which only convinces me more that you're interested."

"Our ten-year age gap is showing. Stop being juvenile," I scoff. "There's a woman named Madison staying across the way from me. She's . . . spunky. And she's starting her own business, so we've struck up a sort of competition on who can accomplish more each day."

Hana facepalms her forehead. "Only *you* could get into a productivity competition with someone. And then call that connection."

"Well, it's at least making my time here more interesting."

"Which is where, again?" Hana asks, eyebrow quirked.

I'm saved from skirting her question by Hamlet jumping onto my lap and meowing loudly at Hana's face on the screen.

"Heya, Ham, you sweet boy," she says in a high-pitched voice.

"Hana," I groan, emphasizing the Korean pronunciation of her name, which sounds similar to *Han*—like Han Solo—followed by an *ah* sound. Hamlet meows along with me. "Just call him 'Hamlet,' for goodness' sake."

"I'll stop calling him 'Ham' when you tell me where you are and confess your undying love for Madison," Hana counters.

"I love . . . you. Go to sleep," I say and end the call with an exaggerated jab at the phone screen.

CHAPTER TEN

Madison

"What can I say? It was the straw that finally broke my back," I conclude. Syd is wiping tears from the corners of her eyes after laughing so hard, and Becky takes a sip of water to calm the flush in her cheeks. Clara has already heard the story of Ivy's durian catastrophe—albeit the emotional breakdown version as opposed to the polished comedy sketch.

Davis pats Syd's back as he says, "Don't die laughing there, beautiful. I love you too much."

Clark rolls his eyes at Davis, as though he's not constantly being just as lovey-dovey with Clara. Now that Becky has her laughter under control, she says, "Well, I'm sorry that you were forced to move, but it's our gain. We're glad to have you in Noel, Mads, for however long you can stay."

I give an appreciative wave in her and James' direction. "Thanks to you two for giving me an affordable place to stay for now."

Conversation is interrupted by the delivery of three large pizzas. Every Tuesday night, Clark and Clara have dinner with Davis and Sydney, James and Becky, and Beau and Abby. All the grandparents watch their respective grandkids so the parents can have a weekly get together—a tradition they were kind enough to include me in this week. With an open invitation in the future, although I'll have to feel out how much of an intrusion I am tonight.

"Abby texted to go ahead and start eating. They'll be here in five minutes. Beau was late getting home from the factory today," Syd says, putting her phone down. My ears perk up at her mention of Beau and the factory. How could I casually pull information out of Beau about what Liam is like at work? Strictly in the name of our competition.

Today was technically a very productive day for me—I opened a business bank account, which took far longer than I'd anticipated. I also enrolled in an online course to brush up on the Chicago Manual of Style guidelines, since we followed the Associated Press Style rules at WritInc. If I'm going to get hired to proofread books—both nonfiction and fiction—I'll need to switch my brain to Chicago Manual mode.

I also emailed the friend who's working on designs for me, plus revamped my résumé to be ready for use on my website. But while those were all crucial tasks, I'm worried that Liam will come home today waving a smoking gun of productivity.

Not being around tonight to compare notes with him is the one downside to saying yes to this group dinner. But maybe an inside scoop from Beau will counterbalance that downside.

We begin the process of serving pizza slices onto plates. Syd makes a big show of waving her olive-laden pizza in front of Clark and Clara, who both dramatically crinkle their noses in disgust. Abby and Beau join the table with a flurry of greetings and grab their own slices of pizza.

I don't even have to lead the way in prying information out of Beau—Davis is on the ball with questions to satisfy my curiosity. Davis asks Beau, "How's it going with the new corporate guy? What's he like?"

Yes, Beau. What is Liam like at work?

Beau swallows a bite before answering. "To be determined, I guess. He's very direct and gets straight to the point with his questions and observations."

Syd chuckles and says, "Well, that's not very Southern of him, is it? Someone needs to tell him to beat around the bush and politely back his way into pointed questions."

Everyone laughs in response, and Beau says, "Yeah, it's a bit of a culture mismatch, for sure. Then again, every time he asks a pointed question or makes a critical observation, it makes me realize how screwed up things are. I thought everyone would seamlessly pick up their new roles at this facility after working at the meat-packing plant in the past, but it's a totally different operation."

There's a collective murmur of understanding and support from the group. I'm somewhat shocked when Clark is the next person to voluntarily speak up. "But he—what's his name again?"

"Liam Park," I interject. Eight pairs of eyes look my way.

Beau says, "I forgot he's staying at the cabins with you, Madison. Put a pin in that—I'm circling back to you after Clark's question. When Clark speaks, we must listen."

Clark grunts annoyance but continues his question. "This Liam guy isn't talking about firing people, though, right? Or pulling the plug on the factory?" Clearly, Clark still has some PTSD from the meat-packing plant shutting down and his town nearly dying out as a result.

All eyes are on Beau, now, who shakes his head. "I really don't think so. Even though I don't doubt that Mr. Park is the type to do whatever needs to be done—including firing people—he's gone out of his way to assure employees that cutting jobs isn't his priority. He's trying to identify where things are going wrong so he can optimize processes to make the plant more profitable, instead of just blindly cutting positions. At least, that's what he's said."

Relief is palpable around the table. Beau points at me. "He's living right across from you. Have you talked to him much?"

"Yep," I state, then take a drink of water.

Clara waves a hand and says, "What was it you said about him, Mads? Confident but not an arrogant piece of work?"

Nodding, I say, "Can confirm. I mean, I don't see Liam at the plant, obviously, but that's my impression from our casual conversations the past few days." I don't bother to explain that "casual" may not be quite the right descriptor for our repartees.

"I have a hard time picturing a casual version of Mr. Park, what with his power suits and full-throttle approach to everything," Beau says.

Unable to explain exactly why, I bristle on Liam's behalf. "A full-throttle approach isn't necessarily a bad thing. Maybe the lack of full throttle is what got the factory into this mess in the first place. From what I've seen, Liam seems to be working awfully hard to fix a problem he didn't create. His efforts could save Noel from a second brush with death."

Everyone eyes me with varying levels of shock and confusion. I'm not usually one to explain myself, but I see a glimmer in Clara's romance-filtered eyes, and I need to shut that right down. "Liam and I have a friendly competition going over who can accomplish more on our missions each day—me with my new business and him with fixing the factory. I've seen how early he leaves and how late he comes back—only to spend even *more* hours each night reviewing the pages of notes he took during the day. I really do think he has good intentions of whipping things into shape with as little collateral damage as possible."

"Well, that's good to hear," Abby quietly interjects. She seems the shyest, and I don't know her as well as the other women here, since she and Beau moved away from Noel when the meat-packing plant shut down. I got to know Syd and Becky much better during past trips to visit Clara. Abby looks up at Beau and says, "The last thing we need is to uproot our family again. I hope he gets things running so smoothly that Pure Fur All would never dream of cutting jobs or shutting things down."

"I'll toast to that," James says, raising his glass.

"To Liam Park's master improvement plan," I chime in, raising mine.

"Here, here."

It's late when I arrive home to my cozy little cabin. I'm torn between feeling satisfied from a good time with friends versus chastising myself for the wasted hours that could have been spent moving the needle on my new business.

Liam is sure to win the competition today. Again.

Light glows from the windows of his cabin, but it's a faint light—more like the warmth of a bedside lamp than the full overhead light. Even though Liam stopped by my cabin yesterday, it's late tonight, and I feel hesitant to randomly knock on his door. Especially if he's in bed reviewing notes. Based on the ridiculous hitch in my chest seeing him with his tie undone last night, I don't think I'm at all ready to see dressed-for-bed Liam. So I lock my car and walk the few steps to my cabin with mild disappointment blooming in my chest.

Until I see a piece of paper taped to my front door. I step inside and flip on a light so I can read the note.

Madison
Coffee hour is at 7:00 a.m. sharp. Text me at 713-555-6184 if you'll be sleeping in and won't make it.
Liam

I reread the short note, examining the neat print. *He does have impressively legible handwriting.* Smiling, I pull out my phone and save his number.

ME

Please. There's no sleep for the determined.

This is Madison, by the way.

I don't have to wait long for the conversation dots to begin bouncing.

MR. EXEC

Noted.

I roll my eyes at his succinct response. *Ever the efficient communicator.*

ME

I'll take the L for today. Tasks took way longer than expected, so I didn't check off my entire to-do list today.

MR. EXEC

What took a long time?

Opening a business bank account effectively wiped out half of my day.

Banks are the worst. I'll give this one to you out of sympathy.

No, no, no. I earn my wins. I assume you have 78 pages of notes today?

Not quite 78, but plenty to keep me busy. Been reviewing notes since I got home a couple of hours ago.

There's a pause in the conversation as I try to decide what to say next. But Liam's bouncing dots eventually halt my debate.

Had big plans tonight? Or burning the midnight oil working at some tea shop I don't know exists?

I snort a laugh.

Zero tea shops in Noel, sadly. Becky's Brews coffee shop is open most of the year, but she's taking a break between busy seasons.

And neither. No big plans or midnight oil. Just a casual dinner with my best friend, Clara, and her husband, plus some of their other friends. One of them you know. Beau Olson.

Ah, yes. Beau seems like a solid employee.

I decide to poke the bear. Just a little.

ME

> Curious to know what he thinks of you?

MR. EXEC

> I don't care what he thinks about me.

ME

> Careful. You might veer from confident to arrogant territory.

MR. EXEC

> It's not arrogant to not care what people think. I'm here to do my job. A job I happen to be very good at, which will benefit your friends when the factory doesn't shut down. I'll do my job and then leave. I don't need people to like me in the process.

My stomach ties itself in knots at the matter-of-fact statement regarding his temporary presence in Noel. Which is nonsense because my life will continue on just fine without Liam's presence. Not to mention I'm *also* a temporary resident of Noel.

I tap my thumb on the side of my phone as I debate whether to continue the conversation. *Liam made it pretty clear that he's not here to make friends—which logically means he doesn't see me as a friend. Maybe what I thought was a mutual enjoyment of our back-and-forth was actually him humoring me, and now he's tired of it. Tired of me. I should stop annoying him.*

I've just set my phone down on the table when it *pings* again. I pick it back up with embarrassing speed.

MR. EXEC

> But you can tell me if I ever cross the confident/arrogant line with you, MJ. As my neighbor, I do care a little what you think about me.

I purse my lips, clamping down a smile.

ME

> You forgot fierce competitor in addition to neighbor.

MR. EXEC

You'd better get on the ball tomorrow if you expect me to attach the term "fierce" to your competitor title.

ME

Good thing I have an extra-strong cup of caffeine scheduled to start the day.

MR. EXEC

7:00 sharp. See you then.

CHAPTER ELEVEN
Madison

Since I had already ceded yesterday's victory, I went to bed early instead of working last night. Which was a good decision, considering I'm now wide awake at 5:45 a.m. without the assistance of an alarm. I'm still snuggled under the covers when I hear a crunch on the gravel outside, startling me out of bed.

Pushing aside the curtain and separating the blinds on the side window, I catch a glimpse of Liam's retreating form, running away from the cabin complex. *I guess the running is a consistent thing. I suppose he has to keep that body in shape somehow when he's moving all over the country. And he's doing an awfully good job of it.*

The observation is simply an acknowledgment of fact, nothing more. Still, I make a mental note to add more barre sessions with Clara to my to-do lists.

I'm on day-three hair, and while I frequently push it to four or even five days with the help of quality dry shampoo, I decide to take a fast shower before going to Liam's cabin. After all, they do say to dress for the day you want to have—and I'm gunning for a win today.

While I shampoo and condition my hair, the eucalyptus and tea tree oil scent wakes me up even more. *I may not even need caffeine today. But I'm not turning down the chance to count Liam's suits, assuming his cabin has the same open-concept feel. I bet he has at least six.*

I don't bother to blow-dry my hair since it air dries mostly straight all on its own. I do take a few minutes to apply some light makeup, including the mini cat-eye eyeliner that helped maintain my token "sassy" aura at WritInc. I even go so far as to slip on a pair of jeans and a sage-green sweater in lieu of leggings and a sweatshirt. Because I have an extra few minutes, I repaint my nails, choosing a coral pink as the main color. After painting my right thumb and index finger, I pause. *Should I switch back to ring finger accent nails now that I'm no longer secretly sticking it to Chad?* After a momentary debate, I skip over my middle fingernail, leaving it blank. When the coral nails are finished, I decide I may as well just go bold and paint my accent nails stark black. Call it a power move.

Dressing for the day you want to have—check. Maybe I'll actually add that to my to-do list for the day so I can officially check it off.

At 6:57 a.m., I cross the few yards of gravel between our cabins and knock on Liam's door. He swings it open almost instantly, and holy moly, I was not prepared for freshly-showered Liam Park. He must not have sprayed any cologne yet because I'm hit by a scent of masculine body wash instead. I physically bite my tongue to stop myself from telling him to ditch the cologne altogether.

His black hair has been styled but holds that still-wet sheen, and the black dress shirt he's wearing with light gray slacks should be the poster look for business professional dress codes. He isn't wearing the matching blazer yet (although it's hanging on a hook by the door), and it has me picturing what the shirt would look like with the sleeves rolled up on his forearms and paired with jeans.

All of these observations have flooded my brain in the split second it's taken Liam to say, "Good morning, MJ."

I'm a fish with its mouth hanging open. I'm about to be caught acting like a total psycho if my brain can't manage to remember some common greeting phrases, stat. Something streaks across the room behind Liam, causing me to scream, jump, and narrowly avoid psycho-staring territory.

"You have a cat in here?!" I exclaim just before I realize I have a death grip on Liam's arm.

It's a very firm arm.

His eyebrows form a wry line as he looks down at my hands wrapped around his bicep, then back to my face. "Are you . . . afraid of cats?"

I release his arm only to give it a firm swat. "No, I'm not afraid of cats. I was just startled. I didn't expect to see any animals running around the tiny cabin." His amused smile remains in place. I huff. "Are you even *allowed* to have pets in here? Does James know you have a cat?"

Liam shrugs. "I assume so. I didn't book the lodging—our executive assistant did that. She's good about finding places for me that allow pets, so I'd imagine the landlord is aware of Hamlet's presence."

In response to his name, the cat gives a loud *meow* as it brushes up against Liam's ankles. It sits down at his feet and eyes me with a look of utter contempt.

"Um, hi there, Hamlet," I say uncertainly as I bend forward and reach out my hand. The cat hisses and swats at my fingers, causing me to jump back in alarm. *Maybe I am afraid of this cat.*

"Don't take it personally," Liam says. "Hamlet doesn't really like people, but he's harmless."

"Duly noted," I say, pinning my own haughty glare on Hamlet. He narrows his eyes at me before trotting across the room to curl up on the bed. I turn to Liam. "I was promised a cup of coffee that would tempt me to change my mind about hot beverage rankings."

Liam claps his hands together, a boyish grin spreading across his face. "Indeed," he says as he walks the few steps to the kitchenette. "If you think tea is better, it's probably because you haven't had a high-quality cup of coffee yet."

He places a hand-crank coffee grinder on a kitchen scale. With practiced movements, he turns on the scale and a goose-neck water kettle. He opens a vacuum-sealed container and pours coffee beans into the grinder, measuring out the right grams. While the water heats, he grinds the coffee beans, retrieves a coffee mug from the cabinet, and covers it with a pour over contraption. He places a cone-shaped filter inside but doesn't add the coffee grounds yet. When the water has been heated to the set temperature, he pours hot water through the filter over the sink.

"Why are you doing that?" I ask, stepping closer in my curiosity.

He looks down at me as I stand next to his shoulder. "Pouring water through first gets rid of any lingering taste of the filter," he explains as he dumps the coffee grounds into the damp filter. He places the whole pour over setup onto the kitchen scale and zeros it out before slowly pouring hot water over the grounds in a controlled swirling pattern.

As he stirs the water into the grounds with a tiny spoon, I can't help but think this entire process is rather soothing to watch. Even if it turns out to taste bitter and disgusting. Liam continues to swirl more water over the grounds in intervals as he asks me about my to-do list for the day.

"I'm hoping that my friend who's designing my logo and other graphics will get them back to me today. Then I can finish the web design and get some social media accounts created. I also have an editing course to start, and I'll get through as many of those video modules as possible so I can add the credentials to my résumé ASAP," I answer. I'm still mesmerized by Liam's sure movements making the pour over coffee.

He sets the water kettle back on the heater, and I look up to meet his eyes. He asks, "I thought you had several years of proofreading experience? Why do you need to take an editing course?"

"Well, the specific style guide we used at the company I worked for is different than the style guidelines used for books. Thank goodness I get to embrace the Oxford comma again," I reply. I launch into the differences between style guides, and he doesn't even look bored as I explain.

"What company did you work for, and why did you quit?" he asks.

Although it's a reasonable question, I feel embarrassed to answer. Ashamed to admit that, apparently, I wasn't irreplaceable. I give a brief description of WritInc as a company, but shy away from answering his second question.

"And?" he asks, holding intense eye contact.

Sighing, I say, "And last month, my manager decided to save the company money by replacing me with a robot." Liam raises an eyebrow, and I say, "They're using AI to run the final proofreads instead of a human proofreader."

Considering Liam's job description—optimize processes and get businesses running more efficiently—I expect him to side with Evil Chad. So I'm surprised when he shakes his head in disapproval.

"Were there ever any complaints from customers about typos or errors?" he asks.

"I resent your insinuation that I would let a mistake slip through!" I huff. "Zero complaints in the seven years I worked there."

Liam shakes his head again. "I understand the manager's logic, but that's a short-sighted decision. They could lose more money than they save in the long run if they start having errors. Customers don't like 'efficiency' if it means mistakes—they could lose some clients," Liam says, miming air quotes.

I resist the urge to hug him. Enthusiastically.

"Thank you!" I say instead. "That's exactly what I said. Apparently, I'm not very persuasive. Or, I'm not very essential."

"Untrue," Liam says as he removes the pour over funnel from the mug, now that the water has finished draining through. "You're both."

He hands the mug to me with a gleam in his eye. "I think you'll find I'm also very persuasive. I used my favorite coffee beans, just for you," he says. "Moment of truth."

"Don't I at least get some cream or sugar in here?" I ask, scrunching up my nose. Even though the coffee smells divine.

Liam mimics my dramatic reaction to his hunt-and-peck typing confession two nights ago, covering his ears and squinting his eyes closed. He begins in a falsetto voice, "I think you ruptured my ear—"

I smack his arm again to cut him off, which causes him to fully laugh. It's a deep, comforting sound, especially paired with the smile lines around his eyes.

"You need to try it black," Liam says when his laughter dies out. "Quality coffee doesn't need to be drowned out with milk or sugar. You'll get the full-bodied tasting experience by sipping it black."

Eyeing him with suspicion, I raise the mug to my lips and take a slow sip.

I'm offended by how not awful it is.

Faking a cough, I give Liam my best accusatory eyebrows. "I don't know—tastes pretty bitter to me."

He gives me a smug smile in return. "You are such a liar." I roll my eyes but take another sip.

Gosh darn it, this is actually pretty good.

"If you enjoy the variety of teas I saw on your kitchen counter, then I know you have the refined palate to taste the different notes in the coffee," Liam says. I stand a little straighter at the compliment. And mentally glitch over his casual snoopiness when he was in my cabin the other night. I shouldn't be surprised that he's matching my game.

He motions toward the mug. "What do you taste?"

I take a longer drink, paying close attention as I swallow. "Warm, earthy undertones. Like chocolate or nuts or something. It's not acidic or fruity at all." Liam gives me an approving look, and I can't help but smile. "I'm right, aren't I?"

Liam nods as he says, "Cocoa, hazelnut, and caramel—it's a single origin bean from Brazil. It brews really smooth without any acidity or bitterness. You can go ahead and admit that you like it," he adds as I'm taking a full drink.

I groan as I turn away from him, holding the mug with both hands. "Fine. I admit it. But I don't necessarily like it *better* than tea." My eyes scan the space of his cabin. It's larger than mine with a spiral staircase leading to a loft, but otherwise the layout is the same, simply bigger. The bed is neatly made, and I notice (with smug delight) several suits hanging on the bar by the bed.

Swiveling around, I lock eyes with Liam, which could be a bad idea for my runaway hormones. "I'm seeing an astounding number of blazers hanging up over there."

Liam leans against the counter, crossing one ankle over the other and folding his arms across his chest. The casual pose is doing nothing to corral my hormones. Neither is the self-assured smile on his face. "I already told you I like suits. That's not a dirty secret."

I swallow hard before plastering a smirk on my face. "How many?"

"I have enough," Liam says, his lips twitching slightly. I raise my eyebrow in challenge. "Eight," he finally admits on a sigh.

"Here—but you have more that you left at home?" I prod. He makes a "whatever" face. I *tsk* my tongue, turning a full circle in the room as I take another appreciative sip of coffee (and keep an eye out for the cat that is no longer on the bed—that gray devil might sense my sarcastic teasing of his master and attack me).

When I turn back to Liam, he's restarted the coffee brewing process with an insulated to-go mug. "You're taking coffee with you to work, or is that a second cup for me?" I quip.

He looks over his shoulder at me with a smug smile. "Told you I'd convert you."

"You did *not* convert me," I snap back. "I'll be happily drinking tea the rest of the day while I accomplish twice as much as you do, Suits."

Liam fights a smile as he swirls water over the coffee grounds. "We'll see about that, MJ."

CHAPTER TWELVE

Liam

As I drive the seven minutes to the factory, I do my best to wipe Madison's face from my mind's eye. I have a long list of questions that need answers, and that's what I should be focusing on.

Not the scent of tea tree and eucalyptus that emanated from Madison's damp hair. The fragrance knocked me off-kilter when she bent closer to me trying to pet Hamlet, reminding me of the stash of essential oils that Halmeoni kept as remedies. I was always drawn to those particular smells that were so bright and fresh—the pure aroma waking up your brain.

I was almost grateful for Hamlet swatting Madison's hand, since it snapped my brain out of the enchantment. When she stepped so close to my shoulder to watch the coffee brewing process, I had to breathe through my mouth just to keep myself from being spellbound again.

Hana has it all wrong—I'm not in love with Madison, nor will I ever be. It would be stupid to fall for someone who's destined to only ever be a temporary acquaintance.

But I can acknowledge that Madison is slightly hypnotizing.

Which is not what I need right now. Or ever.

What I need is to figure out how this factory has managed to deviate so far from standard operating procedures in a matter of a few months. Pure Fur All is a newer pet food company, but its other two production plants seem to be running light-years better than this one, at least on paper.

When I walk inside the facility, I drop my bag off in my office before heading to view the production line. I'm hoping to catch a glimpse of everyone in action when they don't expect my presence there. I stay up on the stairs out of the way, happy to see that the production floor is efficiently humming along. Turning to leave, I notice something new on the giant whiteboard hanging on the wall of the production floor. *Target production goal: 60,000 pounds per day.*

Assuming that this was Beau's work, I make a mental note to commend him on the initiative. And then I make another mental note to get a TV screen where hourly updates of numbers can be displayed so that employees know if they're on pace or falling behind.

After interrogating the sanitation specialists and engineers about their processes, I head to meet with Mark, who's in charge of HR and finance. I'm a little surprised that one person is covering both departments, but at this point, I should stop being surprised by any level of mismanagement at this facility.

I purposely arrive fifteen minutes ahead of our scheduled meeting, so Mark is surprised when I walk into his office. And catch him playing a game on his phone in the midst of chaotic piles of folders and papers spread across every flat surface.

My eyes narrow in proportion to the way Mark's widen. He abruptly stands and stammers, "Mr. Park, I, uh, I wasn't expecting you for a few more minutes. I had just finished up some . . . things and was waiting for you before I moved on."

I'm confident that my face is broadcasting the irritation I feel because I make no attempt to cover it up. Mark's face reddens in response.

"How long have you worked here, Mark?" I ask.

He swallows hard. "Mr. Wilson hired me in December. We met through an acquaintance in Bentonville, and he offered me the job shortly after."

An hour later, I have all the information I need to draw a proverbial red line through Mark's name on the employment list. For some reason, Mr. Wilson had fired the original employees assigned to finance and HR, replacing the two of them with Mark.

According to Mark, he was promised an easy job because Mr. Wilson would be carrying much of the workload in order to "save the company money."

I smell a rat.

After having Mark sign in to his accounts, I essentially take over his mess of a desk and email myself all of the finance and human resources reports that I want. On the way back to my office, I stop at Amanda's desk.

"I need you to let the quality control team know that I won't be shadowing them this afternoon. And block off my schedule from any other meetings today," I say. As soon as Amanda nods in acknowledgment, I turn away and stalk to my office.

I have some reports to review with a fine-tooth comb. *Several* reports.

"What exactly are you saying?" Cal asks. I have him on speaker, my phone sitting on my desk in the midst of several marked-up reports. It's after eight in the evening, and a headache is blooming behind my exhausted eyes.

"I can't tell you *exactly* what's happening yet. I'm on the verge of figuring that out, I think. But in general, I'm telling you that the plant manager was up to some shady practices. I don't think we're looking at a casual breakdown in procedures or accidental lack of efficiency here," I say, leaning both hands on the desk. "Don't let Pure Fur All make any moves filling the manager position here until I figure out exactly what Mr. Wilson was up to and who else knew about it."

"You know that means you staying there longer to keep things running. In podunk Arkansas," Cal states, as if I didn't already know that.

My natural instinct would be to sigh in frustration at the reminder, but a series of images flashes through my mind—Madison's smug smile when she asked about my suits this morning. The look of pleasure she tried to hide when she took a sip of the coffee I made for her. Her small fingers clenched around my arm. Suddenly, the frustration evaporates.

"Yeah, I know. It's what needs to happen, though," I say. "I'll keep you updated on everything I find out."

"I expect that update soon," Cal says before ending the call.

I straighten up my desk, organizing the papers into folders and storing everything in my satchel. I power down my laptop and add it to the bag along with my tablet. Looping the bag over my shoulder, I head out for the day.

The second shift employees are working hard on the production line, but all of the office staff are long gone for the day. As I walk through the abandoned lobby, my phone lights up with a text.

MJ

> No amount of overtime hours from you could defeat my accomplishments today.

I can't help but grin at my phone. Even though I need to curb this smiling reaction to Madison.

ME

> Is that so? I'm just walking to my car. Are there any good places we could eat dinner while comparing notes?

MJ

> That depends on your definition of "good." Your big city snobbery has me hesitant to offer suggestions.

ME

> Didn't you come here from Kansas City? That's not exactly a small town.

MJ

> Yes, but we've already established that I'm Noel-resident adjacent thanks to my bff.

ME

> I think you're just avoiding a negative answer to my question.

MJ

I just made dinner and have plenty. Why don't you come over here?

ME

Ok, but I'm not awarding pity points for productivity because you took time to cook food.

MJ

I don't need the pity points. I have an ace. Prepare my congratulatory flowers, please.

I practically jog to my car, happy that Hana isn't here to see the smile on my face.

CHAPTER THIRTEEN

Madison

Why did I just do that? Why would I spontaneously invite Liam to join me for dinner in my tiny cabin? My very *tiny* cabin? Especially when I just cooked stir-fry? If he grew up with any amount of homemade Korean food, he's going to judge this meal so hard.

I blame my tired brain for making such an irrational decision. Or, maybe I should fault the town of Noel for only having three dinner options during the offseason—pizza, the Deer River Bar, and a fried catfish joint I could never imagine Liam setting foot in. Actually, I should blame the town gossips (everyone) who would quickly broadcast that Liam and I were out to dinner together. Although, Liam looking so dang good in that gray suit and black shirt this morning might hold the most culpability.

There's so much blame to go around, but there's no time to divvy out responsibility for my poor choices. Nothing in Noel is farther away than a few minutes' drive, which means I have mere moments until Liam arrives.

I rush to stack the dirty dishes in the sink, at least giving the illusion of the countertop being clean. After saving the document of notes I took during the course sessions today, I power off my laptop and move it to the side table next to the bed. I hear the sound of a car pulling in and whip around the room looking for any other messes that need to be cleaned up.

My phone *pings* from my back pocket, and I check the text from Liam's new contact name.

After closing the door to the bathroom, I snatch the throw blanket from the back of the chair I was sitting in. I quickly fold it and drape it across the foot of the bed. I used my tablet to watch the editing courses, so there's no Christmas ambience video currently playing to cast doubt upon my productivity. Still, I close the Christmas tab on the browser for good measure, since I'll need to show Liam the tablet as evidence later.

There's a firm knock on the door, and I reach up to smooth down my hair. *What are you doing, Madison? Stop acting like you're interested in Liam. That's dumb.* I purposely dishevel my hair and move to open the door.

Liam stands outside, deep brown eyes meeting mine. The hint of smile lines curb the intensity of his everyday stare. He's ditched the jacket to his suit and rolled up the sleeves of the black dress shirt. The top button is undone, and so am I.

"Where are my flowers?" I ask, embarrassingly breathless. I need a second to pull myself together—to program my brain to stop romanticizing the man in front of me. And there's nothing like a little verbal skirmish to reset my brain back to its normal settings.

Liam's eyes flash with the challenge, and that does nothing to reconfigure my brain's malfunction. The right side of his mouth twitches in an antagonizing smile as he says, "I'll bring congratulatory flowers when I know flowers are due. Prove it."

Rolling my eyes, I gesture him inside. "No judging the microwave rice, okay? It's hard to cook properly with only one burner and no oven."

He holds up both hands as he pivots to face me. "Zero judging the food. I'll reserve my judgment for your work output."

"Judge away. I have a trump card," I scoff. After handing him a plate, I pull the lid off the bowl of brown rice and place a spoon inside. "Help yourself."

Liam motions a hand toward me and says, "Ladies first."

Quirking an eyebrow, I mimic his gesture. "No, guests first. I'm absolutely positive that 'guests first' is the gold standard of East Asian hospitality."

A half-groan escapes Liam's throat as he narrows his eyes. "Fine. You've got me there."

"Ha," I boast. "Benefit of proofreading thousands of articles over the course of seven years—you pick up helpful tidbits of knowledge along the way."

Liam smiles as he spoons rice onto his plate, followed by a heap of stir-fried veggies. "I'm impressed you made this with such a small kitchenette setup," he says. "I haven't even attempted to cook anything outside of microwaving noodles."

"Is that typical for you?" I ask as I dish up my own serving. "Do you ever cook?"

"If I'm in one place for a while, I cook some of the time. At least, I'll make a meal with enough leftovers for a couple of days so I'm not ordering takeout every day," Liam says as we walk the few steps to the table. "No one is breaking down the door to eat my food, but I can make enough basics to eat healthy-ish most of the time."

I avert my gaze as Liam takes his first bite, focusing on mixing the veggies and rice on my plate. When I dare a glance up, he swallows before saying, "This is good. Thanks for inviting me to eat with you."

Blowing out a breath, I say, "Okay, let's just address the elephant in the room. How much authentic Korean food did you grow up eating?"

A stifled chuckle morphs into a full laugh as Liam covers his mouth full of food. He takes a sip of water before asking, "There's no elephant. Have you really been sitting here worried that I would judge your stir-fry?"

Glaring at him, I think my silence is enough of a confirmation.

He smiles as he answers. "I swear I won't judge your cooking. Well, unless you attempt to make *kimchi*. That I would judge. I ate a lot more homemade Korean food as a child when we lived close to my paternal grandparents. My *halmeoni*—my grandmother—would cook for us several times a week. When we moved, my mom attempted to cook some of the same dishes herself for a while, but that effort slowly fizzled out. My dad burned anything he attempted to cook, so we didn't eat Korean food as consistently."

"Do you speak Korean?" I ask.

Liam nods. "I can, but I don't very often anymore. Mostly just with my grandparents when we occasionally talk on the phone."

I continue prying. "You don't visit your grandparents often? How far away are they?"

"Across the pond," Liam says, amusement in his eyes. "They live in London."

I abruptly stop chewing. Covering my mouth with my hand, I ask, "Wait, you lived in London?" Liam nods. "For how long?"

"First eight years of my life," he says. "We moved to the US when my mom's father was in poor health, about a year before he died. And we just . . . stayed."

There's something wistful—or pained?—in his voice as he says it. I'd continue meddling, but his body language tenses to a not-open-for-further-questions vibe. Instead of asking any follow-up questions, I sigh heavily. Liam looks up at me quizzically.

"It's really disappointing to discover that you could have had a British accent, and here you are, speaking all neutral American English. What a pity," I deadpan.

He smiles as he looks down at his plate. Without meeting my eyes, he murmurs, "I can recall the British accent when I want to."

Oh good gracious. Add that to the list of things that won't help my brain act normally. I need to get this conversation back on track and *stop* imagining Liam speaking with a British accent.

"I completed eight of the ten modules in my editing course today," I proclaim. "Plus, I started working out a pricing guide for my services. Beat that."

Liam leans forward in his seat. "I can't tell you specific details, but I uncovered a *lot* about the factory's issues today."

My heart stutters with a pinprick of disappointment and hurt. "Why won't you tell me any details?" I ask, masking the hurt with annoyance.

Rather than answering my question, Liam gives me a pointed look. I shrug. "What? Because I'm friends with Beau?"

Liam tilts his head in a "you said it, not me" gesture, and I fold my arms across my chest in response. Slouching back in my chair, I say, "It's a stretch to even say I'm 'friends' with Beau. Acquaintances. Friends by association. Current acquaintances who could be friends in the future."

"Still," Liam says before taking another bite of food.

Now I'm really and truly annoyed. Running my hands through my hair, I twist it up into a ponytail. "It's not like I'm going to say anything to anyone. You think I can't keep information to myself? I'm a steel trap when I want to be."

"Don't take it personally," Liam says. The exact phrase to use when you want someone to take something extra personally. He takes a drink of water before continuing. "I'm on the cusp of uncovering the root of what's been going wrong at the factory. I can't risk messing up my investigation."

I aggressively spear a piece of broccoli with my fork. "You make it sound like you're a police detective," I grumble under my breath. I hold the forkful of broccoli in the air to punctuate my statement. "Well, if you can't tell me any specifics about what you did, then I'll have to assume you're bluffing and didn't actually accomplish much today. I'll be waiting for those flowers."

Shoving the broccoli into my mouth, I glare at Liam as he stifles a smile. "I concede," he says. "So how does an editor go about pricing her services?"

I cover my face and lean my head back. "What a great question," I groan. "Turns out that's more difficult than opening a bank account," I say as I sit back up and return Liam's eye contact.

"Impossible," he replies. "What's so hard about it?"

Pulling my legs up to sit crisscross in my chair, I say, "I spent a couple of hours today searching through freelance editors on social media. I looked through their posts and websites, making a chart of all the varying rates people charge."

"How do they price their services? Is it by an hourly rate?" Liam asks before scraping the final bite of rice and veggies together on his plate.

"No, most charge a certain rate per word. Line editing is rightfully a higher rate than copyediting or proofreading since that requires more work helping the author to smooth out wording and readability flow. But there's still a wide range of how much people charge for copyediting and proofreading," I explain. "I spent forever waffling about where in the range I want to fall."

"What's your first instinct?" he asks.

That I'm making a huge mistake and never should have thought I could be successful at this on my own. The genuine thought is not the one I say out loud.

"I think I'll charge on the low end of the spectrum until I have some experience under my belt," I respond.

Liam gives me a disapproving look. "No. You already have experience. You shouldn't be undercharging."

My cheeks heat. "Well, I don't have experience doing *this* specifically. Independent editing. I'm brand-new to this scene, so I have to charge a low rate to get my foot in the door and build up some clientèle."

A firm head shake from Liam. "You have seven years of full-time professional proofreading experience. With no complaints against you. And, I assume, some sort of related college degree?" he asks, and I nod my head. "I'm sure you're more qualified than a lot of the freelance editors out there. If you charge a low rate, you're going to attract the clients who are looking for the cheapest rate over the highest quality of work. Price your rate higher to attract the clients who are serious about quality."

I break eye contact, looking down at my fingers tapping on the table. "I'm not sure that's how this works. Any paying client is better than no clients."

Liam taps the table close to my fingers, drawing my attention back to his eyes. "Don't undersell your expertise with a low rate. Charge what you're worth, MJ."

Heat burns through my chest, up my throat, behind my eyes. *I wasn't worth enough to keep around at WritInc now, was I?* I blow a slow breath through my nose and glare at Liam. "You're so bossy, Suits."

A self-satisfied smirk spreads across Liam's face, further contributing to my brain malfunction. His confidence is so maddeningly attractive. "That's why they pay me the big bucks," he says, shrugging his shoulders.

"I found three typos on your company's website," I announce. He's already conceded victory today, but I'll play my trump card anyway. Simply to get my brain back on track.

"Huh?" Liam's brow furrows.

"The Pure Fur All website. I found three typos," I say.

"First of all, let's set the record straight—I am *not* employed by Pure Fur All," Liam replies. "I work for Holden Incorporated, a corporation that owns several companies, including the newly-acquired pet food company. I won't let my good name be associated with Pure Fur All as an employer."

I roll my eyes at his offended reaction.

"Secondly, I find myself completely unsurprised by any mistakes made by Pure Fur All at this point," Liam says, pinching the bridge of his nose. "Show me," he demands.

As the person used to being the one bossing everyone around . . . I'm surprised to realize that I don't dislike being on the receiving end. At least, not when it's Liam.

I take our empty plates to the sink and retrieve my tablet. After opening the web browser, I type in Pure Fur All's website. When I sit back down at the table, Liam scootches his chair around to sit next to me. I practice even breaths.

"Right here on the home page, it says, 'Only the purest ingredients make their way in to our pet food,'" I say, pointing to the location on the screen. "'Into' should be one word. Because the ingredients are physically going into the food."

Liam hums. "And?"

Clicking the menu at the top, I navigate to the page about the company founders. "When it talks about the husband and wife who started the company here, it says, 'The Williams' had a vision.' Never, ever, in any universe of grammar, does an apostrophe make a plural. It should say, 'The Williamses had a vision.' Although, that honestly sounds clunky, and I would change it to 'The Williams family.'"

Liam nods and says, "Okay. There's another one?"

"Here, it says, 'Pets of every kind deserves quality food.' Whoever wrote this probably thought that 'deserves' was modifying the word 'kind' that comes right before it, which is singular. But 'kind' is part of a prepositional phrase modifying 'pets,' which is plural, so it needs to say, 'Pets of every kind deserve quality food.'"

I give Liam a triumphant look, which brings a whisper of a smile to his face. "Like I said. Zero percent surprised at incompetency in the Pure Fur All company at this point," he says. "This is not under the parameters of my job description, but will you email these to me anyway? I'll pass it along."

Biting back a smile, I open my email. Of course, I've already saved screenshots of the errors. I'm about to compose a message when the newest email in my inbox catches my eye. I gasp before I can stop myself.

"What is it?" Liam asks with concern. "Is something wrong?"

"No," I say, a bit breathless. "My graphic designer friend just emailed me the designs for my logo to add to my website."

Liam nudges my shoulder with his. "Well? Let's see it."

I open the email and click on the file titled "MJE logo1." My breath catches when the image pops up to fill the screen. *My* logo.

The word "Joy" is the focal point, large and centered in the angled design. It's written in a brushstroke handwriting font, and the words "Madison" and "Editorial" are in a lowercase typewriter font. The words tuck underneath the top stroke of the capital "J" and to the left of the dip of the "Y" in joy, creating a frame around my middle name.

I blink to neutralize the burn pricking my eyes.

"It's really good," Liam says. "What's the second version?"

Clearing my throat, I minimize the file and click "MJE logo2." It's the same design as the first, but where the initial version was in a muted sage green and gray, this version pops with a bright coral and teal color scheme.

"This one," Liam says before I can say anything. "This one is much more you."

"Is it now?" I ask, giving him a sass-laden look. He sass-looks right back. "Okay, yes, probably so." I stare at the image for a moment longer, taking it in. "I do kinda love it."

Liam drums the table. "All right, get your laptop. Let's get that uploaded to your website and add your 'I'm a professional and deserve to be paid as such' price guide so you can land your first client tomorrow."

Swiveling my head toward Liam, I raise a panicked eyebrow. "Seriously?"

"Of course," he replies.

As if it's that simple. Wave a magic website wand and, poof, I have a successful business on my hands. The reality of this task—of finding clients, of creating a stream of income—suddenly weighs down my shoulders.

Why did I think I could do this? If my boss of seven years didn't think it was necessary to keep me around, why would a complete stranger hire me? This is a saturated market—there are plenty of freelance editors for hire. Who am I to break into the scene and expect instant success?

Liam's voice calls me out of my crippling thought spiral. "MJ?"

Huffing, I stalk away to retrieve my laptop from the bedside table. "It's Madison, Suits. And I don't think finishing my website is going to conjure a first customer out of thin air on day one."

When I return to the table, Liam is standing with his arms crossed. He gives me a pointed look. "I'll let you keep calling me 'Suits' if you stop doubting yourself and get to the real work."

Planting a hand on my jutted hip, I raise my chin defiantly. My reaction seems to be exactly what he was hoping for, if the gleam in his eyes is any indication. "I *have* been doing real work. Everything I've been doing has been to create a business that I can get off the ground. I can't recruit clients to a business that doesn't exist."

Liam makes a show of considering my answer before pinning me with his stare once more. "Maybe. Or maybe you've been checking off practical tasks that are important, but not critical, because you're afraid to take the leap. Afraid you'll fail."

Pursing my lips, I refuse to respond. Because I don't want to give him the satisfaction of confirming his assessment.

"But I don't think you're going to fail, Madison Joy. So let's get to it," he says before he clicks on the lights of the mini Christmas tree. He takes a seat and dramatically cracks his knuckles.

I swallow my smile before I sit down next to him.

CHAPTER FOURTEEN

Liam

I'm startled awake by Hamlet swatting my face. When I crack my eyelids, his seafoam eyes have a murderous look in them.

He wasn't happy with me last night when I came home for two minutes to feed him before leaving again. When I finally left Madison's cabin after midnight, I could hear his irritated yowling from across the gravel path. He gave me the cold shoulder as I changed clothes for bed, then he chose to sleep on the small loveseat instead of on the pillow above my head like usual.

I was too tired to go for a run this morning, so I'm late filling his food dish. Clearly, a swat to the face is what he thinks about my tardiness. Propping up on my elbows, I look Hamlet in the eye. "You still upset with me?" I ask. He meows in response, and I reach a hand to try to scratch his chin. He hisses and scampers off the bed.

"I guess that's a 'yes,'" I mumble, throwing the covers off.

After giving Hamlet breakfast, I take a shower and try to wash away thoughts of Madison. We accomplished a lot last night getting her website finished and creating social media profiles. She tried to claim everything as her own productivity for our competition. But I insisted that half the credit was mine since I was coaching her through how to optimize the flow of her website to entice clients. I also helped her update her LinkedIn account and strategize a series of social media posts to introduce herself and her editing services.

It was a ton of fun.

It was also gratifying to watch her confidence slowly grow with each task we accomplished and strategy we outlined. Then again, that could have been the lateness of the hour contributing to her loosened-up mindset.

Now, I need to center my thoughts on pet food production. And suspicious former plant managers.

I style my hair and pair a pale pink button-up shirt with black pants, dressing as quickly as possible. After I tie my dress shoes, I bend down to one knee to give Hamlet some attention. He allows me to run my hand down his back and scratch his chest. "I promise I'll be home tonight, okay?" I say.

Meow.

He blinks slowly at me before jumping onto my shoulders.

I guess I'm forgiven.

Giving him a quick scratch under the chin, I pull him off and nuzzle his face before setting him down on the floor. After lint-rolling my shirt, I slip my arms into the sleeves of my blazer and head out the door.

I'm thankful that Madison isn't sitting in the Adirondack chair this morning because I don't think I'd have the willpower to leave straightaway. And I need to leave—both this morning and, eventually, forever.

CAL

Where's my update?

I stare at the text as I set my bag down in my office. I've been inside the building for less than sixty seconds and already have an impatient message from Cal.

Scrubbing a hand across my jaw, I pause to think before responding.

I've screwed up.

Normal Liam would have spent three hours at home last night poring over the reports I printed off. Combing through the information I've compiled to find the through lines that explain everything.

Normal Liam would have had answers for Cal this morning.

Instead, Madison has a website, and I have nothing.

Taking a deep breath, I dial Cal.

"I expect something good, Liam," Cal says without preamble.

I clear my throat, then wish I could retract the sound. It's nothing but a stall tactic.

"I'm afraid I don't have an update yet, Cal. I wasn't able to review the information from yesterday to draw any conclusions yet, but I should have something for you by end of day," I state.

I'm met with silence. It makes my blood itch.

"See that you do," Cal finally says before ending the call.

I close the door to my office and lightly pound my head against it.

What are you doing, Liam? Why are you letting yourself get distracted by a woman you're never going to see again when this job is done? This job needs to be your focus. Not Madison's business. Not her piercing eyes, or her shiny hair, or her sharp wit.

"Do your job, Liam," I say aloud.

And I do.

By the time Beau pokes his head into my office to say he's leaving for the day, I'm shaking my head at my laptop in utter dismay.

"Everything okay, Mr. Park?" Beau asks.

I bark a laugh. "Uh, no, everything is not okay."

"Anything you need from me?" he asks. I appreciate his response—not pressing me to share more while still offering up his assistance.

"I'm sure I will eventually. But for tonight, no. You can head home," I say. Beau gives me a nod and retreats. I double-check to make sure that Amanda is also gone and close the door before I call Cal.

When he answers, I ask, "Hey, you have a few minutes? Because you're not going to believe what I found."

What I found is that John Wilson was embezzling money from the company. I'm not a police detective (as Madison so kindly pointed out), so I don't have the authority to dig into his personal finances to discover *why* he was embezzling money. But I do know exactly why this plant has been underperforming and overspending.

"It started with doctored expense reports that he submitted using receipts he created with generative AI," I explain to Cal. "Those were for smaller amounts the first few weeks that the facility was open. But then things start to get really wild. They had a forklift driver who quit in November, but the offboarding paperwork was never filed. The bank account for paycheck deposits was changed the week after the employee quit—and I think we can safely assume the new bank account is tied to Wilson.

"Apparently, getting away with that move made him even bolder. When the floor manager quit at the beginning of December, his offboarding paperwork was also never filed, although the direct deposit account was changed. That's around the same time that Wilson fired the HR and finance positions, replacing them with his new buddy from Bentonville, Mark. While Mark is receiving the salary due to the finance position, the HR paychecks are still being deposited to—you guessed it, a new bank account."

The personnel files I received didn't indicate that the floor manager position was sitting empty—as far as I know, those "fake" employees' bank accounts are *still* receiving bi-weekly paychecks. Which means the company has been paying three salaries to employees who don't work here anymore. And because they were never replaced, their workload was never picked up, resulting in disarray on the production floor.

"You've got to be kidding me," Cal growls.

"You know I have a knack for uncovering messes and broken systems, but I have to say, this one's next level, even for me," I say. "I can't believe that no higher-ups at Pure Fur All took the steps to investigate what was happening here. Do they have any contact with Wilson?"

"Not that I know of, but we'll be turning this information over to our lawyers to get some legal action started. That will track him down," Cal says. "This is good work, Liam."

"I know it is," I reply. It's not arrogance—just facts. Which Cal understands.

He says, "I'm not sure how much I trust the decision-making of any of Pure Fur All's leadership right now. Are you okay staying there as acting plant manager for a little while to get things whipped into shape? I'd prefer our company not bleed out any more unnecessary cash. Investors tend to get prickly about things like that."

A jumble of feelings churns in my gut.

On the one hand, I came here ready to get out as quickly as possible. I *should* be chomping at the bit to leave ASAP.

On the other hand, my time has been shockingly brightened by the brunette living across from me.

Which presents a different challenge—how to resist getting pulled under by my fascination with Madison. I've already spent too much time distracted by her, so am I asking for trouble by agreeing to stay longer in her proximity? But I'd be lying if I said I didn't *want* to be around her a little longer.

I might be playing with fire, but I can handle the heat. I just need to create some boundaries to keep the alluring flames confined to the fireplace.

"Not a problem, sir," I answer.

CHAPTER FIFTEEN

Madison

"Mads, I can't believe how much you've gotten accomplished already! It's been less than a week!" Clara exclaims. We're gathered around a table at Becky's coffee shop along with Becky and Syd, where I've been showing them my website and social media accounts.

"This looks so professional," Syd says as she untangles Addie's fingers from her hair. Addie is basically Sydney in three-year-old form, with the same blonde hair and long, full eyelashes framing her light-brown eyes. Syd's son, Davis Jr., is in school along with Becky's son, but Addie tagged along for our soft-opening of the coffee shop. Becky's Brews will be open Thursdays through Saturdays for a few weeks until full-time hours start for tourist season.

We happily play the guinea pigs for her new drink ideas—although, I'd secretly be much happier if she offered some tea options.

"Now I just have to find some actual clients," I say with a sigh.

"Are you hoping to edit fiction or nonfiction?" Becky asks.

"Honestly, anything. I might have a preference for nonfiction, but there don't seem to be as many independent nonfiction authors looking for editing services. I might have to be hired by a publisher to get that kind of work," I say. "I'll do just about anything at this point, at least to get started."

"Well, your website looks good. And the first posts you created for social media are appealing and informative, so hopefully you'll get some inquiries soon," Syd says. "I'm impressed by everything you've done so far."

A tiny *ping* of guilt zips through me that I'm taking all the credit for what I've accomplished, considering that a lot of this was based on Liam's suggestions. But I'm not about to confess to these three married friends that I've been spending late nights with him.

Especially not when Clara knows every detail about my failed attempts at finding someone via dating apps. There were a lot of guys who weren't interested in a second date. And of the ones who were, I tended to sniff out their annoying flaws by the second or third date, successfully thwarting any long-term future. Clara would think something is up if she knew I've spent solo time with Liam on multiple occasions and haven't blacklisted him yet.

And nothing is up. Nothing can be up.

"I spent an hour this morning following a web of editors, publishers, and authors on social media in an effort to network and get my information out there. I don't love the idea of cold messaging authors, so I'm really hoping to get a few inquiries soon to get the ball rolling," I say. "I don't know what I'm going to do if I don't gain some traction. My severance will only hold me over for so long before I need some income."

"Why don't you work some hours here at the shop?" Becky offers. "It wouldn't be full time or anything, but it could give you a little bit of cushion while you get things rolling."

"Really?" I ask. "Would you really need help?"

"I'd take your help over high school girls any day," Becky responds with a laugh. "I have a feeling your ability to follow directions would be much better. I could train you before tourist season picks up."

"I'll be your best customer," Clara says sweetly.

"And I'll be your worst customer to make sure you have what it takes to handle the rude tourists," Syd adds mischievously.

"I might take you up on that, Becky," I muse. "Sure beats moving back home with my parents."

"Do they live in Kansas City?" Becky asks.

"Oh, no," I say. "They live on a farm in rural Nebraska. My brother and his wife also have a house on the property because they're going to take over when my dad retires. *If* he ever retires."

"No farm life for you?" Syd asks.

I shake my head. "I enjoyed growing up there. I know that a lot of my work ethic and attention to detail come straight from that upbringing. So I appreciate it, but I've been eager to get away from the small-town life ever since high school."

Clara motions around. "And yet, here you are," she says with a sly smile.

I shake my head slightly. "Noel is different. You're here. You're all here," I say. "It's a good break from KC while I get my life figured out. Then I'll be out of your hair and back on my way to city life."

"You don't need to leave anytime soon. We like having you around, Mads," Syd says.

Is she just saying that because she's close friends with Clara? Are they all just tolerating me because I'm Clara's best friend?

Clara is the type of person that attracts friends like flowers attract bees. She's kind, thoughtful, and generous—who wouldn't want to have her in their corner? I, on the other hand, haven't always had the easiest time keeping close friends. Apparently, I'm too abrasive for some people's taste. Often, I'll lie awake at night replaying conversations I had that day, only to realize too late that something I said out loud probably should have stayed an inside thought.

Clara's been the exception, accepting and loving me for who I am. At least, after we'd spent lots of time together—I think her naturally non-confrontational demeanor forced her to be nice to me in the beginning until she came to appreciate my blunt personality. She certainly needed someone to tell her the hard things when she was too nice to stand up for herself.

But I don't expect that all of her friends here will share her opinion of me. Becky may rescind her employment offer after spending hours upon hours together training me.

"By the way, do you want me to come get the Christmas decorations from your cabin?" Becky says.

I don't miss Clara's expectant look as she turns her attention to me. Like she *knows.*

Sighing, I answer, "No. They've turned into a good luck charm of sorts. The Christmas ambience somehow helps me get in the zone to be productive."

Clara raises her hands victoriously. "Christmas always wins. I told you, Mads—you just needed some Christmas magic."

I fight a smile as I tell her, "Okay, but could you please request that the Christmas magic send me a paying client now?"

After dropping Clara off at her cabin (and being subjected to Clark practically kissing the lips right off her face after a mere five hours apart), I head back to my tiny corner of the world. Liam's SUV is still gone, and I can hear that darn cat howling through the door like its life is about to end. I cross the gravel path and peek through the window, only to be startled by a hiss and a paw swiping at the glass.

"Well, I guess you're alive, little devil cat," I huff. Leaving the animal to its misery, I kick off my shoes in my cabin and heat up some leftover stir-fry. While the food is microwaving, I turn on all my Christmas lights and open the ambience video on my tablet.

Screwing up my courage, I spend my dinner time sending cold direct messages to authors and emailing small publishing houses offering proofreading services. An hour later, I hear Liam's car pull up. Peering out the window, I see the lights come on inside his cabin.

I shouldn't be expecting him to stop by. I shouldn't be crossing my fingers that he'll text me about his day on the job. I definitely shouldn't be hoping he'll tell me the details of his "investigation" into the plant.

But I'm maybe a little disappointed when he *doesn't* do any of those things.

Flopping onto my bed, I stare at the ceiling and debate with myself. Make contact or wait for him to contact me?

Sitting up, I decide that one short text won't hurt anything.

> **ME**
> I got a job today!

There's no instant response, giving me plenty of time to pick apart my decision to text him first. Finally, after five minutes that feel like a root canal, he texts back.

> **SUITS**
> You landed your first client? Well done.

> **ME**
> Well, no. Still on the hunt for a proofreading client. But Becky offered me a job at her coffee shop.

The message is instantly read, but the response dots don't immediately start bouncing. It's a few minutes until his next text comes through.

> **SUITS**
> Why are you wasting time working at a coffee shop instead of focusing on getting clients? Or are you bailing on MJE and last night was a waste of our time?

My eyes read and reread his text over and over, trying to process a different meaning than the words on the screen. Heat prickles in my chest, a kernel of anger whirring to life inside.

> **ME**
> Um, rude. No, I'm not bailing. I spent most of the day on MJE tasks and reaching out to potential clients. It's not a waste of time to accept a part-time job that will give me a little bit of stability while I get things off the ground.

> **SUITS**
> Not trying to be rude. I just don't want you to chicken out on something you were excited about.

> **ME**
> I'm not chickening out. But I promise not to risk wasting any more of your precious time. I've got things covered on my own from here on out.

I toggle my phone to silent and click off the screen.

Then, I sit down at my laptop.

I'll show you, Mr. Exec Suits Park.

I start sending more emails about my proofreading services, and I'm deep in the zone when there's a knock at my door.

Crossing my arms, I glare at the offending knocker on the other side of the door. I take my time getting up to answer it.

"Yes?" I ask curtly as I open the door a crack.

"I'm sorry," Liam says. He's wearing the same brand of athletic apparel he had on the first time we met, and it's really rather annoying that he can look so attractive in both suits and athleisure. Especially when I'm very annoyed with him.

"Sorry for what?" I prompt.

He huffs an exhale through his nostrils. "I'm sorry I insinuated that you wasted my time and that you were chickening out."

I make a show of looking at my phone. "Um, last time I read your words with my highly-trained eyeballs, pretty sure you outright said I wasted your time and I was chickening out. There was zero insinuation or subtlety."

Liam rolls his eyes, then leans a forearm against the door. "Okay. Sorry for *explicitly stating* the above. I was in hot water for not having a report ready to go for my boss this morning. Normally, I would have had an update to share first thing."

Guilt twinges my gut. "But you were helping me out, instead," I state flatly. Liam shrugs. "Sorry," I say.

"It's fine," Liam replies. "You're in good shape now, and I had a full report ready for my boss by the end of the day. All's well that ends well."

"Thanks for telling me what happened that made you act like a jerk. 'No legacy is so rich as honesty,'" I quip, playing on his Shakespeare reference, even though he probably doesn't realize he was quoting the Bard.

Liam raises an eyebrow, amused. Then, he catches me entirely off guard when he quotes, "'Our virtues would be proud, if our faults whipped them not.' I'm afraid you were caught in the crosshairs of my faults whipping my virtues, keeping me from getting too prideful," he says. "I'm sorry for being a jerk."

"Why do you know so much Shakespeare?" I demand.

Liam merely smiles, a sly, mysterious smirk. "Wouldn't you like to know? Goodnight, MJ."

I watch his retreating figure, listening to the crunch of the gravel under his feet. Then, I close the door and groan.

CHAPTER SIXTEEN

Liam

It's been two weeks since I discovered Mr. Wilson's embezzlement scheme. Two weeks of slowly whipping the factory into shape, despite the fact that no new hires have been authorized yet. Two weeks of realizing that the expiration date to my time in Noel is nowhere in immediate sight.

Two weeks of trying to keep my interactions with Madison short enough to not become a distraction, while long enough to not cross over into jerk territory again. My enjoyment of our conversations and time together creates an uncomfortable tension, considering nothing good could come from growing too accustomed to her company.

I'm in the middle of a conversation with Beau about one of the ovens that's been acting up when my phone rings with a call from Cal.

"I need to take this," I say, gesturing my phone in the air. Beau nods, and I walk away. "Cal, give me just a second to walk off the floor to my office where it will be quieter."

Once I make it to my office, I shut the door. "Okay, what do you need?" I ask Cal.

"I need you to make a short trip to Houston to meet with our lawyers and investigators. I want you to personally walk them through all the discoveries you've made so that they can present their case for criminal charges against Wilson. Can you be here tomorrow night ready to present the next morning?" Cal asks.

"Um, yeah, I can figure that out," I say.

"Good, I'll have Angie book a flight for you from Bentonville to Houston. We just need you here for one day of meetings, unless you want to stay an extra day as a break from small-town hell," Cal says.

"No, if I'm gone too long, my cat will tear apart the cabin. I'll just stay the one night," I say. Cal confirms and ends the call.

I sit down to review my notes, not wanting to risk appearing unprepared when I talk with the legal team. As I look through the reports and papers, I debate whether to get an extra layer of certainty about my findings.

Thus far, I haven't clued in Beau or any of the other employees to the fact that Wilson was embezzling funds. I didn't want to risk jeopardizing the legal team's actions if rumors started spinning out of control to the wrong ears. But in the weeks that I've been here, Beau has proved to be not only a reliable employee but a competent leader as well. He also had more interaction with Wilson than most other people here at the plant. Confirming some facts with him may not be such a bad idea.

Making up my mind, I page him to come to my office. When he arrives, I invite him to close the door and take a seat. Standing up from my chair, I walk around to the front of the desk, leaning against it and crossing my legs at the ankles.

"Beau, I need your help to answer some questions, but I have to ask for your absolute silence about the things I'm going to share with you. You've proved to be an honest, reliable leader here, which is why I decided to bring you up to speed on some information. But I need your word that you won't repeat anything we talk about," I begin.

Beau sits up straighter in his seat. "Yes, sir, you have my word. I'm glad to help with any questions I know the answers to."

Nodding, I add, "One more thing. If I loop you in and get your eyewitness confirmation on some things, this could mean that you'll be contacted by the Holden Inc. legal team in the future. Is that something you're okay with?"

A flash of concern crosses Beau's face. "I'm not in any trouble, am I?"

"No, not at all," I reassure him. "This is all regarding some of Mr. Wilson's actions while he was here running the plant."

Relief crosses Beau's face, followed by a hardened expression. "If I can do anything to set right what Mr. Wilson mismanaged, I'm happy to do so. I care about the success of this factory because I care about the success of this town and the families here. Plus the surrounding towns that rely on Pure Fur All for employment—a lot of people have a lot to lose if this plant goes under. Please let me help."

So I do. I fill him in on the general details of my discoveries about Wilson's embezzlement, and I watch the quiet fury on his face grow less and less quiet with each new detail.

"That low-life excuse for a man," Beau growls when I finish my explanation. "He jeopardized the jobs and futures of so many good people here. He made us all think we were inept and unqualified, when he was the one stealing from our labor."

For the first time, it hits me how this whole ordeal must feel to the employees here. How confusing and frustrating it must have been for them to be doing honest work but never quite hitting their marks—because no one told them what marks they should be hitting. How unnerving it must have been, thinking they're failing and fearing for the future of their employment. People like Beau and Amanda who are genuine, hardworking humans.

Suddenly, what was once simply another broken puzzle to fix feels personal. Wilson wasn't just stealing money from Pure Fur All or Holden Incorporated—he was stealing from these people. Stealing their money, their security, their peace of mind.

"Beau, I'm going to shoot you straight—the Pure Fur All executive suite has kind of been a mess in all of this. Their people should have caught what was going on a long time ago," I say. Beau's eyes flicker with fear. So I give him the only reassurance that I can. "I can't promise that the Pure Fur All brand is going to come through this unscathed. But I can promise that I'm going to do everything in my power to make sure this factory keeps running and your jobs are secure. I'll stay as long as it takes to ensure that the Noel production facility is an irreplaceable component of Pure Fur All's success, okay?"

Beau clenches his jaw and nods in appreciation. He thanks me and then says, "On that note, I had an idea to run by you. I know this may not be the best time to bring this up when you're still trying to fix what's already here, but I've been thinking about something that could benefit both the plant and the brand in the long run."

Leaning one hand on my desk, I motion for him to go on with the other. "Hit me with it. I always like to hear proactive ideas, not just reactive moves."

"Well, I've been seeing some commercials for freeze-dried pet food recently. It has all the benefits of the fancy, fresh pet foods, but it's more cost effective because it doesn't have to be refrigerated to ship to consumers," Beau explains. "I looked up some of the machinery on a supplier's website, and the specs look like a production line could fit in the empty warehouse space that we have. Being located in Arkansas, we're really close to a nationwide retailer. We could get our foot in the door with retail stores as well as selling online."

The visionary gears of my mind pick up speed as Beau explains his idea. It's brilliant, actually. If we could pull it off from an operations standpoint, it could be the next big leap in Pure Fur All's brand. Not to mention solid job security for everyone at this plant.

"What about personnel? Do you think there are enough potential employees in the town to man a whole new production line?" I ask.

Beau nods enthusiastically. "Yes, sir. We're constantly turning away applications from people from all the surrounding towns. This plant is a stable income opportunity for a lot of people. It would take some training, of course, for a different type of production. But we could have the manpower if there was the demand."

I can't contain the full smile that escapes as I nod at Beau. "This is an excellent idea. I'm heading to Houston to meet with the legal team about Wilson's case, but I'm also going to pitch this idea to the powers that be—pitch *your* idea."

He smiles back at me. "Thank you, Mr. Park. Thanks for everything you're doing."

Beau stands when I do, and I hold out my hand to shake his. "Beau, call me Liam."

When I pull up to my cabin, I notice Madison sitting outside with her laptop balanced precariously on the arm of the Adirondack chair. We're currently experiencing those final few weeks of spring in the South when the weather is perfect, just before we plummet into the miserable summer heat. A breeze picks up strands of Madison's long hair, blowing them across her face. She reaches up a hand to tuck the strands behind her ear, and I notice the ear bud that must have drowned out the sounds of my arrival.

I take advantage of the moment to watch her for an extra few seconds while she's oblivious to my presence. From what she's told me, she's landed two clients in the past week on top of working a few shifts at the coffee shop. I haven't visited her there, mostly because of work, but also because the menu sounds entirely like frou-frou drinks as opposed to real coffee.

If I'm honest, I hope she doesn't work at the coffee shop for very long. Because I hope Madison Joy Editorial starts taking up all of her time as soon as possible.

Bending down, I scoop a few pieces of gravel into my hand. As I walk toward her, I toss a small rock close to her chair, hoping to get her attention without startling her by suddenly hovering over her. The second pebble I throw successfully interrupts her focus, and she looks up at me with those dagger eyes that I like so much.

"What's with the stone throwing?" she chastens.

My lips quirk in a half-smile. "Just wanted to snap you out of that laser focus before I dared approach."

Madison drops her head back with a sigh. "Puh-lease. I'm not that scary. I wouldn't have ripped your head off too much if you'd startled me. I'm perfectly level-headed."

"*Hmmm*, 'The lady doth protest too much, methinks,'" I tease.

Her eyes narrow. "You still owe me an explanation of why you know so much Shakespeare."

"Puh-lease," I mimic. "Practically everyone knows that line. Hey, I need to ask you a favor."

She sits up in the chair, closing her laptop. "I'm listening."

"I have to fly to Houston tomorrow for one night. Could you check in on Hamlet for me a few times? Fill up his food and water dishes tomorrow night and then the following morning and evening? Make sure he hasn't destroyed anything?"

"That's not a very good selling point, you know," she counters. "'Could you make sure my devil feline hasn't destroyed the world?' Super appealing request."

"He's not that bad," I say. "He's just . . . distrusting. But I swear he won't hurt you. Please?"

Madison pauses to pull her hair into a ponytail, and the devilish gleam in her eye concerns me. "I'll do it. On one condition," she says. I motion for her to continue. "Explain Shakespeare. You're quoting obscure lines. Your cat is named Hamlet. Explain yourself."

"I think you're going to be disappointed by the non-sensational reality of my answer," I say, although I'm inwardly panicking with my knee-jerk aversion to sharing personal information. "My mom is a professor of early modern English literature with an emphasis in Shakespearean study. We heard a *lot* of Shakespeare growing up."

Madison's jaw drops open, and it's kind of adorable. I purse my lips to stop a smile.

"All right, I didn't expect that answer," she says. "Also, you said, 'we.' That means you must have at least one sibling."

Shoot. How does she keep luring me into sharing personal details?
I shrug. "I answered your question already."

"Ah, but that question just got your first Hamlet feeding secured," Madison quips. "Siblings?"

I growl. "One younger sister."

Madison holds up two fingers. "There's your second feeding. Now, what shall I ask for the third?" She taps a finger on her chin with mischievous delight, and I decide to disrupt her little power play.

Placing a hand on either arm of the Adirondack chair, I lean in close. Her sharp intake of breath and stiffened posture assure me that I successfully stole back the upper hand. "Choose your final question wisely, MJ. Because you won't be trapping me in personal questions again."

Her eyebrow arches, and I have a sinking feeling in my gut that I'm in for it with this one. Her voice is steady when she asks, "Why don't you like small-town Arkansas, Suits?"

I mentally scramble for some version of the truth that wouldn't admit the truth. But, my value of honesty trumps my self-preservation instinct, and I tell her, "Because I grew up in small-town Arkansas, and I hated it."

Her eyes widen, and I see a thousand newly-hatched questions forming on her tongue.

"That's it. Three answers for three times checking on Hamlet. I'll drop the key off tomorrow before I leave," I say, rising to my full height. Motioning toward her laptop, I ask, "How's the editing going?"

She can't stifle her smile as she responds. "Good. I landed another new client today, so I'm up to three. The new one today won't need me to start for another couple of weeks, but it's still another contract."

"Keep it up. Madison Joy Editorial is ready to skyrocket," I say as I take a few steps backward. "See you tomorrow, MJ."

Chapter Seventeen

Madison

"**I**'m coming in, and I'm providing you with basic living necessities, so you'd better not give me any attitude!" I call loudly through the door. Perhaps if I announce my presence to Hamlet, he'll be less threatening.

Opening the door a crack, I poke my head in to look around the cabin. I'd like to assess the position of my enemy before I step onto the battlefield. A mild panic sets in when I see zero signs of life. *Liam only left this afternoon. Surely Hamlet hasn't figured out how to unlock doors to escape?*

"Hamlet?" I call out as I tentatively step inside—right into a trap.

I nearly jump out of my skin when Hamlet loudly hisses right next to my ear, where he's perched by the door on the built-in bookshelves that Liam repurposed as a shoe holder. I clap a hand over my racing heart and narrow my eyes. Pointing a finger at Hamlet, I say, "You are the type of cat that gives cats everywhere a bad name."

As if to emphasize my point, Hamlet swats at my finger, hissing a second time. I jump back, glaring at the feline. "You're lucky I'm a rule-follower who believes in doing the right thing, or I'd walk right out of here and let you fend for yourself for the next twenty-four hours."

He leaps to the floor and haughtily pads away from me, leading the way to his food and water dishes. There's a bag of bougie-looking cat food on the counter along with a note from Liam.

One scoop for each feeding.
Thanks,
Suits

I openly smile, since there's no one here to hide it from. Direct and to the point, just like I've come to expect from Liam. But his embrace of my nickname for him makes my stomach do a weird flutter kick.

Carefully measuring out the scoop of food, I pour it into Hamlet's food dish, pulling my hand away quickly to avoid any more swatting. I dump out what's left of the water and refill it in the sink.

As Hamlet munches away on his dinner (keeping watchful eyes on me while chewing), I turn a slow circle around the cabin. I've been here before, but it's worth pausing to see if there's more information to gather. As much as I'd love to full-on snoop around, I have moral boundaries. So I settle for absorbing anything in plain sight—which is disappointingly little. A set of adjustable dumbbells sits on the floor by the loveseat, but that only serves to confirm Liam's commitment to fitness. Which his regular runs already indicated, so that's nothing new. There are no family photos or personal memorabilia of any sort.

Unless you count the suits.

The past couple of weeks have been an odd contrast to our first week as neighbors. Liam has kept more distance ever since the night he helped me get my business launched instead of working on his own reports. In theory, I *know* that he has simply been absorbed by his actual job. That he remembered his focus needs to be on what Holden Inc. is paying him to do rather than on me launching Madison Joy Editorial.

But I have a hard time not assuming the worst—assuming that he got tired of my company, tired of my sass. After all, he wouldn't be the first man to do so.

I have a whole litany of reasons people shouldn't enjoy being around me. I'm the chairwoman of the "Madison's Critics Club," ready at the drop of a hat to give a lengthy speech about everything that's wrong with me.

Too direct.
Overly critical.

No filter when speaking.
Has unrealistic expectations.
Annoyingly perfectionistic.
Quick to judge.

The disappointing part is that, at least for a few days, it *seemed* like Liam was hanging with me. Dishing out just as much as I did—and enjoying it as much as I did.

But either my initial assessment was all wrong, or he moved on to more important things.

Either way, I've been matching his distanced vibes, at least until our conversation last night—when he confessed that his mom is a Shakespeare expert, he has a little sister, and he grew up in small-town Arkansas. And now, I have a zillion curiosities about Liam Park's life. I might literally go insane if he keeps withdrawing and never gives me answers. Alas, what's visible in the cabin gives me zero new clues.

I decide to send a slightly probing text. First, I send a photo of Hamlet by his food dish.

ME

The devil eats.

SUITS

You're being a touch dramatic.

ME

Your evil companion is the dramatic one. I have the minor heart attack to prove it.

Just showing that I followed through on my end of the bargain. If there's any other personal information you'd like to divulge, I could be convinced to stay and shine a laser pointer around to keep Hamlet entertained.

SUITS

I'd advise against that idea. It's unlikely to end well for you - Hamlet sees right through laser pointer nonsense. He'll only look at you like you're an idiot.

As if he could sense our text conversation, Hamlet looks over at me with a death glare.

Huffing an exasperated sigh, I pocket my phone. On my way out the door, I pause to stick out my tongue at Hamlet.

"Iced white lavender latte for Clara!" I call loudly, despite the fact that Becky's Brews is only large enough to accommodate four tables. And despite the fact that Clara is standing directly in front of me.

She gives me an amused look. "This barista power is going to your head, Mads."

I grin at her. "Just living out my barista dreams. I've gotta get the hang of it in time for tourist season."

Clara rolls her eyes with a scoff. "Never have you ever dreamed of being a barista, Miss 'Tea Is Better Than Coffee.' Do you think you'll be working here over the summer, or will you be too busy with proofreading clients?"

There are no other customers here, so I round the coffee bar and sit down with Clara. "We'll see. Of course, it would be nice to have a mile-long waiting list of potential clients. But until that happens, I'll keep slinging the inferior caffeinated beverage that I disdain so much."

I haven't confessed to Clara that Liam made me a cup of coffee I actually enjoyed. I haven't confessed to myself that I wish he'd invite me over for another cup sometime. When he came to retrieve his key last night, he offered zero exposition on his time in Houston. Beyond ensuring that Hamlet behaved himself, Liam also asked zero questions about my life or business or feelings, so I one-upped his aloof attitude as I shut the door without a goodbye. I don't anticipate any more pour over coffees with Liam, and I'm working hard not to care.

Becky walks in the front door, arms laden with cartons of various milks. "Morning! How are you lovely ladies today?"

Clara and I both jump to our feet to lighten Becky's load, and together we restock the refrigerators. As we organize milk cartons, Becky says, "Mads, I need to talk to you about the cabin." The apologetic expression on her face makes my stomach sink.

"I talked with James last night, and I'm afraid we really need to open your cabin up for rentals as soon as possible," she says. "We've sold out all of the cabins for the upcoming opening weekend, and we just had another couple email asking if there were any available. I'm so sorry for the short notice, but the month of April is when tourist visits start ramping up."

"It's okay. You guys were already more than generous to let me stay there for the past few weeks. You have no reason to feel guilty about running your actual business," I assure her. Even though I've grown to love my cozy Christmas cabin and feel an unreasonable level of sad feelings when I think about vacating the space.

"Do you need to come stay with us?" Clara asks. "We could blow up an air mattress in the sunroom."

"No way," I say. I have zero desire to live with newlyweds, but I don't tell Clara that. Instead, I reason, "You need your sunroom office to continue writing the greatest Christmas romances ever told." She smiles at my compliment, her blue eyes lighting up with warmth. I sassily add, "Plus, you'd have to sell off half of your jungle in there to make space for an air mattress."

She huffs, but she can't deny it. Clark has only enabled Clara's obsession with plants—her sunroom truly looks more like a jungle than a house. He's the perpetrator who bought the shirt Clara is currently wearing, which says, "Just One More Plant." Except the word "One" is crossed out and replaced with an infinity sign above it.

"How does one go about finding a rental house or apartment in a town like Noel?" I ask Becky.

"*Hmmm*, your best bet would probably be to work with Rhonda, the real estate agent in town," Becky replies. "She handles rentals as well as home sales. Just text her what you're looking for."

"What are the odds of finding a small, furnished apartment in Noel?" I ask, already knowing the grim answer. "Or should I be relocating to Kansas City or Nebraska?"

Becky and Clara exchange an anxious look. Clara is the one to answer. "Please don't leave Noel! I promise it wouldn't be an intrusion for you to stay with us. We could turn the sunroom into our shared office space during the day. It would be fun!"

I raise an eyebrow, crossing my arms. "Would Clark find this plan fun?"

Clara's smile fumbles. "He'll come around."

I turn to Becky. "What's Rhonda's number?"

CHAPTER EIGHTEEN

Liam

APRIL

"I can't tell you how unusual it is for a rental like this to come available here," the real estate agent tells me. "Ever since Christmas Fest started and the pet food plant opened, rentals have been practically nonexistent in Noel—especially furnished spaces."

My first order of business this morning had been to contact Rhonda, the town's only real estate agent, to inquire about a longer-term rental option. As comfortable as the cabin has been for a short stay, if I'm going to be here for a few more months, Hamlet and I need a little more room to stretch our legs.

I *really* don't want to commute in from Bella Vista or Bentonville every day, but finding a furnished apartment in a town like Noel isn't exactly easy. Luckily for me, Rhonda messaged me back almost right away letting me know that a rental property had just come available. I left the factory to meet her here a mere hour later—a pro of small-town life, I suppose. It's an unremarkable ranch style house made of reddish-brown brick with dark shutters framing the windows.

"The owners of the house will be back at the beginning of next year when they return from visiting their kids abroad. So, as long as you're out by the end of December, the place could be yours," Rhonda says.

It's a more-than-adequate space with a split floor plan, the primary bedroom on one side of the house and two small bedrooms on the opposite end. One of the rooms is being used to store the owners' more valuable and sentimental items, so it will remain locked. But the other is open and set up as a bedroom. There's a single garage that's also locked, but I can easily park my SUV in the driveway.

The space is an odd juxtaposition—the interior of the house looks like it was recently remodeled, with hardwood floors, white granite countertops, and dark wood cabinetry in the open-concept kitchen and living spaces. The furniture, on the other hand, looks straight out of the 80s with mismatched floral prints and pink velvet chairs. Although the furniture is outdated and not at all my personal taste, I could live with it for a few months. Hamlet will certainly appreciate having more room to roam while I'm gone at work.

"What do you think?" Rhonda asks. "I have someone else interested who's coming to see it today, so let me know as soon as possible if you want it."

"I'm not sure that I would need it all the way through the end of the year," I say as Rhonda and I walk back to the front door and onto the porch. "But even if I wind up leaving town, the company could still pay to rent it out for the full duration of time. I'll take it—I can sign the rental agreement right now and move in this coming weekend."

A shocked gasp draws my attention to the driveway, where I find Madison frozen, a look of dismay on her face.

"Oh, you're a little early for our time, Madison," Rhonda says. Her voice sounds apologetic as she adds, "But also too late, I'm afraid."

Madison half huffs, half screams and literally stomps her foot from her place on the driveway. She spins around to retreat back to her car, but not before I see a sheen of tears in her panicked eyes.

"Text me your office address, and I'll meet you there to sign the papers," I call to Rhonda over my shoulder as I jog down to the curb. Rhonda's expression looks equal parts confused and intrigued, but she shrugs and pulls out her phone.

I manage to make it to the driver's side of Madison's car before she can get in, and I catch her elbow. "Madison, wait. Talk to me."

She yanks her arm from my grasp, but I block the entrance to her car with my other arm. She glares at me. "No, Suits. Sorry if I'm not interested in talking when you've been very *uninterested* in talking the past couple of weeks, right up until you snatch the only rental property available in Noel right from under my nose. Move your arm so I can get in my car and drive away with dignity."

Her voice is full of bluster, but I can see the very real tears she's fighting to hide. I feel an unusual wave of guilt wash over me—for the rental house issue on top of my intentionally distant behavior.

"Come on, MJ. I didn't know that you were also coming to look at the house. I'm staying in Noel for a few more months and need a bigger place, but I'm sure there's another option for you," I say, trying my best to soften my typical no-nonsense tone.

Madison blinks rapidly and bites the corner of her lip, clearly composing herself before she flips on the dagger-eyed expression. "What option, exactly? If you're here with Rhonda, then you must know that there are *zero* other rental properties available in Noel. I have to be out of the cabin so James and Becky can start renting it out for the season. I was finally starting to get my feet under me here, and now I'm going to have to start all over again somewhere else. Because—so help me—I cannot stay under the same roof as Clark Noel, the world's most anti-social recluse who also cannot manage to keep his hands off of my best friend for more than five seconds at a time! I'd rather move back to my parents' farm in Nebraska, which I thought was the one thing I would never, ever do with my life!"

She pauses to take a deep inhale after her tirade, and the fire in her eyes flickers out again. She theatrically removes my hand from her car door and turns away, saying, "Goodbye, Liam."

Her use of my given name triggers a red alert in my brain, and I blurt out, "You can stay with me in the rental house."

Madison's head jerks sideways to meet my gaze again, a bewildered expression in her eyes. "What?"

I motion my head toward the house behind us. "The house is more than I need. It's more than enough for both of us. It's a split floor plan, so we could have bedrooms on opposite sides of the house and work out a plan for the shared spaces."

As she bites her lip again, I see the wheels turning in her mind. "I don't know . . ." she says. "What would people think? It's a small town. People are bound to make assumptions."

As if I needed a reminder of why I despise small towns so much.

I shrug. "Who cares? We both know that we're simply sharing the only rental space available in town. Besides, it will only be for a few months until my work here is done. Then you could have it all to yourself until the owners come back in January."

I'm surprised to feel a balloon of hope in my chest—hope that Madison will agree to this. Hope that she could remain a regular fixture in my life for the duration of time I'm here. Even if that's a dangerous hope.

Madison drums her fingers on the roof of her car. I glance back to the house, where Rhonda is standing and very conspicuously watching our interaction. No doubt she'll have planted the rumor seeds to grow wild by the end of the hour.

"Fine. I'll pay half the rent," Madison says, squaring her shoulders. "How much is it?"

"No need. Holden will be footing the bill anyway. You don't need to pay anything," I say. It's a true fact, but I also hope that a few more months of fewer expenses might encourage Madison to truly take the leap with her business and stop playing it safe at the coffee shop.

"That's ridiculous! I'm not just going to live here for free!" she exclaims. "I'm not a charity case."

"What if you cover groceries?" I offer, hoping to appease her sense of pride.

She's back to chewing her lip. "I'll buy groceries, *and* I'll cook dinner," she states.

I hold out my hand to shake hers. "Deal," I say.

Madison looks down at my hand and moves to take it with hers. She stops short and glares at me again, "But you are cleaning your own room and bathroom. I'm not your maid."

"Agreed," I reply with a shrug, still holding out my hand.

She again stops short before she takes it. "*And* your devil cat is not allowed in my room."

I roll my eyes. "Hamlet is actually very well-behaved and easy to train on boundaries. I promise he'll stay out of your room."

Madison finally shakes my hand. "Fine, then. It's a deal."

I'm not easy to intimidate. In fact, I'd almost be so bold as to claim that it's *impossible* to intimidate me.

But as I stand in the living room with Clark—arms folded across his broad chest, eyes shaded from view by a baseball cap, deep scowl on his lips behind his beard—I find myself internally squirming ever so slightly. He's only a few inches taller than I am, but he exudes a towering presence beyond his physical height.

I adopt my "command the room" posture I use when addressing employees with a plan they won't want to hear.

From the other room, Madison's and Clara's cheerful voices can be heard as they debate where to place the desk in Madison's room. "I think it should be facing the window so I can look outside," Madison says, but Clara quickly counters, "But if you're facing the window then the sun will be too bright in your eyes! Let's put the desk perpendicular to the window."

A throat clears next to me. "Just so we're clear—you'll be treating Madison appropriately, like a landlord with a tenant?" Clark phrases it like a question, but I know it's a statement.

I narrow my eyes. "Of course."

Clark grunts. But his tone is slightly softer when he says, "Beau's had decent things to say about you, which is the only reason I'm okay with this plan for Madison to stay here." I nod, not sure how else to respond. Clark leans closer when he adds, "But, for the record, I'm very protective of my people. And, as my wife's best friend, Mads qualifies as one of my people. Got it?"

"Noted," I reply. Clark's expression narrows, but he leans back and turns around as Clara walks into the room. The way his hardened scowl melts into a besotted smile at the sight of her hits me with an unexpected wave of envy.

"We promised Pops we would be over in time for dinner tonight, so we've got to get going," Clara is telling Madison. "But text me if you need help with anything tomorrow."

"Who's Pops?" I ask, suddenly wanting to be included in the conversation.

"He's like the town grandfather figure," Madison says. "A very cantankerous grandfather."

Clark snorts. "Probably why you two get along so well," he says to Madison. I find myself bristling at his insinuation about Madison, but she responds with a wry smile.

"That makes three of us," she says, punching Clark's arm. "Tell the old man 'hi' from me."

After Madison walks them to the door, she returns and claps her hands. "First things first—we need to teach Devil Cat to stay away from my room."

Rolling my eyes, I chide her. "You're so dramatic." I walk to the primary bedroom, where I'd closed Hamlet in while Madison's few belongings were moved in by Clark and Clara. Opening the door, I find Hamlet waiting to be let out. I moved in this morning, so he hasn't had enough time to do a thorough inspection of the new space yet. He immediately wanders off to continue sniffing everything in sight, but I call for him to follow me.

I walk to the doorway of Madison's room but stop Hamlet when he tries to walk in. "No," I tell him firmly. He looks up at me and meows loudly in protest. "No," I repeat as I gently redirect his body away from Madison's room. He meows again and tries to turn back toward the room. "Hamlet," I say in my firmest disapproving parent voice. He knows that tone. After one final disgruntled *meow*, he turns away, resuming his investigation of the living room.

"That's it?" Madison asks. "That's all there is to it?"

Nodding, I hold my hands up in a shrug. "When he was a kitten, I would squirt him with a spray bottle of water to teach him what was off limits. But now, he comprehends the tone of my voice. So that's all there is to it."

I can't tell if Madison looks impressed or disbelieving when she asks, "How do we know he won't sneak in to claw me in my sleep?"

"Well, for one, you could sleep with your door closed," I say, a smirk on my lips. She huffs. "For two, Hamlet always sleeps on the pillow above my head. He won't bother you at night."

"Interesting," Madison says. "With all your rules about him not getting on the counters or tables, I'm surprised you let him sleep in bed with you."

I simply shrug. "I don't want him crawling around where I'm going to prep and eat food. But sleep is different, somehow. I like knowing he's close by when I'm asleep."

Madison's looking at me with a curious expression, and I wish I could delete my last comment. I decide to redirect before she asks any personal questions. "Why don't we go to the grocery store to stock up on food for the week?" I suggest.

Ten minutes later, we're walking the aisles of Noland's Grocery, the only store in town. It's busier than the other times I've been here, which makes sense considering more tourists have started flocking to the town for river float trips. The water would still be too cold for my preference, but to each his own.

"Did you make a list of what you'll need for whatever recipes you're making this week? We can divide and conquer if you give me half the list," I tell Madison as I push the grocery cart next to her.

"That's not how I roll as a cook," she responds. "I take a more minimalistic approach to cooking."

"Why am I not surprised?" I muse under my breath, earning a glare from Madison. "Please, do explain."

"I don't cook from recipes—I simply keep a supply of basic seasonings and sauces on hand. Then I pick a protein, vegetable, and carb to mix together in some combination. Almost anything can taste good in a tortilla, over rice, or mixed with noodles. Less waste that way since you're not buying some obscure ingredient to use one time."

I have to hand it to her—it is a practical approach to cooking. And the stir-fry she made the one night I joined her for dinner tasted great. I guess she's on to something.

"Now that we have a regular-sized fridge and freezer, we can actually stock up enough to not have to make grocery trips every few days," Madison says as she tosses ground turkey into the cart. Her use of the term "we" sends a warm buzz through my veins, but I shake it off as I follow her.

"How do you feel about tofu?" Madison asks as we approach the fresh produce section.

"I'm fine with it," I say. "One of my favorite dishes my grandma used to make was a pan-fried tofu." I kick myself for offering up the information as I see Madison's eyes flare with interest.

She quickly reins in her expression, though, before nonchalantly asking, "Oh? When's the last time you had it?" She busies herself adding two packages of tofu to the cart instead of making eye contact.

Giving in, I say, "I haven't seen my grandparents for about three years. It's harder for them to travel so far now, but I can't really break away from work long enough to make a trip to London worthwhile."

Madison peruses the lettuce options as she says, "Not being able to see them must be tough. Will you see your parents and sister while you're in Arkansas, at least?" She's forced a casual tone of voice that does nothing to hide her intense interest in my answer.

Fighting a smile, I shake my head. "I see what you're doing, and I'm not biting."

She drops the carefree pretense and pins me with a stare. "You're no fun. Why don't I get to uncover the mystery of Liam Park's family and childhood?"

"It's not like you've told me anything about your family or child-hood," I counter. "Aside from never wanting to go back to live at the Nebraska farm, you've said nothing about your upbringing. I don't even know if you have siblings."

She huffs as she adds a bag of romaine hearts to the cart, along with carrots and bell peppers. "I have an older sister and a younger brother. My sister lives in Omaha with her husband and daughter, and my brother lives on the farm with his wife. They have a separate farmhouse from my parents, but they'll swap houses someday when my dad decides to retire and my brother takes over the farm." She glances up at me, placing a hand on her hip. "There. My family history."

I snort a laugh. "I hardly call that a 'family history.' More like a recitation of the members of your family tree." She rolls her eyes as she turns away to lead us down an aisle of dry goods. I ask, "Why don't you want to go back to the farm?"

She chews her lip and doesn't respond as she reaches for a bag of jasmine rice. "Why didn't you like growing up in a small town?" she asks instead of answering.

We face each other there in the aisle, Madison's hands death-gripping the bag of rice, and mine the bar of the grocery cart. Neither of us says anything.

There's a war being waged in the limbic system of my brain, opposing emotions fighting against each other. Tell Madison more about myself—deepening our connection into a genuine friendship—or guard anything that could be used against me in the future?

After a long minute of silence, Madison plops the rice into the cart and moves down the aisle to the pasta.

In my core, there's a sinking disappointment over which side of the war won out.

CHAPTER NINETEEN

Madison

Liam hovers over my left shoulder as I move the pan-fried chicken onto a plate and dump chopped zucchini into the same pan I used for the chicken. I wipe the back of my hand across my forehead, attempting to move a strand of hair that freed itself from my ponytail. When Liam leans even closer to peer into the pan, I jab him with a sharp elbow to the side. Hamlet meows dramatically at Liam's feet, acting as the guard dog version of a cat while also maintaining his disdainful cat caricature.

I give Hamlet an evil glare before glancing up at Liam. "Are you going to hang around watching me every time I cook dinner?" I ask, forcing annoyance into my tone. Because, really, his proximity is flustering me in an entirely different way than annoyance.

Especially when he's dressed in jeans and a maroon T-shirt that fits perfectly across his chest and biceps. This casual look is far different than the suits or athleisure I've seen him in thus far. It's unfair that something as basic as a T-shirt and jeans would be stopping my lungs from fully inflating.

"I'm just trying to learn from your cooking process. This is almost like creating a standard operating procedure, but for food instead of a company," he says, sounding genuinely intrigued.

I can't help but smile at his comment as I scoop out a half cup of pasta water before draining the cooked rigatoni noodles in the sink. After dumping the cooked zucchini onto the same plate as the chicken, I add butter to the pan and crack lots of fresh pepper into it.

"Does this dish have a name? Or just . . . minimalist pasta?" Liam asks.

I shrug as I stir the pepper and butter around the pan. "Eh, I suppose it's a version of *cacio e pepe*."

"Caci-what?" Liam asks. I look over to see his furrowed brow.

"*Cacio e pepe*—it's a simple, classic Italian pasta dish. Surely you've seen it on a menu at one of your many fancy business dinners," I say.

Liam shakes his head. "Ah, nope. I'm not the schmoozer taking clients out to wine and dine their business. That's a different department."

"What are you, then?" I ask.

He narrows his eyes and looks up, as though lost in thought. "I'm the diagnostic specialist coming in and telling people what they don't want to hear. Or maybe the emergency room doctor performing triage and the surgeon correcting what's wrong all rolled into one."

I give him a skeptical look. "*All* the expert doctors rolled into one, huh? So important."

Liam's lips twist into a wry smile. "I mean, doctors are notorious for having poor bedside manner, so I suppose the illustration fits."

Turning back to the stove, I dump the pasta into the peppered butter, followed by grated Parmesan cheese and the reserved water. "Bedside manner doesn't always matter when you're saving someone from certain death, though. I'm sure the people you work with are grateful you come in and save their company from destruction."

He leans his back against the counter next to me as he says, "Yeah, as long as you're not one of the limbs getting amputated. They generally don't appreciate being told they're getting cut off."

My stomach lurches. "Is that going to happen here?" I ask tentatively, avoiding eye contact as I stir the chicken and zucchini into the pasta.

"That's not my goal. Beau and I are actually trying to graft on a new limb, if possible. I think the execs are going to go for it," Liam says.

"All right, we've taken the medical metaphor too far. Normal words explanation, please," I demand. After turning off the stove, I hand a plate to Liam and scoop pasta onto my own plate.

"We're hoping to expand production here, not cut it back. More jobs, not less," Liam says as he dishes up food. He follows me to the table as he continues explaining, Hamlet at his heels. "It's not official yet, so don't go around getting anyone's hopes up, but we're trying to get a second production line started for freeze-dried food. I pitched the idea while I was in Houston. The Pure Fur All exec team already has their work cut out for them trying to recover from their incompetency, though, so it's not a guarantee they'll go for the idea."

"Is that why you're staying here longer?" I ask.

Liam makes an appreciative sound as he takes his first bite of pasta, and I absolutely let the indirect compliment go to my head. He swallows before answering, "Yes. Well, partly yes. My extended presence was already on the table simply to fix what was broken at the plant and give Pure Fur All time to get their act together. But suggesting this idea would certainly make a longer stay even more necessary."

"And how do you feel about that? I seem to remember someone being rather eager to get out of backwoods Arkansas," I press. Hamlet meows from under the table.

Liam's fork pauses midway to his mouth, just long enough for me to notice the hesitation. "Situations evolve," he answers cryptically. We chew in silence, but I watch for any sign that he might offer up more information.

Unfortunately, the dictionary of metaphors would have a photo of Liam Park next to the "steel trap" entry. And I'm more disappointed by that than I should be.

"I don't want to live on the farm because I don't like the idea that making a mistake could literally derail your entire livelihood," I say. Maybe he'll be more honest about whatever past he's running from if I open up first.

Liam looks at me quizzically. "What are you talking about?"

"At the store, you asked why I didn't want to go back to my family farm. That's why," I say.

"Okay, but that statement requires a lot more explanation before it makes sense," Liam says.

Taking a deep breath, I sigh out a long exhale. "My older sister and I are flip-flopped as far as birth order stereotypes go. I'm the responsible one, not her. Well, she's much more responsible now as an adult and mother. But in childhood, I was the one always picking up the slack and keeping everyone in line."

Liam pauses eating, setting down his fork and leaning in. I continue explaining. "As kids, one of the responsibilities on the farm that we helped out with was watering the corn during the hot summer months. In the morning, you ride a four-wheeler out to the fields to tap open the 'gates' on the irrigation system with a hammer, but you have to remember to close them a few hours later. One time, when my dad was out of town at a farm equipment auction, my sister was assigned to the task. But she never remembered to go close the gates. The water ran for three days straight and rotted the roots of the corn. It ruined the entire field, not to mention creating an astronomical water bill."

I can hear my dad's voice yelling at my sister, clear as day. Clear as if it were happening right now, not decades ago. "My dad drilled into us that mistakes like that can cost a farmer everything. And, of course, in a small farming community, everyone talked about it for weeks afterward. It didn't seem to bother my sister that much, but I was mortified that people were talking about her failure. As the more responsible child, I became the one tasked with the irrigation job, and my dad constantly reminded me of the importance of not messing it up."

Spearing a piece of zucchini with my fork, I say, "I don't like making mistakes, ever. But I don't want an entire livelihood riding on my ability to not mess up."

Liam leans back in his chair, watching me. I'm suddenly very self-conscious of my chewing. Finally, he says, "That's intense. No wonder you don't want to go back."

Swallowing, I add, "Don't get me wrong. My family is great. I love my parents and my siblings. I don't hold it against my dad in the slightest—farming is an extremely stressful profession. There's so much beyond your control, and profit margins are slim. My parents raised us in a loving environment, and I always enjoy seeing them when I go back to visit. It's not like they traumatized me or anything. It's simply the explanation for why farm life isn't for me."

Liam takes another bite, and I wait for him to offer up his own "why I hate small towns" explanation.

I wait. And wait. We eat in silence until Liam asks, "How's Madison Joy Editorial going? Everything running smoothly with your clients so far?"

All right then, no reciprocal sharing happening tonight.

Stabbing a large bite of pasta with my fork, I use the lengthy chewing process to give myself time to decide how to answer his new question. Just last night, I'd painted a rose-colored version to my parents when they called to voice their concerns *again*.

Don't worry! I've had three clients so far who gave glowing reviews! Things are poised to take off! I'm making more than I'm spending on bills!

I did *not* mention that my bills are extremely small because I moved in rent-free with my former temporary neighbor. I also didn't mention that after my current client, my editing schedule is as wide open as Nebraska farmland.

Which version do I tell Liam?

"It's . . . crawling, I guess, as much as I wish it were running," I confess. "The clients I've worked with so far have been wonderful. They've written positive testimonials that I've posted on social media and the website, but I'm still waiting for a burst of momentum. I don't know why I thought that I could suddenly have a thriving independent business on my hands when the real-world job I had didn't think I was good enough. Delusions, I suppose."

"Stop it, MJ," Liam practically snaps. "Negative self-talk isn't going to get you anywhere. You're good at your job, period. Keep working every avenue to connect with potential clients, but don't sell your abilities short in your mind. Clients want to hire someone who's confident in the value they bring to the table—focus on the value you bring."

"That's easy for you to say, Suits! You with all the job security in the world since there are always problems to fix. You make it sound so simple—but it's not!" I snap back. "It's not like I'm not trying."

"Maybe you could try harder if you weren't spending your time working at a coffee shop," Liam says. "Maybe you could up the intensity of going after clients if your focus wasn't divided. You should take advantage of this period of time having fewer expenses to double down your efforts on MJE."

As my blood pressure rises, a tremor slips into my voice. "I *am* trying with MJE. The coffee shop is simply a temporary solution to be able to tuck some money into savings. It's the more responsible choice."

"You already made the riskier choice when you decided to start your own business. Second-guessing at this stage of a start-up is a death knell," Liam says, leaning forward. Movement under the table catches my eye, and I glance down to see Hamlet anxiously weaving back and forth around Liam's ankles.

"Trust me, I'm *well aware* that I made a risky decision. That's not the point," I respond icily. My palms are firmly planted on the table as I glower at Liam—if only to stop them from trembling.

"You want to know the point?" Liam asks, though it's not really a question. He leans back in his chair, casually crossing his arms. "The point is that I think you're hedging your bets in case MJE fails. But if you keep doing that, it's going to become a self-fulfilling prophecy. I'm telling you to put all your chips on the table if you really want to succeed."

He says it so coolly, so matter-of-factly, like he didn't just gut me entirely with his honest assessment. I guess this is the diagnostic specialist who tells people what they don't want to hear. The one with terrible bedside manner.

I don't know what to say that won't lead to a breakdown of tears or an outburst of rage. So I simply mumble, "Noted."

Gathering my fork and napkin onto my plate, I mechanically scrape my leftover pasta into the trash, rinse the plate, and place it in the dishwasher. As I turn in the direction of my room, I call over my shoulder, "When you're done eating, put whatever pasta is left in the fridge. I'll come wash the dishes after I edit a couple of chapters."

I hear Liam's deep sigh. "Madison . . . come back. Please?"

"I'm gonna go focus on not failing, okay?" I announce without looking back.

Resisting the urge to slam my bedroom door like a petulant teenager, I pull it shut behind me. My body shakes with the anger I'm working so hard to suppress.

If I'm really honest, it's probably less anger and more fear. Fear that Liam is spot on with his diagnosis. Fear that I really *will* fail because I'm too afraid to put all my eggs in this basket. Fear that I'm not doing the right things to make this work *because* I'm afraid.

Fear that this was never the right thing in the first place.

Why did I let Clara talk me into this? Why didn't I just stay in KC and search for jobs? Why did I let her convince me to come down here and go out on such a precarious limb? Clara was always the one with big dreams, not me. I just wanted to keep my head down and keep doing good work. Why was that too much to ask out of life?

Why did I let Clara convince me that was too little *to ask out of life?*

Plopping down at my desk, I open up the manuscript I'm editing and half-heartedly read a few sentences. Pausing to rub my eyes, I look around my room.

Nothing about the decor is what I would have chosen for myself, especially the old-fashioned quilt on the bed. The furniture looks like something passed down from a great-great grandmother—meaning they may very well be sentimental pieces for the homeowners. But it's hardly an inspiring atmosphere for my jumbled thoughts.

I miss the cozy ambience of my tiny cabin. I try to turn my attention back to my laptop, but it's hard when I'm feeling ragey and uninspired.

I miss the Christmas lights, I think. *Darn you, Clara Jane Noel.*

ME

Never thought the day would come that I admit this, but I think I need some Christmas magic back.

CLARA

<GIF of Buddy the Elf jumping>

You have come to the right place, my friend.

ME

Duh.

> Thrifting trip to Bentonville tomorrow? I'm not working at Becky's. And I'm way ahead on the manuscript I'm editing. Can you take a little writing break?

CLARA

> Absolutely. I'll drive.

After a few more minutes of unsuccessful attempts to concentrate, I give up and decide to go clean the kitchen. Maybe restoring order to a space will clear my mind.

Padding my way out to the kitchen, I find zero signs of the meal I just cooked. The dishwasher is running, and the pot and pan I used are clean, dry, and back in their appropriate cabinets. There's not even a crumb on the shining countertop—but there is a scrawled note.

I won't apologize for being honest and telling you what you needed to hear. But I am sorry if my approach crossed over into jerk territory. You're not a failing company—you're my friend, and I'm sorry.
Suits

I stare at the note, rereading the few lines. *You're my friend.*
But are we? Can Liam qualify as a friend when he still won't tell me anything personal about himself without me needling it out of him?
I return to my room and shoot off a text message.

ME

> Apology accepted, I suppose.

SUITS

> I'm relieved, I suppose.

ME

> Watch yourself, or you'll owe another one.

SUITS

> I really am sorry, but also, I really am serious. Chase the dream, MJ. Don't wait for it to come to you.

Chewing my lip, I tap the side of my phone with my thumb.

ME

What if I'm not sure if this is the dream? If I'm not sure I care about having a dream?

I immediately regret the text and wish I could unsend, but it's already showing as read. The three dots start bouncing in reply before I can ruminate too much longer on it.

SUITS

I don't think you would have even started if it wasn't a dream. Maybe admitting that it IS the dream is the first step to making it happen.

ME

When did you get to be so philosophical?

SUITS

Byproduct of growing up with Shakespeare, I suppose.

ME

Then why are you out dissecting companies instead of waxing poetic on mountaintops?

SUITS

I guess I was balanced out by my biology professor father.

ME

!!! A family life clue dropped without me manipulating it out of you?! What's next - your sister's name?

SUITS

Consider it an apology gift.

Hana.

That's it, though. Goodnight, MJ.

CHAPTER TWENTY

Liam

I pick up my pace to a sprint as I run up the final hill. Once it plateaus, I'll reach the turn to the street that the rental house sits on. I'm already exhausted from the extra-long route I took today, but I needed to burn out as much agitated energy as possible.

Usually, I'm not one to rehash my interactions with other people. I'm a direct communicator, take it or leave it. The bonus of my career is that I literally get to leave when the job is done, so other people's reactions to my communication style isn't something I lose sleep over.

But last night, I laid awake in bed arguing with myself over whether or not I was too harsh with Madison. Because I want her to take it, not leave it, with me. In the past, she's seemed to dish out the honesty and sarcasm as readily as she's accepted it from me, but I may have crossed the line last night.

I tried to find a comfortable sleeping position that would turn off my thoughts, to no avail. Hamlet was *not* happy with my mental thrashing that turned into physical fidgeting. His irritated hiss directly in my ear forced me to still my body, even if my mind wouldn't turn off.

After walking a few extra circles around the driveway, I pause to stretch my quads and calves. It's technically still spring, but the stifling Arkansas humidity is already starting to set in. I wipe sweat off my forehead with the hem of my shirt before opting to pull it over my head altogether. There's no way Madison is up yet, considering I got up to run after waking even earlier than usual, unable to fall back asleep.

As I open the door, I find that Madison *is* awake. She's perched sideways on the lumpy floral sofa with her laptop balanced on her knees, a steaming mug in one hand. Her gaze turns to me when I come through the front door but abruptly snaps away. She swivels her body so her back is to me, but not before I glimpse the flush heating her cheeks.

I cover my smile with one hand, even though she's no longer looking my direction. At this point, pausing to put my shirt on would call more attention to the fact that Madison just saw me without it, so I simply walk to the kitchen to fill up a glass with water. "Morning. You're up early," I observe before chugging the water. Hamlet scurries over and paws at my feet, so I scoop breakfast into his food dish.

Madison is awkwardly fighting to keep her eyes locked on the laptop screen in front of her—fighting and failing. Her frequent glances in my direction make me smile again, which I hide by turning to put my glass in the dishwasher.

"Yeah, well, some of us have things to chase and dreams to do," she says, then smacks her forehead. "Dreams to chase. Things to do. Whatnot and et cetera," she amends.

As adorable as fumbling Madison is, I don't *actually* want to make her feel uncomfortable, so I slip my shirt back on before I join her in the living room, taking a seat on one of the pink chairs. "What are you working on?" I ask.

Madison's cheeks are still red, but she manages to maintain eye contact with me as she answers. "Trying to get a few chapters proofread before Clara and I go on a little adventure to Bentonville today."

"Oh, really? What's in Bentonville?" I ask.

"Hopefully some decent thrift stores," she says, crisscrossing her legs. "But don't worry—I'll be hard at work cold contacting more potential clients later today. No lectures required."

"Hey, you accepted my apology. Are you retracting?" I tease.

"Ugh, lucky for you, I'm a woman of my word. You're still forgiven," she says as she moves the laptop from one knee to the other. "Doesn't mean I won't still sass you about it," she adds under her breath.

"I'd expect no less," I reply. Standing to my feet, I ask, "If you had your number one pick of the type of material to proofread, what would it be?"

Madison leans her head back to maintain eye contact. "I'm not exactly being picky right now, Suits."

"But if you *were* being picky, what would you pick?"

She purses her lips as she considers the question. "I would love to edit nonfiction books in the leadership and self-development genre."

"Why?" I ask.

"Because . . . well, because it feels especially important that those kinds of books not contain stupid errors. Why should I take your advice if you don't know when 'full time' should be two words or hyphenated? It drives me absolutely *crazy* to find typos in personal development books," she says. "But before you even suggest I just 'go after those authors,' *those* authors are primarily working with publishers who have in-house editors."

"Then why didn't you apply for an editing position with a traditional publishing house?" I ask.

Madison pauses to pull her hair back into a ponytail before she rises from the couch. "Because . . . I don't know."

I give her a pointed look. She glares back at me but doesn't say anything else. Taking a step closer, I prod. "Why didn't you apply to publishers, Madison? Why create Madison Joy Editorial?"

She crosses her arms and matches my step forward, erasing more of the space between us. "Maybe I didn't like the idea that I could put years of honest work into a company and have my job stripped away in an instant again. Maybe I liked the idea of having a little more autonomy and control."

"Okay," I say with a nod. "Do you think there could be authors out there writing the kind of books you want to edit who *also* like the idea of having more autonomy and control than they could find with a traditional publisher? And do you think they could be on the hunt for experienced proofreaders who will make sure their work is just as high quality as any traditionally published book?"

Madison's nostrils flare as the gold flecks in her eyes catch fire.

Fiery Madison is my favorite version of any human I've ever met. The thought flashes through my mind, but I sweep it away to my subconscious, unwilling to acknowledge what it could mean.

"Fine—you have a good point. I'll try to find *those* authors later today," Madison says. She swivels on one heel to turn away from me, her ponytail swishing across my bare arms in the process. "I'll report back tonight. You might owe me a second round of flowers in addition to the first bouquet you never got."

As Madison picks up her mug of green tea with one hand and her laptop with the other, an idea floods my mind. Something far more useful than flowers.

Scooping Hamlet up from where he's lurking behind the chair, I head to my bedroom. Before showering, I send off an email to our assistant back in Houston.

Angie,
I need an upgrade on my reMarkable tablet to the newer model with more storage space. Expedite the shipping if you can. Thanks.

When I arrive home after work, I walk through the front door to discover that the North Pole exploded in the entryway. There's a three-foot Christmas tree lying on the floor along with tangles of lights, boxes of ornaments, and a faux pine and eucalyptus wreath. Hamlet is sniffing his way around the piles of greenery, and the Jonas Brothers' voices fill the house as "Like It's Christmas" blares from a Bluetooth speaker.

"What is going on here?" I yell, expecting Madison to pop into view. Apparently, my yell is no match for Nick, Joe, and Kevin, though, because Madison is nowhere to be found. I turn to the right and peer my head through her open bedroom doorway. She's shoving her full body weight into an antique dresser that has to weigh twice as much as her tiny frame.

"What are you doing?" I ask, finally catching her attention. "Why are a bunch of Christmas decorations cluttering up the entryway?"

She stands and brushes a strand of hair out of her eyes. "Oh. I bought some Christmas decorations at the thrift stores today."

"How? It's April. No stores have Christmas decorations out already," I say.

"You underestimate my powers. I didn't receive my 'Queen of Thrifting' title as a participation trophy," Madison scoffs. "You'd be surprised to find that thrift store owners are more than willing to give you access to their storage rooms and offer discounted prices if you're promising to offload their currently unsellable merchandise."

"Um, I don't think that's actually a thing. Thrift stores don't just take customers to the off-season storage rooms," I say, brow furrowed.

"Like I said—you underestimate my powers," Madison says, eyebrow quirked. "Particularly when combined with Clara's Christmas obsession."

"Let's circle back to the 'why' question. *Why* are there a bunch of Christmas decorations here?" I ask.

Madison sighs and leans against the dresser that hasn't budged an inch. "Clara and her spell on this town have me under the Christmas curse. I can't get in the inspiration zone without being surrounded by Christmas. I've been off my game ever since I moved out of the cabin and into the house."

She averts her gaze from mine, as though she's cognizant of the fact that there are *other* reasons she could be off her game in this house, but she's unwilling to acknowledge as much.

I'm also unwilling to acknowledge as much.

"Well, you may be a goner, but I am under no Christmas curses. We are not putting up a Christmas tree in April," I say.

"Duh," she replies. "It's all going in my room, not the living room. Have no fear." She pushes off the dresser and stands, gesturing to me. "Are you going to make those muscles useful, though, and help me move this so I have room for the tree close to my desk?"

"I think you've lost your mind," I say instead of moving.

Madison stalks toward me, eyes narrowed. The movement is not dissimilar to how a disgruntled Hamlet slinks across the room, as much as she claims to hate him.

She pokes me in the chest, which is right at her eye level. "*You* are the one who told me to chase the dream. If a Christmas wonderland is what it takes for me to run, then you should be the first in line handing me an energy gel pack."

The jacket of my light gray suit has been draped over my arm for this conversation, but I move to lay it on Madison's desk chair. Unbuttoning the cuffs of my white dress shirt, I start rolling up the sleeves when I catch Madison's eyes tracking the movement. With a wry half-smile, I ask, "Where to, boss?"

Madison snaps to attention and motions to move the dresser as far down the wall as possible. Her room has an old-fashioned twin bed with a trundle underneath along one of the walls, and the dresser is across from the bed. "I moved the random dining chair and side table that were here to the living room so the dresser could move over. It's on those slidey-thingies, but I still can't get it to budge. If you push from this side and I try to lift it up a little on the other side, maybe it will move. Or maybe it has grown roots into the floor."

Huffing a laugh at her statement, I motion her aside. "I got it." Bending my knees, I place one hand on the bottom of the dresser and the other near the top of the side. Giving a forceful shove with my shoulder, I walk forward as the dresser slowly slides toward the opposite wall where Madison wants it to go.

"Good?" I ask after standing to my full height.

Madison huffs and rolls her eyes. "Showoff. You can carry the tree in here if that's how you want to be."

I have a mile-long list of things I should work on tonight. Employees I want to shift around on the production line. Standard operating procedures to update based on recent outcomes. Research on the potential new freeze-dried production line equipment.

Instead, I change into shorts and a T-shirt and spend the next hour helping Madison "floof" the tree branches, hang strands of twinkle lights all over her room, and hand her ornaments like a surgeon's assistant. Her pop Christmas hits playlist continues on loop, and I pretend to be a lot more reluctant about the whole thing than I actually am.

For his part, Hamlet is a curious spectator from the doorway, obediently staying out of the room.

When we finish, Madison heats up leftover pasta, which we eat while she fills me in on the list of independent authors she emailed today.

"I decided an email with my résumé and client testimonials attached would be more professional than sliding into someone's DMs on social media. We'll see what comes of it," she explains. "But I put myself out there for twenty authors writing the type of material I'd dream of proofreading, so even if I get completely ghosted, I think you still owe me flowers."

Swallowing a bite of chicken, I rise from my chair. "Actually, I have something I think you'll like better than flowers." She raises a confused eyebrow as I cross the room to where my satchel is sitting on a barstool. Her eyes widen when I cross back to her holding out my reMarkable tablet.

"What are you doing?" she asks, holding up her hands as though I'm pointing a gun at her.

"My company is sending me the new upgraded version that has more storage capacity. I cleared this old one off today, so you may as well have it," I say.

"You can't just give me this," Madison tries to protest. "Is this ethical? Legal? Is your company going to come after me for this?" She asks the questions in earnest, but I see the desire sparkling in her eyes.

"I told you—I'm getting an upgrade. I get new office and tech supplies all the time without returning the old stuff. And I recently turned down the upgraded laptop they offered because I didn't need it. They won't ask for this one back. Just take it," I insist, practically shoving it into her hands.

Her slim fingers wrap around the thin edges of the tablet, and she caresses the fingertips of one hand across the smooth screen. She looks up at me through squinted eyes. "Don't think I don't know what you're doing here. But it just so happens that my covetousness over this particular item is going to win out over my pride."

"I don't know what you're talking about. I'm just passing along my leftovers instead of throwing them away," I insist.

Madison's lips turn up in a real, genuine smile without any hint of smirk or sarcasm or satire. And as much as I enjoy all of Madison's sassy expressions, this smile sucks the oxygen out of my lungs.

"Will you show me the basics of how it works?" she asks.

I help Madison transfer the manuscript she's editing over to the tablet, then give her a guided tour of the capabilities. She grins like a kid at Disney World the entire time, and she promptly curls up on the sofa to dive right into proofreading.

Rather than retreating to my room, I pull out my laptop and sit at the dining table to work on the operating procedures handbook. Hamlet jumps onto my lap and curls into a ball of lightly purring fur.

I try to focus on my computer screen, but my eyes can't help but bounce up every few minutes to glance at Madison across the room. She's lounging back against the side of the couch, one ankle propped over her bent knee. I watch as she fidgets, flipping the reMarkable stylus over the back of her hand in between making marks on the page.

The sight of her so happily using the "gift" I gave her melts something in my chest.

After tonight, I need to go back to maintaining some distance and boundaries—stay late at the office or work in my room instead of the shared living spaces.

Because I can't afford to soften to someone. Not when we're both leaving.

Our stars may have crossed temporarily, but they're not fated to stay that way.

Facts are facts.

CHAPTER TWENTY-ONE

Madison

"**I** think I'm going to need to cut back to just working two shifts a week, if that doesn't put you in a bind," I tell Becky. I'm at the Deer River Bar with "The Marrieds," as I've come to call the collective group. I've become a semi-regular ninth wheel to their weekly dinners, and they all *seem* unbothered by my presence, at the very least.

Becky nods as she chews a bite of her chicken sandwich. "I'll move some shifts around and figure it out. I hope that means you've been taking on lots of new clients!"

I can't help but sit up a little straighter as I answer, "I have! Three new clients have signed contracts in the past week. And one of them is literally my dream type of client. I can't wait to start reading her manuscript when she's done with her final revisions."

"I'm so excited for you, Mads!" Clara exclaims. She and Clark ordered matching cheeseburgers sans any condiments, and they're also somehow managing to hold hands while eating said burgers.

"How have the past few weeks been living in the house with the exec guy?" Clark asks. "He hasn't done anything inappropriate, has he?"

I swiftly shut down the mental image of Liam walking into the house shirtless the first morning we lived there. The flush the memory would bring to my cheeks would only invite intrusive questions from Clara.

Instead, I turn up the sass dial as I roll my eyes at Clark. "Please. Zero inappropriate things are happening. We're simply coexisting in the only rental space your tiny town has to offer."

Clark glowers at me, as he always does when anyone dares insult his precious city. Or with pretty much zero prompting whatsoever.

As it turns out, coexisting really is the best description of the past three weeks between Liam and me. We haven't had much personal interaction since the night he assisted me with the Christmas decorations and handed me the greatest gift I've ever, *ever* received. I've been working hard to chase the dream that I think is really and truly my dream, and he works very long hours at the factory every day. Even on the weekends, we have short conversations during the brief times that neither of us is working.

I've continued cooking dinners most nights of the week, but Liam's only been home to eat together a couple of times.

Which is *fine*—because we're just roommates and sort of friends. Nightly dinners together are not required or expected. But I feel like I'm earning my keep, so, it's a win.

"Hey, sorry we're late," Abby says as she and Beau join the table. "You're not gonna believe what we have to tell y'all tonight. Well, what Beau has to tell."

My attention is piqued, along with everyone else's. Abby's not one to take the lead in conversation, so for her to sit down and immediately draw attention to herself must mean there's some serious tea to spill.

And if Beau is arriving late from work, I have a hopeful feeling that it has to do with Liam's work at the factory. Am I still salty that Liam has remained entirely tight-lipped about his so-called "investigation" at Pure Fur All? Absolutely, I am. I'm a grudge-holder, 100 percent.

"Please, do tell," Syd says, propping her chin on her hands.

Davis laughs next to her. "Syd's always ready to board the gossip train." Syd smacks him in the chest but doesn't deny the statement. We all lean in a little closer as Beau begins talking.

"Okay, all of the official charges have been filed, so I can finally tell y'all what's been going down at Pure Fur All these past few months," Beau begins. There's a brief pause while the waiter takes a food order from Beau and Abby, but we listen in rapt attention as Beau details the former plant manager's embezzlement scheme. He speaks in a hushed tone as he explains the fraud and misdirection that Liam uncovered, and I find myself inordinately filled with pride over Liam's accomplishment.

"That's outrageous!" Syd exclaims as Clark and Davis mumble violent suggestions about what the plant manager deserves.

"The plant's not in danger, though, is it?" Clara asks. Everyone's most pressing question.

"No, it's not. Mr. Park has worked really hard to get our production line in shape. We're hitting all of the target numbers now, even though we're short-staffed," Beau says.

Abby squeezes Beau's shoulder. "Because my man here has essentially been shouldering the work of two people the past few months," she says with pride.

Beau smiles at her but is quick to dismiss the praise coming from the group. "Not just me. Lots of people are pulling extra weight. But no one more than Mr. Park. I wasn't sure about him when he first arrived, but he's whipped everything into better shape than I could have ever imagined. That demanding attitude sure gets things done. And he's pushing hard to get a second production line added to open up even more jobs."

"What do you mean, another production line?" James asks. Beau explains his idea to add the freeze-dried food line in the empty warehouse space and how Liam is doing everything he can to make it happen—including extending his stay here in Noel.

The more Beau shares, the more the conflict of emotions escalates in my mind. Pride, awe, and admiration for Liam battle the sense of aggravation, bitterness, and hurt over the fact that I'm hearing this from Beau. Not from Liam.

My smile is a frozen fixture on my face as I scoot French fries around my plate, pretending to listen to Beau answer everyone's follow-up questions.

"Wow, has Liam said anything about this to you, Mads?" Becky asks. "I mean, I don't know how much y'all talk at the rental house."

I swallow an imaginary French fry to hide the injury I feel at her reasonable question. "Not really. We do talk some, but he's very hush-hush about work stuff. Probably because of the legal charges."

Everyone accepts my answer at face value and returns to sharing and dissecting each other's thoughts and speculations. If anyone notices that I'm uncharacteristically quiet, they're either too relieved or too polite to point it out.

When I arrive home after dinner, I see Liam's SUV parked in the driveway. He's rarely at the house by himself between the long hours he works and my work-from-home situation. Suddenly, I find myself desperately curious to see how he spends his solo time.

In full-on stealth mode, I quietly open the front door, slip off my shoes, and tiptoe the few feet through the entryway until I can peer around the wall to see the open living room and dining room. I hear Liam's voice before I see him sitting on the couch, talking to his phone screen.

As I approach Liam's back, a deep male voice with a British accent is saying, "It's very late over there. You need to get some sleep, Hana. We'll figure this out and call you tomorrow."

I can make out a dual-screen video call with a couple in one half of the screen and a young woman in the other half. Right about the time I realize I maybe shouldn't be intruding on Liam's personal conversation, a young female voice exclaims, "Who is that? Is that Madison?"

Freezing in place, I'm confident there's a very guilty look on my face when Liam whirls around to face me, turning his phone screen away. Although, shielding the video screen doesn't mute the voices.

Older female voice—"Who's Madison?"

Young female voice—"Wait, I want to talk to her! Madison, this is Hana, Liam's sister!"

British male voice—"*Who is Madison?*"

Liam stands as he yells, "I'll talk to you tomorrow."

Meow. Hamlet yowls with disapproval at me as he comes slinking around the couch. He gives a disdainful scowl in my direction before trotting off to Liam's room.

Liam, for his part, gives me an equally disdainful, narrow-eyed look as he crosses his arms. Which has the opposite effect of intimidating me, considering how attractive he looks in his baby blue dress shirt with rolled-up sleeves and two open buttons.

I'm too busy talking myself out of being attracted to scowling Liam to be intimidated by him.

"Pursuing a career in espionage, are we?" Liam asks.

Raising my chin, I say, "Exhausting all my vocation options, I suppose. Looks like I could hack it as a spy, if required."

"You know, most people consider it rude to eavesdrop on private conversations," he states.

I give him an annoyed look. "Yeah, well, most people don't have to eavesdrop to learn basic information about their friends. What's the family meeting about? Is something wrong?"

"Everything will be fine," Liam says.

Cocking my head, I observe, "That's an evasive non-answer."

"Well, I was never planning to fill you in on this *private* family conversation, so evasive is what you get," Liam says. I continue glaring until he sighs and adds, "My grandmother will be undergoing a medical procedure next week. It's nothing too serious, and she should be just fine. My uncle—my father's older brother—lives close to them and is handling everything. But my sister is living with my grandparents in London while she's doing her postgraduate study, so she was calling to fill us in and suggest my dad fly over to visit soon. That's the story."

I process this sparse information that told me more about Liam's family than I've learned in the past months of knowing him. "Why wouldn't you just tell me that? You get all huffy about me eavesdropping, but most people don't have to spy on their friends to find out that something big is happening in their family. Most people don't have to hear from third parties about the embezzlement schemes that their roommates have been uncovering at work."

A muscle ticks in Liam's jaw. "Talked with Beau, did you?"

"He said it's public information now that charges have been filed," I say, not wanting to get Beau in trouble. The town would never forgive me if I was somehow responsible for getting him fired.

"He's correct. We shared the information with all of the employees today. They deserved to know why things had been running so poorly and to understand why operating procedures are changing," Liam says matter-of-factly.

I grit my teeth to prevent my chin from trembling. "But you didn't deem it worthwhile to fill me in on everything you've been doing? You've had the inside scoop to everything I've been working on since we met—since we started egging each other on about work—but I don't get a single sliver of information from you?"

Liam's face is impassive. "I didn't think you'd care that much. It's not like your life or future are directly tied to Pure Fur All in any way."

"Friends tell each other things like this. Friends tell each other about their families—friends don't have to walk in on a family video call to find out their younger sister lives in London. *You* are the one who said in your note that I'm your friend," I say, heat building in my chest. "Friends share personal information to get to know each other."

Liam shrugs. His voice is cool when he says, "Well, I don't."

"*Why?*" I ask. "Why do you hold everything about your life so close to the chest? I opened up and told you about my childhood and why I didn't want to go back to my family farm. It wouldn't kill you to reciprocate even the tiniest bit."

Deep down, I know his refusal to open up to me as a friend only hurts this much because I might want to be *more* than friends with Liam. But I keep that knowledge shoved down where the light of admission doesn't shine.

We stand off in silence. Only Hamlet's *meows* from the bedroom pierce the quiet.

I sense the heightened pounding in my chest, the quiver of adrenaline in my fingers.

Taking a few steps closer to where Liam stands—arms still folded across his chest—I raise my chin. "You know, I'm usually the one who winds up being too abrasive for people. I get told I'm too direct, too honest, too blunt. So coming from *me*, you should really consider this. You're crossing the line. You're very, *very* far over into 'jerk territory.'"

His nostrils flare, but otherwise, he gives no response.

Pivoting on my heel, I walk to my room. "I hope your grandma's procedure goes well," I call out without turning back.

CHAPTER TWENTY-TWO

Liam

MAY

Despite the unseasonably warm temperatures, the atmosphere of our house has been icy.

Madison's been giving me the silent treatment ever since our "fight." Honestly, I know I deserve it. I've barely caught a glimpse of her the past few days, as she's either holed up in her room with the door closed or out of the house when I come home from the office.

It should be fine. I should not care. She's more of a roommate than anything, and this is acceptable roommate cohabitation.

But it's not fine, and I do care. Which exponentially increases my frustration about everything in life.

After Hana saw Madison in the background of our family video call, I was forced to explain to my parents why there was a girl in the house. Which then forced me to explain that I am currently working a job in Arkansas, a mere three hours away from them. I was narrowly saved from an imminent visit by the plane tickets they purchased to go visit my grandparents and Hana for a few weeks.

Since both of my parents are college professors, the beginning of summer break here means that they can take an extended trip to London. But once they're back stateside, I'll now be forced to plan a trip to visit them in Conway, if only to ensure they stay far away from Noel.

I can't handle them meeting Madison right now. Because *I* don't know how to handle Madison right now.

I make decisions based on my gut instincts, and 95 percent of the time, my gut doesn't steer me wrong. But Madison seems to fall into that outlying 5 percent, because my gut is telling me that I want more with her. That she's meant to be more than just an acquaintance or roommate.

More than just a friend.

But that makes absolutely zero sense. Sure, I've been in Noel longer than most job locations—I arrived at the beginning of March, and it's now May. Even if I'm here a few more months, though, the job will eventually end. And I'll move on to pull the next factory back from the brink of catastrophe. Noel is not my long-term destination.

Not to mention who even knows how long Madison will be here? She seems to care about the people of this town, but she's a self-named city dweller. How long would this small town hold her?

So I'm fighting against my gut rather than going with it. An unusual reversal that's been throwing off my whole week.

Checking the clock next to my bed, I see that it's a little past 7:00 a.m. It's a Saturday, but this is sleeping in for me. Hamlet has been stretched out on my chest dozing for the past twenty minutes, and I absentmindedly stroke his fur as I contemplate what to do. Even if I won't give in to that instinct to open up my life to Madison, I do want a level of peace between us. I *don't* want her seeing me as a jerk.

Throwing on some running clothes, I quickly brush my teeth and head out to the kitchen to see if Madison is awake. Hamlet trots after me, and I pause to scoop food into his bowl before casually looking across the open living space to see if Madison's door is open.

Her room is dark. Peeking out the window to the side of the front door, I see that her car is gone. Frustration blooms in my chest, and I run a hand through my hair.

After drinking some water, I lace up my running shoes and head toward the river, intending to take an extra-long route today.

There's a break in the humid heat this morning, so I push myself harder than usual while running. As I follow a path along the river, I'm surprised when I see Madison sitting at a picnic table on the riverbank.

The reMarkable tablet is propped in her hand, but her gaze is fixed on the water.

Well, here's my chance for an olive branch.

I slow way down, allowing my breath to even out before I approach her. A montage of emotions flashes through her eyes when she sees me, finally landing on glacial indifference.

"Hey," I say. *Wow, super smooth, Liam.*

Madison cocks her head to one side. "Hey."

I'm staring, trying to figure out what to say, when Madison asks, "How's your grandmother?"

"Oh, yeah, she's doing fine. The procedure was more of a preventative thing than an emergency. But my parents are flying there next week, so . . ." I trail off.

"That's good," Madison states, then turns her attention back to the tablet.

"I'm actually glad I caught you here," I begin, but I'm interrupted by Madison's snort.

She gestures out to the river and asks, "Here as opposed to our shared rental house?"

"Well, you haven't exactly been around the house a lot this week," I say, bristling.

Madison scoffs. "I'm surprised you noticed."

I blow out a measured breath. "Look, I'm sorry about the other night. You caught me by surprise, and I didn't handle it well. Could I have a turn cooking dinner tonight?"

She raises an eyebrow. "Why?"

"Because I'm trying to find the exit from jerk territory, okay? Making you dinner seemed like a nice gesture," I answer.

Madison stares at me for a long moment without answering. "I already have dinner plans with Clara and Clark," she says, gathering her stuff and throwing it into an oversized tote bag. My chest tightens, but then she adds, "If you really want to get out of jerk territory, you'll think of *one* personal thing you could share about yourself tonight. Just one, Suits. I'll be home around eight o'clock. You have all day to prepare yourself."

She doesn't say the words aloud, but her subtext is crystal clear. *"This is your last chance."*

I pace the room while I wait for Madison to arrive home. Hamlet is mimicking my motion, meowing in his whiniest tone. I'm not sure if he's picking up on the threat of severe weather in the air or my anxious energy.

I've thought all day about what I could tell Madison that would be enough to pacify her need for personal connection without handing over vulnerable information she could use against me. It's been my least productive day in a long time because I can't seem to focus on anything but the inner turmoil I've felt since her ultimatum this morning.

Headlights momentarily light up the dark sky—unnaturally dark for a little past eight on a summer evening. I'm relieved that Madison has made it home safely, even if it means my time is up. Hamlet is glued to my ankles as I walk to the entryway to wait for her. When she opens the door, I realize it's pouring rain. Her long hair is dripping water as she toes off her shoes.

"Shoot, I should have moved my car earlier so you could park in the driveway tonight. I didn't know it was going to start raining this early," I say, stepping toward her.

Madison waves me off, but I see her shivering from the cold rainwater. "No, no, I'm the one who insisted you park in the driveway. Since you're the paying renter and all."

"You want a towel or something?" I awkwardly ask.

"Yeah, I'm going to change clothes real quick and wring out my hair," Madison says. When she meets my eyes, hers are filled with mischief. Between that sassy look, the water glistening on her face, and the half-smile twisting her lips, my lungs stall out at how beautiful she looks. They freeze altogether when she closes the distance between us and points a finger in my face.

"Don't think you're getting out of share time. I'll be out in a few minutes ready to hear every detail of your life story," she says. I give her an annoyed look. "Okay, okay," she amends. "To hear one solitary detail of your life story. It better be good."

I retreat to the kitchen as she closes her bedroom door. I've already eaten dinner and washed all the dishes, so there's nothing for me to do but stand here. Her bedroom door opens, followed by the sound of the bathroom door closing. Hamlet meows at my feet, so I lean down to pick him up. He nuzzles his face against my chin, as though trying to calm my nerves.

"Maybe I should tell her about the day I met you. About the animal shelter adoption drive when you were the last kitten left, cowering in the corner of your cage, hissing at anyone who came close to you. Maybe she'll think that's personal enough. If I tell her that I saw myself in you and knew I couldn't leave that day without you coming home with me—would that be enough to satisfy her curiosity?" I muse to Hamlet as I rub beneath his chin.

"It's a start." Madison's voice startles me so completely, I literally jump. Hamlet hisses at her in response, and I swivel to see her smirking at me.

Flustered, I mutter, "Maybe we should ship you off to Langley for CIA training." Hamlet leaps out of my arms and runs to my bedroom.

"I guess I could stop calling him 'Devil Cat' now that I know your history," she says. "But that doesn't count as your personal insight of the night since you weren't intentionally telling me."

"If we're going to be friends, we need to axe the eavesdropping," I say with a mild glower in her direction.

"I won't have to eavesdrop if you just start telling me things," Madison counters as she saunters closer. She's wearing an oversized sweatshirt with shorts—a combination I've never quite understood. Either it's cold enough for a sweatshirt or hot enough for shorts. Not both.

The combination on her, however, is making my tongue swell in my throat. I swallow hard.

A booming clap of thunder interrupts the moment, causing both of us to jump. Madison's brow furrows, and I move to look out the window to the backyard. Tree branches are wildly dancing as rain continues to pound.

Suddenly, the distinctive *plink, plink* of hailstones sounds, mere seconds before the blare of tornado sirens.

When I turn back to Madison, her face has gone white. Her muscles are tensed, and she suddenly starts pivoting in every direction with frantic energy. "Where do we go?" she asks in a warbled tone.

"Aren't you from Nebraska? And Kansas City? They have tornadoes there," I say.

There's panic in Madison's eyes when she looks back to me. The panic dissipates just long enough for her expression to fill with sarcasm. "Yes, but we have *basements* in Nebraska and Kansas, genius. Where do you go during a tornado in Arkansas?!" Panic has refilled her tone, and I step forward to place two firm hands on her shoulders.

"We're going to be just fine. It's probably just a precaution. We'll find the most fortified room that's not on an exterior wall, like one of the bathrooms," I say, voice calm.

"But your bathroom has that giant frosted window and mine is also on the exterior," she says, voice shrill.

Taking her elbow, I steer her to the laundry room. It has one door leading to the primary closet and one opening up right next to the garage. "We're going to sit here in the laundry room until the sirens stop. I'm sure this isn't going to be anything serious, okay? Do you want to grab your phone?"

Madison shakes her head. "It was down to two percent. I just plugged it in, so it won't have much battery yet anyway." She follows me to the laundry room, and I call out for Hamlet to join us.

The sirens are still blaring as we step into the laundry room, and I close both doors once Hamlet is inside. Madison paces tiny circles around the space, which only makes Hamlet meow with more alarm.

Sitting down on the floor with my back leaning against the wall, I tent my knees and tug Madison's hand to pull her down next to me.

She pulls her knees up to her chest, breathing heavily.

"You okay?" I ask, peering down to try to meet her eyes.

"I don't like storms," she confesses. She's trembling, and I can tell this isn't just a run-of-the-mill dislike of thunder.

"MJ, we're going to be okay," I try to reassure her. She nods in acknowledgment, but she's still shaking. I ask, "Can I put my arm around your shoulders?"

Her eyes dart over to mine, searching my expression. When she nods, I drape an arm around her shoulders and tuck her to my side, trying to still her full-body shivers. I'm grateful that I'd already offered her that physical comfort when the power cuts out a second later, leaving us in the pitch-black. Madison flinches under my arm, so I hold her a little closer.

"I especially don't like storms in the dark," she whispers.

Pulling my phone from my pocket, I see that the battery is at 26 percent. Frowning, I switch on the flashlight anyway. Hopefully, the power won't be out long, and I can plug it in to charge. I set the phone face down on the ground, illuminating the small room with the beam of the flashlight.

Hamlet squeezes his way between us, looking for his own comfort, so I stretch out my legs so he can sit on my thighs. I scratch his chest with my free hand to calm him down. Madison is still shaking, so I lean my cheek against the top of her head and do the only thing I can think of to distract her.

I talk.

"We lived in London until I was eight years old. My mom is American, but she did her postgraduate studies at Oxford, where she met my dad. He was doing his postgrad in biology, and they were such an unlikely match. My mom, the American woman studying Shakespeare, and my dad, the British-Korean science nerd. They didn't make sense on paper, but as my mom would always quote when sharing their love story, 'The very instant I saw you, did my heart fly to your service.' She always said she was a goner from the moment they met."

Madison's trembling begins to subside, so I continue. "Their relationship wasn't always easy. My mom had a lot to learn about Korean culture and family dynamics, and my dad tried to figure out when to hold on to those traditions and when to defer to my mom's more independent American culture. My paternal grandfather actually chose my and Hana's names, which is traditional in Korean families. But he'd lived in the UK long enough that he made sure to choose names that were easy to pronounce in both Korean and English. Still, it was a different family mindset for my mom to get used to. My dad is the second son, so the level of expectation on him isn't quite as high as my uncle, but there's still a unique relationship between Korean mothers and their sons.

"Of course, I didn't know any of that as a child. I simply knew that I saw my *halmeoni* and *harabeoji* almost every day. Halmeoni cooked full Korean dinners for us, and she'd take me with her to a tea shop down the street that fused British and Asian tea cultures. In my mind, my nuclear family was my parents *and* my grandparents. Then, one day, we left. And we never went back," I say.

In the muted light, I see that Madison is absent-mindedly stroking Hamlet's back as he sits on my leg. And he's allowing it. Maybe he assumes I'm the one petting him, or maybe he can somehow sense that Madison needs the comfort.

That's all I had originally intended to tell Madison tonight, but for some inexplicable reason, I continue sharing. "My mom's parents had moved from Iowa to Arkansas while she was living abroad, and when her dad's health was failing, we moved here so she could be close to him. My father had been doing research in London, but he was willing to take on a teaching role if it meant my mom could spend some time with her father before he passed. It's not exactly easy to find open biology and Shakespeare studies positions at the same university at the same time, but Conway, a small city in Arkansas, has multiple universities. My dad was offered a biology professorship at the state school, and my mom got a position at a private university. Even after my grandfather passed away, they both enjoyed their jobs enough that they decided to stay."

Madison speaks for the first time, her voice quiet. "That must have been a rough transition. London to Arkansas."

I huff a laugh. "To say the least. And throw in the half-Korean culture, and it was just a mess for a little kid to navigate. Third graders aren't quite as enamored with British accents as adult women are," I tease, giving Madison's shoulders a slight squeeze. Her quiet laugh encourages me to continue.

"I didn't understand the thick Southern accents any better than they understood my British English. There were zero other Asian students in my grade, and kids can be ruthless to people who are different from them," I say. "I was trying to adjust, to do well at school—after all, I was the child of not one, but two college professors. And you have to understand—in Korean culture, eldest sons are expected to do everything with the utmost excellence in order to bring honor to the family. It's not bad or wrong, necessarily, but it's not an easy expectation to live up to when you're totally floundering in a new culture with no friends."

The tornado sirens are no longer blaring, but the power is still out. Madison has stopped shaking, so I continue talking rather than disrupt the peace.

"Conway isn't tiny like Noel is, but it's certainly not a big city, either. And small towns love their gossip. So any time I did something remotely wrong or subpar, word would somehow always make its way back to my dad. In fifth grade, I finally felt like I was getting my feet under me. There was this bully in the grade who was always picking on kids, and one day, I caught him being especially cruel to one of the girls in class, and I stood up to him. Another one of the cool kids buddied up to me, acting like he was so impressed that I'd stood up to the bully. I sensed something was off, but I ignored the instinct because I was so desperate to have a friend. We started hanging out after school, and he asked so many questions about my upbringing in London. One day, he invited me to his birthday sleepover party. I was so excited, and my dad gave me this huge lecture about how to act with respect in someone else's home."

My chest starts to tense at the memory, and for a second, I wonder why I'm still talking. Madison is calm. The storm has passed. There's no reason to share the rest of the story. But as I move my head to glance down at Hamlet, Madison nuzzles a little closer against my neck, even as she continues stroking Hamlet's back. Resting my cheek against her hair again, I continue.

"It was all a huge setup. The kid who I thought was my friend was actually best friends with the bully I stood up to. All the kids at the party ganged up on me to make fun of every personal thing I'd shared about myself with my so-called friend. I wanted to leave, but all I could think about was my dad's lecture about being respectful in someone's home. Leaving the party early didn't seem like it would be respectful, at least in my mind at that moment. So I stayed. And the next week at school, the boys spread all sorts of rumors about how weird I was, which circulated to my dad, who scolded me for making the family look bad."

Pausing to take a deep breath, I appreciate the weight of Madison against my chest as it inflates and deflates. I focus on the grounding quality of her presence—not on the roiling in my stomach at the memories I've shared.

"Liam . . . I'm so sorry. I'm sorry that those kids treated you that way and that your father didn't understand," Madison says, voice just above a whisper in the intimate space.

Sighing, I say, "I don't blame my dad. Truly, I don't. In retrospect, I think he was still wrestling with his own sense of lost culture after moving to the US, and he was probably harder on me than he wishes he would have been. They definitely weren't as hard on Hana by the time she was in school," I say.

"How much younger than you is she?" Madison asks.

"Ten years. My parents had only planned on having one child. Hana likes to say she was the surprise party we all needed," I say, and Madison laughs.

When she quiets, she whispers, "'Now I see the mystery of your loneliness.'"

I recognize the quote from *All's Well That Ends Well*, but I still ask, "What do you mean?"

"I get it. Your aversion to opening up to people. Your hostility toward small towns. I understand," Madison says. She tilts her head to look at me, so I raise my cheek from her hair and angle my face toward her.

Her lips are so close to mine. A breath away. The dim light of the phone flashlight casts shadows across her face, and I cease breathing, afraid of what I might do. Afraid of what it would mean to eliminate that inch of space between us.

"But the message you internalized as a little kid isn't always true. You *can* have friends who won't hurt you. I'm not going to hurt you, Liam," Madison whispers. "You can show me who you are, and I won't use it against you."

Maybe. Until we leave. And never come back.

Clearing my throat, I slightly shift my body away from Madison. She suddenly sits up straight, and Hamlet jumps off my lap.

I've officially broken the spell.

"I'll leave the light here, but I'm going to see what it looks like outside," I say. I hear Madison murmur "okay" as I stand and open the door, walking away from the tension between us.

I open the front door and look around. There are tree limbs down all over the place, and rain is still pouring in sheets. Closing the door, I turn around to see Madison walking across the living room with the phone flashlight.

"How's it look?" she asks.

"Lots of tree limbs down. I wouldn't be surprised if the power is out all night, especially in a more remote town like this," I say. The light is illuminating Madison's face enough that I see the look of fear pass over her face.

"Why don't we sleep out here in the living room? We can turn on the gas fireplace and at least have a little bit of light," I suggest. Madison is quick to agree, and we push the lumpy couch out of the way so we can move the mattresses from her bed and the trundle out to the living room. We line them up in front of the fireplace, and I flip the switch to turn it on.

After we alternate taking my phone with us to go to the bathroom and brush our teeth, I power it off to save some battery for tomorrow morning. We lie down on our respective mattresses, Hamlet stretches out on the pillow above my head, and I stare at the ceiling.

"Liam?" Madison's voice says, barely audible.

"Yeah?"

"Thank you."

I turn my head to look at her. "For what?"

Her voice has more strength, more sass, when she says, "You know what."

My lips twitch in a smile. "Goodnight, MJ."

"Night, Suits."

Minutes tick by as I try to fall asleep, but I can't even keep my eyes closed. Tired of staring at the ceiling, I fold my arm under my head, propping it so I can watch the fire. As Madison's breathing evens out, I give up the fight to not look over at her.

Madison Joy might very well be the fiercest woman I've ever met. But staring at her now in the dim firelight—curled on her side, hands tucked under her chin, hair splayed on the pillow behind her—she looks so delicate.

My chest heats with the phantom sensation of her tucked against my side, that eucalyptus-scented hair caressing my neck.

I roll to my side, facing away from Madison.

My gut is wrong. Madison is a bad idea. My gut is wrong. It's wrong, I tell myself over and over, until exhaustion finally drowns out my consciousness.

CHAPTER TWENTY-THREE

Madison

T he pillow I'm holding suddenly turns into a motor engine. Its rumbling hum grows louder, vibrating my arms. I must have fallen asleep in the tractor for some reason.

But that doesn't make sense. I don't live on the farm anymore.

My eyes suddenly snap open, awakening me from my dream. The engine pillow in my arms isn't an engine *or* a pillow at all.

It's a cat.

Hamlet is lying under my arm, his back snuggled up against my chest, purring softly.

The events of last night crash through my waking memory. The storm, the laundry room, the comfort of Liam's arm around me. The soothing timbre of his voice as he talked—really *talked*.

My gaze moves from Hamlet over to Liam lying on a mattress a few feet away from mine. He's sprawled on his back, one arm angled above his head and the other stretched out across the space between us. His eyes are closed, his hair is disheveled, and the early morning light illuminates the faint brush of stubble across his jaw. *Will I ever catch him in a state where he doesn't look attractive? Is it even possible?*

His chest rises and falls with deep, even breaths, and I remember what the movement of those breaths felt like beneath my cheek last night. I also remember the cold vacuum of air left behind when he abruptly left the room. And all at once, this moment feels too intimate.

Glancing down at Hamlet, I telepathically question him, *Will you punish me if I move right now?* I stroke his striped gray fur until he raises his head and looks at me, seafoam eyes narrow with sleepiness. As he stares at me, I don't see any sort of transition to ill intent in his expression. I give him a quick scratch under his chin, and then I slowly, silently stand up from the mattress. I turn off the fireplace, making a mental note to give Liam some cash to help cover that utility bill this month. Slowly tiptoeing, I ninja my way to my bedroom.

Away from Liam.

When I try to turn on the light in my room, I discover that the power is still out. *So much for texting Clara. Guess I'll just have to drive over.* I quickly change clothes and brush my teeth as quietly as possible.

As I quietly step out of the bathroom, I see Hamlet staring at me from where he sits perched on Liam's chest. Liam is awake now, rubbing Hamlet's back with one hand and his eyes with the other.

Clearing my throat, I say, "Morning."

Liam drops his hand from his eyes and props up on an elbow. "Morning. Did you sleep okay?"

"*Mmhmm,*" I hum. "The power is still out, so my phone is dead. I'm gonna drive over to Clark and Clara's and see how the town is doing. If there's anything I can do to help."

Liam sits up fully, scooping Hamlet into his arms in the process. I extinguish the flicker of jealousy that flares up.

"Is it safe for you to be out driving? If the power is out, there could be electric lines down," Liam says as he rises to his feet. He crosses the room to look out the front window. "If you give me a few minutes to get dressed, I can drive you. I should probably go over and check on the factory."

"Oh, I didn't even think about that. Will it be a total disaster without power?" I ask.

"Nah, there are backup generators for this reason. But we definitely don't want those going out, so I should go make sure everything is still running smoothly. Give me five?" Liam asks.

I don't have a good reason to say no, so I nod. "I'll feed Hamlet while you get dressed."

He looks at me as though he can somehow sense that Hamlet and I have buried the hatchet. "Thanks," is his only response as he heads to the opposite side of the house.

As I open the container to scoop out Hamlet's breakfast, he rubs against my ankles, tail swaying in the air. "This is a real truce, right? You're not going to turn on me when my guard is down?" I ask as I pour food into the dish.

Meow.

"Well, I don't know what that tone means, but rest assured that you do not want me for an enemy. So no double crossing me. *Capisci?*"

Meow.

Hamlet busies himself with the food, so I refresh his water dish. By the time I'm done, Liam emerges wearing a pair of jeans and a polo shirt.

"I'm honestly shocked that you own a polo, Suits," I sass, trying to recalibrate our vibe.

Liam simply rolls his eyes. "You and your pigeonholes. Let's go."

Liam dropped me off at Clara's cabin before heading to the Pure Fur All plant. He took my cell phone with him to charge at his office and promised to find me after he made sure things were okay at the factory.

"Although Noel wasn't directly hit, there was a tornado a few miles away. We got hit with high winds, enough to knock out several electric poles," Clark explains as he navigates his truck around a large branch in the road. "Being such a small town, we don't have the same resources to get the power back online right away. It might take a couple of days for the power company to get everything fixed."

"What are we going to do?" Clara asks from the passenger seat. I'm sitting in the back seat, an enthusiastic Chase crowding my lap and licking my face every few seconds. I rub my hand over his golden fur, which increases the speed of his wagging tail.

"We can't do anything to get the power lines restored, but we can clean up limbs so the electric company has better access to the roads. And generally get the town back into shape," Clark says. "Just watch—we'll get to Main Street, and there will already be a crowd gathered to get to work."

Sure enough, when we pull into the parking lot of Noland's, Davis is already standing on his truck bed, talking through a bullhorn to organize work parties.

"All of the power should be dead, but if you notice even a hint of a power line being live, stay away and call the electric company to report it," Davis says as we step close enough to hear. "Those without chainsaws buddy up with people who have them to haul away the cut branches. Let's get our town cleaned up!"

A cheer rises from the crowd of townspeople, and everyone quickly disperses into small groups. I turn to Clara and ask, "What should we do? I wouldn't mind manning a chainsaw."

"Absolutely not," Clark states, zero nonsense in his tone. I glare at him. "There's a group that's going to assemble some sandwiches for lunch inside the grocery store. Why don't you two help with that?"

Popping my hands on my hips, I tell Clark, "You can't tell me what to do. I grew up on a farm. Maybe I'm great with a chainsaw."

He mimics my intimidation pose, but his twelve extra inches of height make his stance a little more threatening than mine. I fake a sigh and say, "Fine, fine. I'll just pretend I'm back on lunch duty for harvest."

In no way should anyone trust me with a chainsaw today. Not when I'm mentally on edge after last night with Liam.

Sydney and Becky are already inside of Noland's organizing an assembly line. Syd greets Clara with a hug, and I'm caught off guard when Becky does the same to me. "Hey heyyy," Syd says. "Emily is off doing mayor stuff trying to get the town up and running again. But she gave me free rein to pull food supplies from the store as long as we keep records."

"Good thing they have a generator here too," I say. "I didn't even think about backup generators until Liam mentioned the factory having one."

Clara and Syd exchange a look as I pull on food service gloves. "Stop those looks. I'm allowed to say Liam's name without it meaning anything. We are roommates, after all."

"Yeah, he did seem super pleasant when he dropped you off this morning," Clara says. Syd perks up and gives me a suspicious look.

"He didn't want me driving over to Clara's in case the roads were unsafe after the storm. He just dropped me off on his way to the factory. No biggie."

"Sure, okay," Syd says, and Becky chuckles.

Maybe Liam had a point about small-town gossip.

"Maybe you should invite Liam to join us on the float trip the first weekend of June," Clara says innocently. "He might enjoy a little time off experiencing the town's scenery."

"Yeah, invite him!" Syd agrees. "I'm sure the guys would love to grill him a little more on his grand plans for the factory."

A protective lion roars to life in my chest. "No grilling."

Everyone pauses in the middle of assembling sandwiches to look at me. I soften my tone. "They could just be friendly without grilling him about the factory. I'm sure he deals with that enough from corporate."

"Good point, Mads," Clara agrees. "I promise I'll make Clark be nice."

I level her with a stare, and she amends, "Well, I'll *try* to encourage him to act friendly. Ish."

"Don't worry, Davis can balance out Clark's grump factor. And Beau would be there, so Liam would have a familiar face, at least," Syd says. "I mean, no pressure, but feel free to tell him he's welcome to join."

"I'll talk to him about it," I mutter, slamming the top piece of bread down on the turkey and cheese. Because it *would* be good for Liam to see how great people can be. To experience what real friendship looks like among some of the best people I know. To get a peek into the sweet side of small-town life.

I'm just not sure how well my heart could handle it if he actually lets his guard down again. Vulnerable Liam captivated me. But I don't want to be a captive if the guards shoot back up.

Clara changes the subject, filling us in on the movie script she's currently writing for Heartmark. This one won't be produced until next year, as she already has one in production for this upcoming Christmas. I'm so proud of her for grabbing hold of this dream, I could burst.

As people start trickling into the store to grab food and take a break, I'm surprised when I see Liam come in alongside Davis. In a sea of men bedecked in flannel or T-shirts, Liam sticks out like a sore thumb in his pale blue polo. But his jeans are covered with specks of sawdust, a sure sign he's been assisting with the limb removal.

He's listening intently to whatever Davis is saying, that laser-focused look on his face. When Davis pauses mid-step to turn toward Liam with a huge smile on his face, Liam breaks into a laugh. Davis slaps Liam on the shoulder, howling with laughter at whatever story he just told.

My heart is twisting itself into funny knots at the sight of Liam and Davis laughing together, just in time for Liam to look up and make eye contact. I drop my attention to the bags of chips in front of me, rearranging them for the people coming through the food line.

"*Hmmm*," Clara hums next to me, not saying anything else.

"Shut that hum right up, Clara Jane," I mutter.

When Davis and Liam approach us, Liam pulls my phone out of his pocket and hands it to me. "Here you go. It charged to eighty percent, at least."

"Thank you," I say, pocketing the phone.

"Liam here is gonna join us on our float trip," Davis says, clapping Liam on the back.

"That's great!" Clara exclaims. "From what Beau has said, you're putting in long hours at the factory every day. You deserve to enjoy the fun side of Noel, too!"

"Speaking of the factory, was everything okay there?" I ask Liam.

He nods. "Yes, the generators were doing their thing. But since the power could be out for another day or so, Beau came in and we cut back part of the production line to conserve power, just in case. It will hurt our numbers for the month, but you can't avert natural disasters."

Our numbers. He claimed the plant so naturally, I wonder if he even realized he did it.

"We'll come eat with you guys!" Clara says, giving me a serious side eye. "I just saw Clark walk in, so we can all take a break together and figure out what to do next."

After filling plates, we head outside to Clark's truck in the parking lot. Chase's tail goes into hyperdrive mode as we approach, and he gives Liam a cheerful greeting when we climb into the truck bed. We spread out and sit along the edges, chatting as we eat. Liam freely shares an update about where they are in the approval process for the new production line—information everyone is eager to lap up.

"I was thinking that we should take some food over to Pops," Clara says as we finish eating. "I know he said he was fine when we called this morning, but it wouldn't hurt to go over and check on him."

"Davis and I still need to pitch in to cut up and haul away a couple of the bigger trees that fell on the main road into town," Clark says. "We could go after."

"Clara and I can just drive over there," I assert. "We are strong, independent women, after all."

"I don't know how well the road to Pops' house has been cleared yet," Clark counters. "Just wait a couple of hours and we'll go over there."

"I could drive them," Liam offers. "I've heard about Pops but haven't met him yet."

Clark gives Liam an assessing look but agrees.

I could protest more about Clark's overprotectiveness not letting us drive alone, but I know it's just his nature. Plus, I'm a little giddy about the prospect of watching Liam meet Pops for the first time.

"Prepare to meet one of the greatest human beings on planet Earth," I say from the back seat. Clara is sitting up front, giving Liam directions to Pops' house.

"What's so great about him?" Liam asks as we pull into the long driveway.

"He's a straight shooter, in the most endearing way," Clara replies.

I laugh. "I don't think Pops ever had a filter to begin with, but add on the phenomenon of elderly people losing their filters, and you get the most unfiltered remarks ever."

Liam smiles and puts the SUV in park. "Sounds like my kind of man."

"If it weren't for Pops, Clark and I may not even be married," Clara says, a sentimental tone to her voice.

"Yeah, because that dummy McScrooge needed some sense knocked into him," I add, hopping out of the car and closing the door.

"I get the sense there's a long story there, and I hope you'll tell me about it later," Liam says. "But for now, we should probably try to get some of those tree limbs cleared away from the walkway and porch."

I carry the bag of food, and Liam pulls a large limb off the sidewalk so we can make it up to the front door. Clara knocks on the door and calls, "Pops? It's Clara and Madison! We brought you some food."

"And a new friend to meet!" I add, smiling slyly at Clara.

A minute later, the door opens. Pops stands there leaning on his cane, smiling at Clara. "Well, now, Miss Clara, I told you I'd be just fine. You didn't need to trouble yourself to come out here."

Clara leans in to kiss Pops' cheek. "You know it's never any trouble to come out and see you."

"Miss Madison, how are ya?" Pops asks. With his stooped stature, he's pretty much at eye level with me.

"I'm doing just fine," I reply. Liam has stepped up behind me, so I gesture to him. "Pops, this is Liam Park. He's been overseeing the pet food factory for the past few months."

Liam holds out a hand, and Pops angles his neck to meet Liam's eyes. "You're the one who came in telling everyone where they were wrong?"

"Um, yes?" Liam answers, a hint of uncertainty in his voice.

"And now things are working the way they should and won't shut down?" Pops asks.

"Yes, sir. That's the plan," Liam says, hand still outstretched.

"Good thing for you," Pops mutters. He vaguely nods and says, "You can come in." Leaning heavily on his cane, he turns to lead us into the house.

Liam mimes shaking his hand up and down, and I snort a laugh. His eyes dance as they meet mine, and I mouth, *"Told you so."*

I catch Clara watching us and give her an evil eye before I follow Pops into the house. "You got any sweet tea, Pops?" I ask.

"Sure do," Pops says. "Might not be as cold since the fridge has been off, but I'll get y'all a glass."

Liam gives me a concerned look, aggressively shaking his head. It only makes me smile with even more evil glee. He has no idea what he's in for.

I see the horror Liam tries to hide when Pops hands him a glass of brown liquid so thick it's more syrup than tea. Pops eyes Liam distrustfully, waiting for him to take a drink. Liam's eyes dart to mine—as though I would save him from this trial instead of thoroughly enjoying my spectator experience.

I give him my Grinchiest grin.

He takes a gulp, and his Adam's apple bobs as he stifles a cough. *"Mmm,"* he says. "Thank you."

Clara has graciously played along and not interfered with my little game, but I don't miss the "I'm on to you" look she gives me.

We help Pops out to the front porch, where there are several wooden rocking chairs he crafted decades ago. Pops was a master carpenter in his day, and the whole town is full of his signature furniture creations. Now, he spends his time whittling small animals and knickknacks to sell at "Santa's Workshop" during Christmas Fest.

Liam makes a big show of insisting that he clear away all of the tree branches littering Pops' yard, but I think it's just his way of getting out of drinking any more of the sweet tea syrup. Clara is the only person who can drink it without exerting great effort to swallow.

I find I have a much easier time stomaching the sugary drink when I'm able to watch the muscles in Liam's arms and back as he hauls tree limbs into a pile.

Clara chatters away with Pops, and I throw in a comment here and there. I decide to do Liam a solid and pour out half of his sweet tea into a nearby bush when Pops isn't looking. When Liam joins us on the porch, he takes one look at his glass and mouths, *"Thank you."*

I get Pops sharing about his carpentry experience, and Liam listens with genuine interest (in between forcing down swallows of tea). After an hour has passed, Clara announces that we should get back to see if Emily needs more help.

"Would you want to come stay at our house tonight?" she asks Pops. "I don't love the idea of you staying out here by yourself with no power."

"Oh please, I've survived a lot worse than a couple days without power," Pops says. "I'll sleep much better in my own bed next to Bev's picture."

Clara's eyes mist over like they do any time Pops mentions his late wife. Clara never met Bev, but even I have to admit I get emotional when I hear Pops talk about his beloved soul mate.

"Thanks for stopping by," Pops tells us. He holds out a hand as he adds, "It was nice to meetcha, Liam."

Liam's smile is genuine as he shakes Pops' hand. The genuine quality of the grin slips when he thanks Pops for the sweet tea, but who could blame him?

After dropping Clara back at Noland's and purchasing some flashlights, we drive to our house. Hamlet greets us with chill enthusiasm, even allowing me to scratch his chin. We eat up anything still edible in the fridge for dinner, since everything will spoil with another day of no power. As the hour grows later and the sunlight sneaks away, I feel my anxiety rise slightly. Which is stupid. The nightlight on my clock is so faint, it hardly even counts as light. I should be capable of sleeping without it.

Catching Liam's eye, I see him watching me thoughtfully. His voice is quiet when he asks, "Why don't you like storms? Or the dark?"

My eyes narrow as I consider the question. He opened up and shared a *lot* last night, so I suppose it's only right to return the favor. Still, I drop eye contact as I begin.

"When I was twelve, there was a big storm that came through. The tornado didn't wind up hitting us, but it did destroy some of the outbuildings on the farm next to ours. When the sirens went off, my sister and I went down to the basement and got in the closet under the stairs, like we were supposed to," I say. I can feel the darkness closing in around me as I recall the story.

"My parents joined us, but my brother, Chris, wasn't there. Dad went out to look for him and took the flashlight with him, leaving us in the dark when the power went out. Turns out Chris wanted to go save the barn kittens and bring them to the house with us, which is *not* what we were supposed to do. My dad found him but stayed in a small cellar in the barn with Chris rather than risk getting hit by any debris. We had to ride out the sounds of the storm in the pitch-dark basement, not knowing if Dad and Chris were okay. Mom cried the whole time," I explain, swallowing a lump in my throat. "But they were fine. We were all fine. And now I'm twenty-nine and shouldn't be afraid of storms or the dark anymore."

When I glance up at Liam, there's a look in his eyes I've never seen before. I don't know how to characterize it, but I know it makes me feel both warm and shivery simultaneously.

"Why don't we sleep out in the living room again tonight? Save the batteries in our phones and flashlights in case we need them later," he suggests.

Biting my lip, I nod. "Yeah, good thinking," I say, pretending that his suggestion isn't solely to save me from being alone in my dark room.

Now that we both have flashlights, we get ready for bed and reunite in the dark living room, lit solely by the glow of the fireplace. When I bend down to straighten the sheet on my mattress, Hamlet leaps onto my shoulders.

Half screaming, I jerk upright and yell, "I thought we were friends now, Hamlet! Why are you attacking me?!"

Liam's lips are curled in a soft smile when I turn to him, Hamlet precariously balanced on my shoulders. "You are friends," Liam says. "He's not attacking you. It's a sign of affection." He pauses to clear his throat. "Hamlet has never done that with anyone other than me."

There's a deep well of emotion in his eyes when he meets my gaze. Too deep for comfort. I tilt my head to meet Hamlet's eyes instead. "Well, Hammie, you have an odd way of showing affection."

Liam groans. "Not you too."

Raising a quizzical eyebrow, I ask, "What?"

He shakes his head. "Never mind. Doesn't matter."

CHAPTER TWENTY-FOUR
Madison

SOS. I'm having severe writer's block. What do I do?

Something Christmassy, obviously. Christmas is always your inspiration.

You're right.

Duh.

Okay. Are you free tonight? We could do a girls' night, Christmas style.

I will always clear my schedule for you. What do you need me to bring?

I can't help but laugh as I read Clara's text. Her Christmas spirit seriously goes from zero to infinity at the drop of a hat.

Of course, I'm not going to arrive empty-handed. I make a quick phone call to Lenore, one of the bake club ladies, to ask about the possibility of a rush order of orange cranberry scones. They're one of the most popular baked goods at Christmas Fest, and Clara loves them so much, they were one of the featured desserts alongside cake at their wedding reception.

Thankfully, everyone in this town *loves* Clara. And the bake club ladies keep extra cranberries stocked in their freezers to have on hand for Christmas in July. Lenore promises to dip into the supply and have a batch ready for me to take to Clara tonight.

This girls' night is coming at the perfect time. It's been over a week since the storm and town cleanup. Liam and I have skirted around discussing the time we spent together huddled in the laundry room and then sleeping by the fireplace. The air is heavy with the increased level of intimacy that neither of us is addressing.

I'm not working at Becky's today, so I make great progress on the manuscript I'm editing. Which is good news, considering my dream manuscript should be arriving in my inbox any day. I want to be fully focused when the time comes so I can put my best foot forward with this author.

If I know Clara Jane Noel in the slightest, I know that she will be wearing her flannel Christmas pajamas for this girls' night. Even though it's ninety degrees outside, I pair my long-sleeved Grinch pajama shirt with the regular shorts I'm wearing. Compromise.

As I gather my things to leave, Hamlet pads over, meowing loudly. When he rubs up against my ankles, I bend down to stroke his back. "Hey, Hammie," I croon. "I'm gonna go relax and try to stop thinking about your daddy, okay?" Hamlet responds by leaping onto my shoulders, so I reward him with a little scratch on the chest.

"I really have to go now. I have fresh scones to pick up," I tell Hamlet as I pull him off my shoulders and cradle him in my arms. Liam chooses that precise moment to come through the front door, halting suddenly at the sight of Hamlet snuggling me.

"You're not allowed to like her more than me," Liam tells Hamlet. I ignore the possible double meaning of his statement.

Meow.

Liam's brow furrows when he takes in my appearance. "Isn't it a little warm for fuzzy Christmas pajamas? And early? You're really taking this to the next level."

Shaking my head, I pass Hamlet off to him. "We're having a girls' night at Clara's. She's suffering from writer's block, and considering that she writes Christmas movie scripts, a little dose of Christmas spirit is just the inspiration she needs."

"So you're leaving for the night?" Liam asks. I don't miss the way his face falls with the question, and I don't know what to do with that.

"*Mmhmm*," I reply. "Don't wait up for me. I mean, not that you ever do. Or ever *should* wait up for me. Or . . . whatever. I'll see you tomorrow."

I dash out the door, chastising my stupid brain on the way to my car.

"How in the world did you manage this in the past six hours?" I ask as I step inside Clara's cabin.

It is *fully* decked out for Christmas. I'm pretty sure every decoration that she owns is currently on display and illuminated by hundreds of lights. There's a four-foot Christmas tree set up by the fireplace, and even the stockings are hung on the mantel. Chase is excitedly prancing around the room, wagging his tail with exuberance, clearly loving the Christmas spirit as much as Clara.

Clara shrugs. "Just a little Christmas magic." I narrow my eyes at her, and she confesses, "Clark didn't have any jobs this afternoon. He finished fixing the patio he was working on this morning, so I contracted his handyman hours to help me get all the decorations put up."

The man himself walks out of the sunroom and through the living room. "I drew the line at starting a fire in the fireplace, though," he says. Clara pouts her lower lip. While I do see her point—the tall stone fireplace is certainly the central feature of the room—I also see Clark's point.

"Clara, it's like, ninety-five degrees already. We can imagine a fire in the fireplace in our hearts, okay?" I say, deciding to back up Clark. "And to counterbalance that disappointment, I have orange cranberry scones!" I announce, holding up the container in my hands.

"Thank you, voice of reason," Clark says to me. "And, on that note, I'm outta here."

As he exits the front door, Sydney comes in. "Let's get this party started!" Her eyes widen as she takes in the Christmas wonderland. "I will never get over the fact that you turned Clark from, well, *Clark*, into a man who will decorate his house for Christmas in May."

Clara sighs with lovey-dovey eyes as she responds, "He really is the best."

After Clara makes cups of whipped-cream laden hot cocoa for each of us, we kick back on the couch, and Chase curls up at our feet. When Clara starts *White Christmas*, I give her a confused look. "I was expecting a Heartmark Christmas movie," I say.

"I was afraid if I watched a Heartmark movie that it would just send me deeper into my writing rut. Or make me second guess if what I'm writing is original enough. So I decided to go with a classic instead," Clara replies.

As the night wears on, we alternate between paying attention to the movie (mostly for the musical numbers) and chatting about life. Syd updates us on an interior design project she's doing for a couple in town. We needle Clara until she tells us the basic plot of her work in progress (extremely sweet and very Christmassy). And then the tables turn to me.

"So, Mads, you and Liam seem to be getting along well," Syd says just before taking an enormous bite of a scone, effectively handing me the proverbial microphone.

"Yep! He's turned out to be a decent roommate," I reply, giving her nothing to work with.

Syd groans, mouth still full. She talks around the food. "Come onnn, Mads. Just tell us if there's something going on between you two. The people want to know!"

I spear her with a look. She swallows the scone in her mouth.

"The people in this room, and exactly no other people," Syd amends, miming zipping her lips.

If only it was a straightforward answer.

I sigh and flop back against the couch, covering my face with my hands. "I don't know. I literally don't know what to tell you because I don't know if there's anything going on!"

Clara flops back next to me. "Would you like there to be something going on?" she asks softly.

"I honestly don't know. Logically, no. But . . ." I trail off.

"But your chemistry is off the charts?" Syd teases.

I sit up straight, pinning her with a glare. "How would you even know that? You saw us interact for all of—what?—thirty minutes at the town cleanup?"

"Clara had a few observations from your time visiting Pops as well," Syd adds with a twinkle in her eye.

Clara chokes on a bite of scone as I swivel to her. "How dare you, Clareeey?!" I only pull out the "Clarey" name when I really want to display my annoyance at Clara.

She coughs longer than I think is actually necessary, and then she tries to give me her sweetest puppy eyes. "Don't hold it against me! I just made a casual comment in passing to Syd about how cute you and Liam were together."

Now I *really* glare at Clara, because there's no way the word "cute" could be what she used to describe Liam and me.

"I believe her exact words were, 'Finally, Mads found someone who matches her sass,'" Syd cuts in, eyes dancing. "In the absolute *best* way possible. I can't wait to see for myself on the float trip."

"Do not make this a big thing, or you will scare Liam away," I state firmly. Clara and Syd look at me with twin expressions of confusion. "He's not the type to open up to people easily. Or at all. Kinda like Clark, but . . . different. Just, don't push him too hard, okay?"

"We won't," Clara vows. "I promise. And we're not pushing you either, okay, Mads? You know I love romance, but I love *you* more."

I nod at Clara, but then Syd adds, "Well, I'm maybe pushing you a *teeny* bit, but only because I know you can take it." She winks at me, and I smile in return.

Maybe I wasn't able to avoid thinking about Liam all evening, but this girls' night was still exactly what I needed.

CHAPTER TWENTY-FIVE

Liam

JUNE

I wasn't sure what to expect out of a river float trip in Arkansas, but I'm having a shockingly enjoyable time. The other guys here—Beau, Clark, and Davis—are comfortable in a way that suggests this was an integral part of their childhood and young adult years. Although I grew up three hours from here, I was never invited on any float trips (not that I would have accepted an invitation). I suppose I could have experienced something similar during college, but the vibe at the University of California, Berkeley was a different world than northwest Arkansas. Kayaking at Albany Beach is very different from lazily floating down a small river in an inner tube.

By the time I was getting my MBA at Pepperdine Graziadio Business School, I was too focused on learning everything I possibly could about the business world to bother with recreational activities. Aside from a daily morning run, at least.

As I watch the easy camaraderie between these lifelong friends, there's a dull pain behind my ribs. An uncomfortable feeling, like I've missed out on something. I shift in my inner tube, my attention catching on Madison and Clara twirling each other's tubes in circles.

Being in close proximity to Madison in a bathing suit adds a different layer to the subtle torture of this event. I've tried to maintain distance from her in the weeks following those nights together during the storm. Fought to shut down the instincts that scream at me to pursue her the way I dream about.

Watching her interact with this group of friends—the way she radiates energy as she volleys sarcastic banter with everyone—only makes my gut instinct even harder to ignore. I've never fought this hard against my gut in my entire life, and it's an infuriating battle.

"So, Liam, tell us some of your job's greatest hits. Surely there must be some other companies that were more screwed up than our very own pet food factory," Davis says with a grin.

"Yes, please tell me we're not the worst train wreck you've ever seen," Beau adds.

Laughing, I respond, "I don't know how to answer that in a way that doesn't disappoint you. This was definitely my first time uncovering an embezzlement scheme. It just might take the cake."

Beau groans, splashing water over his face.

"But that was definitely a Wilson screw-up, not the employees," I amend, trying to soften the blow. "But I do have stories for days of general incompetence and idiocy, if not outright criminal activity."

As I share examples, there are shocked exclamations, howling laughter, and pleas for more horror stories. It feels easy conversing and connecting over stories of work that I'm good at without having to share any intimate details of my personal life.

By the time we reach the end of our float route and cook dinner over an open campfire, I realize just how comfortable I felt with this group of friends today. The knowing smile Madison is giving me from across the fire seems to indicate that she can sense my thoughts.

As we sit around the fire, Syd makes a comment about the significance of this annual float trip that everyone picks up on but me.

"Wait, Liam doesn't know about this," Madison says. "Clara, Clark, fill him in on the history of float trips and Christmas and your love story."

I appreciate her looping me in, and the rest of the group seems eager to throw in their two cents as Clara and Clark share—well, mostly Clara. Clark offers minimal verbal additions, but he stares at Clara with mesmerized eyes the entire time.

I catch Madison's eye as Clara talks about Clark finding her by the giant Christmas tree in Kansas City to confess his feelings, and I see something new glimmering in her gaze.

Is it envy? Discontentment? Longing?

Or am I just projecting my own emotions onto her?

Madison is uncharacteristically quiet for the remainder of the evening, and I'm content to sit back and listen to the natural flow of conversation between the friends. The evening dies down along with the embers of the fire, and everyone makes quick work of packing up the day's supplies. We left our vehicles here at the end of the float path this morning and carpooled up to the start of the route, so Davis and Sydney will give Clark and Clara a ride to retrieve Clark's truck. As we disperse to our cars, Clara and Madison talk in hushed tones before Clara gives Madison an extended hug goodbye.

The conflicted look on Madison's face when she turns to me only adds to my own conflicted feelings.

What am I doing? What are we doing?

It's a bad idea.

Right?

Madison's pensive mood continues on the drive home, and I don't have any spare mental energy to drum up conversation. I'm too busy trying to beat my gut instincts into submission.

We ride the few minutes home in tense silence.

The quiet remains a heavy blanket as we head inside the house. Madison kicks off her sandals at the door and sets down the bag holding her phone, sunscreen, and empty water bottle. She pauses to give Hamlet a "hello" scratch on his chest, then pads to the kitchen for a glass of water. The domestic familiarity of this scene between us makes my chest ache.

I follow her, standing a few feet away, watching her motions. She's still wearing her swimsuit underneath a pair of cutoff jean shorts and a T-shirt, and her long hair is pulled up into a high ponytail. The coral strap of the halter top is visible above the collar of her T-shirt as she stands by the sink. The vision of her holding Clara's hand to twirl their inner tubes around on the river dances through my mind. The memory of her teasing laugh is so tangible, I expect her to be grinning when she turns around.

Instead, there's that same unfamiliar, guarded look in her eyes when she pivots toward me, leaning her back against the counter. Wisps of hair that escaped her ponytail frame her face, and her cheeks are perfectly sun-kissed.

The tether I had on my gut is stretched too far, too thin. It starts snapping strand by strand, adrenaline surging through my system as I stare at her. I shift my weight on the balls of my feet, clenching and unclenching my fists.

I don't know what exactly changed in my expression, but Madison looks at me with concern.

"What's wrong?" she asks. She takes in my fidgety energy. "What's going on? Did you not like hanging out with everyone today? I thought you were having a good time, but was I wrong?"

Barking out a half-laugh, I take to pacing back and forth. "No. That's not it. I did have a good time today. I enjoyed being with everyone."

Rubbing a hand over my jaw, I glance at Madison. She frowns as she asks, "Is it . . . bad that you enjoyed it?" When I shake my head, she holds up exasperated hands. "Then what is it? Why are you acting all psycho-antsy?"

"Because—" I start but catch myself. Pausing my pacing, I turn to face Madison. She sassily raises an eyebrow, and that's it for me. "Because I'm tired of convincing myself not to kiss you."

The confession hangs in the air between us, and her other eyebrow raises in shock. The drumming in my chest is so hard, so fast, I think my heart could literally burst any second. I'm surprised it doesn't explode out of my chest altogether when Madison takes a step closer to me.

So, so close.

Her chin is raised, her eyes are locked on mine as she murmurs, "Maybe you should stop convincing yourself."

That's all it takes to snap the final strand of restraint. I instantly step toward her, gather her face in my hands, and lean down to finally claim her lips with mine.

Madison meets my kiss with the same explosive intensity raging through me, zero to sixty with no warm-up lap. Like gunpowder and a spark, our lips meet with eruptive chemistry.

I'm immersed in her scent—eucalyptus and sunscreen and campfire smoke. Immersed and happily drowning, putting up no fight to save myself. I want *more* of her passion, *more* of the taste of her lips, *more* of this volatile alchemy between us.

I make a conscious effort to slow us down, to relish the softness of her lips against mine, the smooth skin of her cheek beneath my thumb, the tangle of her hair between my fingers.

But she wraps her arms around my waist, hands roaming the muscles of my back, and my foot backs off the brake. Looping one arm around her back, I lift her onto the kitchen counter, bringing her lips to my level. She fluidly moves her hands from my back to my neck, pulling my mouth back to hers. I can't hold back a moan at the sensation of her fingers against my scalp, her unrestrained passion almost a challenge.

All that feisty, sassy energy bundled up in Madison's tiny frame reverberates in the way she kisses me, and I could so easily get lost in it forever. The power of her kiss could become my addiction, my energy source, my sanctuary.

So easily.

But the logical part of my brain claws its way back to consciousness, reminding me of why I fought against this attraction to Madison in the first place. Because it's *not* actually easy or simple.

It takes concerted mental effort, but I break away from Madison's lips. We're both breathing heavily, and I remove my hands from her waist and her hair, placing them on either side of her on the counter.

We stare at each other, gulping in oxygen, until I catch my breath enough to speak. "What are we doing?" I ask.

"Ummm, I was kissing you, Suits. That's what I was doing. Pretty sure it was a mutual action," Madison deadpans. Her response reignites the gunpowder, and my body screams at me to continue that mutual kiss. I settle for dragging my thumb across her lips instead.

"It was very mutual. You might recall that I'm the one who started it," I murmur. Under my thumb, her lips curve into a classic Madison smirk. "I like you, MJ. I feel . . . different with you. Different than anything I've ever experienced. You're fiery, you say exactly what you're thinking, you're determined, and you don't take crap from anyone, myself included. I like *this* attitude," I say, holding up her hand to point out the way she always has her middle fingers painted a different color from the rest. She coyly bites her lip as I release her hand.

"There's also the fact that you're so freaking beautiful I can hardly stand being in the same room without touching you." My thumb traces down to hold her chin. "I like you. But how can this work? There's an expiration date to our proximity. We've always known there was. So what are we doing?"

Madison's lips turn down as she whispers, "I don't know."

I return my hand to the counter, because I'm not sure I can withstand any tiny point of physical contact with the woman in front of me. Not if I'm going to have a level-headed conversation.

"I don't know how it's going to work," Madison says softly. "And normally, a lack of clear plans makes me queasy. I'm not a fan of forks in the road without an obviously right direction to follow."

Disappointment and fear sizzle in my chest at her words, causing my muscles to tense. But Madison reaches a hand up to my cheek, smoothing her fingers down my jaw as she adds, "But right now, I don't want to take a path that isn't toward you. Because I like you. I like your self-confident, take-control-of-the-room swagger. I like the secret tender side you do a very good job of hiding. I like that you don't back down when I try to push your buttons, and I like who you push *me* to be. So I can figure out how to make the path work. I'm very resourceful."

That sassy glimmer is back in her eyes as she finishes the sentence, and I lean in closer to her again. "We carve out the path as we go?"

"As we go," she whispers.

I decide that's enough level-headed conversation for the night and crash my lips back into hers.

Seconds or minutes or hours later, we're interrupted by Hamlet leaping onto the counter.

"Hammie!" Madison exclaims as I pull out my disappointed dad voice to chide, "Hamlet, *no* counters."

He jumps onto Madison's shoulders, yowling for attention. Given our proximity, it's an easy few steps for him to cross from Madison's shoulders to mine, meowing incessantly in my ear.

Although initially annoyed, I recognize his interruption for the necessity it is. My default speed setting may be more Formula 1 race car than minivan, but I don't want to kill the engine of whatever is happening between Madison and me. I want this to be a cross-country road trip, not a drag race. So I need to recalibrate my momentum accordingly.

Sighing, I pull Hamlet off my shoulders and hold him in my arms between us. She leans in and kisses him on the head, then plants a soft kiss on my lips.

"To be continued when we've had some sleep and can think straight," Madison says.

"Just to be clear, are we talking 'to be continued' on the kissing or the 'how does this work' conversation?" I ask wryly.

She bites the corner of her lip before replying. "Both. Obviously."

Chapter Twenty-Six

Madison

My mind rouses to consciousness before I open my eyes. My first waking thought is of the wild look in Liam's eyes when he confessed he wanted to kiss me. My next thought is of how electrifying it was to have those very passionate lips against mine. I keep my eyes closed, replaying every detail of Liam's kisses in my mind.

I sigh with happiness and open one eye to check the time. It's 7:34 a.m. on a Sunday, so I could linger in bed if I wanted to.

Or I could get up and see Liam again as soon as possible.

It's an easy decision. I leap out of bed, pulling up the quilt and tidying the pillows. Not bothering to change out of the tank top and shorts I slept in after showering last night, I go to the bathroom to brush my teeth and hair. I make sure there are no sleep crusties in my eyes and pad out to the living room, hoping Liam is awake.

He's standing in the kitchen, chugging a glass of water. By the look of his sweaty athletic shirt, he just returned from a run. As I approach, Hamlet meows from his place at Liam's ankles, and Liam turns to face me.

If I had any hint of trepidation about how our interactions might go following the events of last night, it's dissolved completely by the sensual smile he gives me. My pulse races as I step closer to him, close enough to see the beads of sweat still dotting his forehead.

His eyes quickly roam down and up my body, and he clears his throat. "We might need to have a conversation about what you are and aren't allowed to wear around the house. Especially first thing in the morning."

My brows pinch into a sarcastic look. "Oh really? Well, if that's the case, you're going to have a very miserable time going for runs in baggy sweats and oversized, long-sleeved T-shirts all summer. Not to mention how difficult it will be for you to get ready for work if you're not allowed to wear any of your suits around the house."

Liam's smile has turned positively wicked, his eyes glimmering. "Is that so?" he asks as I invade his personal space, intending to resume physical contact immediately.

He steps away, though, holding up his hands. "Hold on, you don't want to touch me right now. I'm drenched in sweat—the Arkansas humidity is awful already, even though it's only June." He reaches out to softly drag a finger down my jaw. "Doesn't mean I'm not thinking about kissing you, though. I just need to shower first."

Taking a step forward to erase the space he put between us, I lift my chin as I say, "Liam? Now that we're being honest about how we feel, there's something I need to confess." His eyes dilate as he holds my eye contact. In my peripheral vision, I notice his hands twitch at his sides. "I've been dreaming," I slowly enunciate, taking my sweet time, "about you making me another pour over coffee."

I give him my most mischievous smirk. He exhales a sharp breath just before wrapping me up in his arms and pulling me against his *very* sweaty chest. "Have you?" he asks, an evil laugh in his tone. "Forget showering first, you deserve this."

"Ack, gross! What? Were you running through a sauna?!" I exclaim, squirming in his embrace. He tickles my sides as he rubs his sweaty hair against my face, and I squeal. "Gross! Gross! That's disgusting!" I yell, pretending to gag.

Is Liam really and truly drenched in sweat? Yes.

Am I legitimately upset about being in contact with his sweaty body? Not even a little.

He finally releases me, his teasing grin lingering. I make a big show of wiping off the imaginary sweat he left behind. But when he suddenly takes my face in his hands and kisses me, my hands instantly latch on to his chest, sweat and all.

After a short but very thorough kiss, Liam pulls back. Whatever starstruck expression he sees on my face must be exactly what he was going for, because his self-satisfied smile widens. "Good morning, MJ," he says.

"*Mmhmm*," is the only response I can muster. Liam traces a thumb across my lips before releasing my face. He turns toward his bedroom, calling out over his shoulder, "I'll make coffee after I shower."

I might just need a cold shower myself. You know, to wash off all of Liam's gross sweat.

"Now we're going to raise our right legs into an arabesque, and hold. Bend both knees, and lengthen. Bend, and lengthen." The barre instructor's voice coaches us through the video screen, and I find that I'm struggling far less to keep up this time.

Probably because my mind is distracted thinking about Liam.

"Did Liam have fun yesterday? It seemed like he was having a good time, but I don't really know him well enough to be able to tell what he's thinking," Clara says between even breaths. Her arabesque form is still far superior to mine, but at least I'm holding my own.

"He did. I think it was good for him to be around the guys and see some close friends interacting," I say. It takes me far more effort to talk and also remember to breathe than it did for Clara. She raises one hand into second position, balancing herself on the barre with just one hand to increase the level of difficulty on her core muscles.

Showoff.

"I think he also had a good time when he kissed me last night," I casually comment.

Clara falls right out of her arabesque relevé, and I grin in victory.

"'Scuse me, what?" she exclaims, turning to face me. I glance over at her, a smug look on my face as I continue bending and lengthening my trembling leg. Clara crosses her arms. "Mads, tell me everything *right now*!"

Sighing, I say, "We should probably do the cooldown so our muscles don't get—"

Clara cuts me off with a light shove, forcing me to plant both feet on the floor. I simply laugh.

"I will lead us through a cooldown while you tell me every single detail," Clara says.

We sit on the floor, and I half-heartedly mimic Clara's stretches as I expound on the events that unfolded after Liam and I got home last night. Her love for romance is second only to her love for Christmas, so she sighs and swoons and squeals as I describe our kiss and subsequent conversation.

Clara places the back of her hand to her forehead and dramatically "faints" to the floor. "Mads, I'm dead. You've killed me with happiness for you."

Lying down on the floor next to her, I stare at the Christmas lights still strung around the room. Her Christmas magic certainly seems to be extra magical at the moment. I tell her, "I'm pretty happy too."

"So . . . how *will* you make this work? What happens when you're not in the same city anymore? Long distance?" Clara asks, turning her head to look at me.

I shrug. "I don't know yet." I try to tamp down the edge of panic that creeps in over not having an ironed-out plan for the future. *As we go. As we go. As we go*, I mentally chant.

Clara props up on one elbow. "What city will *you* even be in?" she asks. "Are you going to go back to KC or stay here in Noel?"

Sputtering a breath through my lips, I repeat myself. "I don't know yet."

"You know you could stay here! You can proofread books from anywhere. Why not join me as an official Noel resident?" Clara prompts, eagerness in her voice. "We've loved having you here for so many months."

Rolling my eyes, I say, "I know *you've* loved having me around. I'm not sure if the sentiment is widespread." The self-doubt slipped out before I could corral it as an inside thought, and I wish I could take it back.

Clara's brow furrows. "What do you mean? Of course, everyone loves having you here. I mean, you know Clark—he's not going to openly display any affection, but he's happy you're here. And Becky, Syd, and Abby are thrilled. Not to mention Pops and Emily and—"

Waving a hand to cut her off, I say, "I'll give you Pops. We're kindred spirits. But we all know you're the real town transplant sweetheart, and I just get included in the kindness on your behalf."

"Mads, what are you even talking about? Everyone loves you for *you*," Clara insists as she sits up. She smacks my stomach when I don't respond, and I sit up to face her. She continues, "You have no idea how many conversations I've had with people about how glad they are that you've been sticking around. About the energy and laughter and joy you've brought to town by being here. You're Becky's favorite employee at the coffee shop, even though she knows your time working there will be short-lived as your business takes off. Your spunk is the spark the town needed to cheer everyone up again after the Pure Fur All fiasco. Everyone is hoping you decide to stay permanently."

I fiddle with a loose string on the hem of my leggings, avoiding eye contact. "Are you just being your typical, sweet Care Bear self, trying to help me feel better?"

The movement of Clara's hand rising catches my attention. She holds her flattened hand straight up, palm facing me. "I swear on my Hindu rope hoya that I'm telling the truth."

I gasp. "Not your favorite plant! This is serious."

"I'll throw the ficus tineke onto the swear pile, just for good measure," Clara adds solemnly.

"Wow. You're not kidding around," I say, a hint of a smile playing at my lips. I can't quite hide the joy that's inflating my heart. "Well, if the tineke is on the chopping block, too, you must be telling the truth."

"In all seriousness, Mads, people really do love you and want you around. So, if you want to stay, I'll help you find a great long-term housing situation. I'll make Clark build you your own cabin in the woods next door," Clara says.

Huffing a laugh, I say, "Actually, can we tell him to do that, just for fun? I'd like to watch his reaction."

Clara rolls her eyes. "All right, now that we've officially established you as a permanent resident, what are we going to do when Liam's time at the factory is finished?"

Her question is the pinprick that slowly deflates the joy ballooned in my heart. I sigh. "I don't know. I really don't like the idea of a long-distance relationship. At least, not for an extended time. I also *really* don't like the idea of moving to Houston. A relationship with Liam doesn't actually make very much sense. Maybe starting something with him is the wrong thing to do."

I pause, trying to find words for how I feel. Clara waits patiently for me to continue. "But cutting him out of my life feels *more* wrong. It's like my gut knows we're supposed to be together, even if my head can't wrap itself around how we're going to make it work on a practical level. I guess we'll just cross each bridge as it comes. Forge our own way forward."

Clara smiles at me. "I have to say, I'm impressed at your willingness to go with the flow here. Are you sure you don't have a secret Excel spreadsheet somewhere with check boxes mapping out your future relationship?" she teases, and I laugh heartily.

"Now that you mention it, maybe that's not a terrible idea," I quip back.

"Would Liam want to join us for Tuesday dinner this week?" Clara asks hopefully.

"Ehhh, that might be a stretch. Close friendships haven't really been his . . . thing in the past. I might need to slowly ease him into the friend group," I say. "But I'll work on it."

Clara gives me an impish grin. "If he kisses you anything like you claim he does, I have a feeling it might be easier than you think to convince him to play along with any request from you."

After my abbreviated barre workout and lengthy conversation with Clara, I head home to get some work done on the dream manuscript

I'm editing. Elizabeth, the author, contracted me to do both copyediting and proofreading. She sent it to me last week, and I'm taking extra time to ensure I don't miss a thing.

Although I shouldn't be surprised, I'm disappointed to see the empty driveway, meaning Liam's probably at the factory putting in some extra hours on this Sunday afternoon.

It's a good thing he's gone, Madison. You need to get some of your own work done. You have *to nail it with this author if you hope to land more clients like her.*

I decide to take an extra few minutes to make a cup of matcha for an afternoon boost of energy. Filling Liam's water kettle and programming it to the green tea temperature, I begin sifting the matcha powder into a bowl. When the kettle chimes, I pour a small amount of water into the bowl and whisk it side to side with my bamboo whisk. Once it's frothy, I pour it into a mug to add the rest of the water.

When I make matcha in the mornings, I usually add half milk and half water to make a matcha latte, but I settle for just water this afternoon. I drizzle maple syrup into the tea to sweeten it. Carrying the steaming mug to my bedroom, I set it on the desk and turn on all of the Christmas lights.

I pull up a snowy Christmas ambience scene on my tablet, and compare it to the hot, sunny summer outside the window. *If I did move here permanently, I would sure miss snowy winters.*

Turning to my laptop, I drill down my focus on Elizabeth's manuscript. I'm about a third of the way through and loving every second. About an hour later, I'm distracted by Hamlet's loud *meow*. He's sitting just outside the door to my bedroom, looking at me with those intense eyes of his.

Meow.

"You want to come in here, Hammie?"

Meow.

Rising from the desk, I move to the doorway and scoop him into my arms. "I suppose since we're friends now, you can come into my room. As long as you promise to behave. Remember—no double crosses, okay?" I tell him.

Meow.

After nuzzling him briefly, I set him down on the floor so I can resume editing. He trots over to my Christmas tree, giving it a thorough sniff inspection. When he's satisfied with his findings, he crawls under the tree and sprawls onto his side, looking up at the lights.

Smiling, I tell him, "That used to be my favorite thing as a kid, too, Hammie. I'd lie under the tree and look up through the center to see the rainbow of lights filtering through the branches. Sorry that these are just white lights and not multicolor. Maybe I should have gone with my kid taste instead of refined adult preferences."

Meow.

Hamlet quietly keeps me company for another hour as I continue reading and making corrections to the manuscript. I'm just thinking about pausing to make dinner when I hear the front door open.

"Madison? Hamlet?" Liam's voice calls.

"In here!" I yell back. He steps into view in the doorway, taking in the sight of Hamlet curled up under the tree beside me.

"Off limits, huh?" he jokes.

"You know that Hammie and I have an understanding now," I say, not missing his flinching reaction to my nickname for Hamlet. I stand and saunter toward him. "What? Am I really not allowed to call him that?"

Liam sighs. "Hana always shortened our cats' names to girlie nicknames—Ophelia, Rosencrantz, and Guildenstern became Ophie, Rosie, and Gilly. I've tried to hold my ground when she calls him 'Ham.' He's a dignified cat. It's insulting."

"Wow, your family really is serious about Shakespeare," I remark. Liam smiles and shrugs in response. "Okay, so Hana isn't allowed to shorten his name. Buuut, does the ban extend to me as well?" I slowly wrap my arms around his waist as I ask, tilting my head back and giving him sad eyes.

"Those puppy eyes won't get you anywhere with me," he chides. But I feel the muscles in his back tensing in response to my touch.

I glare at him.

"That fiery gold spark in your eyes might get you somewhere, though," he says before threading his fingers through my hair and pulling my mouth to his.

Every time Liam kisses me, it gets better and better. Like our lips were meant for each other, and every time they meet, they fuse together more perfectly. This kiss is more playful than last night's urgent, desperate kisses, but it's just as intense. Just as consuming.

When Liam releases me, I inhale a deep breath, gathering my wits from the corners of the earth he just scattered them to. "That was a yes to calling him 'Hammie,' right?"

"You're relentless," he sighs.

"I thought you liked that about me," I tease.

Liam smirks. "You are absolutely right. It might just be my demise. Or, at least, the demise of Hamlet's dignity."

On cue, Hamlet snakes between our feet, loudly meowing on his way to the kitchen.

"Dinner time?" I ask.

Liam leans closer to me and murmurs, "I mean, we can pause to eat dinner if you want to."

I'm having a hard time thinking about anything other than the feel of his lips when they're hovering so close to mine. "Hammie could practice a little patience for a few minutes," I say, voice breathy.

Rather than meeting my lips with his, Liam gently brushes kisses along my jaw, leaving a trail of shivering fire on his way to my neck. "He hasn't learned a lot of patience, I suppose," he murmurs in my ear, "since I don't have much patience myself."

"Me either," I say as I turn his face to bring his lips to mine. Liam steps closer, my back pressing against the door frame, our lips soldered together just like they're meant to be.

Milliseconds before I lose all sense of reality, I press Liam's chest away from me. Gasping a breath, I say, "Okay. We need to lay some ground rules."

"Okay," Liam says, eyes locked on mine. "Rule one: Hamlet's name is Hamlet, not Hammie."

"Ha ha," I huff, lightly punching him in the chest, and he laughs. "I'm serious. This is a little unconventional, us being roommates first and then starting a relationship. Rules must be made."

He stands up straight, a smile still playing at his lips. "That's reasonable. Here's rule number one for real: you sleep in your room, I sleep in mine. No sleeping together in any sense of the word. I need the firm boundary line drawn, or the intensity of kissing you is going to derail all self-control. The nights by the fireplace nearly did me in."

While I'm usually the direct one in conversations, my heart pounds and heat floods my cheeks at his blunt declaration. Swallowing hard, I nod agreement. Narrowing my eyes, I say, "Rule two: no coming into the house shirtless after your morning runs."

A devilish smile spreads across Liam's face, and he leans an arm on the door frame above my head. "Rule three," he says, "no stealing any of my clothes to wear."

I give him a quizzical look. "What? I've never stolen any of your clothes."

"This is a preemptive rule," he says. "I'm telling you in advance that I couldn't handle seeing you wear my clothes. If I leave a hoodie lying around, you keep your grabby little paws off."

I give him a sultry smile. "Well, now you're just giving me ideas."

Liam growls, and says, "You're adding it to the list. At least, I'm pretty confident your Type-A brain was planning to write down these rules. Are we signing an official contract? Should I be calling a notary?"

"*Mmm*, don't threaten me with a good time," I tease in a low voice, and I see the spark in his eyes that's a precursor to his lips finding mine. I cut him off before he can distract me. "Rule four: you have to keep talking to me."

He backs away a touch, searching my expression. I clarify, "We're starting a real relationship. This is *not* a physical fling. It's pretty evident that both of us could easily spend all day making out, but you have to keep talking to me. Keep sharing more about yourself. I want to know you better. I want *you* to know *me* better."

Between the silent pause and the contemplative expression on his face, I know he's seriously weighing my demand. He finally says, "Okay. I swear I'll try. I might need a little help in the opening up department, but I'll try. I promise."

"Rule number whatever number we're on: I'm gonna need you to resurrect that British accent," I say, grasping his shirt and tugging him closer to me.

"Aren't you demanding?" he murmurs, leaning in. I detect a hint of posh English as he adds, "Good thing you're also irresistible, love."

Before his lips can reach mine, there's an alarming hiss as Hamlet's paw aggressively swats at Liam's ankle.

"All right, all right, we'll feed you," Liam says, giving Hamlet an evil glare. Hamlet glares right back.

"Let's go, Hammie!" I call on my way to the kitchen, voice obnoxiously chipper.

Liam groans.

CHAPTER TWENTY-SEVEN

Liam

Getting in the car to leave for work is an act of torture.

Last night, I distracted Madison while she made tacos, and then we wrote out a formal list of rules while we ate dinner. Then, she distracted me while I washed the dishes. After a brief pause from productivity to make out, we sat on the couch with our coordinating reMarkable tablets in hand, each working on our own projects.

I never thought that I would enjoy such a domestic scene.

Turns out, it was the best evening that I never imagined.

But it's made it very hard to drive away from the cocoon of domestic bliss, even for nine to ten hours. Especially after we enjoyed coffee together following my run this morning.

We also enjoyed a few rushed kisses on my way out the door, which was the final nail in the torture coffin.

I spend the seven-minute drive to the factory focusing my thoughts and reviewing my to-do list for the day. Because it's an important one. I have clearance from my superiors to make some key personnel moves, so I need to be locked in on work, not memories of Madison's lips.

When I walk through the door, Amanda calls out, "Good morning, Mr. Park."

"Morning," I reply. "Could you have Beau come to my office as soon as he can?"

Amanda nods and picks up her phone, so I continue walking to my office without stopping. About fifteen minutes later, there's a knock at the door, and Beau appears.

"You wanted to see me?" he asks. I motion him to come in and close the door behind him. When he sits down across from me, I lean forward on the desk.

"Beau, I'm going to cut to the chase. It's no secret that you've been a large part of this factory's success. Mr. Wilson made his best attempt to sabotage the facility, but people like you kept it from completely folding. And you've been an integral part of getting things back on track these past few months," I say. "Things have been in a holding pattern as we waited on further investigation into how Wilson was able to get so far without anyone noticing. But I've been given the green light to start making some necessary moves as we look to the future."

Beau's been nodding along, elbows leaning on his knees with his hands clasped. I can't hold back a smile as I say, "The first move I requested was to shift you into the position of floor manager." He sits up straighter, a look of genuine surprise on his face. "I know that all your experience has been with the machinery as head engineer, but you've shown that you can step up to the plate and lead the team. If you'd like the position, it's yours—along with the pay raise and bonus structure."

There's a pause as Beau collects his emotions. The look of gratitude and pride on his face brings me a unique sense of pleasure—so often, I'm the one coming in and dismissing employees, eliminating positions, or altering job descriptions. It feels really good to be the one offering a promotion to someone so deserving.

"I don't know what to say, Mr. Park," Beau says. I give him a pointed look. "Liam," he amends with a laugh. "I can't tell you how honored I am. I would love to take on that responsibility."

Standing up, I reach across the desk to shake Beau's hand. "You deserve it," I say. "Now, your first order of business is to choose your replacement. Which of the engineers do you think has what it takes to fill the head of machinery role?"

Beau and I spend the next hour discussing who to shift into which roles and crafting a job listing for an open engineering position. I ask him to weigh in on other personnel that might need to be moved around, noting his thoughts on my tablet.

We call in the woman he recommended as his replacement to offer her the position, and I craft an email to the company alerting everyone to the changes. After sending it, I begin filling out the paperwork for the position changes to have ready for signatures by the end of the day. *Sheesh, I can't wait until we can actually fill these HR and finance roles so I'm not the one doing this stuff.*

As I'm printing off the official package offers for Beau and the new head engineer, Amanda steps into the office.

"Mr. Park? Could I ask you about something?" she questions.

"Sure, have a seat," I say, motioning to the open chair across from me.

Amanda's hands are fidgety as she begins. "I was reading the email about some of the role changes, and it got me thinking . . . well, I guess I was just wondering if there might be any possibility of me stepping into a different role," she says. She rushes to add, "Not that I don't enjoy being the receptionist, because I do. But I was just thinking that if there are opportunities to advance into different positions, that I'd like to explore that."

She looks up at me when she finishes speaking, and I ask, "Do you have any training for roles outside of the receptionist position?"

Her cheeks color. "Well, no, not really."

"Have you taken any steps to further your education or experience that would qualify you for a position with more responsibility?" I press.

Amanda's eyes drop to her hands in her lap. "No, I haven't. I guess I didn't really think through this. I'm sorry for wasting your time." She quickly stands and rushes out of the room.

Out of habit, I pick up the tennis ball from my desk and start bouncing it off the wall.

Why would she think she should just magically get a different position if she hasn't done anything to earn it? I'm not a promotion fairy.

Leaning back in my chair, I can picture Madison's face. I *hear* her voice accusing me of crossing over into jerk territory. And I know that phantom voice is right.

Rising from my desk, I walk out to the reception area. Amanda's eyes are puffy, a sure sign of recent tears, but she tries to hide it as I approach.

"Listen, Amanda, I'm sorry I was too short and direct with you in there," I say. She sniffs and darts a glance up at me. "Look, I can't make any promises about open positions. I had to beg to get today's changes approved. But you could be proactive in seeking out training and building up your résumé. There are all sorts of low-cost courses that you can take online that will train you in administrative tasks that could give you an edge to stand out for a different role. Eventually, we're going to need to hire some HR and finance roles, so if you have any interest in those fields, you could start working through some training courses."

Amanda's eyes are hopeful, and she nods. "I do think that human resources could be really interesting. I'd really like to do something like that."

Holding up a hand to slow her enthusiasm, I emphasize, "Like I said, no promises. But being proactive to further your education and experience is never a bad idea if you want to climb the ladder."

"I understand," she says, nodding with even more fervor. "I'm going to go home tonight and look for some courses. Thanks for the advice, Mr. Park."

"Any time," I say, tapping my knuckles on her desk. "Thanks for all your hard work, Amanda. You've made my job here easier."

She beams at the praise, and I mentally note that I should make more of an effort to dole out deserved recognition.

CHAPTER TWENTY-EIGHT

Madison

My heart races when I see an email from Elizabeth in my inbox. I sent the marked-up manuscript back to her a few days ago, and I've been holding my breath waiting for a response. I hope she thinks I did a great job, and I hope she'll be willing to write a positive testimonial for my website.

My inner voice of doubt grew each day that passed with no response.

You aren't anything special, Madison. She probably thinks she overpaid you. She's probably had better experiences with other editors. You never should have tried this editing venture in the first place.

I blow out a long breath as I hover the mouse over the unread email. *I wish Liam was here for moral support. To celebrate with me if it's a positive response or rage rant with me if it's negative.*

Over the past three weeks, Liam has slowly become as close of a friend as Clara in a lot of ways. I mean, there are some very key differences—the making out being a major one. Liam also stokes my energy in reverse proportion to Clara's calming effect. So it's probably a good thing I have *both* of them in my life, evening me out.

But his intensity somehow soothes me just like Clara's gentleness does. He's cheered me on every time I land a new client, and he's talked me out of lowering my prices or giving up altogether when the clients haven't come in as frequently as I'd like. When I told him about a rude comment I received on social media, he was saddled up and ready to ride at dawn in vengeance. Who knows what he'd be ready to do if Elizabeth's response is negative?

I'm probably putting too much stock in Elizabeth's opinion, but something about this email feels like it could either be the true beginning or the beginning of the end for Madison Joy Editorial's future. I can't put off the inevitable, so I click on the email.

Madison,

Wow, this is by far the most thorough editing job I've seen. The fact that you went to the effort to research standard terminology in medical journals AND approved collegiate Greek life lingo blew my mind. Thank you for correcting those mistakes before this book went out into the world! I would have been so embarrassed if a reader pointed them out after the fact.

With this being my first crossover to nonfiction, my mind was still used to some of the stylistic freedom of the fiction genre. Thank you for explaining the editing guidelines behind those corrections you made—it will certainly help me avoid repeating those mistakes in the future.

I will absolutely be enlisting your services again with any future books. I'll also pass along your information with a resounding recommendation to all of my author friends.

Thanks again,
Elizabeth

"Yes!" I yell, slamming my hands on the desk.

Hamlet screeches and bolts out from his place under my Christmas tree. However, his paws get caught on the tree skirt in his haste, and he trips, which scares him even further, if his possessed race around the room is any indication. He pounces on my bed but spooks when a throw pillow moves, so he leaps onto the dresser. Liam must include dressers in the "no counters or tables" rule, because Hamlet abruptly leaps back off the dresser, looking guilty and frightened.

Finally, he finds the door to escape from my room, and I chase after him as he scampers across the house to Liam's room. "Hammie, I'm sorry I scared you. I didn't mean it," I say as I approach him. He's hiding under the bed and hisses when I come close. "I was just excited. I shouldn't have made that loud noise. I'm sorry," I say, trying to coax him to come out.

He mewls pitifully from the darkness.

When my repeated apologies do nothing to lure Hamlet out from under the bed, I trot back to my room to retrieve my phone. As I reenter Liam's room, Hamlet is still whining. I hit the call icon next to Liam's contact and plop down on the floor.

My call is interrupted by an auto-text message coming through.

HOT BRITISH BOYFRIEND

I'll call you right back.

Liam massively rolled his eyes when he discovered his new contact name. "I'm not *only* British. I'm also Korean and American," he'd pointed out.

But "Hot British-Korean-American Boyfriend" would be an absurdly long contact name. Besides, I think of him calling me "love" in that sexy British accent every time I see his name pop up on my phone. So "Hot British Boyfriend" stays.

I flip to my stomach on the floor, continuing my efforts to reconcile with Hamlet. "Come on, Hammie. Don't hold it against me. I won't do it again. I swear," I say. I try to reach a hand under the bed, but I'm met with a swift swat to the fingers.

"Hamlet. Don't make me take back all the nice things I've said about you recently," I chide. My phone starts ringing, so I roll to my back and answer it.

"You okay? What's wrong?" Liam immediately asks.

"Oh. Yes. I'm fine!" I reply.

"Then what's up? You've never called me at work before," Liam observes.

"Sorry, did I interrupt something important? Hang up on me if you need to," I say, although I might be the teensiest bit mad if he really does hang up.

"No, I have a minute. I just had to leave the production floor to call you from my office. It's too loud in there to have a phone conversation," Liam says.

"I'll try to make this quick. I accidentally startled Hamlet, and now he's sulking under your bed. I thought maybe you'd be able to coax him out of his cocoon of resentment," I explain.

Liam chuckles. "I mean, I can try. I can hear him yowling in the background, though. Sounds like a serious offense. I may not be able to mend this bridge for you."

"Well, I'm going to put you on speaker so you can give it a shot," I say. I hold the phone closer to the bed. "Come on, Hammie. Your super-hot daddy is on the phone."

A snort comes through the phone. "I'm just not even going to address . . . any of that," he says, and I grin. He clears his throat and says, "Hamlet, why are you hiding, my friend? I know Madison can be scary sometimes."

"Hey!" I cut in, fake annoyed.

I hear the grin in Liam's voice as he continues, "But she's *mostly* harmless. Come back out and keep her company so she doesn't go off the rails."

The tone of Hamlet's *meow* changes slightly, and I try to peek under the bed without moving too abruptly.

"Come on, I hear you, Hamlet. You don't have to be scared," Liam continues in a soothing voice. Hamlet has crept a few inches closer to the edge of the bed but is still hesitating.

I suggest, "Maybe you should try the British accent."

"That works on *you*, not Hamlet," Liam says. *Geez, I wish he were here to kiss me senseless right now.*

"Has he come out yet?" Liam asks.

"No. He's a little closer but still hiding," I say.

"You might just have to give him space and wait him out then," Liam says. "Hamlet is in a dark place right now. Whatever did you do to offend him so egregiously?"

"I was excited and slammed my hands on the desk. He did not appreciate the sudden loud noise," I explain, rolling to my back again.

"What were you excited about?" Liam asks.

I fill him in on the email from Elizabeth and what it could mean for the future of MJE. I can't stop myself from grinning ear to ear as I talk.

"MJ, that's incredible!" Liam says. "That's it—we're celebrating tonight."

"Celebrating how?" I ask.

"You'll find out when I pick you up at five-thirty," Liam teases.

I groan. "You know exactly how much I hate surprises!"

"One hundred percent. Which is why it will be even more fun to not tell you where we're going," he replies, mischief in his voice.

Hamlet emerges from under the bed and stands on my stomach. *Meow*.

"Hammie has forgiven me, it seems," I say, and Hamlet meows again loudly enough for Liam to hear. "He says that you should tell me where we're going so I know what to wear."

Liam *tsks*. "I'll be wearing the suit I wore to work today. Match accordingly."

He left this morning in his charcoal gray suit and black dress shirt. I remember because that particular combination is my personal kryptonite.

"Fine, fine," I sigh. "Now go back to being all important and stuff."

"See you in a few hours, love," Liam says.

It's a good thing I'm already lying on the floor, so there's no damage done when I melt.

I don't have a full-length mirror in my room, so I drag a chair into my bathroom and stand on top of it to get a view of myself in the mirror. The deprecating inner voice that typically nitpicks everything about my appearance is oddly silent as I consider my reflection.

When Liam refused to tell me where we were going, I briefly considered raiding his closet to steal a hoodie as payback. *You're not going to let me mentally prepare and dress appropriately for the situation? Fine, I'll wear your clothes on our date then, just to irk you.*

But we've been taking our list of rules very seriously, so there's no way I would actually break the "no stealing his clothes" rule. I haven't needed to worry about what to wear with him since we haven't gone on any real dates—considering we see each other any time we're both at home. And the fact that there aren't a whole lot of date-worthy locations in Noel.

Also, there's the fact that we haven't really publicized our relationship. Naturally, Clara told Clark, but it's not like he's the hub of the rumor mill. Otherwise, our official relationship is still under wraps. I don't think either of us consciously feels like it's something to hide, but it also feels a little odd to widely report to a town that isn't exactly home for either of us.

Due to our lack of official dates, Liam has only ever seen me in casual shorts, leggings, and jeans on rare occasions. I stare in the mirror at the coral flared mini dress that Clara had admired when I first moved here. I don't know why I brought the summer dress in the first place when I came here at the tail end of winter, but I'm grateful to my subconscious for packing it. It perfectly hugs my body (a necessity since there are no straps to hold it up), accentuating my waist but flaring out with a little fun. I smile. Because I think Liam isn't going to know what hit him.

I applied makeup with my signature cateye and painted fresh nail polish—mint green with a matching coral color as the accent. I also curled a few waves into my hair, which was probably pointless given the summer humidity. Still, I'll have one "wow" moment when Liam walks in and sees me in all my styled-hair glory.

Hamlet meows from the floor, looking up at me like I've lost my mind.

"Short girl probs, dear Hammie," I tell him as I climb down from the chair. I select some tan wedge sandals to add a few inches to my height tonight. I'll make my lips slightly more accessible for Liam.

Liam better be taking us somewhere nice after I went to all this effort. If he drives us to the Deer River Bar, so help me.

After securing the straps of my sandals, I practice walking around the house. It's been a while since I wore any sort of heel, and the last thing I want to do is trip while walking next to Liam. Although, if I trip, he would catch me, so that's not such a loss after all. I just need to make sure he doesn't catch me walking around inside with shoes on—Liam's number one house no-no.

When I hear the sound of a car door, I bend down to remove my wedges and toss them over by the front door. My timing happens to coincide with Liam opening the door, and one of the sandals hits him in the shin.

"What? Why are you assaulting me with shoes? Is this because I wouldn't say where we're going?" he exclaims, looking at my sandals on the floor. The amused smile falls off his face when he looks up and sees me. His expression darkens as his eyes roam over me, and I'm shocked when he leaves his shoes on and crosses the room.

In the space of a breath, he strides over, possessively pulls me to him with a firm hand on my lower back, and claims my lips with his. My hands reflexively find the nape of his neck as he arches me backward. *Who cares where we're going tonight? Actually, do we even* need *to go anywhere? This kiss might be all the celebration I need for the day.*

When Liam's fingers start to thread through my hair, my senses snap back to attention, and I move my hands to his chest to push him away.

"No, sir. I spent precious time adding those curls to my hair for the night, so you're not allowed to mess them up. At least, not until after the humidity ruins them," I assert. With one hand, I give an exaggerated hair flip. "Please pause to appreciate the effort."

Liam's eyes drink me in as he says, "Trust me. I am *most* appreciative."

Now that I'm free of the spell his lips cast over me every time we kiss, I have the wherewithal to notice *his* appearance. His sleeves are rolled, and the top button is undone on his black dress shirt—most likely due to the summer heat. Or he's fully aware of the effect this look has on me, and he's done it on purpose.

I suppose we'd be even, then.

"I was not accounting for that dress when I scheduled our dinner reservation, so we need to hurry if we're going to make it on time now," Liam says, tone still laced with attraction.

My cheeks heat, and I self-consciously smooth my hands down the skirt of my dress. Liam leans in to kiss my cheek and whispers, "You look stunning, in case my reaction didn't make that clear."

After I put my sandals on, Liam takes my hand and leads me out to his SUV. He opens the passenger door for me, then slides into the driver's seat. It only takes a few minutes of driving to figure out that we are, indeed, leaving the town of Noel and heading in the direction of Bentonville. As we drive the thirty minutes to the "big" city, Liam asks more questions about Elizabeth's email and my plans to capitalize on the potential momentum.

"So what are you going to do when you have more clients interested than you have open slots in your schedule? Work more hours to take on more clients or raise your prices to keep your schedule tighter?" Liam asks.

I snort. "I think you're getting way ahead of things here. My booking calendar is not in any danger of filling up yet. I'm focusing on doing great work for the handful of clients I already have in the pipeline."

"Well, that's necessary, of course, but you have to keep the big picture in mind too. Plan for future growth," Liam says. "You could always hire an assistant for a few hours a week to handle communications for you so you can focus on the proofreading work."

His line of thinking has me sweating. I turn up the air conditioning.

"I don't want to celebrate today's success by freaking out over tomorrow's problems. Let's talk about you. Tell me something about College Liam," I say. My suggestion is met with a frustrated groan. I poke him in the side as I toss him an easy question. "Who was your favorite professor and why?"

Liam starts drumming the steering wheel, a sure sign he's thinking. Just like he said—he's needed some help (i.e. very specific question prompts) to get him to share more personal information about himself. But he *has* followed through and tried to be more open over the past few weeks.

It's how I've learned that he was fiercely protective of Hana growing up, not wanting her to endure the same "other" feeling that he experienced. Despite the ten-year age gap between them, he took the role of protective older brother to extreme levels for the eight years they lived at home together. I pity the other kids in Hana's grade.

I now know that his love for running started in middle school when he joined cross country and track. Although he still kept his teammates at arm's length, he found some level of camaraderie with the other runners. A team sport that's largely based on individual performance seems to fit Liam's personality pretty perfectly.

It required several very pointed questions on my part, but I found out that he hasn't been back to London in about seven years—not since he started working for Holden. In the handful of years between college and starting at Holden, he only accompanied his parents and Hana on one annual visit for *Chuseok*, a major holiday in Korea when families gather for a special meal, similar to American Thanksgiving.

Many teeth were pulled to get him to admit that he struggles feeling caught in the middle of the complicated family dynamics—traditional Korean familial roles clashing with independent American values. I'm honestly not sure he even recognized the reason he's been avoiding visits until I pried the emotions out of him.

I've reciprocated with more farm life stories, outlandish tales of my former roommate, and more background about the nightmare of working for Chad. Liam also heard the short-story-long version of my history with Clara. How she was still just a copywriter when I arrived at WritInc, and she took me under her wing as the self-appointed sole welcoming committee member. How I latched on and refused to let her go until we were all-the-time best friends and not just work besties by the time she became the manager of the writing department. But Liam seemed to find particular amusement in the chronicles of High School Madison—like the time I discovered stolen answer keys to chemistry tests junior year and turned over the perpetrators to the teacher.

What can I say? Right and wrong matter—they've *always* mattered to me. Snitches get the moral high ground.

As we pull into a busy public parking lot in Bentonville, Liam is wrapping up his answer to my "who was your favorite college professor" question—his Entrepreneurship and Ideation professor who taught him the diverge/converge method of brainstorming. Such a Liam answer.

"Dr. Cox was a brilliant professor. So much of what he taught was useful and practical—I've implemented his strategies with just about every company I've straightened out," Liam says as he turns off the engine.

When I move my hand to the door handle, Liam reaches across and stops me. "Wait and let me get it," he commands. I'm tempted to kiss him as he leans in so close to me, but I pretend to be annoyed instead.

He comes around and opens the door, holding a hand out to steady me as I step out of the SUV. I quip, "I could have opened my own door, you know."

Stepping a little closer, Liam threads his fingers through mine. "First of all, my *halmeoni* raised me to honor and respect women, and my mother raised me to be a gentleman. But if that wasn't reason enough, do you see that group of guys over there?" he asks, motioning his head to the side. There are several men locking their cars and walking our direction. Liam continues, "There's no way I was going to let you open your own car door and give any of them a reason to think they could have a chance to charm you away from me."

While gentleman Liam makes my heart warm, his possessive power move makes my blood heat to a boiling point. In lieu of openly fanning myself, I jest, "I don't think you have any competition to be worried about."

Liam cocks his head to one side. "Did you look at yourself in the mirror tonight? I absolutely have competition, and I absolutely will do whatever it takes to win. There's no way I'm letting you go," he says, skimming a strand of my hair between his finger and thumb.

"Well, the plethora of guys I dated in Kansas City would seem to disprove your competition claim," I say.

His eyes spark. "Are you trying to make me jealous talking about the other guys you've dated? Because it's working. I hate the idea of any guy but me being on the receiving end of that electric kiss."

I roll my eyes. "I'm telling you—you have nothing to worry about. No guy ever lasted longer than a couple of dates before making excuses to never see me again." I make the statement with a hefty dose of nonchalant dismissal in my tone, but the reality stings. "You sure you're not scared away by me too?"

Liam's eyes spark with a different emotion now. Rage that he's not attempting to conceal. He takes my face in his hands, and his tone is hard when he says, "Madison, any guy who was intimidated by you was a boy who could never possibly deserve you. Don't you ever think about dimming that fiery spirit just because some weak excuse for a man couldn't keep up with you."

His eyes are locked on mine, watching my expression to make sure I accept what he's saying. To make sure I believe it.

Liam makes me think I could believe it.

When I give a slight nod, he leans down and kisses me slowly, with restraint appropriate for our public setting. I fist his shirt in both hands and pull him closer, deepening the kiss, greedily demanding more. Liam obliges, pressing my back against the car—this time, I don't stop him when he buries his fingers in my hair.

"Mads?" a familiar voice says. Breaking away from Liam's lips, I turn to the side and see Becky's extremely delighted smile. She says, "Fancy seeing you here."

I'm not sure if her "you" was meant in the singular or plural sense. Limits of the English language. However, I have zero hesitations when I respond, "Hey, Becky! So, FYI, Liam and I are dating now. Feel free to alert the masses!"

As soon as the words are out of my mouth, my brain flinches that I just encouraged the exact kind of small-town, intrusive gossip that Liam hates so much. I glance up at him to gauge his reaction. His arm is leaning against the car above my head, his body still angled toward me in a possessive posture.

But his lips are smiling—a full smile that makes its way to his eyes. He doesn't break eye contact with me as he says to Becky, "Be sure to make it clear that I was the lucky one to snag Madison's attention."

When I turn back to Becky, her grin is somehow broader. "I'm so glad today was the deadline for me to return that dress I bought at the boutique here. It was *lovely* running into you," she says, a twinkle in her eyes. "I really and truly love this for you two."

After telling Becky goodbye, Liam takes my hand and leads me to an Italian restaurant known for its mozzarella bar. Our conversation is light over dinner, and we're not at all surprised to receive matching "congratulations" text messages from Syd and Davis (although Syd's text to me included a long string of "why didn't you tell me, how could you keep this a secret, you're dead to me" additions).

As we leave the restaurant, Liam says, "Before we head home, we have one more stop to make. We're going to that store that puts out Christmas decorations seven months in advance. We need a Christmas tree for the living room."

I pull his hand to a stop. "What? Why?"

He turns to face me. "I'm tired of Hamlet always hiding out in your room. He barely pays attention to me anymore—he's too obsessed with your Christmas tree."

I quirk an eyebrow. "How do you know he's not just obsessed with me?"

Liam loops an arm around my waist. "Fair point. He wouldn't be the only one. But I guess we'll have to put it to the test with a Christmas tree on neutral ground."

Laughing, I say, "Fine, but we're not going to go buy a new tree from the store. We'll go back to my favorite thrift store." I glance at the time on my watch. "They close in fifteen minutes, but I'll sweet talk Bob into letting us have a quick look around the storage room."

"*Ooo*, I'll finally get to see the Queen of Thrifting in action," Liam says, rubbing his hands together.

Two hours later, a thrifted five-foot tree stands tall in our living room. Christmas music blares as we string multicolor lights and hang ornaments. Hamlet micro-manages our decorating, attempting to climb the branches when we hang something in the wrong spot. When the final ornament is placed, we stand back to survey our work.

"Not bad," Liam observes. "Five stars, I'd say."

"Hold on," I add. I lie down and scootch under the tree so I can look up through the center. A second later, Liam is beside me, our temples touching. Hamlet sneaks in between us, lying down and sprawling on his back.

I lace my fingers through Liam's and murmur, "Five stars, for sure."

Chapter Twenty-Nine

Liam

July

"Remind me to never, ever guide a group again. I'm officially passing off all guide responsibilities to my college-aged employees," Davis says with a groan.

"Your good looks got you into this mess," Sydney replies with a mischievous smile. "Stop being so ruggedly handsome, then groups of middle-aged single women won't request you as their tour guide."

The group of friends gathered around the table howls with laughter, myself included. Madison convinced me to join them for Tuesday night dinner at the pizzeria to hard launch our relationship now that the entire town of Noel (and probably the entire county) knows that we're dating. Davis shared a horror story of guiding a group of eight women on a kayaking trip down the river over the past few days. His account made me extremely grateful to work in corporate America rather than owning a river experience business.

Everyone talks about their plans for the Fourth of July in a couple of days—Madison is driving to Nebraska to spend the holiday with her sister like she does every year, and I'm trying to act like a mature, supportive boyfriend and not pout about her impending absence. Even though I feel very pouty about it.

"Hey, why are so many people requesting next Tuesday off of work?" I ask. "I've had an absurd number of PTO requests for the Tuesday after the Fourth."

"Oh, that's Christmas in July day!" Clara exclaims. "Has Mads not told you about it?"

"Nope," Madison says with a shrug.

"They're probably too busy making out to talk about town traditions," Sydney says, waggling her eyebrows.

Madison rolls her eyes, but it's my turn to shrug. "I won't deny it," I say, squeezing her knee under the table.

"Every year we have a 'Christmas in July' day to watch a marathon of Heartmark Christmas movies and brainstorm ideas for the town Christmas Fest," Clara explains with enthusiasm. "And then we end the day with a huge crawfish boil down by the river."

"Complete with hot dogs for the squeamish," Clark says with a hint of a smile as he pinches Clara's side.

"Not all of us grew up being told that sucking out the brains of crustaceans is a gourmet meal," Clara retorts. She honestly looks a little squeamish as she says it.

"I'm afraid I'm on Team Clara here," I say, and she reaches across the table to give me a high five. I turn to ask Madison, "What about you?"

She says, "This will be my first Christmas in July, so I'll have to withhold judgment until I try one for the first time."

"This I have to see," I muse, already imagining Madison's very loud facial expressions during her first crawfish eating experience. "What time does the dinner start? Maybe I can make it in time after work."

Beau chimes in, "Why don't you take the day off so you can participate in the full festivities? We came for Christmas in July last year, so I can keep an eye on things at the factory for you."

My knee-jerk reaction is to turn down the offer. Breaking away from work isn't exactly my strength. I haven't taken a single day off since I came to Noel—including doing at least some amount of extra work on weekends. Also, I normally wouldn't touch a small-town tradition with a ten-foot pole.

However, the group of people sitting around this table has me thinking it might not be so terrible to change my tune a little. Especially with Madison looking at me so expectantly.

"I would really appreciate that, man," I tell Beau. "I'm always game for a good brainstorm."

Clark grunts. "We hardly need to continue with the movies and brainstorm every year. Christmas Fest already exists—we don't need new ideas."

"It's all part of the tradition now, and you know it," Clara responds with mock indignation. "Maybe Liam and Madison will have some new ideas for us this year!"

"Liam probably does have some great ideas from the famous Christmas markets in the UK—he grew up in London," Madison says.

Sydney chokes on the bite of pizza she's chewing, and Davis gives her a hearty clap on the back. "You grew up in London?!" she asks, voice still hoarse from the coughing fit.

"Until I was eight," I clarify. I give Madison a dagger-laden look, anticipating the next tidbit of my life history she might share. While these four couples do feel like genuine friends—at least, the beginning of genuine friendships—I still feel hesitant to open myself up to questions about my upbringing right here in Arkansas. I'm not quite there yet.

Thankfully, Madison reads my expression, and she diverts the conversation to Clara's plan to convince the local bar owner to turn his space into a pop-up Christmas bar similar to the experiences in Kansas City. This launches a lively discussion of the drawbacks and merits of such an endeavor, saving me from talking any more about myself.

I give Madison a look that I hope communicates, *I'll be kissing you senseless later as a thank you for that diversion.*

When she bites her lip with a coy look in her eye, I know she's accurately reading my mind.

"I need you to know that I don't hate Christmas. And I don't hate you," the tearful woman says, just before the main characters finally kiss for the first time. Snow magically starts falling the moment their lips meet, and they both gasp as they look up at the sky.

Leaning over, I whisper in Madison's ear, "This is really what this town does for fun?"

She shushes me and smacks my chest, but it's a half-hearted action. This is the second of three movies planned for the Christmas in July marathon, and I'm trying to figure out how Heartmark managed to sell these as two separate movies when they're clearly the same storyline. They must have some serious wizardry going on in their marketing department.

I convinced Madison to sit with me in the back corner of the back row of chairs in the town hall. Partly because I'm still feeling uncertain about inserting myself as a member of the community, and partly because I wanted to run my fingers through Madison's hair and caress her arm in relative privacy. The town hall has been fully transformed into a Christmas wonderland, which I assume can be credited to Clara. There are twinkle lights and fake pine garlands strung around the ceiling, a six-foot tree decorated in the front corner, and a small sleigh filled with wrapped presents and surrounded by fake snow. If this is how seriously they take Christmas in July, I can only imagine what the actual Christmas Fest is like.

Thankfully, there's a stretch break before the next movie, so we mill around to sample cookies from the local bake club and coffee drinks from Becky.

Well, Madison samples some of the drinks. I scrunch up my nose at the outrageous amounts of syrup and toppings masquerading as "coffee."

"Don't be a Grinch," Madison says, attempting to hand me a sample cup of something labeled Christmas Tree Farm. "Here, this one has rosemary—maybe that will be interesting enough for that refined palate of yours."

"No, thank you," I reply to Madison, then turn to Becky. "Don't take it personally."

"Best I can do is take it extra personally," Becky jokes, quoting a popular meme. "I promise we do serve black drip coffee at the booth during Christmas Fest. It's not all whipped-cream-laden drinks."

"Now you just need some tea on the menu," Madison sighs. "*My refined palate is so offended.*"

Becky shrugs sympathetically. "I'm just not sure how well it would sell. Maybe I'll try offering a few different tea bags."

"You should make a drink called 'The Grinch' that's a matcha latte," I suggest. "Sometimes all you need is a little marketing twist to get something to sell."

Madison swivels to Becky. "Yes! Please, yes! I'll teach you how to make them—please, please, please?"

"Fine, fine, we can try it for one year and see how it goes," Becky acquiesces. "Any other bright ideas, Liam?"

"Well, if you really want to bring the European Christmas market flair to Noel, you'd sell mulled wine," I say. "It's only the most beloved beverage at the markets."

Becky bursts out laughing. "That's not a terrible suggestion, especially for all of the parents carting their kids around all day. But that would definitely need to be a separate booth from mine. I'll be sure to bring it up during the brainstorm session."

Madison makes no move to end conversation and return for the third movie, so I happily stay in the kitchenette as well. Becky describes the various special events held on the weekends during Christmas Fest—a parade down Main Street on Friday nights, a Rockettes-inspired musical performance on Saturdays, and the event where they pretend to rocket off all the kids' letters to Santa from a rowboat on Sundays. It sounds like an impressive display, complete with well-timed fireworks.

"And you really change the pronunciation of the town from Nole to No-el for November and December?" I ask. "Like, officially?"

Becky nods. "It's an official town ordinance. Clara's great victory over Clark," she adds with a wry grin. "Will you still be here in November, Liam? I hope you get to experience it all."

"I'm not exactly sure what my future timeline looks like," I say, darting an anxious glance at Madison. For as much as we said we would figure out our relationship as we go, we've pretty much skirted around any conversation about our future geographic locations.

I'm torn between my desire to stay close to Madison and the career advancement Holden offers. Ironically, my apartment in Houston is less and less of a selling point for continuing with Holden—considering I hardly spend any time there anyway. I never would have thought it would be true, but there's a growing piece of me that wouldn't mind staying right here in Noel.

But there's no way that would fly with Cal. Even if I'm constantly on the move to different temporary jobs, he would always want my home base to be the headquarters in Houston.

We're interrupted by Pops slowly ambling into the room. He leans on his cane and asks, "Becky, what's a man got to do to get a cup of black coffee around here?"

"Thank you," I say, feeling validated.

Pops turns to me. "I hear you two are going steady now. Can't say I didn't see that coming a mile away when you came by the house."

I stifle a laugh and smile instead. "Yes, sir. I suppose it was only a matter of time," I say, winking at Madison.

When I turn back to Pops, I'm met with a threatening glare. "Just know that we consider Madison one of our own here in Noel. So you'll have a lot of people to answer to if you don't treat her right. A lot of people with tools and trucks and boats and intimate knowledge of every isolated corner of the Arkansas woods. You understand me?"

"Yes, sir," I answer solemnly. When I look over to Madison, I'm expecting to see some form of sarcastic, amused expression. I'm caught completely off guard by the glisten of tears she's blinking away.

"Shall we go watch the end of the final movie?" I ask her, and she nods. When we return to our seats in the back row, I scoot my chair extra close to hers and wrap my arm around her shoulders. I don't ask any questions about her emotional response to Pops' protective speech—I just hold her close while we both pretend to watch the movie.

I *try* to remain a silent observer during the post-movie brainstorm session. Clara stands at the front taking notes on a white board, but most of the discussion seems to be centered around minor tweaks to what already exists in the festival. Eventually, my brainstorm training from Dr. Cox can't be contained any longer, and I hold up a hand to get Clara's attention.

"You have an idea, Liam?" Clara asks, and the room turns to me.

I stand up and say, "I know you've been doing this festival for a couple of years now and have the basic foundation figured out. But it seems like you're being too quick to converge on the things that have already worked and not taking enough time to diverge on totally new ideas."

"What are you talking about?" someone asks from the second row. "What the heck do converge and diverge mean?"

I give a brief explanation of the concept. "Productive brainstorms include ample time to diverge with every idea you could think of across the board, not eliminating anything right off the bat." I motion my hands, moving them away from each other in the shape of a "V" to illustrate the statement. "Only after a broad exploration of possibilities do you converge and narrow in on the best and most achievable suggestions," I add, pointing my hands inward to bring them back together.

"There are some tourists who will continue coming back every year for the same things out of a sense of tradition," I say. "But there are also a lot of people who will check it off their bucket lists and not come back unless there's a new feature to experience. You should slowly roll out one or two new features each year to keep people coming back if you really want this to be a long-term source of revenue for the town."

Murmurs of discussion echo around the room, and I wonder if I was too direct when I'm still an outsider in this town. I just can't help but point out the obvious flaw in their planning when I see it.

Madison looks up at me with a combination of pride and desire, which I meet with a half-smile as I sit back down.

"Liam, why don't you come up here and lead us through one of these diverge brainstorm sessions," Clara suggests, holding the dry erase marker in the air.

"Oh, no. I wasn't trying to take over the brainstorm," I say, holding my hands up. "I was just making a suggestion."

One of my production line employees stands up in the front row and says, "Yeah, come up here, Mr. Park. You've done a great job of turning things around at the factory. We'd be foolish not to put your skills to use on the town festival too."

Sounds of affirmation build around the room, making my heart beat harder in my chest. Madison kicks off a slow clap that quickly catches on, and she cheers wildly when I finally stand up and make my way to the front of the room.

I might feel embarrassed if I wasn't so busy trying to fight off the unfamiliar emotional response to their enthusiastic welcome. I'm not sure how to deal with the tangle of feelings rising up inside me, so I push all emotion to the side.

"Is it okay if I erase this?" I ask Clara, gesturing to the white board. She gives me the go ahead. "All right. Think big. Think outside the box. Think about any Christmas event you've ever encountered or any experience you *wish* you could have. No idea is too big or too outrageous at this stage. What could make this the greatest Christmas festival on earth?"

CHAPTER THIRTY

Madison

SEPTEMBER

The past two-and-a-half months have been a whirlwind in every sense of the word.

The town is excitedly planning for the biggest and best Christmas Fest ever. Liam and Beau have been overseeing the installation of the freeze-dried food production line while hitting all their goals on the original line. More and more people are milling around the town with the new jobs at the factory, resulting in new restaurants and retail stores opening. There's even a new apartment complex going up on the edge of town, offering more housing options for the many people wanting to move to Noel.

It's a shocking turnaround that Noel can't keep up with the housing demand when, just a couple years ago, families were fleeing the small town.

Liam and I have continued spending every available second together, caught up in the whirlwind of our romance. We've stuck with all of our relationship rules—even Liam's promise to keep talking to me. That doesn't mean we haven't spent plenty of time making out by our Christmas tree, though.

Unfortunately, the only thing that *hasn't* been a whirlwind is Madison Joy Editorial. It's been more of a gentle breeze. Occasional gusts of wind are tempered by weeks with zero wind whatsoever.

I'd been so hopeful that Elizabeth's endorsement would open the floodgates to new clients knocking down my door and overflowing my schedule. Instead, I've started taking on more and more shifts at Becky's just to cover my insurance and tuck a little into savings. I'd *really* like to not dip into my emergency savings. The only reason I've managed to squeak by financially is because I'm not paying rent on the house I share with Liam. But there's an expiration date to the free room and board, and it's looming ever closer.

As the first leaves drain of chlorophyll and fade from green to yellow, my confidence similarly drains. *This was a pipe dream that was never going to work. Either I'm going to become a full-time barista, or I need to apply for jobs at some of the other print marketing agencies in KC. I made a mistake thinking I could make this work.*

I haven't really told Liam about the slow drip of business that MJE is generating. I'm doing everything I can possibly think of to generate more buzz and more clients, but I know that if I tell him, he's just going to push me to do even more.

And I don't really want to admit to him that I'm failing. I don't want to be one of the failing businesses he steps in to save.

So I'm secretly spending more time working at Becky's without him knowing. I'm certainly not admitting to my parents that my business venture is failing—they vocalized enough of their doubts over Fourth of July to last a full year. I was able to keep my sister, Caitlin, focused on my relationship with Liam enough to keep her from asking any career-related questions. Clara has become the sole confidante to my failed entrepreneurship venture, but I'm not even giving her the full picture of my self-doubt.

I'm currently reclining on the couch, reMarkable tablet in hand, proofreading the latest manuscript I received. It's a novella, which is never my preferred form of book, but I'm taking anything I can get at this point. Hamlet has been contentedly sleeping under the Christmas tree, but he suddenly trots over and jumps onto my stomach.

Meow.

He settles in, curling his paws under him as he lies down on my chest, his face inches away from mine.

Meow.

"What? Am I that obviously pitiful?" I ask.

Meow.

I set the tablet down so I can scratch behind his ears, generating a thrumming purr.

"Maybe I am that pitiful," I muse aloud. I'm surprised when a tear slips down my cheek, which Hamlet leans forward to sniff. I wrap my arms around him as sudden sobs unleash.

"I don't even know why I'm crying, Hammie!" I exclaim. "I mean, clearly, the fact that I'm a complete failure as an independent editor is embarrassing. Having to admit to my parents that I made the wrong decision going out on my own isn't going to feel good. I suppose there's also the fact that I think I'm in love with your hot daddy, but we don't have a clear plan for a long-term future together because neither of us wants to admit that we don't know what to do."

Hamlet's next *meow* comes out a little strangled, and I realize I'm maybe holding him a little too tightly. "Sorry, Hammie. I guess I know exactly why I'm crying. I just don't know how to fix any of it."

Sitting up, I wipe the tears from my eyes, and my gaze lands on the Christmas tree. My gaze turns into a glare. "I thought Clara's Christmas magic was supposed to make everything work out. You're broken, Christmas," I yell at the tree.

I stand up and unplug the lights.

I've managed to bottle up my emotions by the time Liam comes home from work. I'm standing at the stove making egg fried rice when he comes up behind me, wraps his arms around my waist, and gently kisses my neck. Something about the sweetness of the gesture stings my eyes with tears again, and I scramble to cork them into the bottle before he sees.

"Hey there, love," he murmurs. "Don't let me distract you," he adds as he gathers my hair to one side, giving his lips easier access to my neck.

I sigh and lean my head back. "You're going to burn our dinner, Suits," I half-heartedly admonish.

"Worth it," he replies, grinning against my neck. But he releases me and scoops up a mewling Hamlet to give him a dose of attention while I finish the rice. Liam grabs two plates from the cabinet for me and then feeds Hamlet his dinner.

As we eat, Liam asks about the project I was working on today, and I try to make it sound more substantial than it actually is. He updates me on all the progress at the factory, expressing gratitude for Beau's help through everything. "Having Amanda move into the HR position has been a game changer," he says. "With all the new employees we're onboarding for this freeze-dried line, I'm so glad I'm not the one drowning in all of that paperwork."

Hamlet has finished eating and jumps onto Liam's lap, meowing softly. Liam clears his throat before saying, "Hey, I kinda have a favor to ask you."

I set down my spoon. In the time we've known each other, I can count on one hand the number of times Liam has asked for help with anything. Actually, I wouldn't even need all of the fingers on one hand.

"So, I told you about how I haven't been back to London for Chuseok in several years," he begins. "And even though my grandma is totally fine after her procedure, it still got me thinking that I should visit them soon. My parents will be going back for Chuseok, and I was thinking about joining them." He pauses, scratching Hamlet's chest.

"I've never trusted anyone enough to take care of Hamlet if I was gone for multiple days in a row. Never had someone I thought *Hamlet* would trust enough to take care of him," he says, eyes sliding up to find mine. "But now we have you. So I wanted to ask if you'd be willing to watch Hamlet for a few days if I fly to London at the beginning of October?"

The bottle of emotions is about to go full Mentos-dropped-in-Coca-Cola with the way Liam is looking at me with so much vulnerable trust in his eyes.

"Of course, I will," I say. "I'm glad that you're going to spend some time with your family."

"About that," he adds, "now that I've suckered you into letting me leave town, I should add that my parents want to drive here to Noel and then fly out of Joplin together. Because they'd like to meet you."

Liam's voice sounds like he's walking on eggshells, like he's afraid of the words coming out of his own mouth. As I watch his face, his hand nervously stroking Hamlet's back, I realize how vulnerable this possibility is for him. For me to meet his parents. For them to meet me. For it to happen here in Noel.

I stand and step next to Liam's chair, cupping his face in my hands. "Liam, I would love to meet your parents," I say before leaning down to kiss him.

Liam gently sets Hamlet on the floor with one hand and pulls me to sit sideways on his lap with the other hand, all without breaking our kiss. When he draws back, he leans his forehead against mine. "Thanks, MJ." He reaches up to tuck my hair behind my ear and says, "There's one more thing I've been thinking about. May as well get it all out there at once."

I lean back, brows furrowed. "What?"

Liam exhales a long breath before he says, "I've been giving some thought to the possibility of staying in Noel."

My mind stumbles over his words, puzzle pieces that aren't fitting together. "Like, *living* in Noel? *Staying,* staying?"

He nods. "Have I gone insane?" he asks, his voice a whisper.

I can't help but laugh. "To be determined," I say. My heart is leaping at the thought that Liam could be staying here permanently—even though *I* haven't determined if I can stay here permanently.

Liam's presence would be a strong argument in favor of staying, though.

"What's made you go from judging Noel as a backwoods Arkansas small town to considering it as your permanent residence?" I ask, eyebrow quirked.

Liam sighs, his head falling back. "I don't know. A hundred little things. I think it started way back when I brought Beau into the loop about what had been happening at the factory. It was the first time that one of the screwed-up situations I've straightened out felt personal.

Like it was more than just restoring a pet food production facility to order—it was about keeping a community intact."

I make an affirming hum, nodding in understanding as he continues, "And then there was the whole Christmas in July deal. Seeing the way the town embraced me during the brainstorm session. I don't think I've ever used the term 'endearing' in my entire life, but the whole experience was endearing. It made me appreciate this town as much as they showed appreciation for me in that moment."

Liam pauses, looking especially reflective before he goes on. "You know I went on that fishing trip with the guys a couple of weeks ago," he says, and I nod. He came back low-key beaming, gushing about the good times they'd had and the fish they'd caught. Well, "gushing," as far as the term could apply to Liam's demeanor. He says, "When we were sitting around the campfire that final night, I had this moment where I realized I felt disappointed when I thought about leaving Noel. For the first time, I felt like I had people I didn't want to leave behind—*friends* I didn't want to leave behind."

Liam looks up at me with a wry smile. "Of course, in the midst of all the small factors adding up, there's this one *big* factor wrapped up in a tiny, feisty package," he teases, tickling my side. I squirm until he stops, but then I bring a hand up to trace his jaw with my fingers.

"What would you do? How would that work with your job?" I ask.

He frowns. "That's the one thing giving me pause. I know that Holden would never let me continue my current position if I wasn't based out of Houston. Plus, it would be back to traveling to new places for weeks or months at a time. This is by far the longest I've ever stayed at one location—and that's just because it was a legal mess on top of a corporate mess. And Beau and I managed to extend my time with the addition of the new production line."

Liam's brow furrows, and I trace the lines across his forehead. "So?" I prod.

He sighs. "I guess I could apply to become the permanent plant manager. Shift my employment from Holden to Pure Fur All. Just stay and keep things running."

Now my brow furrows. "Would you be happy doing that? I mean, I know you *could* do it on a backstroke. But standing around keeping a well-oiled machine running doesn't strike me as the type of challenge you'd appreciate. Or something worthy of your skill set."

Liam sighs again, deeper, longer. Like his very soul is breathing out an exhausted groan. He closes his eyes before he answers. "I don't know. Probably not. But if that's what it would take to stay here, then maybe I could live with it." His eyes open again, locking on mine. "I know we said we would figure things out as we go, but I don't think I want to go anymore. I want to stay. Because I . . ." He pauses, swallowing hard, and I sense what's coming. "Because I love you, Madison."

I should tell him that I'm failing. That the dream of Madison Joy Editorial is probably on the downhill slope to utter demise. That I might have to explore other options for employment. That I'm not the relentless girl he thinks he fell in love with.

I should tell him.

Instead, I whisper, "I love you too, Suits."

I lean in and kiss him.

Chapter Thirty-One

Liam

October

"Do you have enough socks? You never want to be without comfortable socks," Madison says from where she's perched on my bed. We've been pretty strict about sticking to our rule of staying out of each other's rooms, but I gave her a free pass today. She created the most thorough packing list I've ever seen and is taking great joy in checking off the boxes.

"I have plenty of socks, MJ," I reply as I zip up my carry-on suitcase. "I'm only going to be gone for five days."

She sits up on her knees, scooting to the edge of the bed where I'm standing. "Are you sure that suitcase is big enough?"

"You just watched me zip it up with no problem," I answer sarcastically.

"Yes, it's big enough for the trip there, but what about all the souvenirs you're bringing back for me?" she says, the golden flecks of her eyes sparkling.

"Exactly what souvenirs am I supposed to be bringing back?" I ask. "English tea?"

Madison smiles. "*Hmmm*, that's a start. I don't know, maybe miniature figures of Buckingham Palace or Big Ben to display on my desk."

"I think you're supposed to get those types of knickknacks when you've actually *been* to the places yourself," I quip, placing my hands on her waist.

Her hands slide up my chest and her lips quirk as she says, "Well, you could at least bring back a thicker British accent."

I dip into her beloved accent as I murmur, "Such cheeky behavior." Leaning down, I catch her lips with mine, and the flammable chemistry between us takes over quickly, just like it always does. I break contact between our lips long enough to thread my arm under her legs and swoop her into my arms.

"Hey! What are you doing?!" she exclaims.

"I'm taking you somewhere away from my bed to finish this kiss," I say. The words are hardly out of my mouth before her lips are back on mine, and I pause in the hallway rather than completing my intended path to the kitchen.

The sound of the doorbell jolts us back to reality, and I carefully set Madison down on her feet. She reaches up and smooths down my hair.

"Your parents' first impression of me probably shouldn't be signs of me tousling your hair while making out," she says. She's made the statement with her signature sauciness, but I see the nervous way she runs her hands through her own hair and pulls down the hem of her tunic.

Taking her hands in mine, I press a kiss to her knuckles. "They're going to love you," I say, bringing a genuine smile to her lips. We walk hand in hand to the entryway, but Madison hangs back a little as I open the door. My parents stand side by side, and I try to imagine Madison's thoughts as she sees them for the first time. I share my father's height and hair color, but my eyes are a lighter shade of brown than his, thanks to my mom's genetic influence. Her brown hair has started to streak with gray, but she won't dye it. She says the gray makes her look even more dignified as a Shakespeare professor.

Whatever smile lines I have are definitely Mom's influence.

"*Appa*, Mom, good to see you," I greet. My mom lets me shake my dad's hand before pulling me into a long hug.

"It's been too long, Liam. We've missed you," she says, patting my cheek. Her eyes turn to Madison, and the smile on her face widens. "You must be Madison. We've heard so much about you! Well, more than Liam usually shares about people, at least."

"Mom!" I groan. I beckon Madison to step closer. "This is my mom, Jessica, and my dad, Min-ho Park." While we've all become accustomed to the American pronunciation of our last name with the hard "r" sound, I'm sure to enunciate the original Korean *Pak* pronunciation.

Madison holds out her hand to shake theirs, saying, "It's nice to meet you, Mr. and Mrs. Park." I smile with pride at her adjusted articulation of our Korean surname. "I'm glad you could stop through on your way to the airport. Would you like some tea or coffee before we have lunch?"

"Oh, some tea would be lovely!" my mom answers. "What kind do you have?"

"Several," Madison replies with a smile. "Why don't you browse and take your pick?"

"I like her already," my mom says in a dramatic stage whisper, holding a hand up to hide her mouth from Madison.

I purse my lips, shaking my head.

Mom follows Madison to the kitchen, and my dad claps me on the shoulder. "I'm glad you're able to come with us. It will be really nice to celebrate Chuseok all together again."

"Me too, Appa," I say. "How were Harabeoji and Halmeoni when you saw them over the summer? Any big changes I should be preparing myself for?"

"Halmeoni looked a little more frail following the procedure, but the doctors all said she's doing fine. Of course, she *insists* that she's doing fine and hasn't slowed down at all, at least from what Hana reports," my dad says. "Halmeoni is really looking forward to seeing you again. Be prepared to be fawned over."

I huff a laugh. "It'll be like reliving my childhood," I joke, but it falls flat. There's still so much about the changes in my upbringing that we've never directly addressed. After all, it was probably my dad's aversion to talking about personal matters that rubbed off on me.

We walk to the kitchen, where my mom is scanning the different types of tea that Madison has on hand. Madison pulls two mugs out of the cabinet as she says, "An Intro to Shakespeare class was required for my English degree, but I loved the professor so much that I took two more of his classes."

"Then I must know your answer—which of his tragedies do you consider most tragic?" Mom asks. Madison has no idea that she just walked into a literary trap. My mom has very strong opinions on Shakespeare's tragedies, and this question is her measuring stick for how deeply people think about the stories.

"Oh, *King Lear*, hands down," Madison answers with utter confidence.

I breathe a sigh of relief.

Madison expounds as she pours water over the rooibos tea bags. "The ending is so complex and bleak, without any hint of the restoration of order or justice like the other tragedies have. To see Lear so badly misunderstand the character of his daughters and suffer so terribly in response. It's awful." Madison pauses. "And, of course, there's the whole eye gouging scene," she adds with a shudder. "It may be the perfect symbol for Lear's metaphorical blindness, but, *yeesh*."

My mom smiles. "I absolutely agree with you."

Madison looks at my mom with surprise. "Really? I would have guessed your answer would be *Hamlet*, based on your family's cat names."

"Oh no, I could never name my precious babies after the most tragic characters!" Mom replies with a chuckle. "*Hamlet* is my favorite play to discuss in my classes. College students identify so easily with the existential questions about life and death the play raises, which makes for rich discussion."

"The class I took on Shakespeare's comedies was my favorite, though," Madison says as they walk their mugs of tea to the table. "I suppose I'm drawn to the sarcasm and understated wit," she adds with a wry grin.

"You realize you'll never be allowed to break up with this girl now," my dad says under his breath. I laugh through my nose as he checks his watch. "We're going to have to break this up soon if we're going to make it to the airport on time."

We give my mom and Madison twenty-five more minutes to discuss Shakespeare over their cups of tea before insisting we need to leave for lunch. I thought about asking Madison to drive with us to Joplin so we could eat at a nicer restaurant there, but if I'm really considering relocating here to Noel, my parents may as well experience it.

And I am *really* considering it.

Thankfully, there's a new soup and sandwich shop that opened this summer that should be a little easier on our stomachs pre-international flight than the Deer River Bar. I ride with my parents to direct them to the restaurant, even though I would have liked the few minutes alone with Madison. I'm only going to be gone for a few days, but the thought of not seeing her for longer than a day sparks a fiery sensation in my lungs. And not the good kind of fiery sensation she usually sparks.

Over lunch, Madison asks inquisitive but polite questions about my parents' careers and backgrounds. In return, they inquire about her time living in Kansas City and her childhood growing up on a farm.

"What are some of your favorite memories from the farm?" my mom asks.

"*Oof,* that's a tough question," Madison answers. "Even though I left and have no desire to go back to farm life, I still have so many sweet memories of growing up there. When I was really young, my dad would sometimes let me ride with him in the combine during harvest. He would let me think I was driving, even though he maintained control the whole time. It made me feel so important."

"What crops did you grow?" my dad follows up.

"I know this will shock you, but we grew mostly corn," Madison says with a sly smile. "We would rotate soybeans into a field every couple of years because corn draws so many nutrients out of the soil, but we were mostly a Nebraska cliché. Once I got a little older, I was helping my mom and older sister prepare meals to drive out to the farm hands harvesting the fields. Farming truly is a whole-family effort, and I do deeply appreciate that upbringing. My younger brother, Chris, and his wife will take over the farm when my dad retires, so I'm grateful that I'll still be able to go home to visit."

"What was your least favorite task?" I ask, curious to hear the answer.

Madison's face groans even though her vocal cords don't. "Laying irrigation pipes during the summer, for sure. It was hot and hard and awful. I was so grateful when Chris was old enough to take over that particular task."

We wind down conversation when it's time to leave for the airport. Mom wraps Madison in a firm hug, and they exchange pleasantries about meeting again soon.

I walk Madison to her car, taking the opportunity to wrap her up in a firm hug of my own.

"Do you think I passed?" Madison whispers.

"With flying colors. I'm going to miss you," I say, running my fingers through her hair.

She smiles. "There's that secret softie side of you," she says before sighing. "I'll miss you too. But I'm so glad you're getting to do this. Keep me posted on how it goes."

I brush a light, chaste kiss to her lips and squeeze her arms in a reluctant goodbye.

It's a good thing that Madison has been slowly acclimating me to personal questions because my mom uses the international flight to grill me about work, Noel, and mostly Madison. My dad is dead asleep on the other side of her, eye mask in place and earplugs secured.

Somewhere over the Atlantic Ocean, my mom says, "I really like her, just for the record." I sense there's a "but" looming around the corner. "But how are you going to make this work between you? Is she willing to move to Houston? And even if she does, will she be okay with you constantly traveling around from place to place like you have been?"

Leaning back against the head rest, I stare at the dimly-lit ceiling of the airplane for a minute. My gut telling me to stay in Noel—to stay with Madison—is one thing. My mouth telling it to my mom is an entirely different level of exposure.

"I'm . . . I'm considering staying in Noel. Possibly transferring jobs to work at the factory long term. Or maybe explore other opportunities—I don't know," I say, not looking at her next to me. "I think I want to stay in Noel. Not only because of Madison, but because of the rest of the town too. The guys I've met there. The vibe of the community. I think I might like it long term. But I haven't decided yet."

When I finally glance over at my mom, I see her watching me with an appraising look. She observes, "I know how much you hate being in limbo. It's not like you to draw out decisions. What's your gut telling you?"

Sometimes I forget that even though I've chased independence, my family still *knows* me. My mom's question is a comforting reminder that it does feel good to be known by safe, trustworthy people.

"To stay in Noel," I answer.

"Then do it," Mom says.

"But is it that simple?" I push back.

She shrugs. "Why can't it be? It doesn't have to be a lifelong decision."

"You and Appa choosing to move us to Arkansas turned out to be a lifelong decision," I bluntly state before I can think better of it.

Mom flinches slightly, but her expression softens. "That's true. We didn't know at the time that it would be a permanent move. We just knew it was the right thing for that moment. And then, it turned out to be the best thing for our family in a lot of ways, so we stayed."

"How was it the best thing when I was miserable living there?" I ask. I guess the honesty dial on this conversation has been turned up to full blast.

"I don't know about *miserable*," my mom says, and I spear her with a look. She seems genuinely surprised when she asks, "You would honestly say 'miserable'?"

"Well, I wasn't happy. That's for sure. I went from walking home from school to a fresh snack and biscuits with Halmeoni to eating bags of Goldfish crackers at after-school care with a bunch of kids who didn't understand me," I say. "And once Hana was born, even though I came home every day after school, I was so focused on being the good eldest son helping you out that we never talked about the issues I had with kids at school. At least when we lived in London, I had familiar routines and a sense of belonging."

Mom's eyes glimmer in the dim light of the airplane cabin, unshed tears gathered in the corners. "I'm sorry, Liam," she says. "I guess I didn't fully understand how difficult the transition was for you. I was so focused on staying in a healthier place myself that I didn't ask enough questions about your experience."

Eyebrows knitting together, I ask, "What do you mean?"

Mom drops her head back much like I did a few minutes ago, searching the ceiling for an answer. "I probably never talked about this with you, but I really struggled with postpartum depression after you were born," she begins, voice a whisper. "It was a different time then, when you were a baby—people didn't understand as much about PPD as we do now. While having Halmeoni around was helpful in some ways caring for you, it really added to my emotional distress. My success as a mother reflected on the whole family, so it was shameful for me to be struggling to get out of bed or be seen in public. The added pressure only made my emotional state worse."

I stare as she glances over at my dad, double-checking that he's still asleep. She continues, "Your father really tried to help. I know he did. But he was caught between a rock and a hard place—wanting to be supportive of his wife while feeling the weight of his parents' expectations on him. We barely muddled through."

"I'm sorry, Mom," I say when she takes a breath. "I didn't know what it was like for you."

She pats my hand as she says, "You didn't know because I didn't want you to know. And don't misunderstand—I love Halmeoni and Harabeoji to pieces. They're products of their own culture and experiences, the same way I am, so I don't hold it against them. When we left London, we really did intend to go back once my dad had passed. But shortly after that happened, Hana surprised us. And your father knew that I couldn't go back to London then—not with the likelihood of the PPD recurring. So we stayed in Arkansas until I got through the worst of the PPD after Hana, and then we just . . . stayed."

"I wish you would have told me, Mom," I say after a long pause. "I think everything could have been different if I'd known all the facts of the situation. At least, my feelings about everything could have been different."

Mom smiles at me as she says, "You did always want *all* the facts growing up—to know the raw, honest truth about everything. I probably should have been upfront with you about it. 'Alack, alack, for woe. What's done is done.'"

I barely contain a snort of laughter. "Mashing up Shakespeare history and tragedy, huh?"

She smiles at me, and I swivel to give her as much of a hug as possible in the confines of airplane seats. "I love you, Mom."

CHAPTER THIRTY-TWO

Madison

ME

G'day, mate.

HOT BRITISH BOYFRIEND

<eye roll emoji> Wrong country, love.

ME

Well howdy, partner. <cowboy emoji>

HOT BRITISH BOYFRIEND

Wrong state. Did you dip into Hamlet's catnip or something?

ME

Nope. This is just the mental state of me without you now.

HOT BRITISH BOYFRIEND

That went downhill quickly.

ME

You have no idea.

For serious, though, how is it going with your family?

HOT BRITISH BOYFRIEND

It's been great. I had a good talk with my mom on the flight over that gave me a better understanding of a lot of things. I can tell you more about it when I'm back.

ME

<taking notes emoji> Adding to my list of personal questions.

HOT BRITISH BOYFRIEND

Do you actually have a list??

Who am I kidding - of course you have a list.

ME

<screenshot of questions list from notes app>

What have you done today?

HOT BRITISH BOYFRIEND

Big Chuseok dinner is tomorrow, so we did some preparations today. I was in the middle of rolling kimbap with my halmeoni when you texted.

ME

Hold on, I'm catching a flight over. I want that food. Hamlet can fend for himself.

HOT BRITISH BOYFRIEND

<photo of containers in refrigerator>

This is the kimchi fridge.

ME

<GIF of shocked cat>

The kimchi gets its own fridge?!?!

HOT BRITISH BOYFRIEND

Of course, it does. The garlic flavor would permeate all the other food if it was in the regular fridge. There's traditional napa cabbage kimchi, but also cucumber, Korean radish, and green onion kimchis.

ME

<GIF of airplane taking off>

I'm totally jealous.

Okay, but after you finish the whole kimbap thing, could you go walk around the Oxford campus for the rest of the afternoon? I'm really hoping that posh accent will seep its way back into your brain.

HOT BRITISH BOYFRIEND

No, Oxford isn't in London. It's an hour train ride away.

ME

How disappointing.

HOT BRITISH BOYFRIEND

<photo of Buckingham Palace figurine>

ME

YOU GOT ONE FOR ME?!

HOT BRITISH BOYFRIEND

<shrugging emoji>

ME

God save the king. Now, hurry back because I miss my sparring partner. Life is so boring without you.

> Also, I miss you kissing me. And holding me in that tight Liam hug.

> And making pour over coffee. And attempting to circumvent my personal questions with your flirty distractions. And exasperatedly scowling at the heavens every time I call Hamlet "Hammie."

HOT BRITISH BOYFRIEND

> <selfie rolling eyes>

> I miss you too. Give HAMLET a belly rub from me.

ME

> Will do. You may never get your sleeping buddy back. I kinda like having him curled above my head on the pillow every night. I'm keeping him.

HOT BRITISH BOYFRIEND

> No way. I'll reclaim his loyalties as soon as I'm home.

My phone suddenly rings with a video call from Liam, which I answer immediately. Instead of Liam's dreamy eyes staring back at me, I'm met with very similar but much more feminine eyes.

"Hana stole my phone!" Liam's voice yells from the background of the call. "Because she is a *child*."

"Hiiii, Madison!" Hana says, grinning at the screen. I can hear Liam talking in the disappointed parent tone of voice he uses with Hamlet, but he's speaking Korean, so I can't understand him. I might need to add speaking in Korean to our list of rules in addition to the British accent.

I laugh as I greet Hana back. "I can't wait until we can meet in person! I'm about ready to hop on a plane and fly over right now."

"I wish you would!" Hana says. "I've been dying to meet you ever since Liam first mentioned his intriguing neighbor. I totally called this relationship from the start, for the record."

We chat for several more minutes until I realize it's past 8:30 a.m. "Hey, I've got to run—can you tell Liam 'bye' from me?"

"I suppose I could hand the phone over so you can tell him yourself," Hana replies with a playful smirk. "Can't wait to talk again, Madison!"

Liam's face fills the screen, and gosh dang it, I miss that handsome face so much.

"You working a shift at Becky's today or something?" Liam asks.

I try to ignore the shiver chilling my veins as I half lie. "Yeah, she needed a shift covered, so I told her I could. Since you're not around I can work on editing late into the evening."

It's sort of true. I am going into Becky's later for an hour while she has a doctor's appointment. But the more time sensitive issue is that I have a video interview at nine to get ready for.

The interview is for a copywriting job creating social media content. It is absolutely *not* my ideal job by any stretch of the imagination. But it's a company in Kansas City that I'm familiar with, and it might be time to get my foot back in the door for future job opportunities. And who knows—maybe they would be open to remote work.

I don't like withholding information from Liam. But I'm only testing the waters. I'm figuring out if it's time for me to face reality and let go of the MJE experiment. I *will* tell him once I know for sure what I'm going to do.

I will.

Besides, the likelihood of this company even wanting to hire me seems slim. I'm the failure who couldn't keep her last steady job and couldn't make her independent venture succeed. Who wants to hire someone with that kind of lackluster performance?

"I'll text you tonight, okay?" Liam says. "I love you."

"I love you too," I respond before hanging up. Before banging my phone against my forehead.

When I see Liam walk through the automatic doors of the airport exit, I run over to him. Pausing to place the cat carrier gently on the ground, I leap into the air and latch my arms around Liam's neck.

"You're back!" I exclaim.

Liam laughs but drops his bag so he can return the embrace. After briefly kissing me, he says, "I was barely gone. You hardly had time to miss me."

"It was forever," I dramatically state.

Glancing down at our feet, he looks back at me with a question in his eyes. "You brought Hamlet? How did you even get him into the cat carrier? He hates traveling."

"Of course, I brought Hammie! He deserved to be here for our family reunification. I used my powers of persuasion to convince him," I say. When Liam gives me a skeptical look, I amend, "Okay, I maybe have a couple of scratches to show for it. But I think he'll forgive me now that he gets to see you. Because we *both* missed you."

He meets my eyes again when he says, "I thought about you every second, love."

Weak at the knees, I latch on to him more firmly as I murmur, "You brought back the accent I asked for." Liam grins before kissing me more thoroughly.

As we drive the hour back to Noel, Liam tells me all about the time with his family, starting with his heart-to-heart with his mom on the flight over, and ending with the genuine joy and happiness of their Chuseok dinner with his grandparents and his uncle's family.

"I'm really, really glad I decided to go back this year. Thanks for making it possible," Liam says from the passenger seat.

I glance over to see Hamlet still plastered against Liam's chest, paws draped on his shoulders as though he'll never let go of Liam again. The sight makes me melt and laugh at the same time. "It's not like Hamlet is hard to take care of. At least, not once he accepts you into the pack and stops plotting to quietly murder you."

I don't have to look at him to see the eye roll on Liam's face. "He was never going to murder you," he says with an exaggerated sigh. "But also, it was more than having Hamlet taken care of. If not for you, I don't know that I would have been willing to face the complex feelings that resurface when I'm with my whole family. If not for your persistent attempts to get me to peel back my protective layers."

"Aww, the ogre is an onion," I joke, alluding to *Shrek*. Liam rewards my remark with a pinch to my side. "Hey! You're going to make me swerve off the road with that behavior!"

Liam reaches over and curls his fingers into my hair, massaging the base of my neck. "Maybe you need to pull over for a minute. It's been way too long since I've kissed you in private," he says, voice thick.

My voice is breathy when I attempt to scold him. "Just be patient. We'll be home in, like, ten minutes."

"I've told you before that patience is not one of my virtues," he murmurs, voice close, just before he skims a kiss where my jaw meets my ear.

The shiver that skips down my spine nearly does make me swerve off the road.

As we pass the nearly-finished apartment complex, Liam catches me completely off guard with a declaration. "I'm turning in an application for one of those apartments."

Now, I literally do swerve off the road. At least small towns don't have heavy traffic patterns.

"You what?" I ask in shock, putting the car into park.

"I've decided I want to stay in Noel. Or, rather, I think I decided that several weeks ago. But I stopped fighting the decision," Liam says matter-of-factly. "I still need to figure out if I'm going to stay on permanently at Pure Fur All or look at other options, but I know that geographically, I want to be here in Noel. With you."

My breath is stuttered, too short to take in enough oxygen.

On the upside, I turned down the copywriting job in KC. The more they described exactly what I would be doing, the less I wanted to do it. Although they were willing to take a chance on me given my past experience, I just couldn't bring myself to write quippy hooks for Instagram ads. So, I'm not imminently moving away from Noel.

On the downside, I still don't know what my long-term, end-game plan is. Every week, I look for job postings at publishing houses, hoping I'll find a proofreader opening. But the Christmas magic isn't magicking. Most of the remote contract positions I can find are more focused on copywriting, not copyediting and proofreading. LinkedIn keeps feeding me suggestions of open positions at marketing firms in Kansas City, thanks to me applying to the last one. I *want* to stay in Noel . . . but will I be able to make ends meet here? Emily has offered me a temporary job helping to organize details for Christmas Fest, but after the holidays, I could be forced to make a hard decision about my living situation.

You're a terrible person, Madison. You should be honest with Liam about your situation. You should be honest about MJE failing. Admit that you're a failure.

But admitting to Liam that I'm a failure is the last thing I want to do. I'd rather undergo surgery sans anesthesia than admit to Liam that I screwed up on this whole self-rediscovery path. That I picked the wrong thing.

Plus, Liam's love feels so right, like my path was always meant to lead to him. To our paths converging into one. I want to stay here in Noel with him. Surely, I can figure out a way to make it happen.

I think Liam misreads my shocked silence as nothing more than surprise and joy that he's decided to stay. Because his smile grows wider the longer I'm speechless, until he pulls my mouth to his and gives me a different reason to not talk.

I have *to find a way to make it work here. Force my path to lead here. Because I love this man too much to go somewhere without him.*

CHAPTER THIRTY-THREE

Liam

NOVEMBER

"I'm so proud of the contributions that each and every one of you has made to bring this day to fruition. The way you've rolled up your sleeves and jumped into the mess to not only get things on track but ahead of the curve is admirable," I say, slowly scanning the faces of the Pure Fur All employees in the room. "But there's one person who's responsible for this day more than anyone else, so I'd like to invite Beau Olson forward to cut the ceremonial ribbon."

Although the new freeze-dried food production equipment has technically already been used for small test runs and training, today will be the first official day of production. Beau holds the giant scissors over the ribbon for a promotional photo alongside Emily, the town mayor. When he clips the ribbon, a massive cheer rises from the crowd of plant employees.

Beau and I have worked a lot of overtime together over the past month to make today happen, but it's all worth it when I see the elated faces of everyone here. Faces that are sure of their town's future. Sure of their job security. Sure of themselves.

As I walk back to my office, I text a photo of the ribbon-cutting to Cal. He immediately calls me.

"Great stuff there, Liam. Everyone at Pure Fur All is happy with the developments. And everyone at Holden is happy with the projected profitability of this new line. Well done," he says, and I can't help but stand a little straighter. As confident as I am in my own capabilities, it always feels good to have solid work recognized.

"Thanks, Cal. It really was a team effort here. And I do want to have a serious conversation about promoting Beau Olson to the plant manager position. I think he's proved that he could hack it," I say.

"Good—the sooner we can finally get you out of there and on to the next job, the better. The messes have been piling up with you being out for so long," Cal says.

Phone still to my ear, I swing my office door closed and start pacing the length of the room. "I need to talk to you about that, Cal. I never would have expected it, but this town has grown on me. And I've decided I want to move here permanently."

"Have you lost your mind?" Cal asks. The only reasonable follow-up question to my statement.

"Maybe I have," I admit. "But it's what I want to do. I don't want to travel for such huge chunks of time moving forward. I think I'd like to feel like I have some roots somewhere—not be such a nomad anymore."

"Well, I suppose I can understand that," Cal says. "But I don't know what to tell you, Liam. I'm not sure we have any remote positions that wouldn't require travel. Not for your skill set. What do you expect me to do?"

Massaging my temples, I say, "I don't know, Cal. Maybe nothing. I know you can't magically create a new job position for me. But maybe you could give me a positive reference if I decide to pursue something new?"

"You know I would, Liam. You've been one of the best employees I've worked with. Will you at least think about this a little longer before you make the final decision? I really don't want to lose you—I can talk with the right people and see if we can offer you a raise or a better bonus structure," Cal says.

Even though he can't see me, I shake my head. "It's not about money, Cal, although I appreciate that. It's about wanting to have a place that actually feels like home. And as much as it came as a shock, Noel feels like that place. I'll think about it, but I want to be honest that my mind is pretty much made up."

Cal sighs. "That shouldn't surprise me. You've always been one to make decisions quickly and plow ahead. Which has served us well here at Holden. I'll still keep my fingers crossed that you change your mind, but I'll also give my highest recommendation to anyone who calls asking about you."

"Thanks, Cal," I say. "Thanks for being a good boss and pushing me to be my best. I really appreciate it."

"Don't get all sentimental on me," Cal says. "Now get back to work."

He hangs up without further comment, and I smile to myself. I pull up Madison's name to text her.

I know she and Clara are working with Sydney and Becky on some final diagrams of the layout for Christmas Fest, so I'm not surprised when she doesn't answer. It's the third week of November, so the town is transforming into a twinkly wonderland of holiday cheer. Any decorations that don't depend on the temporary booth structures have already been hung, portable toilets have been delivered, and shipment after shipment of supplies have arrived, according to Madison's nightly recaps.

The town truly took our innovation brainstorm to heart and added some key new elements this year. They're going to have live reindeer on site, including two babies that families can pay to pet. They're elevating the food options from a handful of food trucks to multiple booths serving a variety of entrées and snacks. In addition to the big musical performance on Saturday nights, there will be a stage where smaller musical artists will perform twice a day.

The additions I'm most excited about are the collectible ceramic mugs that Becky's coffee drinks will be served in (probably because it was my suggestion based on my experience at European Christmas markets). They were specially designed with the Noel Christmas Fest logo along with the year, so they can become a collector's item designed to lure people back annually. If anyone doesn't want the mug keepsake—or needs multiple rounds of coffee—they can return the mug for a two-dollar refund.

I don't think they ordered nearly enough mugs, but what do I know?

"Wow." It's the only word I can say as Madison and I walk through the doors to the Deer River Bar. Ornaments, candy canes, and glittery decorations hang from every square inch of the ceiling. Multicolor Christmas lights are tacked along the booths and outline the windows. Giant statues of Santa, Rudolph, and Frosty the Snowman greet you as you walk past the host stand.

"This is what you've been up to the past two days, isn't it?" I ask Madison, who smiles smugly.

"I knew that Ben would cave as soon as I laid out Clara's vision for the pop-up bar concept," she says. I narrow my eyes at her. "Okay, as soon as I laid out the financial projections of the increased foot traffic and publicity from tags on social media," she amends.

We make our way to the two tables pushed together, joining Clark and Clara, Davis and Sydney, James and Becky, and Beau and Abby. As we walk, I notice that the notoriously sticky floors aren't suctioning to my shoes. "What magic potion did you clean the floors with?" I ask Madison.

"You don't want to know. I don't think it was FDA-approved for commercial use," she says, grimacing.

"I'm surprised by you, Miss Environmentally Conscious Everything," I chide with mock disapproval.

Madison punches my arm. "You try arguing with Clara about anything related to this festival's success."

These Tuesday dinners have become a highlight of my week for the past few months. They're certainly a heavy contributor to the "stay in Noel" decision. We're carving out one final group dinner of the year before the chaos of the holidays and Christmas Fest hits next week. I'm driving to Conway to celebrate Thanksgiving with my parents, and Madison is going to Nebraska. But we'll both be back the Friday after Thanksgiving in time for the Christmas Fest kickoff parade that evening.

"Ben is testing out his pop-up bar menu this week," Clara says cheerfully, handing us the bright, festive menus.

I make a quick scan of the options, and Madison vocalizes my first thought. "These are all the exact same things he normally serves. They just have Christmas-movie-coded names now." She gives Clara a sassy side eye.

"Sometimes we have to take what we can get," Clara sing-songs. "There's always time to butter him up for next year to try some new dishes."

Conversation is lively as we eat our food—I order the "Uncle Frank, You're a Cheap Steak," which is exactly the same as their regular mediocre steak, but I don't bother pointing that out to Clara. As people exchange stories about funny holiday traditions, I even share some childhood memories without any arm-twisting from Madison.

"I had seen the concept of Thanksgiving in movies, and my mom talked about it, but I don't think anything can prepare you for the blob of cream of mushroom soup getting dumped onto canned green beans when you've never had green bean casserole before," I say, laughing along with the group.

I sit back in my chair, one arm casually draped behind Madison, and observe the easy friendships around the group. As I mindlessly stroke Madison's shoulder with my thumb, I'm struck by a sense of peace. Although most of this crew has spent the majority of their lives together, they've also heartily welcomed first Clara, then Madison, and even me into the group. Made us feel like we belong, like we fit in seamlessly with them.

Yes, I have always loved and will always love my family. But outside of my blood relatives, I've never experienced that phenomenon of "finding your village." Your people. I thought it was a myth that never happened in reality the way it does in movies.

The faces around this table feel like my people.

"I've decided to stay in Noel permanently," I suddenly announce. All eyes look to me with varying degrees of surprise. There's a short moment of shocked silence before *all* of the voices are clamoring with demands for more information.

Beau finally holds up a hand to quiet the cacophony of questions. "What are your plans, exactly? Are you going to stay on as the plant manager at Pure Fur All?"

I answer as honestly and directly as I can. "I haven't one hundred percent decided what I'm going to do job wise. I can't continue in the specific position with Holden that I've had for the past several years—not unless I'm based in Houston and willing to travel the majority of the year. Which I'm not willing to do anymore. I like the community here, so I'll figure something out in order to stay. That might be with Pure Fur All, but I honestly don't think so. I'm leaning toward starting my own fractional business coaching or operations consulting business."

Madison's eyebrows shoot up in a "this is news to me" expression. I haven't told her anything about it because the idea only germinated this afternoon. It may not be a full-grown plan yet, but it's where my gut is pointing.

Davis suddenly pounds the table, making all of the women jump. "This is fantastic news. I'm so glad you're sticking around, man."

There's a chorus of agreement around the table. Clara caps things off with, "I think this calls for a toast. A round of 'He's an Angry Elf' drinks for everyone?"

When the bright red drinks arrive, we clink glasses in the middle as Sydney declares, "To Liam and Madison *both* becoming official Noel residents!"

CHAPTER THIRTY-FOUR

Madison

I've been waking up stupid early for the past six days in a row. Pretty much ever since Liam unexpectedly announced to all of our friends that he's putting down roots here.

Everyone was so legitimately happy. Which made me feel all sorts of warm and weepy inside to see him surrounded and welcomed by friends.

It also made me feel all sorts of panicky since I don't have an ironclad plan to be able to stay in Noel. And I *need* a plan. With Liam committed to staying and all of our friends wanting me here, I have to figure out a way to make it happen.

If only Madison Joy Editorial would take off the way I need it to. I don't know what else to do—I've made every connection I possibly can, sent every uncomfortable "cold" email, consistently posted professional graphics on social media, and received nothing but five-star reviews from all of my clients. I do have a couple of repeat clients with new manuscripts in the pipeline, but I've never had more than two or three clients per month.

And that's simply not enough to pay my bills. I've been able to put off making a responsible move since I'm not paying rent with Liam, but we *have* to move out of this house in six weeks. Not to mention we need to stop being roommates and simply be boyfriend and girlfriend for a while if we're not going to rush the relationship faster than we should.

These are the thoughts that infiltrate my dreams and short-circuit my sleep cycles. I've started applying to every freelance copywriting position I can find that allows remote work. Unfortunately, my honed-in expertise in proofreading is not helping me land any of those positions.

My "how am I going to make a livable income?" anxiety is spiraling to an all-time high. And it's leaving behind a reverberating echo: *Do the responsible thing, Madison. Do the* right *thing, Madison.*

I'm curled up in a not-very-comfortable chair on the back patio, gripping a mug of the English breakfast tea Liam brought back from London. Steam curls up and disappears into the morning fog, a mesmerizing dance of mist. The backyard of the rental house is nothing to write home about, but the crisp, fresh air is helping me think more clearly. Between the tea and the blanket I'm wrapped in, I'm a comfortable temperature, able to appreciate the cool gray of the sky as it slowly changes colors with the sunrise.

The patio door opens behind me, and Liam comes out dressed in joggers and a long-sleeve athletic shirt. Luxury, of course.

"Morning," he says before bending down to kiss me. "What are you doing up so early?"

"Just awake," I say, leaving it at that.

"Want to join me for my run?" Liam asks, a teasing tone in his voice.

I scoff. "Absolutely not. If you ever see me running, I expect you to step in and rescue me from whatever is chasing me."

He laughs heartily, the sound like a sunbeam cutting through the foggy morning. "Okay, I'm heading into the office early. Keep it hush hush, but we're officially offering the plant manager role to Beau today. I can't wait to see the look on his face when I tell him."

Liam's excitement brings tears of joy burning behind my eyes. His contentment in Noel and eagerness to make a friend's day is such a stark contrast to his attitude when he arrived here. Back when he had very vocal judgments about small towns and a total disregard for anyone's opinion.

When he hasn't been at the plant, Liam's been working in a different capacity over the past week. He's officially going out on his own, setting up a consulting business to offer executive coaching and temporary fractional COO services. He let me pretend to be useful by listening to my hard-won expertise in incorporating a business, as though he couldn't have figured it out on his own. I made it crystal clear that this new business venture had better still hinge upon him wearing his fancy suits every day. I might just draw up an official contract.

I have a feeling that his independent consulting firm will literally skyrocket overnight once he puts the word out, very unlike Madison Joy Editorial.

"How much longer will you be officially working for Holden?" I ask.

"We don't have a specific timeline—however long it takes to get Beau running things on his own. Which I don't think will take long—he could probably take the reins right now and be fine," Liam says. "I'm guessing just a few weeks. I'll have to take a trip back to Houston to wrap things up at the office there and pack up my apartment, but I'm hoping to have everything closed down there before Christmas. I don't want to be distracted while celebrating my first Christmas with you in Nebraska."

He kisses me again, and I contemplate convincing him to ditch the run this morning. When I clasp a hand around his neck, he senses my evil plan and smiles against my lips.

"You're trouble," he says with a smirk. "Will you be here before I leave for work or are you meeting Clara early today?"

"I should be here," I reply. "I'm supposed to meet Clara at Emily's office at nine to go over the plans one final time before I leave for Nebraska tomorrow."

"I'll run extra fast," Liam promises. "See you soon."

While Liam is on his run, I take a quick shower and get dressed in jeans and the Christmas sweatshirt that Clara bought for me last year—it has a skeleton wearing a Santa hat beside a Christmas tree, and it is the greatest holiday sweatshirt ever designed. I know it will make her happy seeing me wear it. Maybe Clara can Christmas-magic a long-term job solution for me today.

I eat a quick breakfast with Liam before he dips me back in a dramatic kiss on his way out the door. Hamlet stands in the entryway, meowing loudly after him.

"I know, Hammie, I'm pretty obsessed with him too," I say, leaning down to scratch Hamlet under the chin. He leaps onto my shoulders and makes himself at home there as I walk around putting dishes in the sink and wiping off the counters.

When my phone starts ringing, I expect it to be Clara calling with some last-minute urgent need before our meeting. I'm surprised when I see "WritInc" as the contact name displayed. I never deleted the office number from my phone contacts, but I never expected to hear from them again. Worried that they might need updated contact information for my tax documents, I answer.

"Hello?" I don't try to hide the contempt from my voice, even though, if it's some poor HR soul, they don't deserve my unbridled wrath.

A throat clears before I hear, "Hello, Madison, this is Chad calling from WritInc."

Well, at least we know my unfiltered contempt was deserved.

"What do you want, Chad?" I ask. There is zero reason to dance around with niceties.

He clears his throat again, rather aggressively. Gross.

"I'm calling because our decision to rely on AI at the editing stage of our process may have been . . . premature," Chad says. "I mean, I'm not entirely convinced it was a *mistake*, but we're reevaluating the decision-making process and—"

I roll my eyes so aggressively, I nearly give myself a headache. Even though he can't see me, I hope he can sense the eye roll in my voice. "Cut the crap, Chad. Why are you calling?"

"We'd like you to come back to WritInc. Back into your same position," Chad states.

My mind floods with emotions, thoughts, and hormone chemicals that I can't identify.

"You what?" I clarify.

Chad sighs heavily. "We've decided that it is a worthwhile cost to have a human proofreader doing the final checks on all of our publications. We'd like you to come back to your position. I know it's a holiday week, but if you could come in next Monday, we could talk specific details of your employment package and get you set up to start again right away."

The world is spinning, and I need something grounding to latch on to.

"Why? What happened to make you change your mind?" I ask.

There's a pause. "Chad? You still there?" I demand.

"Yes, still here. We, uh, we had a few complaints from customers about errors going out in the newsletters," Chad admits.

I can't help the smug happiness that spreads through me. *I told you so.*

"What kinds of errors?" I ask, trying to sound nonchalant and not like I am completely reveling in his mistake.

"Most of them weren't significant, just some small things the AI didn't catch that customers felt made the publication look unprofessional," Chad says. I don't say anything, forcing him to continue. "Last week we lost a customer because of a more . . . well . . . sensitive error. And Mr. Douglas insisted that we bring you back."

Curiosity extremely piqued, I take advantage of this opportunity to press my thumb into Chad's pain point. Because *I told him this would happen*! "What was the mistake, Chad?" I ask.

"Well, the client was a Chamber of Commerce for a mid-sized town in Ohio, and the story was about a new commercial retail space opening. Including a new private hair salon that required a monthly membership fee to utilize multiple benefits," Chad says, and I hear the embarrassment rising in his voice. "Um, there was a line contrasting the salon to a public hair salon, but the, uh, the 'l' was left out of the word 'public.'"

I can't help it. I burst out laughing. Because *of course* artificial intelligence wouldn't recognize it as a mistake when it's technically still a word.

When I finally manage to contain my giggles, I can hear Chad's scowl beaming through the silence. "I'm sorry," I say. "Actually, I'm not sorry. I tried to tell you that something like this would happen. This never would have happened if you would have just listened to me instead of thinking you could slash my position to cut costs."

I don't mention that if he had never cut my position, I would have never come to Noel. Or met Liam. Chad doesn't deserve to know that his buffoonery brought some good things to my life.

"I'm going to need to think about it," I finally say. "I'm not quite sure that I *want* to come back to WritInc."

"Yeah, I saw on your LinkedIn that you've been trying your hand at independent editing," Chad says. "How's that going for you?" There's a sneer in his voice that would indicate he knows how *not well* it's been going, even though there's no way he could know that.

"It's been a great opportunity to meet new clients and edit literature I find interesting," I say, emphasizing the good points. I don't acknowledge the panicky failure feelings that start swirling in my stomach.

"Just come in next week and let us discuss your offer. Mr. Douglas would like to present it to you in person," Chad says.

Relenting a little, I say, "Fine. I'll think about it and see you next week."

I'm distracted all day by the WritInc offer as I work with Clara and Emily. As much as I would love her advice, I don't have the heart to tell Clara. This Christmas festival is her baby, her favorite thing in the world—aside from Clark. And me. And Chase.

I can't bring myself to burst the bubble of her joy by mentioning that there's a possibility I could be moving back to Kansas City. Even if it's slim.

Do I want to return to WritInc? Absolutely not. As gratifying as it was to hear Chad wallowing in his misstep, I have zero desire to go back to working with him. And even if my MJE clients have been fewer and farther between than I'd like, I've enjoyed editing their content so much more than endless newsletters and postcards.

But . . . accepting the WritInc offer might be the responsible thing to do. I tried to make it on my own—tried and failed. It might have been the wrong move from the very start, despite the positive side effects of bonus time with Clara and meeting Liam.

Liam.

What am I going to tell him? Would he move to Kansas City if I decided to go there? I mean, he could do his independent consulting from anywhere, right? And the Kansas City airport would certainly make travel easier than living in Noel. Maybe I move back to KC temporarily until I get my feet under me. We could do long distance for a little while—Clara and Clark did. At least, for a couple of months until the distance was killing them and Clara moved to Noel.

I pace the living room as I wait for Liam to get home. I didn't have the heart to tell Clara about the offer, but I need to talk this through with Liam.

When he comes in the door, he takes one look at my energy and immediately senses turmoil. Hamlet is meowing at his ankles, but he quickly takes off his dress shoes and crosses the room to me. "What's wrong, MJ?"

"WritInc called and offered me my job back," I blurt out.

"Huh?" His brows form a confused line in the center of his forehead.

"The company I worked for that fired me. They've had multiple editing errors go out in their content, and customers have been upset, just like you predicted could happen. They want me to come back to my proofreading job," I explain.

"But you told them no," Liam states, certainty in his voice.

"I mean . . . I didn't say 'no' right away. They want me to come in next week to meet with the COO to hear the full employment proposal," I say, my voice wavering slightly.

"But you're going to turn them down." It's a statement, not a question from Liam.

I shuffle my weight on my feet. "Probably?"

Liam makes an exasperated sound that's half scoff, half laugh. "You're kidding me, right? It would be stupid to go back to them."

My defensive hackles rise. "It's not stupid to consider a stable job offer."

Liam gives me an incredulous look. "Madison, they *fired* you. After Chad treated you like garbage working there, they replaced you with a robot. Do you not remember how upset you were about that? How *rightfully* upset you were? You can't possibly be considering going back to a company that mistreated you that way."

Picking up on the changing energy, Hamlet slinks away toward Liam's room.

"I have to be a responsible adult, Liam!" I yell. "I tried to go out on my own, and I failed. Maybe I need to make a mature decision, even if it means swallowing my pride and going back to a company I don't like."

"What are you talking about?" Liam asks. "What do you mean you failed? You haven't failed."

"I *have* failed, Liam!" I emphasize, chest heaving. "I didn't want to admit to you that I'm a failure, that I messed up, but I did. MJE is nowhere near bringing in enough income to pay basic expenses. The only reason I've been able to survive these past few months is because I was picking up extra shifts at Becky's and then helping Emily with Christmas Fest."

Liam's eyes are clouded with hurt. "Why didn't you say something? If you would have told me what was going on, we could have brainstormed some new strategies to bring in more clients. I can't help you fix it if you don't tell me the honest facts of the situation."

"I don't need help fixing it, Liam!" I yell, fists clenched.

"Apparently you do, Madison! And that's literally what I do—I'm a fixer!" he yells back.

"Maybe I just want you to be my boyfriend and not my business coach! Maybe I didn't want to admit to the man I love that he fell in love with the wrong girl," I say, tears stinging my eyes. I latch on to my anger to keep them from trickling down my cheeks. "I'm thirty years old—I have to make a grown-up decision. Be responsible for myself. If I can't hack it as an independent editor, then maybe I need to go back to a job that gives me a steady paycheck, even if I don't like it. Sometimes that's what adults do."

Liam glares at me. "And what about us? How do I factor into this decision? Or am I not a factor at all?"

I sigh, a tiny bit of my anger fizzling. "Of course, you're a factor. This doesn't mean we can't still be together. If I do take the job, we could always do long distance for a little while. Or you could come to Kansas City. I don't know—we can figure it out as we go, right?"

Liam's glare has softened into something that looks more like hurt. And it makes me a lot more uncomfortable than his anger.

"Why wouldn't you have said something about this sooner?" he asks. "I . . . I opened up to you, to this place. I finally started to feel like I had roots somewhere. With someone. How could you just blindside me when I've quit my job to start building a life here? With you."

I bite my lip, still feeling defensive but also extremely guilty.

He's right—how could you, Madison?

"Liam, I don't know what I'm going to do yet. I'm not saying I'm going to accept the position. I'm going to stay in Nebraska an extra few days and hear them out at WritInc on Monday, and then I can figure out what to do," I say.

"So you're just going to miss the kickoff of Christmas Fest, too, then?" Liam responds, his tone laced with sarcasm. "Did you forget that you're supposed to be helping Becky at her booth all weekend? Did you forget that we were going to watch the opening night parade together on Friday? Sure seems like you've already made up your mind about this job offer if you're going to prioritize them over all the friends you have here."

His comment cuts deep. His tone cuts even deeper—not quite disappointed. More like an *"I should have known this was going to happen"* tone.

"Liam, you're not being fair," I start. "I haven't made a decision yet."

"You can lie to yourself about that if you want, but I'm tired of you lying to me," Liam says, backing away.

"I haven't lied to you," I insist, defenses rising again.

Liam snorts a sarcastic laugh as he crosses back to the entryway. "Lying by omission is just as bad." He toes on his tennis shoes, which look ridiculous with his navy suit pants and pink dress shirt. "I guess I'll see you next week when you come back to pack up your stuff."

"Liam," I say, a strangled plea.

He closes the door gently behind him. The quiet click of the latch resounds throughout the room louder than if he had fully slammed the door. Because it wasn't an angry, *"I'm so furious this is happening"* slam—it was a resigned, *"I knew this would happen"* click.

It's the click that breaks my heart.

Because I've messed things up with Liam on top of messing things up in my career. Wrong choice piled on top of wrong choice. And now Liam is the collateral damage.

Maybe Christmas isn't what's broken. Maybe it's just me.

CHAPTER THIRTY-FIVE

Liam

I drive for a long time. Hours slip by as I aimlessly take exits and drive along unfamiliar roads, my mind in a constant state of yelling.

How could she do this? How could I do this—give someone this kind of power over me?

When my vision starts to blur from the tired rage, I finally pull over on a quiet country highway, killing the engine. I punch the steering wheel, unintentionally blasting the horn.

"This was your own fault," I lecture myself. "If you hadn't handed her your trust, she couldn't have betrayed you. This is why you don't let people in, you idiot. And now you've set yourself up for even more disaster—quitting your job, moving to Noel. What were you thinking?"

I drop my head to my hands, pressing my fingers hard against my closed eyes.

You were thinking that you loved her. That any path was worth it as long as she was on it too.

Leaning my forehead against the steering wheel, I groan.

My self-preservation instincts flare up, telling me it's time to cut bait with Madison before things get worse. That maybe I'm just not meant to find the kind of love that heals more than it hurts.

Maybe I'm not cut out for love, period. Maybe I've been right all along—I don't have "people." The concept is a myth, just like love that outweighs risk. Nonexistent.

But then, I think about the way Clark looks at Clara, especially knowing his background. I think about Davis and Sydney two-stepping at the Deer River Bar when no one else was dancing, completely smitten with each other despite being years into marriage. *I want the kind of love I see in them—I want it with Madison.*

I think about everyone's enthusiastic response to my announcement that I'd be staying. Sydney's offer to decorate my new apartment. Clark's invitation to their post-Christmas Fest guys' weekend to decompress at a secluded cabin. Davis asking if I'd like to dress up as an elf on one of the nights to row the boat holding the letters to Santa (a hard pass from me). Becky floating the idea of offering pour overs at her coffee shop if I'd teach her how to make them properly.

I'm surprised by the tears that spring to my eyes. *I want these to be my people. I want to* have *people. Can it all really be true if I just want it enough?*

For all of my adult life, I've been respected—even feared at times. But what I've experienced here in Noel feels a lot more like love. Love that tastes like belonging and acceptance. And I *don't* want to give that up, despite the pain of betrayal I'm currently feeling.

I don't want to give up Madison.

Turning on the ignition of my SUV, I pull up the GPS to figure out how to get back to Noel from wherever I am. As I drive home, I mull over everything Madison said during our fight. That she wanted me to be her boyfriend, not her business coach. That she didn't want to admit to me that she was failing.

She's right. Every time she's brought up her business, I've always pushed her, sometimes harshly. No wonder she was afraid to tell me that it wasn't working. I have to figure out how to turn off the "fix it" switch when she just needs to talk. I need to apologize.

After another hour of driving and reflecting, I pull up to the house at 3:00 a.m.

Madison's car is gone.

Running inside, I check her bed just in case I was hallucinating. Hamlet is hiding under the Christmas tree in her room but comes sprinting out as soon as I step into his view. "Where's Madison, my friend?" I ask, picking him up.

Meow.

He looks at me with sadness and accusation.

Pulling out my phone, I try calling Madison. When she doesn't answer, I send a text.

ME

> Where are you? I just got back and was hoping we could talk more.

After a couple of minutes with no reply, I try calling again. She still doesn't answer, so I send another text.

ME

> MJ. I need to know that you're safe. Where are you?

MJ

> I'm fine. I decided to drive part of the way to Nebraska tonight so I can get to the farm earlier tomorrow. I stopped at a hotel in Missouri a little bit ago.

> I'm not sure what else we have to talk about. You seemed pretty certain about your view of things.

Sighing, I sit down on the couch, trying to think of what to say. I need the tennis ball from my office right now. I settle for tapping my fist against my knee instead.

ME

> I'm sorry I blew up. You caught me really off guard in a way that made me feel like I never should have lowered my guard. I'm sorry that I've pushed you so hard with MJE that you didn't feel safe to talk to me about it. I should have been your boyfriend listening to you and not a fixer prescribing solutions.

> I don't know exactly where we go from here. But I do want to figure it out together. There has to be some sort of solution that gives you financial security while staying in Noel. While staying together.

MJ

> I need some time to think. Time to cool down from being defensive and angry so I can think clearly.

ME

> Ok. You can have time.

> If I call, will you please answer? I need to say something to you not over text.

There's a short pause, but then the phone rings.

"Yes?" Madison says when I answer.

"I just need to explain one thing," I say. "I *am* worried about what this job offer means for us. I *am* anxious about what it might mean for me because I don't want to lose *you*. But, MJ, I'm upset about this job offer primarily because you deserve better. What they did to you was an unjust way to treat one of their most reliable employees. You shouldn't have to go back just because they're crawling to you on their knees now that they lost clients and realized they screwed up. You're worth more than that, love."

There's silence on Madison's end aside from a quiet sniff.

"Please think about that as you're taking time to think, okay?" I plead.

"Okay," she replies quietly. "Bye, Liam."

The call ends.

CHAPTER THIRTY-SIX

Madison

"I don't know why you're still thinking about this, Maddie," my mom says. We're in the kitchen at the farm, mixing up side dishes while Dad and Caitlin's husband are out back deep frying the turkey. Chris and his wife will be over in a few hours to eat dinner together.

Mom scoops the niblets of corn she cut off the cobs into the slow cooker, where butter and cream cheese await to completely cancel out any nutritional value of the vegetable. "It seems pretty obvious that you should take the job. You already know exactly what to do there. It's financial security and insurance—none of which you have with this side hustle," she continues as she adds salt and pepper to the corn mixture.

I mash the sweet potatoes more aggressively. "Does it not matter at all that they fired me in the first place? Maybe I don't want to bail them out. Maybe I don't want to move back to Kansas City."

Mom perks up at my statement. "If you've decided you don't care for big city living, why don't you move back here? We'd love to have you closer to home! It could be just like old times having you help out with harvest and—"

"No, Mom!" I cut her off, frustrated. "I'm not moving back here. If I don't accept the job, I'm going to stay in Noel with Clara and Liam."

She *tsks*. "Are you sure you're still going to have a boyfriend to go back to? Especially after you threw that temper tantrum? That's exactly what happened with Arthur your senior year of high school. You need

264

to learn to get a tighter rein on your tongue if you're going to make a relationship work."

Gripping the potato masher tighter, I hold in the choice words I'd like to yell. I officially regret telling my mom about my fight with Liam.

"Can we not talk about this anymore, Mom? I'd like to enjoy Thanksgiving instead of having my mistakes rubbed in my face."

"Now, Maddie, I'm not trying—"

"*Please*, Mom? Just stop," I beg, a hint of tears edging my voice.

Mercifully, JoJo comes into the kitchen asking for a snack. I abandon the sweet potato casserole and sweep JoJo into my arms, carrying her to the fridge to look for some fruit. Mom takes an aluminum pan outside to my dad, so I take a second trying to corral my emotions in the cool air of the refrigerator. Caitlin comes up beside me.

"Mom?" she quietly asks. An entire one-worded question that we both understand.

"Just meddling with her always-right opinions," I mutter under my breath.

Caitlin pokes me in the side. "You had to get that opinionated nature from somewhere," she teases.

I roll my eyes but crack a smile.

I've filled her in on everything that transpired with Liam—with much more detail than I volunteered to my mom. "I don't know what to do, Cait. Going back to WritInc is entirely unappealing, but I tried doing my own thing, and it's not working. At this point, it seems pretty irresponsible to turn down a stable job."

"Mads, what do you *want* to do?" she asks. "Forget making the *right* choice for a minute. What do you *want?*"

I kiss JoJo's cheek, trying not to cry. "I want Liam. I want Noel. To live there with all of our friends, who seem to actually like having me around. I want Madison Joy Editorial to succeed and not be a failure."

Add "not crying" to the list of things I fail at.

Caitlin pulls me into a hug, squeezing JoJo between us. "Then do it, Mads. What's the worst that could happen?"

"I wind up destitute and homeless, filing for bankruptcy while slowly dying of starvation," I deadpan.

Caitlin smirks. "I have a feeling there are a lot of people in Noel who wouldn't allow that to happen. Liam and Clara topping the list."

Taking a deep breath, I slowly exhale. "You're right," I say.

"Duh," Caitlin replies. "We both inherited that 'always-right' nature."

When I wake up absurdly early the morning after Thanksgiving, I know exactly what I need to do. I shower and get dressed quickly, but as I'm applying eyeliner, I pause to look at my hands. Staring at my fingernails, I make a decision.

Removing the black nail polish from my middle fingers, I repaint them in the same shade of crimson as the rest of my nails. I don't need my form of silent protest against injustice anymore. Because I'm going to confront the injustice head-on.

I say brief goodbyes to my family while shoveling breakfast down my throat. Hopping in my car, I begin the four-and-a-half-hour drive from the farm to Overland Park, Kansas, where the WritInc office is located.

Channeling my inner Clara, I listen to my pop Christmas playlist the whole way, begging for a dose of my own Christmas magic.

I know that Chad will be working the day after Thanksgiving because he always had zero personal life or boundaries to speak of. It's not an official vacation day given by the company, so there are bound to be at least a few people there who didn't have enough PTO to take the day off.

When I arrive at the building, I ring the bell at the reception desk. Either the receptionist did take the day off, or Chad decided that reception was another unnecessary position. Finally, one of the graphic designers I recognize comes around the corner.

"Madison?" he says. "What are you doing here? Are you coming back? Please tell me you're coming back. It's embarrassing the number of mistakes that have gone to print."

"I am not coming back," I state. The words feel good on my tongue—a warm-up for my declaration to Chad. "I'm just here to talk to Chad briefly. Is he still in the same office?" I ask the designer.

He confirms, so I march back to Chad's corner office, head held high. When I walk through the open door, he looks up in surprise.

"Uh, what are you doing here, Madison? We're meeting on Monday. Mr. Douglas isn't here, so you're going to need to come back at your scheduled time," he says. The condescension in his voice assures me that he has absolutely not changed his tune, despite being proven wrong. Very embarrassingly wrong, according to the graphic designer.

"I'm not coming back," I say. "I'm not coming back Monday because I'm not coming back, period."

Chad huffs. "If this is some kind of power play to get a pay bump, you can rest assured that Mr. Douglas was already planning to offer you a two percent increase over your previous salary."

I pin him with my best daggered glare. "I told you that you needed a human proofreader looking over the content you sent out. I told you that AI wasn't a sufficient substitute. But you didn't listen."

He sputters a breath through his lips as he stands to his feet. "What do you want, Madison? For me to admit I was wrong? Maybe I was wrong—or maybe people are way too uptight about some meaningless typos."

"Those newsletters and postcards reflect the professionalism of the clients, Chad. Not to mention WritInc's professionalism. The customers you lost were justified in leaving you behind," I say. I feel steam building, the momentum gathering as I step fully onto my soapbox. "All you cared about was cutting costs and increasing the bottom line, not about the quality of the brands being represented. And you certainly didn't care about the employees who had worked their tails off to make sure that WritInc consistently put out the highest quality. Why do you think we had so many customers coming to us after getting burned by other print marketing firms? Because we had a reputation of excellence. Until you screwed it up. Just because your short-sightedness came back to bite you in the butt doesn't mean I have to bail you out."

I almost think Chad has somehow transfigured into a fish, given his open-mouthed, wide-eyed expression.

"I'm glad someone came to their senses and realized you need a real proofreader—although, I have a hunch that person was Mr. Douglas, not you. But you're going to need to find a different person because I have no interest in coming back to work here after how you treated me," I state definitively. "Not only how you fired me, but how you *treated* me ever since you started here—belittling my position and micromanaging everything like no one was as competent as you. I deserve better."

Pivoting on my heel, I march to the door. Holding up a hand in a dismissive wave, I punctuate, "Bye, Chad."

I practically run to my car, hurling myself into the driver's seat. I calculate time in my head to decide just how much I need to push the speed limit if I'm going to get to Noel before the kickoff Christmas Fest parade tonight.

I need to get home. I may not know exactly what I'm going to do to earn a living, and maybe that makes me an irresponsible excuse for a grown woman.

But I know this much: Madison Joy belongs in Noel.

She belongs with Liam.

CHAPTER THIRTY-SEVEN

Liam

As I pull into the city limits of Noel, I'm shocked by the transformation of the town. Of course, I've watched all of the decorations and booths being installed this month. I helped Clark and Davis build some of those temporary structures earlier this week. I'd seen the vision for what Christmas Fest would be.

But that didn't prepare me to *see* the vision of Christmas Fest.

I've always had slightly more positive than neutral feelings toward Christmas. I enjoy it for what it is without overly obsessing like it's the greatest holiday to ever happen to mankind. But the festival grounds are slowly infecting me with their Christmas magic as I drive past the center of town. Even Hamlet is perched on his hind legs in the passenger seat, watching the twinkling lights out the window.

All the main streets are blocked off to cars, keeping pedestrians entirely safe, so I take a roundabout way to the rental house to drop Hamlet off. I get him situated with some water and food, and then I drive back to one of the parking zones close to the festival.

The magic seeps deeper into my bones as I walk through the thick of it. Thousands of lights, dozens of decorated trees, statues and figurines tastefully scattered throughout the area. Photo ops—some classic and some whimsical—are interspersed along the sidewalks. There's a massive "Merry Christmas" banner of lights strung across Main Street, welcoming people to the true heart of the action.

Santa's Workshop is central to the space, where local artisans sell their goods to tourists seeking gifts or keepsakes. There's a tent set up where children can write their letters to Santa and drop them into the letterbox for Sunday's sendoff. According to the map, there's a Living Nativity close to the reindeer enclosure on the riverbank, along with a small carousel rounding out the children's area. And, of course, there are the food and beverage booths—Becky's Brews with coffee drinks, the bake club stand with sweet treats, and several shops serving various entrées.

I smile when I see a booth advertising traditional mulled wine as well as mulled apple cider. The parade won't start for another hour, but the grounds are already filled to the brim with crowds of families—some looking like they've been here before, and others carefully studying the festival map.

The only thing that isn't magical about this Christmas wonderland is who's missing.

I sent Madison a handful of texts this week—some of which she sent short replies to, and some that were left on read. At this point, I'm not even sure what I'll say to her when she gets back on Monday. I want her to stay so badly—more than I've wanted anything in a long time. Maybe ever. But I don't know how to convince her, especially if she doesn't want my help.

Unfortunately, she didn't tell any of our friends here about the job offer. She made up an excuse about needing to stay through the weekend with her family. No one here even knows to be worried that the spark of joy Madison's presence has brought to Noel might be flickering out.

I don't realize I'm staring off into space until there's a squeeze on my arm. Clara is standing next to me, positively beaming with Christmas spirit. "It's pretty special, huh?" she asks me, her gaze sweeping across the festival grounds. "Better than a dream."

Forcing a smile, I nod in agreement. "It really is impressive seeing it come to life. Well done."

Clara dismissively waves her hand in the air. "I may have had the original idea, but it's the entire town's baby. Everyone has contributed in some way to the magic. Even you," she says, eyes dancing. "Just wait till you see the parade tonight—move over, Disney, Noel is coming for you."

We laugh heartily together because we both know that the tiny town of Noel is never going to be a Disney competitor. But maybe the magic lies in what's different—how cozy and intimate it feels. As though you could come back every year and bump into the same strangers who became friends the year before. Friends who slowly become family.

It's the magic of Noel.

I only hope that Madison decides to be part of the magic—to recognize that she already *is* part of the magic.

"I wish Madison was here for the kickoff," I muse aloud, not showing the true depths of my turmoil over her absence.

"Me too," Clara agrees. "Once you get used to her feisty presence, nothing is the same without it."

I can't respond. My throat is too constricted to give my vocal cords any space to speak.

"Good thing she'll be back next week because Becky is slammed already. I'm going to jump in and help her this weekend, but I think Becky is afraid to hurt my feelings and admit that Mads is a better barista than I am," Clara says. "Despite the fact that she despises coffee."

A laugh erupts before I can stop it. Clara looks at me with a confused expression. "MJ hasn't told you about her dirty little secret, huh?" When Clara's confusion only grows, I conspiratorially whisper, "She drinks a pour over coffee almost every morning now."

Clara's mouth drops open. "Stop it right now! She does not."

I shrug one shoulder with a smug smile. "She just needed the right kind of coffee to figure out that she likes it."

At this, Clara's face softens, and I'd almost swear there are tears in her eyes. "You've been so good for her, Liam. You amplify the best in her instead of stuffing it down to make her smaller. I love seeing her with you."

Now my throat is *really* constricted. *What if Madison decides to stuff down the best of her because she thinks it's the right thing to do? What if she decides to go backward instead of forward?*

What if she picks a different path than me?

"I'm going to go get a drink and walk around a little before the parade starts," I tell Clara, needing an out from further conversation about Madison. "I'll see you around."

I meander the grounds, surprised to find that every nook and cranny off the beaten path has been thoroughly Christmasified. There's even an alleyway between two buildings labeled with a sign that says "Mistletoe Lane." When I take a step in to investigate, I see that there are white Christmas lights crisscrossed from the buildings to form a ceiling of light. Dozens of sprigs of mistletoe hang from the strands, creating the perfect excuse for a first (or hundredth) kiss.

"You know, I'd kiss you without mistletoe as an excuse."

I sharply swivel around at the sound of that voice.

The sound of *her* voice.

That sassy, snarky, cheeky voice.

Madison is wearing a smirk to match her inflection, and everything in me wants to kiss her until she forgets how to ever smirk again. Except, not really, because I *love* that sass on her lips.

But I need to know what she's doing here. I need to know what *we're* doing before I jump right in to kissing her.

"You're here?" The statement comes out as a question. A very loaded question.

Why are you here now? *How* here *are you?*

The smirk falls from her expression as she slowly steps toward me. "I'm here because I owe you the world's most massive apology. I was wrong to not tell you that I was struggling and my future here could be in jeopardy."

"MJ, it's okay—" I start, but Madison cuts me off.

"No, it's not okay. I knew what a struggle it was for you to be vulnerable with people—what a big step it was for you to trust me. I was constantly pushing you to open up, but when I should have been open with you, I hid instead. I was wrong, and I hurt you. I'm so sorry," she says with no hint of sarcasm. My heart drums in my chest, the honesty in her apology filling me with love-fueled adrenaline.

Sass sparks fire in her eyes again as she adds, "I drove to WritInc this morning, and I told Chad exactly where he could put his job offer."

A sly smile fights its way to my lips. "So cheeky," I say, and Madison gives me an innocent look.

"I told him he could offer the job to someone else, obviously. What wicked things are you thinking I'd say?" she asks with a toss of her hair.

I still need her to spell things out—to be fully transparent. But I also can't handle the lack of physical contact between us anymore. I step forward and loop a hand around the small of her back, tugging her to me. Her forest-green sweater is soft beneath my fingers, her warmth seeping through.

"So what are you saying?" I clarify.

"I'm saying that this is home. This is where I want to be. You. Noel. Our friends. All of it. Even if it's reckless, even if it's not the right thing on paper," she says, running her hands up my chest. "I'm saying I love you madly, so I'll do whatever it takes to stay here with you. Because I realized old William was right. 'For where thou art, there is the world itself.'"

I move a hand to cup her face, tracing my thumb down to rest on her chin. "'I do love you more than words can wield the matter.'"

Madison's eyes roll as she drops her head back. "No, no, no, NO! You cannot pull a line about love from Shakespeare's greatest tragedy! *Especially* not from that lying, evil excuse for a daughter! This lady doth protest too much!"

Her protests cease, however, as I solder her lips against mine. She returns the kiss with equal fire, with the fervor that results from coming to the brink of losing love.

I kiss her hungrily, greedily, thoroughly, with zero care for whether any tourists have become unwilling spectators. I finally tear our lips apart but press our foreheads together, murmuring, "I love you, Madison Joy. 'Where thou art not, desolation.' So please don't leave again."

Madison pokes a finger in my chest, pointing straight to my heart. "My path," she says.

And I kiss her again.

My arms are firmly wrapped around Madison as we stand on the sidelines of the parade, cheering for the floats that pass by. She may have promised that she's not leaving, but I'm holding her extra tight tonight, just for good measure.

The parade includes floats depicting traditional Christmas movies, the high school marching band playing "The First Noel" on loop, dozens of costumed town residents throwing candy and trinkets to the kids, and finally culminating with Santa and Mrs. Claus. I burst out laughing when I recognize Clara and Clark on the float—Clark looking far less merry than the jolly old man himself.

"How did Clara convince him to do that?" I ask in Madison's ear.

"It's taken two years of begging. He probably only agreed since tomorrow is their first anniversary. I'll bet you twenty bucks he refuses to do it again after tonight," she replies.

I shake my head. "I don't agree to bets I know I'll lose."

Madison waves her hands wildly above her head, trying to catch Clara's eye. When Clara notices, she beams and blows a kiss in our direction. I catch Madison's raised hand in mine, inspecting her nails.

"All one color, huh?" I observe.

Madison turns to face me, placing both hands on my chest.

"I might go back to painting my ring fingers in an accent color if I feel like it," she says as she stares at her hands. She meets my eyes when she says, "I know you said you liked that attitude the first time you kissed me, but you have only yourself to blame for the turnaround. It started as my way of protesting the way Chad treated me at work. It continued as an outlet for the resentment I felt about the injustice that drove me here to Noel. But I don't have any reason to protest anymore—I have you. I have our friends and this town. I have people I know will have my back while I figure out how I'm going to survive. I confronted Chad and laid it to rest. There's nothing about my life to resent now."

I take one of Madison's hands and press a kiss to her curled fingers. "I love you, MJ. And I'll more than have your back. I'll burn the world down to clear a path for you if that's what it takes. As long as we're on the path together."

"No burning necessary," Madison says with a smirk. "Let's just hope for a little Christmas magic to take pity on me."

"You *are* the magic," I tell her, voice serious. I trace a thumb across her lips as I say, "I still believe in you, Madison Joy."

Her eyes glisten with moisture just before she captures my lips with hers.

CHAPTER THIRTY-EIGHT

Madison

DECEMBER

Meow.

Hamlet's loud voice wakes me from slumber. I crack an eye open to see him perched next to me on my bed, seafoam eyes studying me expectantly.

Meow.

"What are you doing in here, Hammie?" I mumble, voice heavy with sleep.

"I thought you could use a little coffee in bed to help you wake up this morning," Liam says from the doorway. Glancing at the clock, I see it's after eight already. Which explains why Liam looks freshly showered and already dressed in a maroon dress shirt and black pants.

He's looking so attractive, I'd love to run my fingers through that freshly-washed hair and mess it up just a little.

"You were up so late last night, I wasn't sure you'd be able to make it to the kitchen without caffeine," he says, the taunting look on his face offsetting the concern in his words.

Rubbing my eyes, I sit up fully in bed, crisscrossing my legs. Hamlet makes himself at home in my lap, and I hold my hands out toward Liam. "I accept."

I've been working Becky's stand at Christmas Fest almost every day for the past three weeks, only to come home and edit a manuscript I have due back to the author before Christmas. Liam has supported me through the long hours with pour over coffees and shoulder rubs, knowing that padding my bank account over these few weeks gives me breathing room to figure out the next step. As magical as the festival has been, I'm excited that this is the final weekend. Because I need a break.

Liam hands me a cup of steaming black coffee, then sits on the end of my bed. I raise an eyebrow. "Such a rule breaker."

He leans in with a wicked look on his face, looking like he's about to kiss me. I hold a hand up in front of my mouth and say, "Nope. No, sir. Let's add 'Must brush teeth before kissing' to our list of roommate rules."

With a fake pout, he sits back. "I don't know—it seems like an awful lot of effort to get the contract amended and re-notarized when we have less than two weeks left of being roommates."

After we travel to Nebraska so Liam can meet my family over Christmas, he'll be moving into one of the new modern apartments. I will be moving into a rundown apartment straight out of the 70s that is being vacated by a tenant moving to the *new* apartment building. The rent is cheap, so I can continue scraping by with my trickle of editing clients and whatever other odd jobs I decide to take on until MJE takes off.

"What time do you have to be at Becky's?" Liam asks, folding his arms across his chest. The movement draws my attention to the muscles in his forearms, visible below his rolled sleeves. I'm tempted to throw my new "no kissing before toothpaste" rule out the window.

Liam is only one week into building his consulting business, Executive Action Inc., and he already signed his first two clients (and turned down two others). Apparently, word traveled fast that "The Fixer" was available for open hire, and all of corporate America is beating down the door for his time.

Do I exaggerate? Maybe. But barely.

He *has* made good on his promise to continue wearing the suits even while working from home. And he doesn't change until after I get home from my shifts at Becky's and can properly appreciate his professional attire.

"I'm supposed to be at Becky's at ten," I say. "But I told Clara that I would stop by Emily's office first to help her unload the new shipment of collectible mugs."

"I tried to tell them they were going to need more to start with," Liam says, shaking his head.

I smile as I say, "I'll be sure to remind Clara that you told her so." Picking up my phone, I turn off my upcoming alarm and notice an email notification. Swiping down on the notification bar, my eyes widen when I see it's an email from Elizabeth.

Not-so-gently setting my coffee mug down on the side table, I click open the email. Scanning through the words, I gasp, "Oh my gosh!" I scan them again and repeat, "Oh my gosh. Oh my gosh!"

"What?" Liam asks, scooting closer to me on the bed. "What is it?"

I look up at him with what I'm sure is a wild expression. "Do you remember that client I had, Elizabeth? The one whose manuscript was my dream kind of book to edit? The one I thought might be the beginning of things taking off, but I never really heard from her again?"

Liam nods along, clearly remembering this very pivotal and then disappointing client.

"Well, listen to this," I say, clearing my throat. I read the email aloud.

Hi, Madison. I'm so sorry for the long delay in communicating with you. Right after I released my book, I was contacted by an up-and-coming publishing house about signing a contract for two more books. We've been in negotiations, and I mentioned that I would like to retain you as my editor if I signed on with them. They requested to see the edits you did for me, and after reviewing the file, they've expressed interest in hiring you to be one of their in-house editors. I know it's late notice, and you're likely swamped before the holidays, but if you would have time to jump on a video call this afternoon with me and the publishing house's head editor, we'd love to talk to you. If not, please send me your earliest availability for next week, if you're interested. Looking forward to talking and hopefully working with you!

All the best,

Elizabeth

When I look up from my phone screen to Liam, his face is brighter than a sunbeam. He lunges forward, crushing me in a hug, and I squeal in response.

"This is amazing, MJ! I knew something like this would happen for you eventually. You deserve this," he says, taking my face in his hands. "Permission to break rule number eighty-five, or whatever number your new rule was?"

"Permission happily granted," I say, elatedly returning his enthusiastic kiss. Hamlet squirms out from between us, retreating to the Christmas tree.

"I'm so proud of you," Liam says when he pulls away from our kiss.

My heart swells as I say, "I'm proud of me too."

"To Madison's new proofreading position!" Clara declares, raising her glass in the air. The ten of us clink our glasses together and take a drink.

"To Liam's new consulting firm thingie!" Beau exclaims, calling us all to cheers our glasses a second time.

"To Christmas Fest being *over* and the return of normalcy to Noel," Clark practically groans, and we all heartily echo agreement.

Well, except Clara. She pouts a little bit before reminding Clark, "It's still officially No-el through the end of the month, thank you very much."

"When will you start with the publishing firm, Mads?" Syd asks, leaning her elbows on the table. The Deer River Bar is still decked out in all its Christmas glory, and the twinkling lights reflect in Syd's eyes.

"Right after the first of the year," I say. "So I have time to enjoy the holidays over the next couple of weeks, and then I'll do my orientation with them in person for three days before I start taking on projects remotely."

"But Madison Joy Editorial will still exist, right?" Clara clarifies. "We worked so hard on her—you can't just leave her out to die!"

Rolling my eyes at her dramatics, I say, "Yes, it will. Because this publishing house is only doing nonfiction, I can still accept fiction manuscripts for freelance editing, as long as it doesn't interfere with my deadlines."

"You're going to be amazing, Mads," Becky says. "But I'm more than a little bummed to lose my best barista. At least come back next year for Christmas Fest to help me make those Grinch matcha lattes. I had no clue they would be so popular!"

"Deal," I say with a grin.

The guys start talking about their bro trip to the cabin coming up next week, and Sydney is entertaining Becky and Abby with a story about her son. I lean my head against Clara's shoulder next to me as I hold Liam's hand under the table.

"I'm so happy to be here with you, Care-Bear," I say. She huffs a laugh at my use of her parents' nickname for her. "Seriously—thank you for suggesting I come here. I think you might have changed my whole life. I'm so lucky to have a friend like you. So lucky to be here."

Clara shrugs her shoulder enough to get me to raise my head and look at her.

"We're the lucky ones, Mads. I can't even imagine what the past year would have looked like without you. Way more boring, at the very least," Clara says with a teasing smile. "You've brought so much joy to me this year. To all of us."

I raise my glass and give her a sassy wink. "Joy to Noel."

Epilogue

MADISON

Four months later . . .

"Sorry to keep you waiting—I was trying to finish up the chapter I was proofreading," I say as I climb into the passenger seat of Clara's car. She invited me to go out for dinner tonight to celebrate the publishing day for the first book I proofread with my new publishing firm.

It's been everything I'd hoped it would be—proofreading meaningful content, ensuring that every sentence is as polished and professional as possible. I wake up every morning eager to switch on my reMarkable tablet and get to work. Even if I'm working in my stuffy little apartment with a carpet-covered column holding up the kitchen counter. We've taken to calling the apartment "The Cave," due to its lack of natural light, since it's built halfway into the ground on the bottom floor of the ancient apartment building.

Still, I'm paying for it with my hard-earned paycheck from the publishing house, and I'm saving every penny from my freelance editing gigs toward a down payment on a house. That is, if any houses will ever go up for sale in Noel. Stupid successful town with zero people leaving and selling their houses.

Maybe I'll compete for one of the swanky apartments in Liam's building when my current lease is up. He's fully settled into his space there, which is good since he works from home 80 percent of the time. The success of his consulting business means he travels once or twice a month, but he never stays away more than a few days at a time.

When he's gone, I'm on Hamlet duty. And while I'm only officially contracted to come in and out to feed Hamlet each day, I absolutely spend every waking second at Liam's apartment and sleep in his bed at night, Hamlet curled up on the pillow.

It's the only way to make Liam's absence bearable.

"We need to drop off this bouquet of flowers to Becky at the cabin on our way to dinner," Clara says, thrusting wildflowers wrapped in brown paper into my lap.

"Why?" I ask.

Clara answers, "Becky forgot them and texted to see if I could bring them over. I guess the people renting one of the cabins this weekend requested fresh flowers, and she wanted to leave them in there tonight before they arrive in the morning. I told her we could swing by on our way to dinner."

It's an odd request, and even more odd that Clara brought me with her on this quest instead of doing it on her way to pick me up. But Clara loves helping her friends, and I love Clara, so I'm along for the ride.

"Which unit is Becky in?" I ask as Clara drives down the gravel path between the tiny cabins.

"Your old cabin," Clara replies. As she slows to a stop in front of my former living quarters, she gestures for me to open my door. "You can hop out, and then I'll park," she says. Really weirdly.

"Okaaay," I say, opening the car door and taking the flowers with me. As soon as I close the door, Clara takes off in reverse, exiting the way we came.

By the time I've registered that Clara just left me here, the evening dusk is suddenly illuminated by hundreds of lights strung every which way around the outdoor space. It's then I notice the baby Christmas tree that kept me company in this cabin is perched right on the porch, twinkling with lights.

And the door is ajar.

My heart starts pounding as I approach the door to the tiny cabin, met by the glow of candlelight.

Liam is standing inside, dressed in his black dress shirt and charcoal gray suit. His hair is immaculately styled, and his eyes are intense as they take me in.

This explains Clara's insistence on me wearing my coral dress to dinner.

As I step closer to Liam, his gaze remains locked on mine. I raise an eyebrow in challenge. "Suits—care to explain what's going on here?" I ask, biting my lip to contain my smirk from turning into a real smile.

Liam's lips quirk, and he closes the final steps of space between us. "MJ—you're wildly intelligent, so I have a feeling you already know exactly what's going on. But I'm going to spell it out for you anyway because I will *never* miss an opportunity to tell you how much I love you. Or how you make everything in my world better. Or how I never want to waste a single second of my life on any path but yours."

His face starts to blur as my eyes burn with tears, but I blink them away, placing my shaking hands on his chest. Liam cups my face in his hands as he says, "Madison, I love you. I love you with a wild, passionate, intense love. With a tender, soft, whispering love. With an unyielding, unbreakable, forever love. You make me love in every way there is, and I want to keep loving you for the rest of our lives."

Liam's hands slide down my cheeks, down my neck, trailing down my arms to take my hands as he slowly bends to one knee. He releases one of my hands to pull a ring box out of his pocket, holding it up in front of him.

"Madison Joy—MJ—will you be my wife?" Liam asks.

After screaming yes, I pull as hard as I can on Liam's hand to force him to his feet, catching his lips with mine as he stands. He literally sweeps me off my feet and into his arms, kissing me with all that wild, tender, unyielding love he just professed.

"I love you so much, Liam," I say when our lips finally break apart. I trace my finger along his jaw, across his lips. "And I have to say, I think you just gave the Bard himself a run for his money with that speech."

Liam's lips twist into a self-satisfied smile, and he murmurs, "'I would not wish any companion in the world but you,' my love. My very own tempest."

Eyes gleaming, I say, "Let's take the world by storm together."

Bonus

Want to read about Liam and Madison visiting the London Christmas markets along with Clark and Clara?

Check out the bonus epilogue!

Click here

Or scan here:

I thought about the potential family dynamics he could have grown up with. You are amazing, and I love you so dearly, my friend.

Parker, I consider myself so lucky that I stumbled across Author's Best Friend and found you as a cover designer. Thanks for seeing my vision for the tie ins from the *Saved by Noel* cover and bringing Mads and Liam to life. And thank you for passionately agreeing with my "no creepy eyes" policy.

To every reader who has ever read one of my books and shared about it with a friend, posted a review, made a beautiful post about it on bookstagram, or sent me a message about how it impacted you: I don't think I can ever really explain how much you mean to me. Thanks for diving with me into these fictional worlds and characters that feel so real in my mind. I can't believe I get to do this.

My kiddos (can I even still use that term when two of you are teenagers? Probably not)—being your mom is the best. We're five books in, and you all still think it's cool that I'm an author. Something about writing Christmas books makes me think extra of you four, because I sure hope you grow up thinking Christmas is as magical of a time of year as I always have. Landon and Layla, thanks for your extra help during our crazy summer to give me chunks of time to get this book written. I couldn't have done it without you.

Kyle, my book acknowledgments forever revolve around you. You've made this whole path possible. Specifically for this book, thank you for all of the corporate business world insights. Thanks for coming up with the embezzlement scheme on the spot off the top of your head—should the world be impressed or scared by that talent? I, for one, am impressed (and very grateful for the help). I would not wish any companion in the world but you.

The late Dr. Larry Cox was a real faculty member at The Pepperdine Graziadio Business School. My husband, Kyle, met him several years ago through a mutual acquaintance, and they hit it off right away. Larry became a sort of professional mentor to Kyle (as well as a friend), and he taught Kyle the diverge/converge brainstorming method that Liam references in the book. We were deeply saddened when Larry passed away earlier this year, and including him in this book felt like a small way to honor his memory and his impact on Kyle's life.

About the Author

Tracy Baack connects with readers through relatable romance. She enjoys writing character-driven contemporary romance novels with so much character depth and development, you just might think they're real people. Her books are always closed-door but full of heart-melting swoon, and they end happily ever after (after a little dose of angst).

Tracy lives with her husband and four children in the suburbs of Kansas City, Kansas, where she loves supporting indie bookstores. Her primary love language is sending the perfect GIF for any moment.

Tracy is the author of *Love and Other Goals, Love and Other Chances, Saved by Noel, Home Safe,* and *Joy to Noel* (with more on the way because she just might be a writing addict).

Connect with Tracy on Instagram at @authortracybaack or through her website www.tracybaack.com.